Her

Felicia Johnson

ISBN:0615823459
ISBN-13:9780615823454

FOR HOLLY

Published by: 8th Street Publishing
Editor by: Carolyn Flournoy
Cover designer: Lacey O'Connor

PART 1

Her

By Kristen Elliott

Her cries could be heard.

Her smiles were seen.

Couldn't be noticed.

Her ways would have been tamed

By just the right hand.

To touch Her soul

To heal Her mind

Her heart would have desired.

The way she called out

Drew them away

They could ever understand.

Her tears.

Her fears.

Her pain.

Her mind held on to them.

Her hand tried to hold on.

There is a way to save Her.

CHAPTER 1

In order to tell a story there has to be a story to tell. For Her, well, for me, there is a beginning and an end. I will start in the middle of Her story where I remember it hurting the most. I remember anticipating my rest. It started with not being able to sleep for nights at a time. This time I wanted to make myself sleep. I wanted to sleep forever so that I would never have to hurt that much again.

Nick pulled the sheets off of me, and found me hiding. I was lying still on my back with my wrists turned up. Blood stained my sheets and ran down my arms and onto the floor. I could hear soft, mellow cries in the background.

"Is she dead? Oh, God!" His voice faded as I drifted out of consciousness.

There were many pills. There was a lot of blood. There was only one knife.

I could hear him crying for our mother. I could hear them both shouting and screaming. He was screaming my name. I was too exhausted to call out to him and tell him that everything was going to be okay. This pain was going to be over soon. Nick was crying hysterically.
He wouldn't have listened to me.

I felt weak, like I had all of the weight of the whole world on me. It felt heavy at first. The paramedic lifted me up and onto the stretcher, and without any support, my head fell back. I couldn't move my head. I started to feel weightless when he laid me down on the stretcher, like I was floating in the air. It was warm and peaceful.

I didn't hear Nick's screams or the sirens anymore. I was surrounded by darkness. I knew this was the moment I had been waiting for. The pain was almost gone. I felt a big relief, took a deep breath, and let out a sigh. If I were left alone for a little longer, I might have completely fallen asleep…

There was pressure on my chest. The pressure was so hard that I could feel my heart moving without my having any control over it. Air was forcibly making its way down my throat and into my lungs. The paramedic was breathing into my mouth.

I blacked out.

I came back.

I blacked out again and was back in the dark.

The warmth filled me again. I felt still. Everything was quiet, and I could finally sleep. My mind felt like it was finally safe to let go. Soon I would not have to think about it anymore. I could have only dreamed of such a peaceful rest. A sleep of nothing. I felt one step closer to eternal peace.

Then a bright light shattered my moment of peace. I awakened with my eyes opened wide. All I saw was white.

There was a hard blow to my chest. Once again, I felt everything. I heard the cries, the screaming, and the sound of sirens.

Shapes and shadows started to form against the white backdrop, and that was when I saw a man hovering over me, sweating, panting, and pressing on my chest.

I felt myself drift off again.

The paramedic stopped pressing on my chest, and began to punch me.

My eyes opened again. I saw Nicholas, who was staring at me through wide eyes. Shocked eyes. Eyes that were probably damaged forever because of me.

When I saw his face, my heart sank. I could not move my mouth. I could not move my arms to reach out to him. I could not do anything but lose consciousness again. I had lost a lot of blood. However, that was to be expected from what I had done.

It was my fault. Nick didn't understand that. Even before all of this - all of the sirens, the chaos, the pills, the blood, the medical staff, and the events that were to come - I knew. All of those things were useless. They didn't really care for me. They didn't really care why I'd done it. They didn't even know me. If they did know me, they wouldn't have tried to save me. They would have understood and they would have let me go. They would have said that I didn't stand a chance, although they would have been wrong. I did stand a chance. It was just up to me to take that chance to save myself. I didn't feel that I needed the chance. It's not as if she would have cared, or noticed. There were things that were more important.

Maybe, I thought, that's why she didn't answer the phone…

"Doctor?" I felt a deep burn in my throat when I tried to speak.

Suddenly all of the chaos was over. I was wrapped in something white. A bright light shone into my eyes, blinding me, and the air felt cold to my almost-bare skin.

"Are you talking to me?" a sweet voice asked from overhead.

I tried to nod my head, but I was still too weak. I could barely open my eyes. The woman with the sweet voice tucked the white object over me. It was a hospital blanket, thin and white. I felt so cold.

"You shouldn't talk," she told me. "Try your best to just rest."

"Please…"

"Shush now."

She gently placed a warm finger over my lips, and then checked the IVs in my arms, as well as a big, beeping machine with wires connected to different areas of my body. Seeing all this, I felt scared. How did those wires get there? I thought to myself.

"Your doctor will see you in the morning dear. Please just try your best to get some rest. I am going to check your wrists now. I need you to hold as still as you can."

Gently, she pulled my arms out from under the thin blankets. When she looked at my bandages and how they were heavily wrapped, I saw her face go from gentle to just plain sad. I closed my eyes as she did what she had to do. When she finished, I heard her whisper to herself, "poor kids these days…" She must have thought I was asleep because she turned out the light and left me alone.

I couldn't rest. I only wanted to rest the way I had rested before the paramedic had punched me. This wasn't where I needed to be. I didn't need a hospital. I didn't need a nurse or any of those sickening IVs and machines. I tried to lift myself up to see if I could get a look around the room, but my body didn't work. Somehow, with a lot of effort, I managed to get my arms to my chest. I raised my hands and lifted my wrists, which were heavily bandaged. A little bit of blood had leaked through the bandages. After a while, my arms grew tired so I let them fall back down to my chest. I had survived. That meant that the consequences were to come in due time.

I didn't know that it would be the next morning.

I woke up with a bright light shining down on me. Grunting, I pulled that thin, white blanket over my face.

"Rise and shine, Kristen!" an annoying voice demanded.

I slowly pulled the covers down from over my face. I could barely see. It seemed so early in the morning. A figure came to the side of my bed. I rubbed my eyes and blinked. He reached his hand out to me.

"I'm Dr. Cuvo." He said, smiling. His smile seemed kind, but it confused me.

I was sick of him already. I looked down at his hand and realized what he wanted. We shook hands, and Dr. Cuvo continued smiling as he pulled a chair up beside my bed. I was able to get a better look at him.

He didn't look like a doctor. He had on a pair of blue jeans and a dress shirt with a huge coffee stain. He didn't have one of those important-looking white coats with a pocket on the left side and a name tag above it. He didn't even have a stethoscope around his neck. He carried a notebook and a pen, but nothing else. Right away, I knew what kind of doctor he was.

Dr. Cuvo made himself comfortable in the chair beside the bed. He opened a notebook and began writing in it. He kept looking over at a chart that was on the edge of my bed, and it looked like he was copying the contents of that chart into his own notebook. He finally looked up at me, and that same mysterious smile appeared on his face again.

"Kristen, how have you been?"

I wrinkled my forehead in response.

"I know, I have had better days myself," he admitted. He comically gestured to his coffee stain. "Imagine that," he chuckled.

I didn't laugh.

"Don't worry. We'll get to better days. Won't we?"

"How should I know?" I mumbled under my breath.

He heard me.

"I don't know," he responded, looking almost surprised. "I mean, we don't really know but we can always try. Isn't that right, Kristen?"

He was irritating me.

"Why are you asking me? Aren't you the doctor? Shouldn't you know if I'll be okay?" I asked.

"As far as your physical health, telling by your chart, I think you'll be fine. You're lucky. But as far as your safety, that's something I'm concerned about."

I didn't respond. The anger and fear that I hadn't seen coming welled up inside of me. I was awake, and all I wanted to do was sleep. This was too confusing, and too much feeling seemed to be ready to rip its way out of me. I held my breath.

"I need you to tell me if you feel safe, Kristen," he demanded. "Do you feel that what got you here in this hospital was the solution to whatever it is you're going through?"

He didn't miss a beat. I knew what we were talking about. What made me so angry was that he didn't know me. He didn't know a damn thing about why I'd done what I'd done. And I got the vibe that he didn't want to hear it, either. He just wanted me to think about it. He wanted to make me feel stupid for it. But he wasn't going to make me feel guilty or stupid, because I knew what I had done. I didn't feel ashamed. I only felt like a failure.

There was a long silence. He was waiting for an answer.

"You don't know me," I told him with a bit of anger in my voice.

"I never claimed to know you, Kristen," he sincerely said.

"Then, why are you staring at me?"

"Just because I am looking at you, you think that I think I know you? In fact, I think it's quite the opposite. I am looking at you to observe you, and I am trying to get to know you." His voice was still so gentle and kind.

I was not backing down.

"I really wish you wouldn't," I snapped.

I felt uncomfortable. I wanted to disappear. I could not look him in the eyes.

"Well," he said with a sigh. "I am your doctor, and I am required to get some kind of information from you, starting right now. I am here to do my job. I really do want to help you, Kristen, even if I don't know you."

"Why?" I tried to fight the tears from coming out of my eyes.

"To try to understand what's been going on with you to make you want to do something this terrible to yourself."

He gestured to my heavily bandaged wrists. I hid them under the blanket.

"Stop judging me," I growled at him.

"Excuse me?" he asked, sounding shocked.

"You're judging me. You said I did this 'terrible thing'. But you can't say that what I did was terrible if you don't even know why I did it."

"Then why don't you just go ahead and tell me, Kristen. Why did you do it?"

"No. Leave me alone." I felt the tears force their way through.

"Kristen."

I wished I were dead.

"Dr. Cuvo," I cried. "I'm tired. I just want to sleep. Please, leave me alone."

He was leaning on the arm of the chair with his chin in the palm of his hand. He was staring even deeper at me now. I felt sick inside. Then Dr. Cuvo gave up, and sat back in the chair. He looked at me with eyes that seemed to be full of pity.

"Would you at least like to eat breakfast right now?" He offered, kindly.

I looked at him strangely. Did he not understand anything I had said? I shook my head. Giving up, he stuck his handout for me to shake. This time I did not oblige. Dr. Cuvo shook it off and assured me that he would be back. I rolled my eyes and looked away from him.

"You can *not* like me, Kristen. You can *not* talk to me, but there is only one way to get through this. It is not the option that you chose a week

16

ago. In here, that is *not* an option. I'll see you later." He grabbed
his notebook and left me in the room alone.

A week ago? I had been in the hospital for a week. All I could
remember was the chaos of that night. There had been a lot of blood. I
remembered everything going black. And after all of that, I would end
up pulling through. It made me angry to think that all of my effort had
gone to waste. I should have been dead, and not in the hospital I
realized that my family would have to see me there. There would be
more problems, and they would be entirely my fault.

I needed to kill the pain. I needed a razor, scissors, box cutter, or a knife.
Anything to bring Mr. Sharp back to me. Nothing was here to bring him
back. I saw the IV in my arm. The needle was sticking into my veins. I
could see the veins, black and blue.

An overwhelming feeling of anxiety came over me, and I thought back to
what Dr. Cuvo had said, that I could not go back to a week ago. He had
said that it was not an option. I began beating my wrists against
the metal bars on the side of the hospital bed. I kept beating hard so that
I could see the blood soak through the bandages. I banged my wrists so
hard that I broke the needle to the IV.

Somewhere in all of this madness, I lost myself. I felt a dark and familiar
entity within me. It took over me. I was not inside myself anymore. I
was not cold from the room. I was not in pain. I was not even angry
anymore.

The nurses rushed in and grabbed me. Two of them held me down.
I continued squirming trying to break free of them. The real doctor with
the white coat and name tag came in. He had a large needle, which he
stuck into my neck as the nurse pressed my head down to the
bed. Adrenaline and pressure pumped into my brain. It felt like a heat
wave had come over me, and that something was trying to suck me into
hell until I felt the world spin out of control. Then, like at the end of a
movie, everything faded to black.

CHAPTER 2

I used to like to write stories. When I was a little girl, I wrote fairy tales and stories about damsels in distress. The women I had written about, lived in the most terrible situations, and a man would come along and rescue the women in every story. I had written hundreds of stories like that, with the same plot and the same ending. The girl had a hard and miserable life. The prince, or the rich and handsome man, would come to her, and give her all of the gifts and love in the world. Then, he would marry her, they would start a family, and they would live happily ever after.

Mom and I had always been more like partners rather than mother and child. I would sometimes have to make decisions for the both of us. It had been just the two of us until she had met the twins' father. I had been six years old.

She had once described their story as a fairy tale romance. In a way, it was. We lived in California, where we were both from. Mom and I were staying in a basement apartment that was rented out by a church. Mom worked two jobs. One job was a day shift and the other was a late night shift. I saw myself off to school in the morning and tucked myself into bed at night. When I arrived home from school, Mom was there with dinner made. We had a half hour to eat dinner together, but then she was right out the door again to go to her night shift job. I would give myself a bath and put myself to bed, and the cycle would begin all over again the next day.

On the weekends, I sat by myself inside the apartment and just waited. I made myself dinner, which was usually microwaved cooked hot dogs, or cold cut sandwiches and potato chips. I wasn't allowed to go outside when she wasn't at home. TV got boring. The radio got boring. Even writing fairy tales had grown boring.

One evening I thought I could sneak out. My plan was to go outside and play in the park across the street. I had planned to come home before dinner time so that Mom wouldn't catch me out when she would arrive home. I figured that, as long as I brought my watch and kept an eye on the time, I would be safe. I put on my baseball cap, made sure my clothes were straight, and tied my shoes. I tightened my watch around my wrists and made my way to the door. As soon as I stepped one foot out of the door, Mom was standing in front of me with her key stretched out to the knob to unlock the door. There was a look of shock on both of our faces. She was shocked to see me at the door. I was shocked, not because Mom was home early, but because there was a man standing beside her. He was tall, dark, and almost handsome in that rugged, industrious kind of way.

I stepped back, and they entered the apartment. Mom asked me where I was going. I told her that I had heard some noises at the door, and that I wanted to see if she was home early. She bought it, probably because she was in a good mood and did not want to question me further and become disappointed when she found out the truth. She had a way of getting the truth out of me when she knew that I was covering up something. However, the focus at that moment was the stranger she had brought to our home.

"Kristen, this is Jack. Jack is my friend from the factory. Jack." She looked at him with seductive eyes. "This is Kristen."

"Hey there," he said.

He had a thick, southern accent. I wondered where he was from. At the time, I had never heard that accent before, except when I watched re-runs of *The Andy Griffith Show* on television.

"Excuse the mess," Mom told Jack. "It doesn't always look this way. Kristen didn't know that we were having a guest. Otherwise, I would have made sure she cleaned up."

If you had asked me at the time, I did not think that Jack was interested in the apartment. He made himself right at home, sitting down on our one couch and pulling Mom onto his lap. They began kissing.

After that day, Jack came over to visit more often. Mom quit one of her jobs, saying that it was too much for her. I knew it was because she wanted to spend more time with Jack. That was what she was doing when she wasn't at work. I didn't really mind. I was able to go outside and play when they felt like being alone. I didn't favor the evenings when Jack spent the night, because we only had one bedroom in our small place. Those were nights that I didn't get much sleep.

There came a time when Jack didn't come around as often as he used to. When days went by without a call from Jack, Mom buried herself in misery. She became depressed and she missed a few days of work.

One day she came home and said that she was tired, and that she wasn't going back to her job. I knew, deep down inside, they had fired her. Then, about a week after she had been fired, Mom dragged me down to the factory where she and Jack had previously worked together. She told me to wait behind the building for her as she stepped inside through the back door.

She was gone for a while until finally she and Jack came out of the building together. She was smiling, and he looked tired. I was confused. Mom leaned toward me.

She said, "Kristen, everything's going to be okay. Jack and I are getting married."

My mouth dropped wide open.

"You are?" I didn't expect to respond aloud, but I couldn't control myself.

"Yes," she assured me. "And you are going to be a big sister."

I couldn't open my mouth any wider. Mom's eyes were puffy and red. Her face was splotchy, like she had been crying. But she was smiling. Jack wasn't smiling. He lit a cigarette and looked down at me. I closed my mouth.

"Okay," I said calmly.

"Okay? Is that all you can say, Kristen?" Mom pushed at me.

I forced myself to say, "Congratulations."

I still felt a little uncomfortable around Jack. I didn't get to spend any time with him before he and Mom got married. The three of us never did anything together. Even at the wedding, while it was taking place, I didn't feel any connection to him. Nevertheless, I saw that he made Mom happy.

Mom and Jack got married in a church. My grandmother was there, but Jack's parents didn't show up. Jack's only brother, whose name was Jonathan, was there, along with his wife, Mariah, and their only son at that time, Jonathan Jr. All of us went out to dinner after the ceremony. It was considered a reception. Mom wore a maternity wedding gown, even though she didn't look that pregnant to me.

Jonathan Sr. was two years older than Jack. Jonathan and Mariah had been married for ten years at the time. Their son, Jonathan Jr., whom they called John, was eight years old. John was quiet and stayed to himself. His mother made him dance with her a few times at the reception, but he looked like he really didn't want to be there. I sympathized with him.

At the reception, Jack looked at me and smiled. That was the first time I had ever seen him smile at me. It was such a handsome, kind, and gentle smile, and it made me feel safe. Jack asked me to dance with him. I nodded, and he took my tiny hands in his and led me to the dance floor. He let me stand on top of his feet and he waltzed me across the floor. I laughed as he made goofy faces at me and swung me from side to side. He was charming.

That day he told me to call him Daddy. He said that he was a nice man, and that he was going to be my daddy. I knew what a daddy was. Daddies were different from fathers. Daddies took care of their little girls, and protected them from everything. Finally, I was going to have a dad. I had always wanted a dad.

I let him kiss me on my cheek. At that moment, I fell in love with him. Not in love like Mom was, but in love like little girls are in love with their dads. That's when Jack became my Dad. I started calling him Dad that day, as he proposed I should do.

My heart was moved, and I said, "Yes, Daddy!"

At that moment, my *Daddy* lifted me into the air and said, "Your Daddy loves you, sweetheart."

I said, "I love you too, Daddy."

This was a promise. I would never stop loving my Dad.

Dad decided to move us to Atlanta, Georgia, where his brother lived. He said that he had received a job offer from one of the largest car factories in America. He would be building cars for Ford.

Mom didn't hesitate. Two weeks after the news, our bags were packed, and we were ready to go. I was afraid to ask, but before I had a chance to, Mom gave me an opportunity to say goodbye to my real father. Of course, I said yes. I wanted to say goodbye. Dad didn't have anything to say about it.

On our way to Atlanta, we stopped at the garage where my father worked. He didn't even recognize me when I stood before him. He asked me if I was lost. I told him that I was his daughter. He grunted and bent down to my level. He pulled out a twenty-dollar bill and held it out to me.

He asked, "Is this what your mother sent you here for?"

I reached out and took the twenty dollars from him.

"No. I'm here to say goodbye. We are about to move to Atlanta. It's far away."

My father knew that he wasn't getting his money back. He stood up and shifted his weight.

"So, you're leaving," he said.

He looked over at the car where Mom and Dad sat, waiting for me. The car had been packed tight with suitcases and small furniture.

"Who's that in the car with your Mom?"

"That's Jack. They got married. Mom's having twin babies," I told him.

He let out a loud grunt. That was how he let people know he was frustrated or annoyed. I thought it was funny. I giggled. My father hesitated a little at first, but he wrapped his arms around me and hugged me. He lifted me off the ground.

"Be good," he said as he lowered me back to the ground and turned me loose from his grip.

"Okay."

"Hey," he called out to me as I started to walk away. "Give me back my twenty dollars."

I pretended not to hear him and kept on walking. I climbed into the car, and Dad asked me if I was all right. I said I was fine. I really was. We were going to a new home somewhere bright and beautiful. Life was going to be just like in the fairy tales.

It took almost a week to get across the country to Atlanta, Georgia, because we kept stopping and resting in hotels. Jack drove the whole way because he didn't want Mom to get sick at the wheel.

When we arrived in Atlanta, we checked into a hotel. Atlanta was definitely a completely new world for Mom and me. On the day we arrived, the sun was shining and it was warm. I loved the feeling that this move gave me. I thought that we were finally going to be free. I thought our lives were only going to get better.

Jack moved us into a house a month after being in Atlanta and working at the Ford factory. Mom was starting to show her pregnant belly. Jack was the love of our lives. He rescued us just like in the stories that I used to write. This was supposed to be our happily ever after. We were supposed to live like that forever.

CHAPTER 3

I used to like roller coasters. I especially liked the ones at amusement parks that turned me upside down and twisted me from left to right, brought me over a big hump and down the long free-fall, moving so fast that, when it stopped, my stomach felt like I had left it behind. Those rides were so fun.

Life seemed to have become one of those roller coasters, except this time I didn't like it. I didn't like being twisted through life and thrown around out of control, not knowing what horrible thing was going to happen next. One day things were fine, and then everything seemed to start spinning completely out of control. Life became a ride that I wanted to shut down permanently.

I had always kept in mind that there were others in the world that had it worse than I did. I didn't want to be selfish. I just didn't think of it as selfish. Maybe it was selfish of me as a big sister. If I had succeeded in killing myself, my little brother and sister would have been left alone with Mom.

My mind drifted constantly to Nicholas, and his face when he'd seen me in the ambulance. When Nick was younger, he hadn't minded me calling him Nickyroo. Of course, being older, it wasn't a cool thing to do. I hadn't seen Alison there the night I'd tried to commit suicide. I hoped she hadn't been there at the house when it happened.

I was thinking too much. I couldn't sleep, anyway. I kept my eyes closed until I heard the door open.

I didn't want to open my eyes. My head felt like it wasn't attached to any part of my body. It felt light, like it was spinning on an axis in outer space. I grunted and threw the covers over my face.

A voice spoke loudly. "Is that how you're greeting me now?"

I recognized the voice. I was groggy, but I still knew who it was.

"Mom…"

Even though I whispered, she still heard me.

I felt her sit down beside me on the bed. The covers were still over my face, and my eyes were still closed. I was sad and scared because I was still alive. Tears came out of my eyes. Mom was mad, and I knew it.

"Hey," she said in a gentle voice. "Can I have a hug?"

I stayed under the covers. This was a trick. Why was she being so calm?

She didn't give up.

"Kristen? It's okay. Please let me see your face. Kristen, take the covers off of your face." Her voice began to change. She was becoming frustrated. "You could at least…"

I was staring up at her and she didn't realize it. She didn't notice until she almost started yelling at me. I threw out my arms and I let her fall into them. I patted her back as she squeezed me.

Finally, she let go of me and said, "Look at you," with sadness in her voice.

I took a deep breath and prepared myself for what was coming next. It took her a minute to go through her whole act. She sighed. She wiped at her dry eyes as her imaginary tears fell. She shook her head at me and stared down at my heavily bandaged wrists. I kept quiet and let her go through the drama until she was ready.

When she finally pulled herself together, she asked, "Why?"

I shook my head.

"No. You owe me more than that, Kristen! For goodness sake, tell me why you did this!" She yelled as she gestured to my wrists.

Mom was angry. I should have stayed under the covers. I heard her begin to sob. When I looked at her, there weren't any tears coming out of her eyes. There were only dry sobs.

"You know you have to stay here. They said that you have to go to a psychiatric hospital in a few days when you get out of here. They are going to lock you up, Kristen. That's what happens when you try to kill someone. They lock you up."

The last thing I wanted was to be locked up somewhere. I especially didn't like hospitals, and psychiatric hospitals weren't any better, from what I had seen on television.

"When can I get out, Mom?" I asked, afraid.

She looked down at me. Her eyes were dry and serious.

"Why? So that you can get out and do it again?"

I shook my head.

Mom started to say, "Does this have to do with Jack getting--" but she was interrupted.

Dr. Cuvo walked into the room. Mom looked startled and quickly rose to her feet. When she realized he was a doctor, she sighed in relief. She greeted Dr. Cuvo, and they shook hands. Dr. Cuvo looked down at me and asked how I was doing. I lied and said that I was fine.

Dr. Cuvo then turned back to Mom to introduce himself.

"I'm Dr. Cuvo. I am Kristen's psychiatrist. Kristen will be transferred to Bent Creek Psychiatric Hospital in a few days. Do you mind if we step into the hallway to speak?"

He gestured to the door for my mother to follow him. She looked back at me and gave me a sympathetic smile. She touched my face warmly and then followed Dr. Cuvo out the door.

I waited for something. I grew afraid because I didn't know what was going on out there. What was he saying to her that I couldn't hear? I suddenly wanted to go home. I wanted to get away from the hospital. I couldn't spend another day in this place. I knew that if Dr. Cuvo was explaining things to my mom about what I'd done the other day when we had first met, she would get angrier and more stressed out because of me. She had already seen what I had done, or what I had tried to do, at home.

I had always been a problem for Mom. I didn't do these things on purpose. I didn't want to be labeled as her "troubled child," because I knew that she had a lot on her plate.

I hadn't made things any better for her when her life had taken a wide turn. Jack had seemed to change overnight after the twins had been born, and that's when things had gotten worse for her. She'd suffered from postpartum depression.

We'd been a happy family for a little while after the twins had grown older. Mom had started taking anti-depressant medication. She'd asked me to help her out with Nick and Alison. I'd had no problem helping with the twins. I'd adored being their big sister.

That was how I'd fallen in love with Nicholas. I'd reached for Nick first when I'd first seen the pair. He was my favorite. Nick and I were always doing things together. Mom and Alison spent most of their time together, playing in the garden or doing girly things in the kitchen. Nick and I were more adventurous. We played sports and hunted for treasure in our backyard.

Dad still played the role of Knight in Shining Armor. He provided for us financially and he kept Mom happy. He did work a lot. Mom always needed someone to lean on. Dad was her strong arm because he was always there when she needed him.

We were happy those first few years of our lives together as a family. It didn't last very long. It was around the fifth year that life began to change dramatically. Things started going on behind closed doors. There were many arguments between Mom and Dad. This change in our family started slowly around the time the twins were first born and when Mom was diagnosed with postpartum depression. Then the dramatic change crept up into one big mess all at one time.

The big moment was when Dad lost his job at Ford. Money problems began to arise, and Mom had to get a job. I was home with the twins after we got out of school. I had to help in a bigger way, and I did not like that very much. I gave Mom a hard time whenever she asked me to do things like make dinner for the kids and clean up behind them. It seemed like I was being asked to be their mother since she had to work. Mom resented me for my behavior, and she made it known to me by telling me how selfish I was.

Dad worked odd jobs. He had quit the stable jobs he managed to land. He compared those jobs to Ford, saying that the new jobs weren't paying as much as he would have been making if he had still been at Ford. Often times, he and Mom didn't sleep in the same bed because of how angry they would get at each other. Dad didn't seem to care. His head was somewhere else. It bothered me. Dad and I always talked. If I had something on my mind, I went to him and we discussed it. He didn't hold back from me, and I loved him for that.

I remembered the last time it was like that for him and me. It was the last time I remember him being my dad, and our Knight in Shining Armor. I went to him while he was lying on the sofa. Mom had already gone to bed. The twins were asleep.

"Dad?" I called out to him.

He looked up at me. He looked as if he did not know who I was. There was no smile, no expression, on his face. I stood, frozen. I did not recognize him.

"Daddy, are you okay?" I asked him, still standing there.

He stood up, looking larger than ever.

"What do you want, Kristen?" he asked.

He walked towards the kitchen, and I followed behind.

"Daddy? You and Mom aren't sleeping in the same room anymore. Are you mad at each other?"

"No," Dad said with a warm smile. "Mommy and I just have to take a time out for a little bit. It will be okay."

"I'm scared."

We stood in the kitchen. He had started pouring a glass of Jim Beam for himself. He took a sip, stared down at me and said, "There's no need to be scared."

His eyes were glassy. They looked sad.

He sat the empty glass down on the kitchen counter and bent down to my level. He put his arms around me and hugged me gently. Even though he stank of alcohol, I still wrapped my arms around him, closing my eyes and letting myself take in his comfort.

"It will be all right, Kristen...It will be all right..."

What was this pressure? I started to feel his grip on me tighten. He was squeezing me. It started to hurt.

"It will be all right... all right..."

"No, Dad, that hurts. Please, Dad, stop." I started to cry.

He was hurting me. I had no idea what he was doing. It hurt too much. It was too hard to make a sound, because I could barely breathe. He lifted me up off the floor in his tight grip, and he stared into my eyes. My eyes were wide open as I tried to gasp for air. It felt like he was going to crush me. I cried, afraid.

"It's going to be all right...all right..." He kept repeating this over and over.

Tears fell from my eyes. Dad leaned in and pressed his lips against my open mouth. He was breathing heavily. He kept kissing me, but his kisses were different. It wasn't like the time he'd kissed me at his and Mom's wedding. This was like a monster trying to devour a child whose closet it had been hiding in. The monster came out. Before I realized what he was trying to do, I heard Mom's frantic voice.

"Kristen!" she shouted at me.

The monster dropped me to the floor. It felt like a long way down. My hip landed on the hard wood.

"What is going on here?" Mom had a look on her face that scared me.

"Kristen! Now, I told you to have this kitchen cleaned up!" the monster shouted.

Mom looked at him. Then she looked down at me. The monster walked over to my mother and put a hand on her shoulder. She stiffened at his touch.

"What the hell were you doing to my daughter?" she asked him.

The monster leaned into her and began talking to her. He was talking so low that I couldn't hear anything he was saying. It must have been convincing enough for her because, by the time he was finished, she was already like putty in his hands. She wrapped her arms around him and they hugged.

"I'll be to bed in just a minute. Let me finish up here with her," the monster told Mom.

Mom looked back at me and hesitated turning away. The monster kissed her cheek and assured her that everything was fine. He shooed her away gently and watched her disappear down the hall.

When I heard their bedroom door shut, I didn't know what to think. I didn't know what was coming next from this monster whom I had never seen before.

He approached me and said, "Kristen, I have to do this."

"Do what, Dad? What are you talking about?"

"I told your mother that you hadn't done your chores like you were supposed to. Look at this mess." He pointed to the cup that he had just drunk from. "I told you, you have to have this kitchen cleaned by the time your mother and I get home from work."

"Dad, I –" Chunks were rising in my throat. I grew afraid of the monster as he slowly started to come closer towards me.

He wasn't my dad. Who was he?

30

Jack snatched my arm and twisted me around. He raised his large hand at me. I watched as his hand came down and struck my rear end as if it were a piece of dough. He went slowly at first. Then there was a look in his eye. His face changed. The monster had taken over him.

He began hitting me harder and faster. I screamed aloud. He took the other hand and covered my mouth. I couldn't move. The monster was too strong. He somehow held me as still as he could, with that one hand on my mouth, and he kept hitting me with the other. He was sweating, and his breathing was outrageous. His eyes were wide as the sweat dripped into them.

The pain became almost unbearable. I felt like I was going to pass out. Before I could completely black out, he stopped. He fell backward and hit the wall behind him. He was exhausted. I was exhausted. I crawled along the floor to the table to get as far away from him as I possibly could. I tried to sit down, but I was hurting too much. I covered my mouth as loud cries, which I seemed to have no control over, came out of me.

"Kristen, I didn't do this to hurt you," he lied. "I did this to prepare you for what you have to live with. You have responsibilities that you have to uphold. Life is not a handout. You are not always going to get everything you want."

I cried harder, confused.

"Shut up!" he yelled at me. "You don't have anything to cry about. When I was a child, we got it a lot worse than that little spanking you just had. If I even once cried the way you are doing right now, I'd get more!"

He balled his fists up and strained his face to show how intense his punishments must have been.

"You have it way too easy. The way your mom used to let you get away with everything! If I didn't do my chores, do you know what they would do to us? I was woken up from my sleep and I was beaten! Beaten! It was not a spanking, because there is a big difference. Then I would have to stay up and clean until it was spotless. And I still had to get up and go to school in the morning. So, you had better fix your face right now. Fix it!" His voice echoed off the kitchen walls.

I wiped my eyes as fast as I could and sucked in my cries.

Jack, the monster, continued, "I didn't even have my own room. Did you know that? I had to share with Jonathan. I had to share everything with my brother. You should be thankful and stop being selfish. Help your mother out more around here."

His words cut me deep inside. I didn't mean to be selfish. I didn't want to be selfish. Maybe I did deserve it.

"I'm sorry," I said to him.

"Now, go to bed." He pointed towards the hallway that led to my bedroom.

I started walking towards my room. When I got there, I let myself fall onto my bed. I lay there for a while, crouched up. I was useless. I hoped that I wouldn't make him angry like that anymore.

From then on, I stayed on top of my chores and tried my best to stay out of Jack's way when he was in monster mode.

As I tried to stay out of his way, I noticed that Nicholas was getting more in his way. Nick and I were always able to talk to each other, and I told Nick to stay out of Jack's way as much as possible. Nick told me that he would, because it scared him when I told him about the spanking. Truthfully, I wanted to scare Nicholas. It was better I scare him than Jack. This was my way of protecting him. Alison didn't seem to need protection. She was with Mom when Mom wasn't at work, and Jack didn't seem too interested in her, anyway. It was always Nick and I who were being yelled at.

Nonetheless, I wanted to protect both of them as much as I could. I would always hate myself for the day that I decided to hang out with my best friend Lexus and her parents one weekend. When I came home from Lexus's house, I realized I had arrived in the middle of a nightmare. When I entered my house, Alison ran to me with tears in her eyes. She was so afraid that she couldn't even speak clearly. Mom was on the couch, reading a magazine, when a loud scream came from the hallway that led to our bedrooms.

Mom stood up suddenly. "What was that?" she asked Alison. "Where's Nicholas?"

"Daddy…" Alison managed to get out from between her quivering lips. "Daddy, he –" She started stuttering.

I hugged her as Mom walked up beside us.

"Alison, where's Nicholas?" I asked her.

"Daddy ripped the cord out of the TV." She couldn't say any more. She fell into Mom's arms and cried harder.

I stormed toward Nicholas' bedroom. I heard the loud and torturing whacks of the cord going against his flesh. His screams sounded morbid. I grew afraid. I put my hands on the knob to open the door, but it was jammed. I couldn't get in.

Nick screamed in what sounded like agony, "Daddy, no! Please, Daddy, no!"

I started crying with him and Alison. Mom held on to Alison tightly. I ran for the telephone and started to dial 911. Mom rushed over, snatched the phone out of my hand, and hung up the receiver. I looked at her, shocked.

"What are you doing, Mom? He's killing Nicholas! He's killing him!" I could hardly breathe. I was crying so hard.

"No, he's not trying to kill him. He doesn't mean it. You don't know what he has been through. I can handle this."

"No! I'm calling the police *this time*!" I shouted.

That's when I felt her hand go across my face. She slapped me hard enough for me to see stars.

"I'm the adult here. You listen to me. You better not pick up the phone," she threatened. She turned to Alison and said, "Baby. It's going to be okay. Nick is okay." Her voice softened as she leaned down to her youngest daughter.

Alison stood with her hands covering her ears. Tears rolled down her face. I watched Mom storm away towards Nicholas' room. I leaned down and grabbed Alison in my arms. I held her to comfort her, but her cries wouldn't stop.

I heard Mom burst through Nicholas' bedroom door.

"That's enough, Jack! That's enough! You are hurting him too much!"

I heard Jack say, "What do you think I am doing?"

"I don't know, Jack. I don't even think *you* know what you are doing! Look at yourself! You are hitting him with a television cord!" Then her tone grew gentle. "Honey, you can't do that."

"You think I'm abusing him? I would never abuse my own child! What do you think I am?"

"I know, Jack. I know," she calmly said to him. "But I think he's got the point, now."

I let Alison go, and made her sit down. I walked towards Nicholas' bedroom. When I got there, I saw Mom hugging Jack. The television cord was lying on the floor next to Nicholas, who was also on the floor.

What is going on? I thought.

I looked down at Nicholas, all alone and in pain. I wanted to go to him and hold him in my arms to stop his crying. Jack stared me down when I came to the door. His eyes held so much anger. It was as if he was daring me to go to Nicholas. I was afraid he was going to hurt me if I moved any closer.

Nicholas was crouched up with his knees pressed close to his chest. He was shivering. Mucus and tears drenched his face. He was bruised all over his back and his legs. I could see the whip marks, red and deep, on his skin. Some of his wounds were bleeding.

I couldn't stand still. I walked over to Nicholas and pulled him into my arms. I looked up at Mom as she held onto Jack and comforted him. Anger welled up inside of me. I felt my nostrils flare at her the way they did when I was very angry.

I helped Nicholas up and put a robe over him. Alison hadn't listened to me when I'd told her to stay put on the couch in the living room. She stood in the doorway, crying. Jack went over to her and hugged her.

"Why are you crying?" he had the nerve to ask her.

"Because Nick is hurting," she cried.

"Nick only got a spanking," Mom covered up. "He's all right."

I glared at Mom. Mom hugged Alison, and she and Jack took Alison to her bedroom to calm her down. I stayed with Nick. I looked at him as he took a deep breath and wiped his face with his hands.

"Nick," I called out to him once we were alone. "I told you to stay out of his way. I am sorry I wasn't here. What happened?"

"I didn't clean my room, and he…It's hard to stay out of his way, Kristen. He's always -" He stopped.

"He's always what?" I asked.

He didn't answer me. He just looked at me.

"Does Dad try to do things to you?" I asked him as low as I could so that no one else could hear me.

His eyes grew big in shock. "What do you mean?"

"Listen to me, Nick. I want you to know that you can tell me anything. You can tell me absolutely anything you want to tell me. Does Dad ever try to touch you the bad way?"

Nick looked down and shook his head.

"No?" I had to make sure.

"No," he whispered. Then his large, brown eyes looked up at me. He opened his mouth to say something to me. I waited for something - a sound, a word, and a nod - anything to assure me.

"Nicholas!"

Jack called out to him from the doorway behind me. I froze in fear. Nick turned away from me and started picking up his room as Jack entered. Jack stared down at me and then looked at Nick. He put one hand on my shoulder and squeezed it. I wouldn't warm up to him. I tensed in anger, and he let me go. He started toward Nicholas.

"I didn't mean to hurt you like that. Oh, look at you, you're bleeding. I'm sorry, son. I'll clean that up for you in the shower. Why don't you come on in there with me so that I can help you?" He smiled at Nicholas.

I wanted to tell him no. I wanted to tell him to get out and leave us alone, but I couldn't. Nicholas nodded at Jack and said he'd take a shower with him so that Jack could help him clean up. Jack left the room with a sympathetic smile. I wasn't fooled. I told Nick that he didn't have to go if he didn't want to.

"I *have* to," he said.

That was the end of that conversation. I had to let it go. I hated myself for leaving. My plan to protect them was failing.

"What were you trying to do, Kristen?" I heard a voice creep into my thoughts.

I opened my eyes, just realizing that they were closed. I saw Mom and Dr. Cuvo standing over my bed. I was in the cold hospital room with the thin, white blanket over me. I must've fallen asleep while they had been in the hallway talking. I started to feel crowded in with the two of them hovering.

"What? What did you say?" I asked Mom.

She had crocodile tears in her eyes. It was all an act.

"I talked to Dr. Cuvo. I know about the other day, and how you had banged your wrists," she said. "Dr. Cuvo says that it is best that you go to Bent Creek Hospital. You are not well enough to go home with me. I agree with Dr. Cuvo."

"Do you know what Bent Creek is, Kristen?" Dr. Cuvo asked.

I nodded at him, angry, not wanting to talk or see him or Mom anymore. I wanted to be dead. Away, asleep, somewhere, anywhere but here would have been better than the two of them hovering over me. Suddenly I heard the door open. The nurse from my first day in the hospital walked into the room. She said that it was time to change my bandages and that she would help me get cleaned up. Relief washed over me.

Dr. Cuvo did not leave without shaking my hand. He assured me that he'd be back tomorrow. Mom gave me a kiss and said that she'd be back tomorrow too, and that we were going to talk. She assured me that she was not angry with me. She said that she loved me. Then, she and Dr. Cuvo left me alone with the nurse.

When they were gone, I looked up at the nurse, thanking her slightly with a smile. It was the first time I had smiled in a long time. The nurse returned the smile kindly.

She was careful and gentle while she changed my bandages. It was strange to have someone cleaning me like I was a baby. But I knew that I wouldn't be able to wash my own body for a while. Not only because I couldn't bathe myself without getting my stitches wet, but also because I couldn't look down at the horror on my wrists.

I thought deeply about the things that I had done to get myself here. I thought about how much I had screwed up. I thought about my family and the family I used to have. It seemed like it was right for me to breathe and smile at some point in my life. Then everything had just burst to pieces. There had been more downs than ups. But there had been a point when things were up. Then things had fallen back down, slowly at first, and then more quickly. Things had rapidly turned from chaos and confusion to just plain old misery that had made life terrible. It had even been scary sometimes. I was still scared. Just thinking about it horrified me.

I shuddered at the frigid air as the nurse began to undress me. I was sad as the nurse washed me, because I knew that it would have to be like this for a while.

I wanted to be on this type of rollercoaster: Life. I always remembered the fun rollercoasters. The ones that turned you through seemingly endless and almost horrifying tunnels, and yet they were fun. You never wanted them to end, and when they did, you're either ready to ride another one or ride the same one again. Nevertheless, the rollercoaster of Life was never ending until your dying day.

CHAPTER 4

The next afternoon, Mom and Dr. Cuvo kept true to their word. Dr. Cuvo was the first one I saw. He came in with my chart and his usual smile. When Dr. Cuvo said that it was time to go, Mom was ready to bring me to Bent Creek herself, but Dr. Cuvo said that, by law, the police or an ambulance had to escort me to the psychiatric hospital.

Mom said she'd meet us at Bent Creek. She took my suitcase with her. She wanted to drive over to Bent Creek in her car. I was glad because I knew it would be awkward for her to ride with me in a police car or an ambulance. I didn't even remember seeing her in the ambulance on the night I had been rushed to the hospital. She had been holding onto Nicholas to keep him away. I got lost in my thoughts of that night. I must have had a strange look on my face because Dr. Cuvo asked if I was all right.

"Yes," I lied.

"Have you eaten?" Dr. Cuvo asked.

"Yes, I ate," I said as I looked away from his eyes.

We walked down the hallway, followed by the plainly-dressed police officer. The police officer was going to take me to Bent Creek. I began to feel sick inside. That feeling of death came over me. It felt strange to have a police officer following me. I felt like everyone in the hospital was staring at me, as if they knew where I was going and why. My face flushed, and I felt a little dizzy. I tried to keep my head down and stare at my own feet as I walked so that they could not see my eyes. These were my consequences for being so useless and stupid.

"Kristen?"

I looked up at Dr. Cuvo. We stopped and waited for the elevator.

"If there's anything you need from me while at Bent Creek, I can always be contacted. We will have visits every day. I want you to use this time to the best of your ability to try to let me help you work things out."

I stayed silent and nodded at him. What was taking that elevator so long? I looked over at the exit sign that led to the stairs. I wondered if I could make a break for it. The police officer waved his finger at me like he knew what I was thinking. I rolled my eyes at him and looked back at Dr. Cuvo.

Finally, the elevator arrived. We took it down to the lobby and made our way to the exit. When we were outside, the police officer said that he had to get his car, so Dr. Cuvo and I waited for him. Dr. Cuvo suddenly laughed. I was lost in my thoughts, and his laughter startled me. I looked up at him, confused.

"So what do you think of our rent-a-cop?"

He wasn't funny. Nothing was funny. I turned away from him, still angry inside.

"Kristen..."

"Why didn't I just die?" I heard myself say. When I realized I had spoken aloud, I covered my mouth with my right hand.

Dr. Cuvo had heard me.

"There's a reason for everything," he responded. In a situation like this, the reason is not what's important. The point is that you are here. Your brother found you, your mother called 911 in time, and you were saved. You've come a long way, Kristen. Think about that. I learned about how your heart stopped twice because you had lost so much blood, and now you are standing here on your feet just a couple of weeks later. That says a whole lot about you. You're a fighter, whether you like it or not. That is what's going to get you through this. I know you will get through this. You're too strong not to."

I blushed inside. I had never seen myself the way he had just described me. However, I knew that he was wrong. I wasn't strong. I was weak and useless. I didn't know how to feel about what he had said, but I did know that I felt strange. I didn't want him to see that.

I kept my back towards him, wishing he'd shut up, because the police officer was pulling up in a gray Sedan. The police officer got out as Dr. Cuvo was patting my back. I cringed and took two steps away from him. He was only trying to be kind. I knew it, but I didn't want to accept it.

The police officer opened the door for me. I climbed into the back seat.

Before he shut the door, I asked Dr. Cuvo, "Was it my Mom?"

"What?"

"Was it my Mom who told you to make me go to Bent Creek, just like she called the ambulance for me to come here?" I asked.

"Yes," he answered. "She signed you into our care to help you. She didn't do it to hurt you, Kristen."

I nodded. "So, it's up to her whether or not I can go home?" I started to feel hopeless. Mom would probably let them keep her troubled, messed up, useless child forever. Lock me up and throw away the key. I didn't blame her.

"No, it's up to you, since *this is your life*," Dr. Cuvo said as the police officer started up the vehicle. Dr. Cuvo stuck out his hand to me and we shook. "I'll see you tomorrow."

Dr. Cuvo closed the car door and I headed off to my prison chambers.

CHAPTER 5

When we arrived at Bent Creek, I was shocked. It didn't look anything like I had expected a mental hospital to look. It wasn't like on television. There weren't any bars on the windows. There were actually flowers and trees outside, and the people who worked there smiled when they greeted us. My mother handed one of the workers my suitcase. Immediately, she snatched it away and started going through it. I almost laughed at her eagerness, but I wasn't even going to crack a smile in here, especially not around Mom.

It was almost dark outside when we arrived. It had been a fair ride—not too long, but not short, either. It was freezing in the office where they made us wait. Mom and I sat at a long, rectangular table. I tried to sit furthest away from the door. Mom followed me and sat next to me.

Shortly after, a woman came into the room. She had my suitcase in her hand. She placed the suitcase next to me, and then sat across from Mom and me. She spoke in a sweet, high-pitched voice and she spoke very carefully.

"My name is Nurse Habersham. I am one of the psychiatric nurses here at Bent Creek. Kristen, I'm going to ask a few questions to put in your chart." She looked at Mom. "I understand that Kristen has not had a full evaluation. However, this doesn't mean anything, since Dr. Cuvo has already admitted her."

Mom nodded at her while trying to look at my chart. The nurse kept it at an angle so that she could write. Mom wasn't having much success.

"It's just procedure. We have to do these evaluations. It's just an initial one, and then we will do another one before Kristen is discharged." She looked at me and smiled.

I wanted to try to smile back, but I felt too awkward. Mom was sitting right beside me. I couldn't let her think that I actually felt good about this place or what I had done to get here.

Mom squeezed my hand. "Now we'll get you the help that you need. Some *real* help," she said, not looking at me.

The nurse gave me another warm smile. I didn't feel warm. I felt cold. I wished I could go home with Mom. I wished that I could fool them and tell them I was fine, that I was just having a bad night and that I was over all of that mess. I wished.

But there I was, about to be left alone, for God only knew how long, with people who didn't know me. People whom I didn't know, Mom didn't know, and who probably didn't really care about me. They were just people with jobs to me. They were people who needed to make a living, just like we all did. In addition, I had seen how people were treated in these types of places. I had watched television specials and investigative documentaries about old mental hospitals. There was no way I could get sane. Not in this place. Not in prison.

"Excuse me, when will I get to see Dr. Cuvo?" I asked Nurse Habersham.

"You will get to see your doctor tomorrow. Right now, I am going to let you have the things that are safe for you to keep in your room. They are all in your suitcase, there by your feet. We had to remove a few things, but we hold on to them. You will be able to have them when you need them. You can't keep items like hair sprays, nail files, and make-up, things like that. It's just procedure."

"Do I need to take some things home with me?" Mom asked her.

"You can take whatever you don't want us to hold. We just lock up those other things until she needs them. She can ask for her things like make up and nail files in the morning at grooming time, but she just can't keep them in her possession."

I rolled my eyes. Yep, I thought, why didn't I think of that? I could kill myself with a lipstick and some hair spray. I could just picture it. I felt myself chuckle when my stomach jumped. I must have sounded strange, because the nurse said, "Bless you," as if I had sneezed. Better she thought I had sneezed than laughed.

"How old are you, Kristen?" Nurse Habersham asked.

"She's seventeen," Mom spoke up for me. "Her eighteenth birthday isn't for another month and a half."

"Okay. Kristen, you are going to be on the Adolescent Ward with peers around your age." Nurse Habersham explained.

I would have preferred to go to the ward with the adults. Maybe there would be a lot of old and quiet people. They would leave me alone and not tease me like the other kids did.

"Are you still in school, Kristen?" Nurse Habersham asked.

"I'm home schooled, but I will be graduating soon."

"Home school," she repeated. "Well, if she is to keep up with her schooling, you can bring her books and homework to her. Since it is summertime, we don't have study hall during the day. Study hall is only during the school year. If Kristen's home schooling is year-round, then she could take time during her free periods to study."

Mom nodded. I sat still, staring down at my hands. They rested on top of my knees.

The nurse excused herself and went to the door. She spoke very low to someone who was standing out there. I turned to Mom.

"Mom? Where are Nick and Alison?" I asked.

Mom said, "They are with their aunt and uncle."

I shuddered as I thought about what that meant. A sharp pain went through my chest. Jonathan Sr. and Mariah were Nick and Alison's aunt and uncle. Mom hadn't cut ties with them, even after she and Jack had divorced. It was nice of them to look after my brother and sister while Mom couldn't. It just meant that they knew. If they knew, then John knew. If John knew, then Lexus knew.

Something landed on my lap. I looked down. It was a hospital gown. I looked back up. Another nurse had come in and tossed it to me. Nurse Habersham was still there. She was talking to Mom now and showing her out the door. I was confused as to what was going on.

"I need you to take off all of your clothes except your underwear, and put that gown on," the new nurse said kindly. "I'll be back." She stepped out of the room.

I changed out of my clothes, feeling strange. When I was in the gown and out of my clothes, I sat and waited for the nurse to come back in. She had great timing. She came back in with my chart, a pen, and she was wearing a pair of elastic gloves.

She asked me a bunch of questions. "Any stomach aches? Headaches? Do you have asthma? Kidney problems? Vomiting? Diarrhea?

I shook my head no to all of the above. Then she stood up. "I'm going to examine you quickly for any scars or wounds that you have coming in here, and I'll also check your vitals. When I am finished, you can put your clothes back on."

I stood up. She stood before me and raised my arms. She pressed on my tummy, my ribs, and my abdomen. I couldn't help but giggle. She somehow made it tickle. It was funny how she and the doctor were the only ones since Dad who could make me ticklish. They were the only ones who seemed to have that magic, ticklish touch. They knew exactly where to find that spot on my tummy where I was hiding the rest of the little girl that was left inside of me.

I wondered how much of that little girl was left inside of me. Things seemed to happen so fast in life. I'd lost so much time. I had to keep finding the way to make myself deal with things instead of going to Mommy and Dad to help. Dad wasn't there. There was only Jack. The monster had made me too scared. Mom had been blinded by darkness, and I couldn't reach her without any light. It didn't seem like there would ever be any light.

The nurse continued to search me from head to toe. I saw her face as she saw all of my old scars. Her face sank in sadness. I remembered where most of the scars had come from, and how I'd been too angry with myself to leave my room sometimes. I'd taken a piece of something sharp, like the back of my earring, and had scraped it hard onto my skin until it had bled or until the pain had been so thick and satisfying that I could stop. My breathing had been so hard and heavy from my head pounding. I'd felt my heart beat in my brain. I'd sucked in the atmosphere and accepted my punishment for being alive and having to be there. Sometimes I'd even completely forgotten why I had done it in the first place.

The nurse finally finished poking at me. She listened to my breathing through a stethoscope and then she wanted me to drop my gown. Nervously, I did what she asked. There I stood, in nothing but my cotton, white underwear. She did another search of my legs, back, chest, and arms. She seemed to be counting under her breath. She asked me how old some of the fresher looking scars were. She even asked how some of them got there. I wanted her to take a wild guess. She knew, but she was being like Dr. Cuvo, trying to make me think about it.

She stretched out my arms and squeezed my heavily bandaged wrists. I shuddered in pain. "Oh, I'm so sorry," she apologized. Then she stopped and looked at me. "What happened?"

I shrugged my shoulders.

"You don't know what happened to your wrists?"

I stayed quiet and stared down at the floor. I just wanted to go home. Getting frustrated, the nurse gave up on me and told me to get dressed. She left the room.

I started putting my clothes back on. I bent over to put on my shoes, and something fell out of my pocket. It was something shiny. As I looked closer, I realized what it was. It was my sterling silver butterfly pendant. I picked it up off the floor, and stared at it closely. If I had been caught with this, they would have definitely taken it away. I used to have a lace string that looped through one of its sharp wings so I could wear it around my neck. I'd just started carrying it in my pocket so that no one could see how sharp I had kept its wings. It was easy to sharpen on any hard rock. The wings were so sharp that I could run the pendant across my skin without pressing, and a line of blood would break through. I loved it. I could always keep Mr. Sharp near me.

"Who's Mr. Sharp?" Lexus had asked once, when we were kids. Lexus had been my best friend for a long time.

We had been sitting in my bedroom for hours, trying to figure out what we wanted to do with ourselves until Lexus' parents came to get us. They were letting me come over to Lexus' house for the weekend. I was so excited. I loved going over to Lexus' house.

Lexus and I became friends when I was in the sixth grade. She was in eighth grade. We both didn't really like each other at first because she used to be popular in middle school, and I was more like a social reject. She was two years older than I was, and at that age, we thought that two years was too big of a gap for us to have anything in common.

Lexus was beautiful. She had long, flowing hair that she always wore out, and her mom let her wear make-up. I kept my shorter hair in a ponytail, and Mom didn't let me wear make-up in middle school. Not many boys paid attention to me, and the girls made fun of me for not looking like them. It just so happened that one day, at a company picnic for the advertising company that Mom worked for, Lexus and I spotted our parents greeting each other. It turned out that Lexus' dad was on the same work team as my mom. They found out that Lexus and I went to the same school. Days after the picnic, our parents used Lexus and me as a good excuse to meet up and have play dates.

It was a forced, play date thing at first. For about the first year or so, Lexus pretended that she didn't know me at school, but she was nice to me when our parents were around. I didn't care. We didn't have anything in common. She was too boy-crazy, and I was too tomboyish.

When Lexus' dad got promoted to team leader and her family moved uptown, our families still remained close, but Lexus started to warm up to me after we didn't go to the same school anymore. She started private school. She said she hated going to private school, and that some kids were mean to her. I told her I knew how that felt. She said that she was sorry for being mean to me in school, and from then on, we were best friends.

"Who's who?" I asked Lexus, as I walked back into my room with two sodas.

"Mr. Sharp," she said.

"Where did you get that from?" I asked her.

She held out a sheet of paper. "I read it in one of your notebooks. See?" Lexus held out my notebook. I had often written poetry and stories in it.

She continued, "It says, 'crimson seeps out of wounds as Mr. Sharp can remind me again of my doom.' Ha! Ha! That rhymes. Is this one of your poems that you wrote? What is this?"

I snatched my notebook from her and gave her the soda that I had brought for her. I ripped the poem out of the notebook and into pieces of confetti.

"It's nothing," I said. "It's just mumble-jumble that doesn't mean anything. It's stupid."

She looked at me with concern. I smiled at her and shoved her shoulder as she went to take a drink. When the soda splashed on her and she laughed, I knew she had let it go. I was off the hook.

"Do you miss our old school?" I asked Lexus.

"Yeah, a little," she said. "I'm going to be in high school next year. Dad said I don't have to go to private school anymore, since it was too hard. I'm glad about that. Besides, I want to be on the cheerleading squad. I already know I am going to like this a lot more than middle school."

I stayed quiet. I knew I wasn't going to like high school any more than I liked middle school.

"Do you wish we were going to the same school?" Lexus asked.

I shook my head. "No, actually I don't." I was being honest, but I guess she thought I was joking.

"No, for real," she laughed. She shoved me playfully. "I bet you'll like it. Are you looking forward to it? Hey, maybe you could join the cheerleading squad when you get to high school, and we can cheer against each other at competitions!"

"Yeah, sure, Lexus," I told her as she kept laughing. I knew she was kidding. She had to have been kidding. Then again, Lexus was always trying to get me to be like her by wearing make-up and taking my hair out of my ponytail.

"I can't wait to go to my new school. I hear it's gotten pretty hard over at your school, because, of course, they've got more guys around here." She grinned at me.

I made myself smile back.

She got up and went to my mirror to fix her make-up. "Want some?" She held out pink lipstick to me.

I shook my head.

She laughed at me. "You are so funny."

"Why?"

"No reason," she said.

I was curious as to why she had said that, or I could have just been paranoid. I started to get a little on the defensive.

"No, why did you say that I was funny?" I heard myself shout.

Lexus closed up her lipstick and came towards me.

"Calm down. I didn't mean anything by it. You know, you should change your shirt before we go out."

She laughed at me and pointed to a large chocolate stain on my brand new white shirt that Mom had bought me.

"Why? What's wrong with it?" I joked.

Lexus tugged my ponytail playfully. I got up and went to my closet, and pulled out a new shirt. As I was changing, Lexus ran to the window.

"Yay! Mom and Dad are here!" She was so happy about it. "Hurry up and change! I am going to say hi."

She ran out of the room and shut the door behind her. I didn't blame her. I would have been out of that house even faster if I didn't have to change my shirt. Her family was perfect, like my family used to be.

I loved going over to Lexus' house. I liked her family's swimming pool, their nice garden, the fact that they always went out to eat, and that they

48

were genuinely kind people.

I grabbed my overnight bag and ran out of my bedroom. I was just as excited as Lexus about her parents being here. They were rescuing me for the weekend. I tried not to think about Nicholas and Alison. I wanted to get away. I had to go, whether I was being selfish or not. Excited and anticipating, I ran to the edge of the short stairwell that led to the front door and jumped those five steps. I reached out to push the screen door open. Breaking my rush and joy, I ran into Jack. He grabbed me.

"What are you doing?" he asked.

"Sorry," I told him, not making eye contact.

"It's okay. Where are you going with that bag?"

I looked over at Lexus and her parents as they talked to Mom beside their car. They were laughing and not even looking my way. I was just a few yards away from freedom. I started to panic inside, but I had to keep cool.

"Lexus' swimming pool is finally finished. Mom said that I could go up to Alpharetta this weekend to check it out if Lexus' parents didn't mind." I wondered if he was going to make a scene and fuss at Mom in front of them for saying that I could go. He seemed to hate it when I was happy about going over to their house.

"Oh, okay," he said with a smile. "So you'll be back with your own family tomorrow, right?"

"No, I'll be back on Sunday. Mom said I could stay all weekend." I was afraid that he would tell me I had to come back tomorrow.

"Hmm."

"What?" I asked, afraid.

He looked over at Mom and glared at her. "Nothing," he said. "Go, have fun." He gave me a peck on the cheek and then pushed past me into the house.

I sighed, relieved. Alison cried that she wanted to go swim in the new pool. Mom told her we'd all go next time. I hugged Nicholas. He seemed angry.

"I wanted to spend the night in your room tonight. We can watch movies all night like we always do on Fridays," he told me.

I kissed his cheek. I wasn't going to let myself get sad.

"Next time, Nickyroo," I told him.

I didn't say any more. I got in the car with Lexus as she shouted loudly to her father that she was starving. Her parents said goodbye to Mom, Alison, and Nick.

They got into the car, and we were off. As Lexus began telling them about everything she wanted to tell them, I stared at Jack as he watched us from the living room window. The look on his face confused me. I couldn't tell if he was angry or not. He seemed distant. He looked like a little kid who wanted to go out and play, but it was too rainy outside.

"Hmm," he had said. His words had come out dark and hard. He had glared at Mom.

Nick had said that he wanted to stay with me that night. He seemed afraid. I became afraid. What had I done? Selfish and stupid Kristen! I suddenly wanted to go back home. But it was too late. We had already made the turn onto the highway by the time I got myself to calm down inside.

I felt a sharp pain. I looked down and realized I was twisting that butterfly between my fingers. Blood ran down my fingers and dripped onto my clothes. Lexus was so caught up in her conversation with her parents that she didn't notice. I didn't care. It was better that way. Mr. Sharp didn't say much aloud back then, anyway.

I quickly stuffed the silver butterfly pendant into my pocket. The nurse came back into the room just as I was concealing it. She didn't notice. The nurse said that it was time to go. When I came out of the room, Mom was gone.

"Where is my Mom?" I asked.

"She went home," the nurse told me.

"But I didn't get to-" I made myself shut up.

"Come on. I'll show you where you will be staying." Nurse Habersham escorted me out of the examining area and into a different part of the hospital. It was the residential part.

The lights were dim, and it was so quiet in that part of the hospital. The nurse asked me to try to whisper if I had to talk, because it was after hours and she didn't want to wake anyone up. We passed through the residential area and got on an elevator. She used a key to access and operate it. I guessed that they had to use key access so that nobody would escape. When we arrived on the seventh floor, I saw a large sign that read Adolescent Ward.

We stepped off the elevator, and another person came to meet us. This woman said that she was a counselor. Her name was Ms. Mosley.

Before Nurse Habersham left, she told me, "Your mother told me to tell you good night and that she'll see you soon as she can."

I was still confused as to why Mom had left without telling me goodbye herself. I didn't ask Nurse Habersham. I let her go. The nurse didn't have key access to the Adolescent Ward, so she went back onto the elevator and left me there with Ms. Mosley. The counselor escorted me through the double doors and onto the Adolescent Ward.

"Let me explain a few things to you," Ms. Mosley began, as she led the way. "First of all, I know you are probably wondering why your mother could not come up here with you. She had to go because, from the point of admittance, you can't have visitors until the doctor puts it in your chart. You are what we call a Level One right now. That means you are restricted to this ward unless you are going to therapy or to your bedroom. Follow me, and I will show you to your room."

I followed behind her. We walked through a large living room with a television, tables, chairs, and board games sitting on the tables. A large, semi-circular area that was divided from the room by a high counter had a sign that read Counselor's Desk. The desk overlooked the living room. Double doors were to my right with a sign that read Boys' Unit. I shuddered at the thought that there could be boys in this ward too. Through the large living room to the other side was another set of double doors with a sign that read Girls' Unit. Ms. Mosley held the door open for me as I carried my suitcase and almost struggled to tag along. I felt physically and mentally tired.

Ms. Mosley didn't turn on the lights when we walked into the room. She kept the door open and let the hallway light shine in. I sat my bag at the edge of the bed like she told me to. She told me not to worry about putting any clothes away. She said I could put my things away in the morning. She told me to try to get some rest because wake up time was at seven a.m. When I looked at my watch, I saw that wake up time was only six hours away. I didn't realize how late it was.

I lay down in the bed. It was cold in there. I curled up under the useless, thin, white blanket as Ms. Mosley said good night and closed the door. The light from the hallway started to disappear, and soon it became completely dark in the room. My eyes wouldn't adjust, so I closed them.

I tried to take all of this into my memory. I wanted to remember what it looked like and what it smelled like. There was a smell to that place. It wasn't like a smell that stunk, nor was it a sweet smell. You could never forget a smell like that. It was a smell that all hospitals had. It began to creep me out. It was as if the smell was there for me to remember, so that I would never forget where I was or what I had done.

CHAPTER 6

In the morning, I heard footsteps in the bedroom. I still had the thin, white blanket over my face. I lifted the blanket from my face to see to whom the footsteps belonged. When I did, I only saw bright sunlight, shining directly in my eyes. I pulled the blanket back over my face.

"No! Get up!" a loud voice shouted. I looked up, and Ms. Mosley was standing over me. "Come on! Get some socks on your feet, and come get your vitals checked! It's time to get up!" She yelled even louder.

Prison! I knew it! I was already getting yelled at. Ms. Mosley was different from the night before. She was now being loud, serious, and stern. Her hands were cold when she touched my arm while pulling me up off the bed. She had long nails that dug into my skin. She didn't even attempt to leave until she saw that I was up and out of bed.

On her way to out of the room, she tapped on the bathroom door. She yelled, "Janine, you know what's going down! Don't let me come back in here in five minutes and see that you're still in that bathroom. Hurry up so you can get your vitals checked and *eat breakfast.*"

Janine was my roommate. I hadn't noticed her when I had come in last night. I had arrived so late. I hadn't fallen asleep, but I had been tired. I was still tired. I couldn't believe I was expected to be all bright-eyed and welcoming the sun.

I slowly dressed into my socks. I was able to keep most of my things after the nurses had raided my bag. I saw that I had my robe in there, but no robe belt. Oh, that's right, I thought, so that I wouldn't hang myself. I noticed that I was still wearing my clothes from the day before. I wanted to shower and change my clothes, but I knew I wouldn't be able to without wetting the stitches in my wrists.

Ms. Mosley stormed back into the room. She banged on the bathroom door, yelling, "That's enough, Janine! I am coming in."

Ms. Mosley opened the door, and a tall, dark-haired, skinny girl came out. She had rosy cheeks and looked like she could have been one of those teen magazine models.

"See, I'm finished. Here's my make-up kit." The girl handed Ms. Mosley a small pink bag. "Gosh, that's all I was doing. You'd think the world was coming to an end, the way you were screaming."

"Humph," Ms. Mosley grunted. "Five minutes, Janine. That's all it takes. You know better."

The girl rolled her eyes and threw herself carelessly on her bed. She looked up at Ms. Mosley, whose arms were folded across her chest.

Ms. Mosley grunted again. "No! Get up, Janine! You have to get your vitals checked. Come on!" Ms. Mosley yanked Janine up as Janine squealed, seemingly frustrated. It looked like she had a death grip on the poor girl's arm. Janine snatched her arm away, cursing her and storming out of the room.

I swallowed hard as Ms. Mosley started towards me. "Hurry up. We have to get your vitals, too." She turned away and left me there.

I sighed in relief. I was glad that she'd stopped yelling. My head was ringing. I slipped on my shoes and walked out of the room. I was all right until I walked through the double doors and saw a living room full of teenagers. They were standing around, talking, and getting together in groups. Some of them were watching cartoons on TV and some were in line, waiting to get their vital signs checked. I nervously stepped into line behind my roommate, and a tall, somewhat heavy-set boy came up and stood behind me. I started to feel crowded and closed in. I stepped out of the line and sort of stood next to my roommate.

When it was Janine's turn to get checked, Ms. Mosley made her sit down, and she began checking her blood pressure first

"How are you feeling today, Janine?" Ms. Mosley asked.

"Better. Can I go home?" my roommate said as she looked
Mosley with a smile.

"Sure! You can go home, Janine," Ms. Mosley responded. "Just ᴉne
one favor first."

"What's that? Anything for you, Ms. Mosley," she sarcastically
responded.

Ms. Mosley leaned down and looked Janine in her face. "You know
what you can do for me, Precious? Why don't you eat all of your
breakfast this morning, and your lunch, along with your dinner? If you
do that for me today, I will see what I can do about getting your doctor to
let you go home."

Janine rolled her eyes and sat back silently as Ms. Mosley put a
thermometer in her mouth. The thermometer beeped, and she released it
from the plastic probe protector. Janine got up angrily with the plastic
probe in her mouth.

"Throw that away, Janine!" Ms. Mosley yelled to her.

Janine kept walking away. She stopped at the trash can and spit the
plastic probe into it. Turning to Ms. Mosley, she smiled prissily. Ms.
Mosley returned the smile with just as much prissiness. She then turned
to me and motioned for me to sit down where Janine had been sitting.
The boy behind me pushed me along like he was getting impatient. I sat
down. She began taking my blood pressure.

When she finished taking my temperature, she told me to go on so that
the next person could be checked. The boy behind me nearly knocked
me over trying to get me out of the way. I stood off to the side.
Nervously, I watched all of the other kids who were there. They didn't
look sick. Some of them looked pale. Nobody seemed as if they really
cared that they were at Bent Creek. They talked to each other, laughed,
and made jokes. It was just like at school.

I began to feel shy and alone. I wanted to try to sneak back to my room,

Ms. Mosley was watching me. I was starting to think that the kids would look at me and find something to laugh about. They would say that I looked funny, or that I didn't fit in. I hadn't really had any friends in high school. I hadn't even had a boyfriend.

Mom had thought I was crazy for wanting to home school. She had asked, "What about the pep rallies and the football games? What about Homecoming and your Senior Prom? Oh, wait, and the Writing Club? What about the Writing Club? You love being in your Writing Club. I know those were things that you were crazy about."

I was not crazy about those things. Those things made me crazy. I loved the Writing Club, but I hated the pep rallies. I never went to a football game. There was no chance that I'd ever be nominated for Homecoming Queen, and no one would ever ask me to Prom.

I'd told Mom that home schooling would give me more of a challenge than regular school. I'd told her that I had felt that public school just wasn't getting me through, and that I'd work and be able to pay for it myself, and even be able to help her out with a few bills. After I'd told her that, she was excited about it.

I'd been in public high school until the end of my sophomore year. I'd left and had started home school when John had left. He and Lexus had graduated two years before me. I hated school. I hated being stared at and teased by the other kids. I hated to be singled out. I was always alone.

There I was in Bent Creek, feeling trapped. It felt like a school that I couldn't escape. My mind started racing with uncontrollable thoughts. I knew they all could see the bandages around my wrists. They'll know everything. They'll call me weird. They'll make fun of me, I thought to myself.

"Hey," said a voice from beside me. I turned, and big, brown eyes stared back at me.

"We're roommates," said the pretty girl.

"Hi," I said.

"I'm Janine. Bulimic Manic Depressive," she introduced herself. "Come over here with me. Meet our group."

I hesitated. Before I could decline, she yanked my hand and pulled me over to a table full of other people. At the table were three girls and two boys. Janine went over to another table and yelled for one of the boys to help her push the tables together to make room for me. When they finished setting up, Janine and I grabbed a chair and sat down.

Janine looked around at everyone and said, "Hey, you guys, this is my roommate. Her name is – wait, what's your name?"

Still looking down and not making eye contact, I told her that my name was Kristen.

"Okay, this is Kristen. Kristen, this is Daniel, Tai, Chris, Cadence, and Lenni."

"Hey, Kristen, welcome to The Insane Part Two," said Chris. He was trying to be funny and nice.

I couldn't smile. I was too nervous. I looked away from his smile.

"Thanks," I said in a low voice.

"When did you get here?" Janine asked.

"Early this morning," I told her.

"That check in stuff takes way too long," Janine sympathized with me.

"Man, I need a cigarette," a very shaky and sleepy-looking guy said.

I looked up at him. He was the first boy in a long time that I had seen with long hair. He didn't seem to care that it was long and hanging down. His hair half-covered his eyes, but I could see them, very bright and beautiful. His name was Daniel. When Daniel looked up at me, he caught me staring. I quickly looked back down, away from his beautiful eyes.

"I hear that," Tai agreed with him. Tai had a tanned complexion. She was very even-toned and had wild, curly, sandy-brown hair. She was thin. When she smiled, her teeth were yellow. It was obvious that a simple toothbrush wouldn't get the job done.

Cadence was a very pale girl. She had straight, short, black hair. She didn't say much. She mostly stared off into nothing. Her lips were bright pink. She wore heavy eyeliner around her big, dark brown eyes. Cadence held on tightly to a doll. The doll looked like it was made of smooth white resin. It had long, black hair that was all matted up on one side. And it had one creepy looking stitched-up eye. The eye that wasn't stitched up was beady and red. I tried not to stare at it.

Chris had chin-length blonde hair and could pass for one of those California surfer boys with the way he looked and dressed if he had a surfboard in his front pocket.

Daniel, Tai, and Lenni were the angry ones of the group. I sensed that Daniel would have been more pleasant if he wasn't shaking so badly, and if he had a cigarette. Lenni was angry because she felt that she didn't need to be at Bent Creek. She told us the story about how, when she had been twelve, she had written letters about wanting to run away from home. Her mother had found them and had stuck her in Bent Creek. Her mother was somehow convinced that she was going to run away.

Janine seemed sweet. She tried to calm Lenni down by telling her to tell her doctor that the letters were old and that she didn't feel like running away. While Janine was talking, Chris started swearing angrily at Cadence. Cadence looked over at me and stared. Chris stopped and apologized. Cadence didn't care. She and her one eyed doll just kept staring at me. I began to feel creeped out.

"Don't worry about it, Chris," Janine said to him. "We all know about your DID."

"What is DID?" asked Lenni.

"It is Dissociative Identity Disorder," Chris said.

"What does that mean?" Lenni pressed.

"It means that I have four people living inside of me, besides myself." Chris said. He seemed sad. "I'm sorry, you guys. Jake has a bad attitude. He doesn't really like it here, but *I like* you guys. I'm not trying to be rude."

"Who *does* like it here?" Tai commented.

"Look, Chris," Janine said. "Just tell Jake that we're all in the same position here. Chill out. Nobody wants to be here."

I looked past Chris and I saw that Cadence was still staring at me. She was holding her doll against her chest and she was rocking back and forth. I looked away from her.

"So, what did you do? Did you do one of those cry-for-help things and drag your mom's steak knife across your skin to get a little blood? Did you take a razor and do a few cuts across the wrists to make some stains? Come on, tell us," Tai pressed me.

"Oh, shut up!" Janine spat at her. "Why don't you tell us what you did?"

Tai lifted her shirt and showed us her stomach. She had deep stitches from where she said she had stab wounds.

"Guts," Tai boasted. "I had guts to do what I did."

"Yeah, guts that your crazy ass obviously tried to rip out," Daniel commented. I looked over at him, shocked to hear him speak.

Tai smiled and said, "Yeah, but it didn't work this time."

"You think that's funny?" Lenni asked Chris because he was laughing.

"I don't know about Chris, but I do," said Chris' evil personality, Jake. "Look what I did to him." Jake lifted Chris' sleeves and revealed his scarred arms. He had a countless number of scars and burns. He had words carved into his skin. I could make out the words "die" and "for nothing".

"That's messed up," Daniel said.

"What about you, then?" Jake pressed Daniel.

Daniel cocked his head, raised his hand to Chris' face, and gave him the bird. Chris must have come back because he looked at Daniel, shocked.

"Why did you do that to me?" he asked.

Daniel stood up. I watched him as he ignored Chris and walked over to Ms. Mosley. She scolded him for not standing in line like everyone else had done to get his vitals checked. Daniel told her that he liked being the last one so that he could have conversations with her. She seemed charmed and flattered, because she smiled at him. I looked back at Chris. Next to him, Cadence was grinning at me. It was almost as if she was reading me. She knew I didn't feel like I belonged here. I didn't feel like I was like any of these kids. Cadence started laughing harder.

Tai looked at her. "What the hell is so funny?"

"Meds!" someone yelled.

I looked up, and a herd of teenagers was rushing to the nurse's station.

"Those of you who take morning medications, please line up at the medicine counter," called another counselor.

Daniel stayed near Ms. Mosley.

"Don't you have morning medication, Daniel?" Ms. Mosley asked.

Daniel shook his head.

She smiled at him.

Daniel looked up and caught me staring at him again. I quickly looked away. I watched as Cadence stuffed her pills down her throat without drinking the water that the nurse handed out to her. I slowly turned back to Daniel. He was still looking my way. When our eyes met again, he didn't let me turn away from him without giving me a smile. It was warm. I tried to be kind and smile back, but it was hard. I was still nervous. Boys didn't smile at me. They only made disgusted faces. I turned to Janine. She was coming towards me from the medicine counter.

"Come on," she said as she grabbed my hand. "We have to get in the circle." She yanked me up and we walked into a room that was one of many in that ward. There was one love seat and a few hard chairs all pushed together to make a circle. Janine quickly pulled me along to the love seat so that we'd be the first to get it. We sat down.

Janine looked at me and smiled. I tried to smile back, but it was just too early in the morning. Sensing I wasn't quite with it that morning, Janine shrugged it off. Ms. Mosley entered the room and kids poured in right behind her. Tai came in and slid right between Janine and me. As she was sitting down, I saw her give Janine an evil look. Janine rolled her eyes. I guess it was because Janine was sharing the love seat with me and not her. The three of us fit on the couch, but I still felt odd. Both of them were so tiny. I began to get self-conscious over how chubby I felt. Finally, the room filled up with the kids I had seen in the front area, all except for Lenni, who never came in.

"Dr. Finch will be in here soon," Ms. Mosley said. "You guys just sit tight."

Cadence walked past me and sat in the chair next to Daniel. Daniel had a small piece of paper that was rolled up in his mouth. He was sucking on the paper, I guess pretending it was a real cigarette. As he reached up to take the paper out of his mouth, I noticed that his hands were shaking badly.

A tall, dark-skinned man entered the room. I knew he was Dr. Finch because of his professional demeanor. He had a very young face for a doctor. He had a shaved head, a mustache, and a goatee. He was neatly dressed in a pair of khaki pants and a sky blue, button-down shirt with a neatly folded collar. He sat down in an empty chair next to Ms. Mosley. "Good morning, everyone!" he greeted, full of morning cheer.

There were slurred mumbles of a good morning back to him. Some people didn't say good morning at all. I didn't.

Dr. Finch looked around at everyone. He turned to Ms. Mosley and said, "Ms. Mosley, wasn't that the most terrible morning greeting you've ever heard?"

Ms. Mosley nodded her head. She said, "We should try this again."

"Come on guys. *I said good morning!*" he tried again.

Mostly everyone shouted good morning back at him. Tai and Janine shouted as loud and annoyingly as they could. I had to put my hands over my ears. Daniel just sat there with his face in his hands. Cadence stared at him.

"That was much better. Welcome to your Goals Group. Goals Group is your very first therapy session of the day. The purpose of this group is to help you set some positive and reachable goals every day for yourself. It is always good to have a different goal every day. Don't use the same goal that you had yesterday, even if you didn't fulfill that goal. Try it again the day after. When you are choosing a goal for the day, try to make it a real goal. Don't just say what you think Ms. Mosley or I want to hear. Make that goal reachable and something that is really going to help you."

"A cigarette would help me right about now," Tai whispered to Janine and me.

Ms. Mosley seemed not to hear what she said, but she still gave her a stern look that made Tai straighten up.

"Dr. Finch continued, "All right, so we will start by going around the room. Everyone, state your goal for the day and what you will do to try to reach that goal."

"Oh," Ms. Mosley butted in, "I just wanted to say that everyone should state their group goal for the day as well. We discuss group goals in night group with your group counselor. I think that some kids might need a reminder of what their group goal is for the day. So, everyone, make sure that you state that too."

Janine looked over at Tai. They grinned at each other. The odd feeling inside of me was getting worse. It felt like they were making fun of me in some kind of way. I leaned back on the love seat and wished that I could disappear.

Dr. Finch looked at Ms. Mosley and suggested that she go first. Ms. Mosley obliged. "Okay. I'm Ms. Mosley. I am the counselor for Group Two. My goal for today is be on all you all's butts today. You are not getting away with anything."

"Isn't that your goal every day?" Chris blurted out.

Suddenly, out of nowhere, Cadence gripped Daniel's leg and pinched the hell out of him.

"Ouch!" yelled Daniel as he jumped out of his seat. "Leave me alone!"

"Okay, let's get control of ourselves!" Dr. Finch yelled.

"Did you see her just hurt me? She's insane!" Daniel was red with anger.

Tai and Janine were laughing hysterically with everyone else. I seemed to be the only one who thought that this was not funny. Cadence was laughing and she was staring right at me. Her stares were piercing me. I felt my heart beating fast. It could have been the commotion and excitement. It could have been because I was nervous and felt out of place.

Dr. Finch's demeanor went from calm to upset. "Cadence, go back to the front unit with Geoffrey. We don't need this kind of disruption in here." Dr. Finch pointed to the door. Cadence hesitated and looked at Ms. Mosley.

"Now!" Dr. Finch yelled.

Cadence jumped up off the couch as she held her little, resin doll in her arms. As she passed me, she twirled around like she was doing a dance. She stopped and bent down to my level to look me in the eyes.

"Welcome," she said. Then, she strolled out of the door.

I sat still, astounded. My heart was beating faster than before. Janine and Tai were staring at me like I had done something wrong. I slid down lower on the love seat. Maybe, if I keep sliding, I could disappear in between the cushions without anyone noticing, I thought. I was so lost that I didn't even notice that Chris had begun stating his goals for the day.

"I am in Group Three," Chris said. "Our group goal for the day is to try to relate with one of our personalities. I am going to try to relate with Jake. My personal goal for the day is to try to not fight with Jake so much. He thinks that this is his body, but I have to show that I am in control, somehow."

Tai went next. "I'm Tai. I am in Group Two. Our group goal is to be nicer to Ms. Mosley today. That was more her idea than ours."

Ms. Mosley rolled her eyes at Tai.

"Anyways," Tai continued. "My goal for the day is to try not to lose my temper at anyone today. So, I guess in order to do that, I just won't say too much to people that annoy me."

Janine tapped Tai on her arm. They grinned at each other, again.

"Janine, why don't you go next?" suggested Ms. Mosley.

Janine smiled at Ms. Mosley prissily.

"I'm Janine," Janine said, "and I am in Group Two. We have to be nicer to Ms. Mosley today. My goal is to eat lunch and dinner."

"No! No! No!" yelled a boy from the other side of the room. This boy was tiny and had a mousy voice. He was thin. "You can't do that! That was your goal from yesterday."

"No, my goal for yesterday was to just eat lunch. Today I am going to eat lunch and dinner," Janine clarified.

"Yeah, whatever, Janine," the little boy said. "You didn't even eat lunch yesterday, so what makes you think you will eat lunch and dinner today, fat ass?"

Janine jumped up out of her seat and went for the little boy. Dr. Finch grabbed her and made her sit down.

"Shut up, Josh! Look at yourself! Why don't you take a look in the mirror?" I could see tears welling up in Janine's eyes. A few drops fell. Ms. Mosley suggested that Janine go outside with Cadence, but Janine wanted to stay.

"Why don't you make Minnie Mouse leave?" she whined. "He's the one who started with me!"

"No one is leaving," Dr. Finch said. "We are all going to get through this and state our goals for the day. That's what we came here to do, so let's do it." Dr. Finch looked at me. "Why don't you go next?"

I felt a sharp pain go through my chest. "I… uhh… well, I don't know what group-"

"I'll go next," Daniel said.

I felt so stupid.

"I can't believe it, a volunteer." Ms. Mosley said.

"And of all people," Chris said. Or maybe it was Jake.

Daniel showed him his middle finger again. Chris didn't realize this until Jake had disappeared.

"Why do you keep doing that to me?" Chris asked.

"I'm Daniel," he began, ignoring Chris. "I am in Group Two. Our group goal is to be nice to Ms. Mosley, and we have to be respectful and stuff. My personal goal for today is to be more positive when it comes to talking about my future. I have to say better things about myself and not call myself a loser or whatever."

"That is an excellent goal, Daniel," Dr. Finch complimented. "That's real and it's reachable."

Everyone stayed silent. Daniel was picking at his shoelaces. It seemed like he could see me staring at him from the corner of his eye. He looked up at me. I turned away quickly. When I looked back at him, he was looking down and messing with his shoelaces again.

There was another person there, who wasn't afraid to speak up. He shared after Daniel. He was in Group One, and had scars all over his arms and face. He explained that his scars had come from him being burned in a house fire. He didn't seem nervous talking to all of the people that he didn't even know. He was very open, and it seemed like he actually wanted everyone to listen to him.

Josh, the little one who had mouthed off to Janine, was also in Group One. He was in Bent Creek because he refused to eat. He was mean to Ms. Mosley when she tried to help him set a goal for himself. He said that he'd rather they keep the portable feeding tube in him because he wasn't going to put anything in his mouth. I could tell that they really didn't know what to do with that kid, so they gave up on him in Goals Group.

After everyone else had a chance to speak, Dr. Finch dismissed us from Group. Ms. Mosley ordered everyone to get ready for breakfast. Tai and Janine, along with everyone else, jumped up and darted out of the room. Janine left me, but I didn't care. It seemed like she'd been scheming on me in Goals Group with Tai, anyway. They probably didn't like me, I thought. Daniel was still messing with his shoelaces. I looked over at him.

"I really think your goal was good," I heard myself say.

Daniel looked up at me with a shocked look on his face. It was almost as if he had forgotten where he was.

"Oh," he said. "Thanks.'

"Excuse me," a voice said from above me. I looked up and Dr. Finch was standing over me. "Daniel and I have a session now. Would you leave us?" He was nice about it. I nodded and left the room, closing the door behind me.

I wished that Dr. Cuvo were there already. Bent Creek did not seem like the place where I belonged. Sure, I was depressed for a little while. However, I didn't want to be locked up with Bulimics, Multiple Personalities, and Psychos. I just wanted to go home.

CHAPTER 7

During breakfast, Janine filled me in on the way things worked at Bent Creek. She told me that our doctors could come day or night, but we were required to see them every single day that we were here. Then, a rumor started that Lenni was able to go home because she'd had a family session the day before and it had gone well. I figured a family session was a good thing in this place. Today, though, I would dread having to face anyone in my family other than my mother.

The day felt like it had actually begun after breakfast. The first group we attended was Anger Management. It didn't matter if you were an angry person or not. If your group was scheduled for it, then you had to go. Ms. Mosley, head counselor of Group Two, put me in her group. I was somewhat relieved to be in the same group as Janine. Dr. Bent, who seemed like a laid-back person, moderated anger Management. She didn't care if the kids swore or even horsed around a little bit before the session began. She talked with some of the kids as they entered the room, and as we waited for everyone to settle into chairs. She seemed cool because she put up really well with Tai and Janine's constant noise.

"Take a few minutes," Dr. Bent began, "and think of a situation that happened that made you very angry. Now, I don't want you to pick something major, like what landed you in here, but something that could happen to anyone, on any day. You know, just something normal that you figure could make anyone angry."

Tai rolled her eyes. She grunted to Dr. Bent, "I don't think I understand what you mean."

"What's so confusing about this exercise, Tai?" Dr. Bent asked.

Tai flared her big nostrils at Dr. Bent.

She said, "I need to know what you mean by 'normal'. Do you mean something normal like someone making you angry because they cut you off in traffic, or do mean something normal like your step-mother beating the hell out of you for hugging your own father because she is a jealous, old hag who's nothing but a mooching, gold-digger? Is that what you mean by 'normal,' Dr. Bent? Are both of those things something that could happen to just anyone? Or are we just some kind of special group of people where the 'normal' things are just 'normal' things that can happen to anyone kind of things, and the 'really major' things are what we get for not having the 'normal' things happen to us, like it could happen to anyone else? Because if you are asking me to say which is normal for me, and you say that the one I choose is not normal, then I think that's just screwed up, and I don't deserve it, and none of us do."

It took me a minute to swallow all of that. Dr. Bent seemed to be right on basis with Tai. Dr. Bent leaned forward, still making eye contact with Tai. Tai turned her head slightly and looked away from her. Tai had tears in her eyes and she was trying not to let them fall. I watched as Janine scooted away from Tai. Dr. Bent was so calm. She kept her eyes on Tai, even though Tai wouldn't look at her.

She said, "Which one of those two things you mentioned is normal for you, Tai?"

Tai was breathing heavily. She turned back to Dr. Bent with a sharp gaze and wet cheeks.

"Screw you!" she yelled at Dr. Bent.

I thought for sure that Dr. Bent was going to throw her out. Everyone stared at Tai. There were about ten seconds of shocked silence until Dr. Bent opened her mouth and said, "Yeah! Screw me! Screw you! You know what? Screw this! Screw everyone in here! Screw the whole world! Isn't that right, Tai? It works that way in this stupid world! Just screw everything. That's why it's okay to take a knife and slide it across our skin! That's why it's okay to take drugs, drink, and smoke our lives away! That's why it's okay to run away from home, steal, and become junkies! That is why it's okay to kill ourselves, and try to take the rest of the world with us, everyone who cares about us, and everyone who doesn't! Yeah, that's why it's okay, because everything is screwed."

Everyone kept quiet. We stared at Dr. Bent. I never imagined Anger Management to be full of so many angry people. Even the doctor was angry.

Tai had even more tears coming out of her now. She was pouring like a fountain. She sat back in the chair with her arms folded across her chest. She, like the rest of us, was looking right at Dr. Bent. Janine was very far away from Tai. It was as if she didn't even want to be near her. Janine kept looking back and forth from Dr. Bent to Tai.

Dr. Bent finally said, in a much calmer tone, "Everything got screwed up by someone saying 'screw it'. They just give up. It makes it harder on others who haven't. The messed up things in this world are all around us. It's up to us if we are going to give up too, or learn to deal and make it better for ourselves. Tai, one day when you learn to not let your temper get the best of you, and you stay silent, listen, learn, and put it all together in your mind, you'll know the difference between the 'normal' things and what's just 'screwed up'."

Tai wiped her face and didn't say a word. Janine looked at her with a strange expression that I couldn't understand. Tai's face grew dark.

Tai looked at Dr. Bent and said, "Let's leave my lectures in my private therapy sessions, please."

I could tell she was trying to show off.

Janine smiled at Tai for her smart remark and smooth comeback to Dr. Bent. She seemed embarrassed, perhaps because she'd cried in front of everyone.

Dr. Bent remained calm and said, "That's fine, Tai. However, know that I will get deep when you get deep with me. I am going to answer that question if you ask it, whether it's in here or in your private sessions with me. To answer the question you asked me, none of those things that hurt us are normal. You were right, none of us deserves to be hurt by people we are supposed to trust, nor should we be cut off in traffic by rude people, but these things happen. How do we manage to cope and how do we manage our anger when these things do happen? That is what we're here to learn."

69

Tai stared down at the floor. She didn't respond.

"Okay," Dr. Bent said. "Daniel, you want to go next?"

"Sure," he said after clearing his throat. "I remember walking in the grocery store with my mom and my grandmother. My paternal grandmother was with us, and she is Black. Well, my mom is White. Anyways, there was a man, and he had said some racist stuff to us. My mom," Daniel paused and shook his head, "she didn't say *anything*. We walked away from the guy. It made me so mad. I could have just-" Daniel balled up his left fist and punched his right hand hard. I watched as his right hand turned deep red.

Dr. Bent leaned on the arm of her chair and asked Daniel, "What did you do?"

"I stayed quiet too. I just walked out with my mom and tried to keep her calm." He said it as if he regretted it.

"You said you were there with your father's mother and your mother. Where was your father?" Dr. Bent asked.

Daniel answered, "He was in jail at the time."

"What was he in jail for?"

"He was in jail for beating some guy into a coma at a bar for making a pass at my mom." Daniel hid his face from us by looking down at the floor. He started messing with his shoelaces again.

"A lesson within itself. Isn't that right Daniel?" Dr. Bent said.

"Yeah, but I still wish I could have done *something*." Daniel untied and retied his shoes. His face was red like his hand had been.

"You would feel that way," Dr. Bent said. "And you are allowed to feel that way. It was something that caused you to feel angry."

"This is Anger Management, right?" Tai commented.

"What about Screwed Up Life, Management?" laughed one of the other kids.

Dr. Bent laughed and said, "That's a different kind of group."

"What time is that group, Dr. Bent?" Daniel said as he laughed with everyone else.

His eyes squinted slightly when he laughed. When he squinted, it made his eyes glow between his lashes. It was amazing to look at. Those eyes made me smile.

"I don't know, but I think we should all go," Dr. Bent said as the laughter subsided. "Okay, everyone, calm down. Who wants to go next?"

There was silence, and everyone looked around the room at each other. Tai was in better spirits and she kept messing around with Janine. She grabbed Janine's arm and tried to make her raise it in the air.

Dr. Bent ignored them and looked at Cadence. "How about you, Cadence?"

Cadence slid close to Daniel, and Daniel scooted away from her. She licked her lips and nodded at Dr. Bent. Dr. Bent smiled and we all waited, but the weirdo didn't say anything. She just stared at Daniel, smiling.

Daniel finally said, "What's your problem?"

He got up and sat in an empty chair next to me. I shuddered and tried not to look at him. Cadence was staring at me again. This time she looked like she wanted to kill me. I looked down at my shoes. My shoelaces were untied. I started tying my shoes. I zoned out and tuned out everything around me. I didn't know that Dr. Bent was trying to get my attention until I felt someone tap me, which startled me so badly that I jumped, and it made Daniel jump, because he was the one that had tapped me.

"Ouch," Daniel said as he jerked back. "Your shirt's got static. You shocked me."

"Sorry," I whispered, not sure if he heard me. I kept my head down as I tied my shoes.

"Dr. Bent's talking to you," I heard Daniel say. "Are you sleeping?"

I looked up and everyone was staring at me. Cadence wasn't in the room anymore. Dr. Bent must have kicked her out. Dr. Bent asked me my name. I told her that my name was Kristen. She wanted me to go next, but Janine stopped me.

She said, "Dr. Bent, this is her first day. Maybe it would be better for her to listen until she is more comfortable. You remember how I was at first."

Dr. Bent nodded. She asked me if I wanted to listen for now and maybe talk later on. I nodded and looked back down at my shoes. Janine gave me a playful nudge, and I rocked slightly. Dr. Bent made Janine share because she had saved me. Janine started going on about a woman who'd cut her off in traffic while she'd been taking her driver's license exam. She confessed that her response had been yelling out and calling the old woman an "old, stank bag wench". Which Dr. Bent told her was probably the reason she failed her test, not because it was the old woman's fault. She said it was a negative consequence to a negative action.

Daniel laughed when Janine said that she had called the lady an "old, stank bag wench".

Daniel said, "That was definitely not the right way to react, Janine."

"Shut up," she said as she playfully stuck her tongue out at him. "I get to try again next week."

"If you are out of here," Tai said.

I didn't really believe Janine's story. She elbowed Tai in her side and made a silly face at her. Daniel laughed along with them. Everyone seemed connected. I felt out of place.

CHAPTER 8

"Nick? Where are you?"

I felt my chest rise in pain with each breath I took. It was almost as if my heart was trying to escape from my chest. Tears were streaming from my eyes. I was moving in slow motion. Nick was lying on the floor, naked. It was too dark to see him clearly. It was late in the night. I was tired. I'd wanted a drink of water, so I headed for the kitchen. I'd been passing by Nick's bedroom when suddenly I'd stopped.

"Nickyroo? Why are you on the floor?"

I slowly peeked through the door. I could almost see in.

"NICK!"

I suddenly opened my eyes. I looked around, and I saw Janine laughing with Tai on the sofa. I had fallen asleep on the floor in the living room. Cadence was watching television with her doll and Chris, along with a few other kids. Everyone was in his or her place with other people. I was alone in my place. I looked up from under my arm and I saw Daniel coming towards me. I smiled. He sat down on the floor next to me. I tried to sit up and listen to him as he started talking, but as soon as he got out two words that sounded like, "What are-" Dr. Cuvo appeared out of nowhere. I was actually glad to see him.

"Are you ready, Kristen?" he asked me.

I jumped up off the floor and followed him to one of the empty rooms used for group therapy. Before he closed the door completely behind us, I started to give him a piece of my mind.

"I want to go home," I said.

Dr. Cuvo sat down quietly in a chair and opened my chart.

"Come on and sit down, Kristen"

I sat down, impatient and a little upset.

"Please, Dr. Cuvo. I really don't belong here."

"Yes, I heard you, Kristen. I can't do anything about you wanting to go home. You have to stay here until it is safe for you to go home. You have not even been here twenty-four hours yet. The first twenty-four hours are for observation. You haven't even gotten into your therapy."

"What is my therapy? Morning medication? Anger Management? Sessions with you? More of everyone-" I made myself shut up.

"More of everyone doing what?"

"No, Dr. Cuvo." I felt dumb again. I couldn't get out what was locked in my mind. Mr. Sharp was pressing in on me. He was close by; I could feel him creeping in on me.

Dr. Cuvo pressed in on me too.

"What are you feeling, Kristen? What do you feel that everyone in here is doing?"

"Everyone: Janine, Tai, Cadence. They are all talking about me. They are calling me ugly when I am not looking, and they are laughing at me. I hear them, and I can't just go to that place. I can't just go in my room and get away from them. I don't belong here. Can I just go home?"

Warm tears started running down my face. I felt stupid. Maybe they weren't talking about me, or maybe they were, because I'd seen them laughing.

"Let me tell you something, Kristen," Dr. Cuvo began. "I know that kids can be cruel. I know that, in your experience with your peers, a lot people have been very mean to you. If you feel that anyone in here is talking about you, you should go to that person and ask them what their problem is. I can bet that the problem that they tell you is not you. You are probably the furthest from any of these kids' minds. Also, I don't think that any of them have any reason to laugh at you because they are no better than you while you all are in here."

"Why do I keep feeling like they are laughing at me?" I asked him.

"I think it is because you are used to that happening from when you were in school. Understand, this is not school. Bent Creek is not a place where you have the cool clique and the rejects. This is a place where everyone is equal. Everyone has imperfections and feels insecure. There's no hiding it. So, instead of taking the laughter that you hear and using it against yourself, why don't you take it as an invitation to laugh with them? Share yourself the way they are trying to share with you. I think it will help you to see what's really going on."

I nodded and stared out of the one window behind Dr. Cuvo.

"Maybe you're right," I said as I thought about it. His point was valid. I hadn't bothered to think of the situation the way he had described it.

"How are your wrists?" Dr. Cuvo asked.

I shrugged.

"They are okay. I keep them wrapped up. Is a doctor coming to look at the stitches?"

Dr. Cuvo nodded.

"There should be a nurse coming today to take your blood for tests. The nurse should help you get cleaned up so that you don't get your stitches wet. It will be like when you were in the main hospital."

I sighed in relief. I'd been almost embarrassed to ask.

"I talked to your mother, Kristen," Dr. Cuvo said.

"Is she coming here today?" I asked.

"No, you can't have any visitors while you are at Level One. At any rate, while I was talking to your mother, she told me that she was going through your knife collection."

"What was she doing with my knives?" I asked.

"What were you doing with your knives, Kristen?"

"I collected them."

"What else?"

He was looking at my arms. There were old scars from my cutting. I pulled down my sleeves, and kept my gaze towards the window. I didn't feel as trapped when I did that.

"I already know, even if you don't want to tell me." He was still staring at me, but I wasn't staring back.

"She told me about how she'd had problems with you cutting yourself with those knives. Do you want to tell me about the knives, Kristen?"

I didn't say a word. I kept looking out of the window. I was trying hard not to break. She hadn't told him everything. I was sure she hadn't told him the truth behind it all. She was putting it all on me, like she always did. It was easy for Mom to do it that way. Make it twist and turn until it fit the way she wanted it to fit. My mind started racing as the temperature in the room dropped. I wandered off as Dr. Cuvo spoke about the knives. I didn't want to hear him. So, I let myself drift off.

I leaned down, not really sure what it was at the bottom of the tub. I reached in and pulled it out of the drain. Whatever was in that drain was causing it to stop up. When I got it out, I examined its plastic texture and rubbery feel. When I realized what it was, I felt myself gag, and I quickly threw the condom into the toilet. Mom suddenly appeared at the bathroom door, and she stared at me as I stared into the toilet.

"What's wrong?" she asked.

I had been busy cleaning up the bathroom, and trying to get my chores done before she and Jack got home, that I didn't even realize the time. Nick and Alison were in their bedrooms. Mom was now standing next to me, staring into the toilet too.

"Where did you get that?" Mom had fear in her voice.

I put my hands up as if I were under arrest. She looked at the large, yellow, cleaning gloves on my hands.

"It's not mine, Mom," I said. "I was cleaning the bathroom, and I found it in the drain. It was stopping up the tub." Mom looked into the toilet and I watched as her face flushed white.

"Mom, you and Dad haven't taken a shower together in a really long time," I said. "But he and-"

"Shut up." Her voice scared me. It didn't sound like her.

"Huh?"

"I said shut up, Kristen!" she was yelling at me now. She leaned over and quickly flushed the toilet. "Don't come at me with this mess. I am tired. I just got home from work. I can't deal with this right now. What are you trying to do to us?"

I swallowed all the pain that was in my chest and in my throat.

"Mom, I wasn't trying to do anything. I just was saying that I found this in the tub. Jack, he's been-"

"Since when is he Jack?" she asked.

"I mean, Dad's been-"

"You know what, Kristen? I don't want to hear any more of this. Just leave me alone and let me get some rest before your brother and sister realize that I am home, and what little bit is left of my sanity is gone. You really know how to cross that line with me, don't you? You really make things hard on us. Just stay away from me for the rest of the night. I don't want to see your face."

Her words echoed in my head. The feeling that I had gotten so much. That pain that seemed to linger in me wouldn't go away. It was like metal had begun to form in my chest and take the form of a ball. The ball stayed there, and slowly, had begun to turn.

All of this would have been done and over with. I wouldn't have had to remember these things or feel these things if I had just been able to die. Tears started falling from my eyes. I was crying so hard, I could hardly breathe. Mr. Sharp couldn't appear. The talk about knives made him want to come out.

I started screaming, "Stop it! Stop it!" I kept hitting myself in the head as hard as I could while I was screaming. I wanted the thoughts to get out! They had to stop!

Dr. Cuvo grabbed my arms. He was trying to stop me.

"Kristen! What's going on? What is happening? Talk to me, and stop hitting yourself."

I slapped myself in the face, hard. I wouldn't stop slapping until I felt numb. Dr. Cuvo got a tight grip on both of my wrists. He squeezed them. I screamed out in pain as the pain and pressure I felt went through my wrists and out the other sides. The pain that I was feeling inside made it almost unbearable. It made me stop fighting. I looked up at Dr. Cuvo.

His face was the color of a beet. His eyes were huge, and I could tell that he was holding his breath. His large, deep eyes were staring right at me. The compassionate look on his face stung me deeply.

"Stop it," I cried softly to him.

He slowly turned my wrists loose from his tight grip, but he stayed close to me. His eyes still stared into mine.

"I'm trying to make it stop. I want to make it stop, Kristen. Please, you have to help me."

"I don't know how!" I cried to him.

"Let me help you," Dr. Cuvo said.

I couldn't say anything. The pain from the metal ball in my chest made it hurt too much to speak. Dr. Cuvo let me cry. I cried until I felt numb again. When I felt numb, I wiped my eyes, sat back, and looked back out the window. Dr. Cuvo said that he wasn't going to make me talk to him. He could see that I was upset. I didn't want to say anything. I was in the perfect place. I was in the place that Mr. Sharp would let me go when I had my knives, or my silver butterfly, with its sharp wings.

Dr. Cuvo ended my session by telling me that he wanted to start me on a medication called Risperdol. He told me that it would help me get to sleep at night, and it should help me with my worries that the kids in here were against me. I nodded, but I wasn't really listening. I stared out of the window, imagining I wasn't here. I imagined that I was resting somewhere where my ashes would have been scattered or buried in the earth.

CHAPTER 9

When the session was over, Dr. Cuvo stuck out his hand, as usual. I took his hand and we shook. When we were on the main unit, everyone seemed to suddenly appear. Janine ran over from the couch where she was sitting next to Tai and Chris. I thought she was coming over to me, but she jumped in front of Dr. Cuvo with a big smile on her face.

"Are you ready for me?" she eagerly asked him. She seemed really jittery and anxious.

"Not yet, Janine, but I will be with you shortly," he told her as he tried to head for the exit.

"Why not?" She frowned, looking as if she was going to break.

Dr. Cuvo stopped at the exit door. He didn't even look at her while he was talking to her.

"I have other patients to see right now, Janine. I will be back to talk to you later," Dr. Cuvo said.

He pushed past her coldly and stuck his key in the door. The door began to open slowly. Janine tried to stay close to him, and looked at him with anger in her eyes. I watched them closely. Everyone else just seemed to be in their own little world. I watched Janine's lips move as she leaned in closer to him. She wasn't yelling now. I couldn't hear what she was saying. Right when Dr. Cuvo was about to walk out of the half-opened door, he stopped and looked at her. Now he looked her directly in the eyes.

"Later, Janine," he said in a serious, insensitive tone. Then, he walked out the door.

Janine almost followed him out. When she screamed out angrily, Ms. Mosley looked up from what she was doing.

All eyes were on Janine. Ms. Mosley immediately came around from behind the counselor's desk and asked Janine to sit down and join the rest of us on the unit. Janine stood, still staring at the exit door. Her arms were folded across her chest and her eyes were wide open like she was possessed.

"Come on, Janine. Have a seat over here with everyone else," Ms. Mosley tried to encourage her.

Janine didn't flinch.

Losing her patience, Ms. Mosley yelled at her. Janine just stood there.

"Geoffrey, help me with Janine again," Ms. Mosley demanded the young counselor.

Geoffrey stood up from behind the desk. He walked over to Janine and gently grabbed her arm.

Geoffrey said, "Come, Janine. We are going to go sit down."

"Get off of me! Stop touching me, you stupid pervert!" she screamed. She yelled even louder when Ms. Mosley came to help Geoffrey. She was screaming, "No! No! Don't touch me! You can't do this! No!"

Everyone on the unit stared at Janine as she swung her arms wildly. She hit Geoffrey in the face. That's when Ms. Mosley pushed Janine to the ground and pulled her hands behind her back. Geoffrey had Janine in his tight grip. He and Ms. Mosley lifted her off the floor and carried her away as she screamed and shouted. They carried her out of a door and down a hallway that I had not yet walked through. I could hear Janine screaming until the door shut behind them.

I was frightened for Janine after I heard the door slam. After the commotion was over, everyone went back to what they were doing as if nothing had happened. Tai sat on the couch next to Chris, expressionless. I walked over to a seat at a table, near the couch, and sat down. The new guy that I had seen in morning group came over and sat at the table with me.

He leaned over and asked Tai, "Do you know what they are doing to that girl in there?"

"BCR," she told him.

"BCR? What's that?" he asked Tai.

I was curious, too.

"It's called a Behavioral Control Room," Chris clarified.

"Thanks, nobody asked you," Tai growled at him.

Chris didn't respond. Daniel walked into the front room from where Dr. Cuvo had exited. Dr Finch was ahead of him. Daniel smiled and thanked Dr. Finch. He and Daniel fist bumped and then said good bye before Dr. Finch walked away.

"Why did they put her in there?" I asked.

Tai looked at me as if I were stupid. I felt stupid for asking. I guess it was obvious.

Tai answered, "They put her in there to strap her down and shut her up. Don't worry, they don't use shocks here." Tai laughed. "I know what you new people must think when you come in here."

"What happened?" Daniel pulled up a chair to the table. "Janine got put in the BCR?"

"Oh, wow! You are, like, *so* clever!" Tai sarcastically exclaimed.

"What is your problem?" Daniel asked her.

She sighed. "Nothing. I just need a cigarette."

"Me too, look." Daniel stuck out his hands. They were shaking worse than before. "I can't even do any of my drawings. My doctor won't let them give me a patch. Nothing."

"Wow," Tai said. "You're itching for a ciggy really bad."

"She and Janine got into an argument," Cadence blurted out. We didn't notice that she had come over to us. Cadence's creepy little doll was resting on her shoulder.

Tai stood up and smacked Cadence hard across her face. The doll fell to the floor. Cadence grabbed her face, looking shocked, and in pain.

"What? You crazy bitch! You want to talk to me some more? Go ahead, so that I can punch you in your mouth this time," Tai threatened.

Cadence, still holding onto her face, picked up her doll and ran towards the Girls' Unit. She ran through the double doors and disappeared.

Ms. Mosley walked back in and yelled for everyone to go to their rooms and wash their hands for lunch. Tai stormed off. I looked at Daniel. He was laughing.

"She's the crazy one," he commented.

Chris and the new guy walked off through the double doors that led to the Boys' Unit.

"Why did she do that?" I asked Daniel.

Daniel kept laughing. "Tai is pretty messed up. I guess that's what drugs will do to you."

I looked at him, not laughing.

He stopped laughing. He reached out his hand, but he didn't touch me.

"It's okay. It's just that Tai is tired of being here. Much like the rest of us." He tried to make me smile with his smile and his sweet dimple.

"It's okay," he repeated.

His dimple kept smiling at me, so I smiled back.

"So you can smile," he said. "I guess I win the bet." He got up and walked off towards his room.

Bet?

I sat there, letting his smile linger in my mind for a while. Ms. Mosley had to come over and break my pleasant daydreaming. She told me to go to my room and wash my hands. I went to the bedroom. Janine had a big, pink blanket on her bed. It hadn't been there this morning. I threw myself on my bed and began to wander off. I forgot why I had come in here to begin with.

My mind wandered off to Lexus. I wondered what she was doing. I wondered what she had thought when she had heard that I was in the hospital. I wondered what she had thought when she had heard about what I had done. I knew they had told her. He had probably told her. They both knew.

Nick. What was Nick doing? I wondered if Nick was all right. He had been screaming so badly when he'd found me in my room. I did not want him to see me. I could still hear him screaming in my head. I wanted to tell him that everything was fine. Nick was too old and too smart for that. He knew it wasn't fine. I knew it wasn't fine. He'd seen me lying on the stretcher, bleeding and dying.

CHAPTER 10

I remember Lexus having the most beautiful eyes. Her eyes had a sparkle in the colors brown and green, making them almost amber. She had light brown hair, and she always kept her lips painted in cherry lip-gloss.

She turned to me, smiling, and said, "How does this look?"

I looked at her. Of course, she was beautiful. She knew it, and she didn't need me to tell her. I couldn't take my eyes off her as she swayed around her bedroom in her olive green tank top and soft, white Capri pants. She had on the perfect open–toe, white, wedge sandals that showed off her painted toes and pinky toe ring. While looking at her, I wondered how she could possibly be my friend.

I tried to smile at her. I tried to feel happy for her. "You look good," I told her.

Lexus read beyond what she saw on my face. "What's wrong?" she asked as she sat down next to me.

"It's nothing. I'm fine."

"Come on, girl. Don't be like that. I want to have fun tonight. I cannot go out on this date if you are not going to be cool. That's why I wanted you to come over. I need you to help me get ready, and I need you to be my best friend right now. Don't be depressed."

"I know. I'm not being depressed. I told you, I am fine. I am just tired because I'm having cramps or something. I don't know. Okay, you look great! You really do." This time I gave her a wider smile.

She bought it. Her re-applied smile told me so.

"Just make sure you have fun and be safe."

She laughed. "I will," she assured me.

She leaned in and hugged me. Her bare arms brushed my face and I could smell her. She smelled like sweet cherries. Her hair swept across my face. She was soft. She was beautiful. She was perfect.

Lexus pulled away from me slowly. My eyes wouldn't pull away from her. I could tell that my staring at her was making her nervous.

"Quit it, Kristen." She playfully shoved me.

"What? I'm sorry," I said to her. I chuckled nervously.

I still didn't turn away. I moved in closer to her, not sure why.

"You have nothing to worry about. You're amazing," I said.

There was a strange feeling growing inside of me.

"Really?" She pretended as if she didn't know. "That's so sweet, Kristen. I guess I-"

When she went to get up and out of my reach, I felt I had to stop her. So I kissed her. My lips were actually pressed against her warm and perfect lips. The kiss lasted about half of a second before she pushed me so hard that I had to grab my chest.

"I'm so sorry, Lexus. Lexus, please," I pleaded with her as she grabbed her sweater and purse. "I don't know what just happened. Lexus, please wait!"

Lexus didn't say a word. She didn't even look at me. She quickly left me alone in her bedroom without looking back. I ran after her until I saw who was in the living room. I stopped before I could enter the room. I didn't want them to see me. I stayed around the corner and peeked out into the living room where her mother, father, and her date waited.

I watched as everyone complimented her on how beautiful she looked. I watched her date as he stared at her, up and down. He wrapped his arm around her waist. He looked like someone she would have liked back in high school. Her date had big shoulders, he was tall, and he was dark. He had a clean face, and sticky hands. He was dressed nicely, which was a distraction from his mischievous, boyish grin. He was just her type. He wouldn't have asked me out, like he had asked Lexus out. She was beautiful and perfect. She was just his type.

When Lexus returned home, I was still there. She seemed shocked to see me. I tried to apologize, but she told me to forget about it. Lexus said that her night was too amazing to be upset by something silly. She wanted us to forget about it, and to pretend that it had never happened. I agreed to it, but I knew I wouldn't be able to pretend the way she could. I wanted to know what had happened on their date. She said that he had taken her to a nice restaurant downtown and that they were going to go to a movie, but had gotten side-tracked on the way and had parked by a lake. She assumed I knew what had happened at the lake, but I didn't.

"Oh, come on," she said.

"What did you do? Did you have sex with him or something?" I asked her.

She looked at me as if I was insane.

"No! However, we did do some heavy making out. He has an amazing tongue." She had a huge smile on her face that I couldn't understand.

I smiled and said, "That's cool. I have to call my Mom and ask her to pick me up. It's getting late."

"Okay," Lexus said. "Call me when you get home, so that I can tell you more about my date."

"Sure," I said.

When I arrived home, I didn't want to call Lexus and hear about her date with the football player. It made me feel sick. I wouldn't know how any of what she would have told me felt. I did call her, though. I didn't know why I called her. I listened to her as she boasted about all the compliments that he had given her. I listened as she talked about his tongue and his hands. I listened, as I knew I wouldn't ever understand what it felt like to be beautiful and liked.

"Did you miss dinner on purpose?" a voice buzzed into my dream as I was sleeping.

I opened my eyes, and the light from the lamp next to Janine's bed made me close them again. I heard more talking. I slowly opened my eyes this time, expecting the light from the lamp to be on. I saw Janine crawling onto her bed. Tai was standing in front of Janine's bed, looking down at her.

"I didn't feel like eating," Janine said softly.

Janine laid her head down on her pink pillow and snuggled under her pink blanket. She looked comfortable.

Tai asked, "Are you trying to get Ms. Mosley all up on your ass? You missed lunch because you were in the BCR. Now you've missed dinner."

"Leave me alone," Janine sobbed.

Tai turned away and walked out of our room. I could hear Ms. Mosley in the hallway, yelling at Tai for being in our room. I looked over at a depressed girl. Janine looked awful, drowned in her own tears. Her face was pushed into her pillow. Her make-up had come undone. It was smeared all over her cheeks. Her hair was flying wildly over her pink blanket and pillow. I heard her whimpering.

How long had I been asleep? Was I fully awake yet?

Janine stopped crying. She had rolled onto her side, and was looking directly at me.

"You missed dinner," she said.

I nodded, wishing she'd stop looking at me.

"Later, there's going to be group meetings. We usually have a meeting with our group counselor after we take a shower and put our pajamas on." She sighed as if it took a lot of energy to tell me that.

"Are you all right?" I asked her.

Janine smiled with her wet cheeks. "I'm fine," she said. "I'm Manic Depressive or Bi-Polar, whatever you want to call it. It's the same. Blah. I laugh, I cry, I get sad, and I get hyperactive. It doesn't matter what happens. I'm always fine." She sat up and pointed at me. "What's that?"

I looked down and saw my silver butterfly wings shining. The pendant must have fallen out of my pocket and onto the bed. I grabbed it.

"It's just my butterfly pendant," I said.

"Let me see?" Janine said as she reached out for it.

I handed the pendant over to her. She took it and studied it. She smiled and then handed it back to me.

"You should put that on a necklace," she suggested. "It looks special. Did a guy give it to you?"

"No way!" I shouted at her.

Janine shuddered at the tone of my voice.

"Okay," she accepted.

There was an awkward silence after that.

She started laughing and said, "I know it was a weird first day, but don't worry. It's always weird in here."

I forced a smile.

"In a week, you should be allowed visitors. At least then, you will get to see someone you know. That always helps." She paused and studied her fingernails. Then she looked back up at me. "They have this stupid rule that you have to be a certain level to be able to talk on the phone and have visitors. Then, they are over it in about a week. If you get up to Level Two like me, or Level Three like Daniel and Tai, you get to have visitors. They can go play sports and stuff with the other kids off the unit in the gym. I can only have visitors, talk on the phone, and do my laundry in the laundry room. It's stupid, isn't it?"

I didn't say anything. I just let her keep talking.

"When you get your visitors, they can bring you stuff. I bet you want a new blanket. They never tell you how cold it gets in here at night during evaluation. I like visiting hours. Is your boyfriend going to come visit you?"

I looked up at her, and felt anger inside of me. It felt like she was trying me. I couldn't tell if she was serious and she really thought that I had a boyfriend, or if she saw that I was one of those ugly girls who didn't get boyfriends and she was trying to make me feel some sort of way. So, I asked her if her boyfriend was going to visit. To my shock, she said that she didn't have a boyfriend.

I didn't feel like talking to her any more after that.

She kept on, though. "What do you think about Daniel?"

My eyes were fixed on her. "What do you mean?"

"Nothing," she said. "I just wanted to know what you thought about him. That's all."

"He's nice," I said.

"Yeah, well, you know that he's mine," she said.

I just sat there, staring at her. I didn't say anything.

"I'm just kidding," she laughed. "The look on your face! That was too funny."

I looked away from her, embarrassed. How had I been looking at her? Did I look shocked? Angry? Did I look like I even cared? I tried not to. I didn't want to care. I didn't want to care about Janine, just like I didn't want to care about Lexus.

"So, you're one of Dr. Cuvo's patients?" she started again.

Looking back at her, I nodded and yawned.

Janine then yawned too. Her eyes welled with tears.

"Me too," she told me.

I yawned loudly and rolled over so that the yawn wouldn't affect me if she yawned again too. Sure enough, she yawned again. I heard her yawn as soon as my back was facing her.

"Time for night-time groups! Come on, girls!" Ms. Mosley burst through the door. "Up! Up! Up!"

CHAPTER 11

"Meds!" yelled the nurse from the counter.

"Kristen. You have nighttime medication. Come on." Geoffrey was one of the counselors at Bent Creek. He was kind of tall and chubby, and he seemed like one of the nicest counselors here.

Ms. Mosley put on her coat and gathered up her personal belongings. She put an unlit cigarette in her mouth, waved goodbye to everyone, and she was gone. Daniel licked his lips. I heard him whimper like a puppy when he saw that cigarette. He slammed his head into his hands.

Tai gasped at the sight of the cigarette.

"I want a cigarette," she whined. "I hate it when she does that. It's like she's trying to torture us."

Chris laughed at her.

"Shut up," she fussed.

We all went to stand in the long line for night medication. I hadn't expected to start the medication so soon. Daniel stood in front of me. His long, black hair draped down his shoulders, and his soft skin looked moist. He smelled good, like a cool breeze and scented soap. I began to realize that I hadn't bathed since I had left the main hospital.

"Next!" The nurse said. Daniel stepped up. "Hello," the nurse greeted him. "Zoloft." She handed Daniel a small cup that contained a pill. Daniel washed the pill down with a cup of water.

"Open up," the nurse demanded.

Daniel opened his mouth and wiggled his tongue around so that she could see that he had swallowed his medicine. When she said that he was okay, Daniel said good night to her and moved out of the line. I felt awkward stepping up to the counter.

"Last name?" the nurse asked me.

"Elliott," I told her.

She stepped back and went to a cabinet that held all of our medications. She read about four labels before she pulled out a red bottle.

"Here we are. Risperdol for Kristen Elliott, 0.5 milligrams. Wash it down with some water." She pushed the little medicine cup towards me with a cup of water.

I hesitated.

"Is there a problem?" she asked.

"How long does this medicine take to actually work?"

"It usually takes a few weeks, even a month, before you start to feel it working. However, some side effects may start right away. I don't know. It's different with many people. If you start to get any serious side effects like shakiness, stomachache, or a bad headache, then you make sure you tell whatever nurse is on duty and your doctor. Okay?"

"Okay," I said.

"Now take your medicine."

I put the cup to my lips and I let the pill fall into my mouth. I quickly grabbed the cup of water and washed the pill down. I tried not to gag.

"Now, you should rest," said the nurse, as she took the empty cup away from me. "Lift your tongue."

I opened my mouth and lifted my tongue the way I had seen Daniel do it. When she said that I was free to go, I started to ask her if she was the nurse who could help me clean up. However, she grabbed her coat and purse. I could tell that she was eager to leave. So I left it alone and headed toward my room. When I got inside, I didn't see Janine. I felt strange inside that cold room. The light was on, it was nighttime, and I was alone. It was not starting to feel like home. The walls were white in here. In fact, everything was white. My bedroom at home was the absolute opposite. I had painted my room black when I had turned sixteen. It was still black now. Everything in my room was black. From the walls to the bed sheets and pillows. It was all black.

I started to smell myself. I knew that was bad. I looked down at my heavily-bandaged wrists. I wouldn't have dared to unwrap my bandages, and have to look at them. Mr. Sharp's face appeared.

"Stop it," I whispered.

I couldn't bathe without having to unwrap the bandages, but then I'd have to get my stitches wet if I tried to wash myself, because I needed to use my hands to wash, and that would wet my wrists. I figured I could at least get some soap under my arms and pat a slightly damp towel under them.

I opened the bathroom door. Janine was on her knees over the toilet. Her dinner was coming out of her mouth, and it spilled into the toilet like water shooting out of a fire hose. She looked up at me as soon as I felt myself gag. Whatever came up in my throat tasted disgusting going back down. I backed away as she flushed the toilet and ran to the sink. I let the bathroom door swing shut when I backed out. I walked over to my bed. I could hear the water running in the bathroom. Janine came out of the bathroom and stood in front of me. She smelled strongly of vomit.

"Are you okay, Kristen?" she asked me.

I nodded at her dubiously.

"Please don't tell Ms. Mosley," she pleaded. "Please, Kristen."

"Sure, okay," I told her. "I won't tell."

"Thanks," she said in relief. A smile appeared on her face. I could see the worry melt away. She tossed herself onto her bed.

I got up and grabbed a pair of underwear and a set of pajamas out of my suitcase. Then I walked into the bathroom. I tried to wash under my arms and other parts of my body as carefully as I could. I cleaned my face by sticking it under the faucet. I couldn't use the shower because it would've ruined my stitches. I looked up above the sink, and I saw that there was a mirror, but it wasn't a real mirror. It was like a rubbery flat surface that flashed a reflection, but the reflection was distorted. My nose was on my forehead. My eyes were where my cheeks were supposed to be. There was no mouth. It didn't make a difference to me. It was like looking at myself through a real mirror.

A frame sat on my bedroom armoire at home. The frame had once held a mirror. I used to look into that mirror and resent the reflection that stared back at me. I remembered the last time I had seen that mirror. I'd been trying to put on some make-up the way I had seen Lexus do it. I'd had to hurry up and get dressed. Lexus and her parents were coming over to pick me up to hang out at their place for the weekend. I just couldn't get the make-up right. Every time I had put lipstick on, it had caked up on my teeth and it had dried out and cracked my lips. When I had tried to apply eyeliner, I'd almost poked myself in the eye, and it had smeared all over my eyelids. I couldn't make it look right no matter how much make-up I kept putting on to try to cover the bumps and scars. My face would not change, but I'd kept trying to paint it.

Whenever Lexus looked into the mirror, a beautiful image appeared. After she put make-up on, the almost impossible happened. Lexus' beauty was enhanced, and it made her more beautiful than before.

It hadn't worked for me. Angrily, I'd thrown the eyeliner to the floor and smashed the lipstick down on the dresser with my hand. The lipstick had squished red between my fingers and in my palm as I'd punched it repeatedly. I'd looked up at my disgusting face and had seen every pimple and every dark spot that sickened me. I'd raised my lipstick-smeared hands and had bashed them into the reflection of my face. The mirror had cracked. The blow had created a hole in the center, around where shards had shot out like fireworks. It had almost looked beautiful. It had looked better than before. This had made me angry.

My face had been completely distorted. I could still see the ugliness, and I'd wanted to get rid of it. Lexus would have never had to break a mirror just to make herself look more beautiful. No! I *never* wanted look into that mirror again!

Not caring about the blood and the pain that had made my already messed up hand throb, I had pounded into the mirror fiercely until the shards had begun to completely break away and fall apart. I had screamed in frustration as the blood and the lipstick had coalesced and run down my fingers to my arms and dripped onto the floor.

I looked around the unfamiliar bathroom that I now shared with Janine. I sighed heavily.

"Breathe, Kristen... you have to breathe." Mr. Sharp spoke aloud in my ears.

I picked up my blue jeans from where I had tossed them on the floor. I kicked my dirty underwear out of the way and I angrily tried to tear my jeans apart.

My sterling silver butterfly pendant fell out of the pocket of my jeans. I stared in amazement. Mr. Sharp had come to my rescue! I picked up the pendant and pressed the sharp wing to my skin right above my knee.

"If you bleed, you will be able to breathe," Mr. Sharp said.

I dragged the wing across my leg and made a scrape. I didn't cut deep enough to bleed. I couldn't do it. For some reason, I couldn't stand the pain when I tried to press deeper. I stopped and looked around the bathroom. It was as if that moment was when I realized where I was for the first time. I shoved the butterfly pendant back into my pocket. I felt hurried to put on my pajamas in case someone came in to check on Janine or me. They couldn't find the pendant. They would take Mr. Sharp away from me.

After I picked up all of my things in the bathroom and was in a change of underwear and in my pajamas, I made my way back to the bedroom. I felt warmth come over me, and it was heavy and quick. My eyes felt like they were carrying weights. I lay down and, before I could count to ten, I was asleep.

CHAPTER 12

Ms. Mosley busted into the room early in the morning. She was loud, and it made my head pound harder than it already was from the Risperdol. When Ms. Mosley stormed in, Janine was in the bathroom.

"Wake up!" Ms. Mosley shouted. I opened my eyes, and she was standing beside my bed, looking down at me with her hands on her hips.

"Did you get cleaned up last night?" she asked me. She seemed concerned.

"I tried to, but my stitches..." I began.

"There is a nurse that's supposed to come and draw blood from you. She said she'd be here yesterday, but that didn't happen. I'll call over and make sure she comes today. She should help you get cleaned up without messing up your stitches. For now, get up and try to get yourself together for vitals check and breakfast."

She started to leave, but as she passed the bathroom, she realized that Janine was in there. Without knocking, she opened the door and caught Janine sitting on the toilet using the bathroom.

Janine screamed at her, "Do you mind? I am using the bathroom! Shut the door!"

Ms. Mosley shut the door quickly. She looked angry and embarrassed.

"I was just making sure, Janine!" Ms. Mosley said as she hurried out of our room.

Janine came out of the bathroom, furious.

"I wish this stupid place had locks on the doors! That wench has no right!" Janine screamed.

I lay there in bed, not wanting to get up. I had to change into my day clothes, and I needed to put deodorant on. I still smelled dirt on myself. I felt sick. I didn't want to face the day. I didn't want to hear Janine. I just wanted to sleep.

"There has got to be some kind of law against that," Janine continued as she tossed her clothes on.

I started to fall asleep again until Janine yelled that I'd better get up before Ms. Mosley came back and yanked me out of bed like she had done to her before. I pushed myself out of the bed so fast without thinking or taking my time. The world began to spin. I lost my balance and stumbled back into the nightstand. I almost knocked the lamp over, but Janine rushed to my side and caught it. She reached out to me and helped me stand up.

"Kristen, are you okay?"

"Yeah, I didn't sleep well last night. I'm a little tired," I told her.

"Be careful," she warned.

After I got dressed, Janine helped me into the front room. Everyone was sitting around, and some people were waiting to get their vitals checked. Daniel was in the chair, getting his vitals checked by Geoffrey. Janine and I stood in line to wait our turn. Daniel was smiling and talking to Geoffrey.

"Today I have a family session," Daniel told Geoffrey.

"That's good," Geoffrey said. "You think you are ready?"

"Yep, I have been doing pretty well. I want to see my mom. And if it goes well, I might get to go home."

Daniel sounded sure about his family session. He was being open. He sounded like he was sure he'd be well enough to go home. I wondered if that was how I had to be. If I had to be open and sure. If I had to share everything that was inside of me. If I had to sit, face-to-face, with my mother and tell her what she wanted to hear.

"Yeah, and you'll be like Lenni," Tai said. "She got to go home after her family session."

Everyone grew quiet and stared at each other. I gasped when Daniel's large eyes gazed at me. I looked away to ignore him. When I turned back, he was walking away. He sat down at the table where our group sat together. When Janine and I were finished getting our vitals checked, we joined them at the table. I was exhausted from the medicine. I folded my arms across the table and lay my head down.

"Do you really think they'll let you go home?" Janine asked Daniel.

He responded, "Maybe."

"It'll suck if you leave," she told him.

He laughed as he said, "I've got to go home. I'll go crazy if I stay in here another week."

"Oh, goodness, ten days without a cigarette," Tai said. "It's been hell. I need to go home."

Daniel said, "Try three and a half weeks without one."

"And I bet you miss your girlfriend," Janine teased.

I looked up.

Daniel didn't say a word. He looked down and started messing with his shoelaces. I heard someone call my name from behind me. I turned around too fast and had to put my hand over my eyes to keep from feeling too dizzy.

"Yes?" I called out to whoever was calling me.

Then I heard Ms. Mosley say that I needed to come with her. She came over to me, and I took my hand from over my eyes. I looked up at her. She smiled at me and helped me up.

"It'll get easier," she said as she led me out the double doors.

I began to get nervous as we passed a room with a large, steel-bolted door. The door locked from the outside. I assumed that room was the BCR. It had the look of what I imagined it would look like from the outside. It looked cold, and the door was made of black steel. It had three bolted locks on the outside. A small window also opened from the outside. I couldn't see inside the room because the door and window were closed.

We were walking too fast. I had to keep up with Ms. Mosley. She seemed to be in a hurry. When we reached the end of the hallway, she stuck her key in an exit door and led me out. I wanted to ask her where she was taking me, but I got too nervous when I tried to open my mouth. I don't know why I was suddenly shy. It was probably because I had been thinking about when I had first arrived at Bent Creek, and how Ms. Mosley had led me around. She seemed to be the one with whom I should have felt more comfortable, but Ms. Mosley had a look and attitude about her that made me feel intimidated, as if I had to watch every move I made around her.

We stopped at a door that was partially open. Ms. Mosley tapped on the door, and I heard Dr. Cuvo tell her to come in. Ms. Mosley pushed me in first, which made me feel very uncomfortable. Immediately upon entering, I felt a draft of cold air. Ms. Mosley followed me into the room. She smiled when she saw Dr. Cuvo. Dr. Cuvo sat at his desk, wearing that same smile I had seen when we'd first met. Ms. Mosley said that she'd be back to get me when my session was over, and left me alone with him.

Dr. Cuvo kept that smile on his face and said, "Sit down. Stay a while. We have a lot to talk about."

The room was freezing cold. I had an itch. I scratched the back of my neck and sat down. I looked around the office as he started speaking.

"I know that you started taking the Risperdol last night. Keep in mind that I need to know about any side effects that are bothering you. How did you sleep last night?"

"Fine. Waking up was kind of harsh, though," I said, not looking at him.

"Kristen," Dr. Cuvo said.

"What?"

"I'm right here," he said.

When I turned my head towards him, I caught him staring right at me. A shiver went through my spine.

"Please, Dr. Cuvo," I began to speak, but my voice just trailed off. I scratched the back of my neck. I felt like there was a piece of string on the inside of my shirt that was rubbing against my skin.

"Why does it bother you if a person looks at you, or if they want you to look back at them, when you're having a conversation?" he asked, still staring at me.

"You are not looking at me," I said. I lowered my head and stared into my empty hands that sat in my lap.

"What am I doing?"

"You're staring at me."

"Okay. So staring at you is not allowed. Can I look at you?"

"It doesn't matter," I said. "Just do what you have to do."

"No," he kept pressing. "I have to understand this. What's the difference if someone looks at you or stares at you? We are having a conversation. It's like this, right now. I am talking to you and you can't even look at me."

"It is because I know you are staring back at me," I said.

"Right, so why is that a problem?"

I couldn't hold back. I smacked the back of my neck with the palm of my hand so hard that it made a loud noise. It sounded like someone had popped a paper bag full of air. I finally looked up at Dr. Cuvo. He shuddered.

"Are you all right?" he asked.

My nostrils flared and released hot air because I was annoyed. I felt itchy and dirty.

"I'm fine," I lied.

"All right. One of the things I would like to talk to you about is your level. You've moved up to Level Two. This means that you can make phone calls to your family only. We have a scheduled time for phone calls in the evening. In addition, I am going to allow you to have visitors. Do you think that you can handle seeing your family?"

I looked up at him. He was looking at my chart. My insides felt like they were squishing around. A feeling of guilt rose inside of me. I felt anxiety creeping in. The consequences were yet to come. If I faced them, which I knew I would have to do one day, I would be a mess. I would make my family sad all over again.

"Just my Mom," I told him.

"You wouldn't want to see anyone else? Not your brother and sister?" Dr. Cuvo looked up from my chart, trying to catch my eye.

I looked back down at my hands and shook my head in shame. I squeezed my hands together and put them between my thighs to keep them warm. The air conditioner had to have been on full blast. I held back the tears that were begging to fall. I couldn't get the vision of Nick's face out of my mind. I kept seeing his tear-drenched face when the EMTs had closed the doors to the ambulance. Nick was the one who had found me in my bedroom. Not Mom. Nick was the one who had told Mom to call 911. He was the one who had pulled the sheets from over me. Nick had seen everything that I had done first. He had seen me almost die.

I couldn't see Nick. I couldn't let him see me at Bent Creek. I wiped my eyes as the tears started to fall.

"Kristen."

I hated when he said my name with such sincerity. No man had ever said my name with that kind of concern except Jack. It was starting to make me feel a way that I didn't want to feel. It was like when Jack had danced with me. He'd made me feel like he cared for me. He'd made me feel like he wanted to protect me. Dr. Cuvo couldn't have done any of those things. Anger welled inside of me.

Dr. Cuvo pressed more. "Kristen, why are you crying?"

My knees began to knock together.

"Kristen! Kristen!" Echoes were in my head. "Kristen!" He was shouting. "Kristen! Get back here!"

The monster was chasing me. I wanted him to stop. I wanted him to get away from me. My shirt was suddenly around my neck, and I couldn't breathe. I was choking. I dropped the cup of water that was in my hand. The water spilled onto the cold, tile floor, and the ceramic mug broke into pieces. My feet were no longer on the floor. I started to see colorful dots as he pinned me back against the wall. My shirt was getting tighter around my neck. He was going to kill me to keep me from talking. I'd seen him. He was going to kill me because I'd seen him. He was hard and disgusting, and he was breathing in my face.

"How long were you watching?" Jack snapped at me.

I couldn't speak. I was blacking out. Jack saw what he was doing and let go of my shirt. My bare feet hit the tile, hard. I almost fell, but Jack was standing too close to me to let me fall.

"I didn't see anything," I lied.

He knew it was a lie. The tears told too much. I rubbed the back of my neck. It tingled, and it itched. I scratched at it, but the itch would not go away.

"I was tucking Nick into bed. Is that what you saw?" He backed me up into the wall. I moved my hand before the back of my head and neck hit the wall, stopping me in place and leaving me nowhere to go. Jack had trapped me.

I nodded my head. "Yes, sir. I saw you tucking Nick into bed." More tears told a different story.

"Then why were you screaming out to Nick if that's all you had seen? Why are you crying?"

What had I seen? I turned my head to look into Nick's bedroom. I just needed to see that he was in bed. I needed to see that he was tucked in. Nick was under his covers. I could see his feet dangling from under the sheets.

"What are you doing?" It was Mom.

Jack quickly backed away from me. I scuttled next to Mom. I wanted to be as far away from Jack as I could possibly be. Mom looked at Jack, and then she turned to stare at me. I looked away from her.

"Kristen," she said calmly. "Why were you yelling out to Nick?"

"I wasn't yelling," I lied. "I had a nightmare and Nick was in it. Therefore, I went to the kitchen to get some water. I got scared because Jack, um, Dad, scared me when I came from the kitchen, and then I dropped the cup and it-"

I was too nervous. I didn't know whether to tell her what had really happened. Jack was burning holes into me with his eyes. He was staring at me so sternly that it made me choke on my words. The monster was out, and I knew that monster was capable of anything. I believed that monster would have hurt us. He would have killed my family.

"It was my fault," I said. "I should have been careful. I am sorry for waking you up."

"Yes. You should have been more careful," Jack said.

The expression on Jack's face was grim. His stare made me hurt inside. I looked down at the floor. Jack walked over to Mom and kissed her cheek.

"Go back to bed, honey. I will be there in a minute. I just want to check on Alison and Nick. I'll make sure she didn't wake them up."

Mom looked concerned, so Jack kissed her again. She warmed up in his arms. She looked at me and put her hand on my shoulder. She told me to make sure I picked up all of the broken pieces so that no one would get hurt. I tried to. I wanted to pick up all of the broken pieces, but there were just too many. The monster was too powerful. He made it hurt too much.

"Have you been crying?" she asked.

As she looked at me, her eyes began to change. There was concern on her face. She looked at the broken cup on the floor. She stared down at the spilled water, and she then stared up at me. She was not just looking. She saw the shame and fear in my eyes, and at that moment, I felt that this was it. This would be the moment that I had prayed to God for. She'd say something now because she knew. She could see it. Please Mom, I thought. Please, God. Let her do something!

"You must be really tired, sweetheart." Jack said.

Jack laughed and pushed Mom along to their bedroom playfully. He got her to warm up to him without a fight. I could hear him playfully kissing and nudging on her. She was giggling and seemingly happy in her ignorance.

Hating that monster, I began picking up the broken pieces of the ceramic cup. I only wanted to get a drink of water. I only wanted to look in to see if my little brother was all right. There was nothing wrong with that. Right? I'd seen what I'd seen. I'd seen what I wasn't supposed to have seen. He would have killed me. That monster hated me so much that he would have killed me.

As I picked up the pieces, I started to wish that he had killed me. I started to wish that I were not there. I started to wish that Nick was not there. My head felt swollen. The back of my neck itched too badly. I started scratching, but I felt something wet. When I looked at my fingers, there was blood on them. I had scratched too hard, and the itch was still there. It was my nerves. I couldn't calm down. My hands were shaking. I was shaking. I was cold. I was scared. I thought to myself, was Nick all right? Was he asleep? Had I actually seen what I thought I'd seen?

I let the wound bleed. I felt the blood drip down my neck. I didn't want to wipe it. I couldn't cry with the blood running down my neck. It felt like I had missed the last train home. I was stuck in a place that was not familiar. I got all of the pieces up, and threw them in the trash. I wiped all of the water up with a few paper towels. As I went to the kitchen to throw the paper towels away, I peeked in through Nick's bedroom door. I caught him with his eyes open, but he tried to shut them before I could notice.

"I know you are awake," I said to him.

He didn't open his eyes. I whispered his name, but he didn't move. I ignored him, shut his bedroom door, and stood in front of the door. I tried to remember how I had been standing and where I had been standing. I tried to replay what I had done, to see if I could remember to make sure that I was not dreaming. I heard the floor creak behind me. I didn't turn around. I tried to hurry to the kitchen, but something caught the back of my neck. I felt more blood gush down my neck. He could have squeezed it harder and broken it, for all I cared. I didn't make a sound because I felt numb inside.

He led me to the kitchen with his hand wrapped around the back of my little neck. When we got to the kitchen, he shoved me away from him. I slowly raised my head up to look at the monster's dark and rigid face. He was calm, but his expression was frightening.

He sighed and his expression began to soften. This was a look, not of the monster, but of a long time ago. It was my Dad. I almost saw him in that moment. I felt my heart flutter. A sweet, convincing smile appeared on his face. I wanted to believe it was him. I wanted to see my Dad. I missed him so much.

"Daddy?" I called out to him to make sure it really was my Dad.

That sweet convincing smile that Daddy would always give me turned into a grimace. His mouth opened.

He said, "Kristen, I really hate you."

What was left of my Dad was gone. He had completely disappeared. A bolt of lightning had struck through my heart. It came out of his words. Thunder began to crash through my veins. Visions filled my mind.

I saw my Daddy dancing with me at the wedding. I saw my Daddy kiss me for the first time. I saw my middle school graduation where my Dad said that he was very proud of me. I saw my Dad's face when we were all in the room, watching, as the twins were born. I saw our family's first picnic. I saw my Daddy holding me in his arms when told me that everything was going to be okay and that he loved me. It was the first time my Dad had ever made me feel safe. I saw the moment that my Daddy died. I saw the moment my Daddy was devoured by a monster.

He was my Dad. He was a good Dad. He loved me. I loved him. I loved a man, and that man was my Daddy.

I let my blood drip slowly into the tub. Scalding, hot water made the pain worse. There were tears. There was hot mucus. Both drenched my face, my pajamas, and the knife that I had learned to use until I couldn't cry anymore. It was like scratching the back of my neck. The itch wouldn't go away until I bled. Mr. Sharp wouldn't let me breathe until I saw blood. That was the rule. Hold my breath until I saw blood. I told Mr. Sharp that I hated myself, too. Jack wasn't the only one. Mr. Sharp said that I should hate myself because I was useless and a loser. That was why *a monster had eaten Daddy*. That was why Daddy had died.

Mr. Sharp lived in sharp objects. That night he'd come out of the steak knife. He'd introduced himself after the monster had said that he hated me. The monster was now Jack. Jack was the man I had met when I was six years old. Jack was the man who didn't want to get to know me before he and Mom had gotten married. Jack was the man who had been at the factory, smoking a cigarette in the back. That was Jack. He was the man that I didn't know.

I dropped the knife into the tub. Mr. Sharp picked it back up. He made me look at my arms and he made me find a place to cut. More cuts. You need more cuts. That's what he said. I looked around the bathroom. I was scared. I couldn't see this Mr. Sharp, but he had a voice.

"Stop it," I whispered. "Stop it!" I cried.

I lost complete control of what I was doing, and Mr. Sharp took over. He started slicing away at my legs. I watched as my hands gripped the knife tighter. I could hear him screaming for me to die. I cried inside. Not one tear fell out of my eyes. Please, Mr. Sharp! Stop it!

"Stop it," I said aloud.

The knife fell out of my hand and into the tub. I sat still, amazed. It was silent, and I was alone. I was afraid to look down, but I did anyway. My legs were covered in cuts. There was blood on my arms. Scared, I threw myself into the tub. The hot water burned, but it didn't stop me. I let the hot water continue to run. I pulled my knees up to my chest, and hugged my wet pajamas.

"God, if there is a way, please make it stop. Make her see. Please make her see," I whispered aloud. I closed my eyes, and a shadow of a male figure appeared. "No," I said. "Please stop it. I am going to die."

"No," Mr. Sharp said. "You are not going to die."

I looked up. Dr. Cuvo was staring at me. "Were you asleep?"

I couldn't remember what had been the last word said. I wiped at my eyes. I was barely here. I felt like I was still sleeping. I was in the tub of hot water. The water was getting cold. It was cold in the room with Dr. Cuvo. It was cold in the tub with Mr. Sharp. My stitches! I had to get out of the water. I looked up at Dr. Cuvo.

I couldn't get out of the water. Mr. Sharp stared at me from inside. He was laughing. My neck was itching. The knife was no longer in the tub. I couldn't find it. I had no control over this dream. There was no knife, but Mr. Sharp was there. He wanted something. Getting scared, I opened my mouth to speak to Dr. Cuvo, but Mr. Sharp covered my mouth with his hand.

Dr. Cuvo saw that I'd started to say something. He couldn't see that Mr. Sharp was making me stay quiet.

"What is it, Kristen?" he asked with concern. "What do you want to say?"

He was trying to help me. Mr. Sharp wanted me to stay in my place. He wanted me to be angry. Mr. Sharp never said anything to me. He wanted me to know what it was that I already knew, which was everything that he knew, but what he didn't have to say. He dragged me out of the tub and made me stand in the room across from Dr. Cuvo in his office. Dr. Cuvo saw that I was standing.

"It's not time to go yet," he said. "Please sit down, Kristen." Dr. Cuvo's voice shook as he spoke. "What's going on, Kristen?"

I had to say something. The only thing that came out was, "I want to go home."

Dr. Cuvo sighed. He said, "You are not ready to go home, Kristen. We have a lot of things to work through."

I wanted to say something to Dr. Cuvo. I wanted to tell him about Mr. Sharp, but I was afraid. I knew that the whole idea of another person - no, an evil entity - in that room with the both of us would have sounded even more insane than what Dr. Cuvo had already thought I was. Therefore, I sat down and I let myself cry.

Mr. Sharp was starting to leave me alone. He hated when I cried. I hated when I cried. It felt like a weak way out. I would rather cut myself into a million pieces than cry as though I were feeling sorry for myself. Feeling sorry for myself was not allowed. I had to cry to get Mr. Sharp out of me. I had to cry to make that urge to cut go away. It was cold in that room. I pressed my hands between my thighs to keep them warm. Dr. Cuvo passed me a box of tissues. He thought I was crying because he wouldn't let me go home. It was just as well, then. I wiped my eyes and tried to straighten myself up.

"You do understand? Don't you understand, Kristen?" He was looking at me with concerned eyes.

I crumpled the snotty tissues in my hands, and put my hands back between my legs. I nodded silently at Dr. Cuvo while not making eye contact with his eyes. If I looked into those eyes, I wouldn't stop crying.

"Are you okay?"

I nodded and wiped the rest of the tears from my eyes.

"There's an anti-depressant that I want to start you on tomorrow. It is called Effexor. Have you ever heard of it?"

"I've seen commercials," I said as I tossed the tissues into the trash can.

Dr. Cuvo laughed.

"Two medications..." I sighed under my breath. The overwhelming feeling came over me again.

Dr. Cuvo had either amazing ears or just very good senses. "It is going to be fine, Kristen. You are not the only person, especially in here, who takes more than one medication. Remember, you are doing this to get better. Sometimes we can't do everything on our own. Sometimes it is okay to get help, and that is what you are doing. It's a part of your therapy, and it's a part of what is going to help you get out of here safely."

The sympathetic look that his warm eyes gave me while he spoke made my insides tingle. I didn't know how to handle the sincere kindness that he gave me. I looked away from him.

"The nurse put in your chart that you had some concerns about your medication when you first started Risperdol. I just want you to trust me. I am not going to give you something that I know will hurt you. If you feel any kind of discomfort or irritation while taking these medications that you've never felt before, then let me know. I will do something about it right away. All right?"

"Why do you waste your time?" I couldn't hold back.

"What do you mean?" he asked.

"I mean why do you waste your time on me? All of that 'trust me' stuff, and the look that you give me. It's as if you are feeling sorry for me. It confuses me, Dr. Cuvo."

"How does it confuse you?"

"I don't know. It just does." I didn't want to look at him. I felt his eyes burning holes into me.

He got out of his chair, came over, and sat next to me. I still wouldn't look at him. But he wanted me to. "Kristen, what does this confusion feel like? How does it make you feel?"

"I feel-" I swallowed the tears. I swallowed that metal ball that wanted to turn in my throat. I was going to say how I felt, and he was going to listen. He was really going to listen to me, and he was really going to care, even though I didn't. That was what confused me. I realized that. "I feel confused when you stare at me." That was the only way I could get it out at that moment.

Dr. Cuvo put a hand on my shoulder. That touch made me look at him. Looking at him with that tender hand on my shoulder made me even more confused. I couldn't read his face. I had never seen a look like that before.

Dr. Cuvo then asked, "Could it be also that you are not used to opening up this much to anyone?"

"For the most part," I answered. "Especially not with a-" I made myself shut up.

"A what?"

"A man," I said.

Dr. Cuvo nodded. His gentle hand squeezed my shoulder in a kind gesture. "I am a man. I'm your doctor. And I think it's safe to say maybe even a friend."

Looking into his eyes was nice, now that I had heard him say the word "friend". I wanted to trust this feeling, but I was still scared. I saw Mr. Sharp's face in my mind. He was my only friend. He was the only man who was my friend. Jack was my Daddy. Jack loved me. Jack was my friend.

My mind got away from me.

A sudden pain went from my lower abdomen to my lower stomach. It was almost amazing how cold it got in that hospital. My hands and my feet were ice cold, even though I had on socks and shoes. Again, I put both of my hands between my thighs to keep them warm. I wasn't prepared for his next question. Of course, it was a part of his job to pry. I just didn't want to go so deep so fast.

"Kristen, I know that your mother is divorced from your step-father. What about your biological father? Where is he?" Dr. Cuvo asked, removing his warm hand. My shoulder began to absorb the cold air.

"He's alive," I said. "He's back home in California."

"Do you miss California? Do you miss him?"

"California? I guess, I don't know."

"What about your father?"

I heard jack-hammering outside. The sound of construction work was loud. There must be roadwork going on. It was giving me a headache; also, a pain kept shooting back and forth from my lower abdomen to my lower stomach. It hurt more with the sound of the drills.

"Are they doing some kind of work out there?" Dr. Cuvo wondered as he rose out of the chair and went over to his window. He closed the curtains as though that would help muffle the sound of the construction. "I'm sorry about that, Kristen. It is really loud." Dr. Cuvo returned to the chair next to mine. "I bet it's hard with you all the way over here and him in California."

I nodded to humor him.

"Does he know that you are in the hospital?"

"Probably not, unless my Mom told him," I said.

The pain was sharp. I cringed as my lower stomach took its turn hitting the pain back to my lower abdomen. The pain felt as if the goal was to tear my insides apart.

"What is the relationship like between you and your father? How do you feel about him?"

The jackhammer must have hit something it wasn't supposed to, because all hell seemed to break loose. I heard men shouting at each other outside. Something gushed out of me. I felt it push out of me with great pain. My stomach ached. I looked down at my hands that were between my thighs, and they were bloody.

Dr. Cuvo rose quickly from the chair beside me. "Kristen. Oh, my God. Ugh… umm… Just wait a second. Don't move. Please, don't move." He looked like he was going to throw up.

I stared at him. Reality was setting in. I sat still as he had told me to, embarrassed.

Dr. Cuvo dialed someone from his office phone. I could hear Ms. Mosley on the other end. Dr. Cuvo was freaking out as if I were dying. He told her what had happened, and he asked her to come get me to take me back to the unit. He asked her to bring someone from maintenance. When he hung up the phone, he took a deep breath and looked up at me.

"Are you okay?" he finally asked me.

I nodded. I was too embarrassed to look at him, or to say anything to him.

Not long after he hung up the phone, Ms. Mosley knocked on the door. Dr. Cuvo told her to come in. Ms. Mosley saw me and motioned for me to come to her. I stood up and walked to the door. The maintenance man saw the blood on the seat, and he covered his nose and mouth. I'd grossed him out, too. I could have been perfectly fine being dead at that moment. Dr. Cuvo said good bye without the offer of a handshake. He told me to take care, and that he'd see me tomorrow.

Ms. Mosley led me down the hallways that led back to the Adolescent Ward. Once on the unit, she told me to go to my room and that she'd be there. I did as she said. The unit was empty. So was the room. Janine was not there. Everyone must have been in group therapy. Ms. Mosley knocked on the door, which shocked me, before she entered. She had a tampon, a towel, soap, and a plastic bag.

"Here's a bag for your dirty clothes. Just tie the bag up and hand it to me. I will throw your clothes into the wash for you. Because you are not Level Three yet, I can't let you into that part of the facility. I am going to get on the phone today and find out where that nurse is who was supposed to come and do your blood work and help you clean up. I am sorry about this, Kristen. Are you okay?"

I nodded, silent and embarrassed.

"Just try to clean up as best you can. You can change your clothes and take as much time as you need. Let me know if you need my help, or if you need anything."

She seemed nicer than I would have believed on the first day I had met her. I looked away from her, too embarrassed and wanting to be far away.

"Don't worry. All of Dr. Cuvo's patients are female. Hey, at least he doesn't have a white couch." She smiled at me. She was trying to make me smile back.

"Okay then," she sighed. "I will let you take care of yourself. Your group is in Drugs and Alcohol Group right now. You'll probably just have to miss that group today. If you need anything, just come get me. I will be up front on the main unit." She left me alone in the room.

I went into the bathroom. I looked at the tile walls around me. The pain burned in my stomach. Tears fell from my eyes. I began to cry so hard that I heard myself groaning with my pitiful tears. I threw the tampon down. I took my fist and began beating it. I crushed it into the floor.

"No!" I screamed. "No! No! No!"

When the tampon was ruined, I stopped. I took a deep breath, wiped my eyes, and stared at what I had done. I hated him. That's how I felt about him, Dr. Cuvo. I hated him!

CHAPTER 13

I waited as the phone rang. It seemed like forever before the ringing stopped. When the pulsing tones stopped, I got nervous. I almost hung up the phone, but my hand wouldn't take the receiver away from my ear. The area for phone calls was not private. It was at the counselor's desk on the main unit. There were chairs to sit in. I sat still with my legs folded, and I waited. The ringing stopped.

"Hello?" A female voice came in from the other end.

I took a deep breath right into the phone. It made a loud, windy sound. "Uh, hello?"

"Yes," she said. She sounded impatient and annoyed.

I got on with it. "Can I speak to…? I mean, may I please speak to…uh…"

"Who do you want to speak to, honey?" I could hear in her voice that she was irritated and ready to hang up the phone.

"My dad," I forced myself to say. "May I please speak to Christian Elliott?"

I heard her yell, "Christian, pick up the phone! It's your kid!"

I heard a deep, muffled voice in the background. I couldn't make out what he was saying. I pressed my ear harder to the phone.

"It's Kristen!" She sounded angry. "What is your problem? Take the telephone, Christian."

She took the phone away from her mouth. I could hear her yelling. He was yelling back at her. Then the phone was muffled by something, probably her hand. I couldn't hear them clearly. Their words were distorted by the smother.

A few seconds later, there was just silence. It was so quiet that I thought she might have hung up on me. I called out softly, "Hello?"

There was no sound.

"Hello?"

A hard sigh came from the other end.

"Dad…"

"Hi," he calmly said.

"Hey," I said, in relief. "It's me, Kristen." I was smiling. I wondered if he could hear me smiling through the phone. I wished that he could see me.

He didn't say anything.

"Well, I was just calling to say hi. I want to know how you are doing." I was still nervous, but he couldn't know that.

"That's nice."

I felt the metal ball that rested in my chest begin to turn. I took a deep swallow to keep it from rising. "Well, how are you doing?"

"I am doing just fine," he assured me.

I heard him take a bite of something crunchy. He was smacking his lips and crunching down on whatever it was that he was eating. I heard the television blaring in the background. He was watching something with an annoying laugh track that seemed to go off every second. It must have been an extremely funny show, even though he didn't seem to be amused.

"Um, I am doing better now," I told him.

He didn't respond.

I coughed. "Yeah, I was sick for a little while." My hands were shaking and I could feel drops of sweat forming under my arms and in the palms of my hands. I scratched the back of my neck, making it bleed. I wiped the blood and sweat on my jeans.

He continued to crunch.

"Dad?"

His voice came in suddenly, like the sound of unexpected thunder crashing nearby. "Look, Kristen, I don't have any money, if that's what you are calling for. I just got out of rehab two weeks ago. I just don't-"

"No!" I yelled. "That is not why I am calling you."

The tears started building up. I tried not to cry. Geoffrey and Ms. Mosley were behind the desk. I didn't want them to hear me.

"Then what do you want?" He was yelling at me.

"I only want to talk to you," I cried.

"Please," he sighed. "Just stop crying. I know it's been a while. I *just* got out of rehab. When I get my job back, I will send you some money if you need it. Did your mother tell you to call me?"

"No," I said.

I covered my mouth with my hand to keep myself from crying out. I leaned against the back of the chair and unfolded my legs. I moved the phone away from my mouth and wiped my eyes as fast as I could before anyone could notice. I heard the others coming back onto the unit. A few of them were leaning over the desk, asking to use the phone. Janine was one of them. When I looked up, I saw her leaning over the desk. She looked down at me. I covered half of my face with my hand to block out her staring at me. I didn't want her to see. I wished everyone would go away.

"What's that noise?" he asked.

"Nothing," I lied.

I looked back up, and Janine was gone. Two other kids were talking on the phone and sitting in the other chairs. I saw other kids waiting for one of us to hang up so that they could make their phone calls.

"Okay. I have to go. I just wanted to…bye."

I handed the phone over to Geoffrey. Without saying a word, I got up out of the chair and ran to the Girls' Unit. I could hear the kid who was next in line yell to Geoffrey to dial his dad for him. I didn't know why I had asked Geoffrey to dial my father in California. I wanted to tell my father that I was in the hospital, but it didn't seem like a good idea. Once I got in my room, I threw myself on my bed and buried my head under my pillow, where no one could hear me cry.

CHAPTER 14

There was a knock on the door. Before I woke up to realize that I wasn't dreaming about someone knocking on the door, Ms. Mosley was standing over me. She scared me.

"I'm sorry," she said. "I didn't mean to scare you. If you're hungry, there's food. Geoffrey brought your lunch on the unit for you. I know you are not feeling well, but you need to eat."

My stomach growled.

"Come to the front area," Ms. Mosley encouraged.

I rose out of bed and followed her. My head was swimming in pain, but the cramps in my abdomen were worse.

When I arrived on the main unit, I sat at the table where Geoffrey had placed my food. I thanked him, and he told me that it was not a problem. When I saw the food, I couldn't help but immediately tear into it. I was glad that none of the other kids were here. I felt dirty. I needed a bath. It was disgusting to think about what had happened in Dr. Cuvo's office. That made everything worse. I tried not to think about it. I was just going to eat my lunch and go back to the room to lie down. Ms. Mosley surely wasn't going to make me to go group therapy and meetings in my condition. At least I hoped that she wouldn't.

I bit into the triangular shaped peanut butter and jelly sandwich on wheat bread, and I felt the table shake. I looked up. Geoffrey had sat down next to me.

He greeted me with a smile.

"Hey," he said.

"Hi," I said in almost a whisper.

I placed my sandwich down on the tray. Nervously, I looked away from Geoffrey's unfamiliar stare.

He started drumming his fingers on the table. His presence at the table, mixed with my embarrassment and the silence around us, became annoying. I wished he had left me alone.

I looked at him. He stopped drumming his fingers.

"So," he started, "You're taking my group today."

"What's your group?" I asked.

"Drug and Alcohol Group. It is moderated by Dr. Pelchat, but I help out."

"I don't know if my group has that today," I said.

My stomach started growling again. I picked up my sandwich and took a bite. I was embarrassed to eat in front of him. It felt like we were in school. He looked young. He didn't look much older than me.

"You're in Group Two?"

I nodded. I was too hungry to speak. I got down to the last bite of my sandwich and then reached for the small pint of whole milk that sat next to the tray.

"Yeah, okay, so you have that group today," he said.

I drank all of my milk and put the empty carton back down on the table. Geoffrey looked at me as if he was in awe.

"Wow, you must have been really hungry," he said. "You eat like that in school?"

"I don't go to school."

"What do you mean?"

"I mean I home school. I used to go to a public school, but I don't go there anymore."

"Really?" He looked at me differently. "Do you like that better?"

"Yes," I told him.

"Does your Mom home school you?"

I shook my head. "No," I said, "I home school myself."

"Are you taking the summer off right now?"

"No," I said.

"That sounds like it would take a lot of discipline."

I wanted him to stop asking so many questions. I would have gotten up and walked away, but a markedly tall man with a potbelly who was dressed in black suddenly walked through the double doors that led to freedom.

This man was well–dressed, and he had a clean face. He wore his thin, red hair slicked back. He seemed to tower over everything he was standing next to, except the walls. He caught Geoffrey's and my attention.

"Hey," Geoffrey greeted the man.

The tall man looked over at us and smiled. He waved to Geoffrey as he walked around the counselor's desk. He grabbed about six patients' charts.

"How's it going, Geoffrey?" The tall, well-dressed man approached us.

"It's going," Geoffrey said. "SSDD. You know how it is."

The tall man laughed. He put a hand on Geoffrey's shoulder, gave it a squeeze, and said, "I'll be seeing you. I've got to get back to it."

Geoffrey said goodbye as the man started back out the double doors. When he was gone, Geoffrey turned back to me.

"That's the boss," Geoffrey confessed. "That's Dr. Pelchat. He runs this place."

My heart jumped. I hoped Geoffrey didn't hear it.

"He's cool," Geoffrey said. "I hope that, when I am a doctor, I will be as educated as he is."

I looked at him in awe.

"You want to be a doctor?"

Geoffrey nodded with a proud smile on his face. "Yes, I do. I am a full-time student, all year round, just like you. I work here as a counselor part-time while earning my credits, but I still have a long way to go. I am getting my Masters at the end of the year, and I hope to do well enough that Dr. Pelchat will write a letter of recommendation for me to get into State. That's where I want to earn my Doctorate."

"How old are you?" I wasn't in so much of a hurry anymore. I was curious.

"I'm twenty-five. Why?"

I took a deep breath to suppress my shock. "You're young," I let slip out of my mouth.

He laughed. "Yeah, so are you. It's cool that you are home schooling yourself. If I had home schooled, I would have screwed around. You must be very disciplined and focused."

"Home schooling is hard. Well, it's better than being in school. This place kind of feels like it used to-" I made myself shut up.

Geoffrey was staring at me. He was good. He knew how to get me talking. He'd probably learned it in school.

"You know, it's not so bad, though. Everyone in here is in the same position."

"So I hear," I said.

"No, really," he continued. "You don't have to feel like an outcast. I know you are having a rough time right now, but nothing is new here. We have seen and dealt with it all. Moreover, if any of these kids have anything to say about anyone else in here, they need to look at themselves. Honestly, though, I doubt anyone will give you a hard time. Besides, you are here at a good time. Since it is summer, you don't have to go to the classroom."

"Is there a classroom here?" I almost laughed because I thought that he was kidding. I didn't let it come out.

"Yes," he laughed. "There is a classroom here, but it is summer. Therefore, there are no classes. Instead of having study time, you will get to go to the gym, and even outside in the garden. You see, it's not that bad."

"No." I allowed myself to smile at him. "It's not that bad. Not for prison."

"Okay, Kristen. You'll see. It'll get better. It will get better for you in here and out there too." He pointed out the window.

My smile disappeared. "Are you sure about that?" I asked as I watched the sun shine in through the window.

"I'm living proof, because I used to be right where you are. I was here at Bent Creek when I was fifteen. I didn't have a clue. Now, I know where I want to be. I know where I am going. It's all going to work out."

His eyes were glowing. He was smiling confidently. It was almost as though he knew he was going to succeed.

I wanted to ask him about his days in Bent Creek, but I didn't.

"Do you know what you want to do when you graduate?" Geoffrey asked.

I shook my head. "I just need to graduate."

"That doesn't look like that was your plan, Kristen." He gestured to my wrists.

I got up from the table with the empty milk carton and the Styrofoam tray. As I headed for the trash can, Geoffrey got up and followed me. I didn't want to talk to him. I wished that I hadn't even started talking to him.

"I'm sorry," he apologized. "Kristen, please wait." I tossed my garbage into the trash can. I tried to walk away, but he cornered me. "I'm not trying to be mean to you. I am just kind of shocked to see a very smart and beautiful girl like you in here."

I stopped breathing. I couldn't have heard him clearly. Did he really say the word beautiful and refer to me? I felt my stomach turning from the cramps. I heard Mr. Sharp whisper to me. He convinced me that I'd misheard Geoffrey. He reminded me that I was a loser and that Geoffrey didn't know me.

"Kristen." Geoffrey looked worried. "Are you all right?"

"Yes," I told Geoffrey.

"What are you doing in here?" Dr. Cuvo said. Suddenly, he was standing in the doorway. Dr. Cuvo looked at Geoffrey and then he looked at me. I wondered what was running through his mind, because he looked angry.

Geoffrey told Dr. Cuvo that he was about to take me to group therapy so that I could be with my group. He explained that I'd had to have lunch late. Dr. Cuvo seemed annoyed. He was harsh when he told Geoffrey to get me to Group right away. Without argument, Geoffrey hurried me along. I tried to keep some distance behind Geoffrey and me. I followed as Geoffrey led me to my group meeting. I didn't want him to start talking to me again about being beautiful or school or my future. I didn't want to hear it or think about it.

"Here we are," he said as we came up to the door.

"Thanks, bye," I said. I opened the door and entered the room quickly. Shutting the door, I found all eyes on me. I suddenly wanted to be on the other side of that door with Geoffrey.

I saw Tai laughing at me. She covered her ugly, yellow smile. It must have been the embarrassing and scared look on my face.

"Come on in and sit down, Kristen," Dr. Bent said.

I sat down in the chair next to Daniel, since it was the closest empty chair. Daniel was messing with his shoelaces. It must have been some kind of bored habit of his. He seemed to play with his shoelaces in almost every group we had.

Dr. Bent turned to me. "We are doing Coping Skills Group right now. Before you came in, Kristen, we were going around the room and sharing a few facts about ourselves, including what brought some of us to Bent Creek. Tai was just about to share. Tai?"

Tai glared at Dr. Bent.

What were their private therapy sessions like? I wondered.

"Hmm," Tai hummed. "What do I say? I'm Tai. I'm eighteen. I am here because my step-mom made me come."

"Why do you think it is your step-mother's fault that you are here?" Dr. Bent asked.

Tai looked down at the floor. It seemed like she was trying to hold back her anger.

"She just wants my dad to herself. She hates it when I am around," Tai answered.

"Didn't your father agree that you should be here?"

"He only agreed because that wench told him to put me here!" Tai yelled. "She told him that she found pills and needles in my room. He put me in here to lock me up, and he left. They don't care!"

"Calm down, Tai," Dr. Bent said calmly. "Your dad wants you to get help. This is far from being locked up. You're not sitting in some jail cell, vomiting and pissing all over yourself while you are trying to come down cold from drugs. Believe me. It is not even close to anything like that here. You are in the Holiday Inn of psychiatric care. It could be long-term for you, but it's not to hurt you. You know this, Tai."

Tai let her tears fall into her hands. "Well, I wish he hadn't done this to me," she said.

"Your father loves you. That is why you are here. He didn't do this to hurt you. We are here to help you," Dr. Bent assured her.

The whole room was watching her. Even Janine was listening and really taking all of that in. She reached out and touched Tai's hand. Tai grabbed her hand and squeezed.

Tai said, "It's just embarrassing."

I realized that Dr. Cuvo and Geoffrey were right. We were all in the same position here. We all got embarrassed and we were all in here, in need of the doctors' care. I wanted to grab Tai's hand and squeeze it too.

Dr. Bent leaned toward Tai. "You're not the only person in here who has done drugs. You are not the only one who is embarrassed about being here. You are all here because you are all getting help. You will get through this, Tai."

Tai agreed by nodding her head. She wiped her eyes and smiled. She seemed relieved to have been able to express herself. She seemed even more relieved and comforted when Janine squeezed her hand. After a comforting moment of silence, Dr. Bent looked at Janine.

"You're up, kid," Dr. Bent said.

Janine looked dumbfounded. "Me?" She pointed to herself.

"Yes," Dr. Bent answered her.

"Oh, okay." She paused and looked at us. Her cheeks turned pink when she saw Daniel's eyes fixed on her. "Everybody knows me. I'm Janine."

Tai and a few of the others, including Daniel, chuckled.

I shifted in my chair, uncomfortable and impatient. I wanted so badly to be lying down in my bed. I wanted to be away from everyone.

"I am here because I have to start eating my food, and so I have had a hard time, but it will be fine. Someone else can talk now. I am finished." Janine leaned back and kicked her feet up in the air. She seemed nervous and jittery.

Dr. Bent turned her attention to Cadence, who had been sitting in a corner with her strange doll, staring silently at the ceiling. She didn't notice when Dr. Bent called out to her the first time. A girl in our group reached out and tapped Cadence on her knee. It seemed as if Cadence nearly jumped out of her skin. Cadence calmed down when she realized where she was. But she didn't seem too comfortable while everyone was laughing at her.

I wasn't laughing, and neither was Dr. Bent. Dr. Bent told Cadence it was her turn to share. At first Cadence just looked around at everyone. Her face was strange. The tense expression started to melt away as she began speaking.

"I'm Candy. I am seventeen years old, and there are degenerate perverts of the government who are trying to penetrate our minds with unimaginable strengths. We don't know what they are capable of, and there's no way to find out unless you let them get you. My father's friend said that he could protect me, but they got him, too. He tried to get me, but my dad said that this was the only place that they wouldn't get me. They can't find me here. They can't find any of you if you don't talk about it. They'll hack you! They'll hack you all up! They…they said…they will get me…"

She gasped as if someone had tried to grab her. Her left hand stayed between her upper thighs, as if she were trying to protect her crotch. She clutched her doll tightly and pressed it to her chest as she rocked back and forth in her chair. She cried softly.

"I don't want to be a part of it! He said it was for me. It was all for me."

I was confused and scared all at one time. The expressions of fear and paranoia were written on Cadence's face. What was with this girl? She was so afraid that she was shaking. Who was after her? Why were they after her? Who were these perverts? I wondered. I knew I'd never know because they probably didn't exist.

My mind was racing. I looked at Dr. Bent, who looked as calm as the summer wind. I heard Tai and Janine snickering. They probably thought it was funny because they didn't understand. I didn't think it was funny. I thought it was almost horrifying because I didn't understand.

Dr. Bent leaned forward and gave a warm smile to Cadence. "It's all right, Cadence. No one will make you do anything that you do not want to do in here. You are safe, just like we talked about before."

Cadence continued to rock back and forth with her doll clutched closely to her chest. I watched her move her hand down. She placed it between her thighs and she squeezed them together. Someone had hurt her. They had hurt her badly. Maybe she felt that they were still after her. I started to feel bad for her. I got lost in my thoughts; not realizing that the next person had began speaking.

"My name is Rocky," the new person said. "I am thirteen years old. I am here because I tried to…I mean…I…" His hands were shaking and he looked nervous.

"It's all right," Dr. Bent said. "Nobody's going to judge you."

"I tried to kill myself last night," he admitted.

I felt my heart beat faster. Pains shot through my stomach as he spoke. He was so young, and something hurt him enough cause him to want to die. I understood his pain.

"How did you try to do it?" I heard myself ask.

All eyes suddenly shot stares at me.

I sank in my chair, embarrassed.

Rocky looked at Dr. Bent for permission. "Do I have to answer that?"

"You don't have to, but it may aid us all in understanding. Everyone in here has shared his or her issues. It won't make you stand out. If anything, it should help."

"I don't really want to say. I mean, there is nothing to say. I just tried to kill myself. My mom found me, and they made me come here when I got out of the hospital. It doesn't matter." He sighed and looked down at his hands in his lap. I could see charcoal residue on his cheek.

Dr. Bent didn't press Rocky any further. She thanked him for sharing and told him that he'd done a good job opening up. Though she was trying to be nice and encourage him, it didn't seem to work. He kept his eyes on his hands, and had the same depressed look on his face. Dr. Bent didn't pick on him anymore, as she seemed to do with Tai. She moved on to

Daniel.

Daniel looked up, shocked, when she called out to him. His mind must have been somewhere else. Everyone seemed to have been drifting off while other people were speaking. I tried to stay alert in case she called on me.

"What?" Daniel asked.

"It's your turn to share, silly," Janine reminded him.

"What are we doing again? What are we sharing?"

"Are you okay, Daniel?" Dr. Bent asked with concern.

"Can I use the restroom?" asked Rocky.

"Hang on a minute, Rocky," Dr. Bent said. "Daniel, you look pale. Are you feeling okay?"

"I have to use the bathroom, too," Janine interrupted.

Others started complaining that they needed to use the restroom.

"Hey!" Dr. Bent yelled. "Let's get in control here! If you all could just wait a minute, I'll call your group leader to come get you. You all will get a break." She got up and went over to Daniel. She looked down at him. "Daniel, do you feel all right?"

Daniel looked up and his face was ghostly white. His eyes rolled back to where his pupils seemed to disappear and we could only see white. He tried to nod his head.

"Yes," he struggled to get out, "I'm okay, Dr. Bent."

"I don't think so," she said as she began dialing on her phone. She spoke with someone on the other end and asked them to come because Daniel needed help. When she hung up, she went back over to Daniel. Everyone stared at him. Tai and Janine asked him if he was all right, and he kept trying to say that he was fine, but he could barely speak.

Less than a minute went by, and Ms. Mosley entered the room with Geoffrey. Dr. Bent told them that Rocky and Janine needed to use the restroom and that Daniel wasn't feeling well. When Dr. Bent said that Rocky and Janine needed to use the restroom, Tai and a few others said that they had to go, too.

I suddenly felt like I was back in school. I sat quietly in my chair, looking over at Daniel, concerned. Daniel looked like he was drifting off into sleep. Ms. Mosley told everyone to come back to the unit with her and Geoffrey. Geoffrey walked over to Daniel and asked him if he was all right. Daniel insisted that he was fine. When Geoffrey grabbed Daniel's arm and tried to help him up, his lack of balance proved otherwise.

"Easy does it, there. Come on, Daniel. I'll help you back to the unit and we will test your blood sugar. It might be low."

Geoffrey and Daniel headed out the door first. The rest of us lined up behind Ms. Mosley, and we headed out the door, leaving Dr. Bent in the office.

When we were back on the unit, everyone seemed to scramble away to their rooms. Daniel was sitting at one of the tables while he pricked his finger and let his blood drip onto some kind of small machine that looked like a calculator. I sat down at the table with him.

He looked up at me and said, "I guess my secret is out."

"What is that?" I asked, referring to the machine that was sucking the blood from his finger.

"It's a blood glucose testing meter. My blood sugar is low."

He let his head fall onto the table. I looked down at the small machine and saw that the digital screen on his meter read fifty-eight. I called out to Geoffrey, not knowing what fifty-eight meant. Geoffrey came over and tapped Daniel. Daniel looked up. I sighed with relief. I thought he had passed out. Geoffrey gave Daniel half of a chocolate candy bar. Daniel tore into the candy bar immediately.

"Why is your blood sugar low?" I asked him.

He shrugged. "I'm diabetic, so it happens sometimes. Better it gets low than high."

"Why?"

"Because that means I can have candy," he said with a mischievous smile.

"I had no idea you have diabetes," I told him.

"Since I was twelve. It's called Juvenile Diabetes," he shared.

The conversation died right there. It was sad to think that Daniel had to suffer with diabetes, starting from such a young age. It was sad that he had to go through it at all. I'd had no clue that he went through that until he'd gotten sick in our group meeting. I had never seen him take a shot or a pill or anything for his diabetes.

I felt strange inside, just sitting there with him in silence. I didn't know what to say. I didn't know what to feel. I wanted to say something to him, but there weren't any words. All I could do was look at him. His hair was dark and long like John's. I couldn't allow myself to start thinking about John. If I did, I'd get weird right there in front of Daniel. I leaned my head on my hands as my elbows rested on the table.

Instead of ignoring my presence, Daniel began to stare at me. I tried not to look at him. He had a string of caramel hanging from his bottom lip. I debated in silence whether to tell him or not. When I finally made my decision, I looked at him. I didn't intend to say anything, but I couldn't help laughing at the cute expression on his face while he let the caramel hang there. He was clueless.

"What's so funny?" he asked.

"You have some stuff on your mouth. It's just…"

"What?" He was smiling at me.

"The caramel is hanging from your mouth." I kept laughing at him.

The more I laughed, the more it tickled him. He tried to wipe at the caramel, but that only made it worse. He made me laugh harder.

"What? Did I get it?" he asked.

I had to cover my mouth because I was laughing so hard. Daniel kept trying to wipe the caramel away, but was not having much success. I gave in and reached out to wipe it away for him. He noticed me getting closer to him, and he stopped smiling. My thumb touched his chin, and he flinched, quickly turning his face away from me. I immediately knew it was a mistake. Daniel didn't want me to touch him. I pulled my hand away, feeling stupid.

I didn't notice Tai standing nearby. She and Rocky walked over and sat down at the table with us. She gave me a strange look. She was grinning and twisting her lips at the same time. Cadence giggled at Rocky as she passed our table.

"Shut up," Rocky fussed.

"What were you two talking about?" Tai asked.

"Nothing," I said.

"Oh, candy!" Janine exclaimed as she suddenly approached our table. She sat down next to Daniel and she made him smile again.

"How come you can have candy and we can't?" Janine asked him.

Daniel held out the last bite of his candy bar to her and asked, "Do you want it?"

Janine pushed her long hair back and looked into his eyes. It was almost sexy, the way he pushed the last bite of chocolate into her mouth and she chewed it. He watched her enjoy that last piece. Everyone one else watched. We were all shocked that she was eating it.

Interrupting the PG-13 moment between Janine and Daniel, Tai said, "Don't go throwing that back up, Janine. He sacrificed his last bite of chocolate for you."

Janine laughed and stuck her tongue out at Tai. They both laughed. Daniel kept his gaze on her. It looked like he had just noticed the beauty mole on the bridge between her neck and shoulder. Then he poked it with his index finger. Janine squealed in a cute way and poked him back.

Tai looked over at me. She said, "Whew, somebody needs a bath."

Everyone laughed, including Daniel. Janine was still poking at him, but I knew that he was laughing at what Tai had said. I wasn't laughing because I knew that Tai was talking about me.

"Take a whiff," Tai kept on.

"Stop it," Janine kept laughing. "She can't help it. She has stitches, so she can't shower. She can't get the stitches wet because they will melt or something."

That made them laugh even harder. I didn't say anything. I felt exactly what I had expected to feel the first day that I arrived here. They were being just like the people at school. I hated being around other kids. I hated being here at Bent Creek. My cramps started kicking in hard.

Tai hit my arm jokingly.

"Come on, girl," Tai said. "We are just playing with you. We know you can't help it."

They all kept laughing. I felt like such a loser. Janine was sitting next to Daniel, and they were laughing together. Tai got off the subject when Cadence decided to sit near us. Tai started going on about something that had happened at lunch. I missed what was so funny. I stopped listening to her, even though she was really trying to talk to me because I wasn't at lunch with them.

Cadence seemed to like to antagonize new people because she was having too much fun annoying Rocky. Rocky was staring as if he wanted to snap her neck off her body. Cadence found this amusing. Janine and Daniel were in their own little world.

"Are you okay now?" Janine asked Daniel. She was showing her cute, pink dimple on the left side of her face as she smiled.

Smiling at her, Daniel said, "Yes. I am now."

"Why are you being so quiet?" she asked him.

"I am just thinking about stuff," Daniel said as he unzipped a small carry case and packed away his blood glucose meter.

He pushed the carry case aside and looked right at Janine. As soon as Daniel's eyes met Janine's, she blushed. He put his finger on her chin and wiped.

"You had caramel on your chin," he told her.

My stomach burned. I couldn't take it anymore. I got up and went to the bedroom. I stayed there with the door closed, wishing I could lock it and keep everyone else out. I didn't leave to go back to group therapy, and no one came to look for me.

I lay back on my bed and closed my eyes. I wanted to be far away. I didn't want to be here with the other people. I wanted to be back in time to where I was happy. Back when I thought that mental hospitals were not real, and they only existed in horror movies.

I could almost see John's face. I could almost see his hair and his eyes from when we went to the same school, and when he came over to our house with his little brother, James, so that he could play with Nick. He was considered my cousin because his father was Jack's brother, but technically, he was not my cousin. We were not related.

"I remember you," he said to me as we sat on our front porch. "Do you remember me?"

I nodded, picturing him refusing to dance with his mother at Jack and Mom's wedding.

"We go to the same school," he said, referring to the middle school we attended. "I'm about to go to the high school. What grade are you in?"

"I'm in seventh grade," I told him.

I saw his gorgeous eyes, and I remembered his lovely smile so clearly. He looked different in middle school than he did when I'd seen him at Mom and Jack's wedding. He was much taller. His voice was deeper. He was a big brother now. At the wedding, he'd been an only child. My happier thoughts of him were before he knew Lexus. It was the pain of growing up that made me most bitter. Thinking too much made my head hurt. I let myself drift off into sleep.

It seemed as if time had been stolen from me. I fought back tears, which only made my chest fill up with pain. I closed my eyes, confused, and tried to focus.

"God, if you're not mad at me, please help me..." I whispered. I couldn't stop thinking. My mind was racing. I saw Janine's face and I saw Daniel's face. I saw John's face and I saw Lexus' face. They were intertwined. "God, please, please help me."

Ms. Mosley appeared out of nowhere. She had come into the room silently. She must have come in to check on me. I was embarrassed to see her standing in the doorway, staring at me, when I opened my eyes.

"Are you all right?" she asked. She moved closer to me, hesitantly and slowly. "I came in to check on you. Your group is about to go to their last meeting before dinner."

"I can't," I said. "Everyone says I smell bad and I'm just disgusting," I cried. I could smell the dirt on my body. I almost felt sick.

Ms. Mosley sighed heavily. I could see the sincerity in her eyes.

"I am going to call one of the nurses tonight. Someone should have been here to draw your blood and help you with your stitches. I will do everything I can, Kristen. I would help you myself, but I don't want to do anything to mess you up. You're excused from your meeting tonight. Don't worry about it. I will see if Geoffrey can bring your dinner to you so that you won't have to be around them. Just make sure you are at the nurse's station when it's time to take your medicine." Ms. Mosley smiled warmly.

Before she turned away to leave, I sat up in bed and called out to her. She turned back to me.

"How long does it take before someone can really get better and go home?" I asked her.

She sighed. "Listen to me, Kristen. I know it is hard being in this place. But while you are here, you can't let your mind become occupied by the fact that you *are* here. You can't get bogged down with feeling sorry for yourself. You should be pondering on *why* you're here and what it will take so that you can get better, get out of here, stay better, and *stay out* of here. You want to try to get help from your doctors and try to find something that will help you appreciate life."

"Ms. Mosley," I cried. "I am punished with life!"

She put on a stern face and looked me right in my eyes. "Do you believe in God?"

"I believe that there is a God," I told her, confused.

"No," she said with her stern face, "Do you *know* who God is?"

"I've heard of God," I told her. "When I was a kid, my Mom and I went to church. We used to pray together. She always told me that I could pray to Him anytime, even if it was in the middle of the day. I used to know Him, but I think that He's forgotten about me."

Ms. Mosley came towards me again. "Honey, He has not forgotten about you. He knows who you are, even if you don't know Him. Do you know how I know that God has not forgotten about you? You have air in your lungs, you are able to speak, think, and move. This is what you are taking for granted. These are things that you tried to take away that God has blessed you with."

She sat down beside me and continued, "Your life is not yours, Kristen. It is God's. He can never forget about something that belongs to Him. Even though you are suffering with this pain inside of yourself, God is helping you endure it. And He is not letting you do it alone. You are here, and you are getting help from people that He has directed you to. No, God has not forgotten you. He wants you to be alive. That's why you are here."

The beating of my heart was steady and calm. I felt relaxed and secure with Ms. Mosley there beside me. She gently placed a hand on my shoulder as her sternness faded to sincerity.

She said, "He's got you here. There's no way He can leave you and not get you through the rest of the way." She paused and looked at me to make sure I understood.

With dry eyes, I stuck out my arms and wrapped them around her. She hesitated before she hugged me back. Ms. Mosley quickly let me go and smiled.

"You need to rest. We'll talk later," she said as she began to walk away.

Her eyes were always serious, and her tone of voice was strong. I liked that. Ms. Mosley was the most real person I had ever known. I lay back down in the bed when she left the room. I rolled onto my stomach and closed my eyes. There was an ache inside of me. I wanted to get rid of it.

God, get me to endure this.

CHAPTER 15

Ouch. No. Ouch. Stop it. No.

I felt a sharp, pricking pain shoot through my arm. I first felt it when I was asleep. It started on the back of my hand, and then moved to my wrist. When I opened my eyes, I could hardly see because the bright light from the sun was shining through the bedroom window. I tried to lift my hand to cover my eye, but when I tried to move, I realized that the pains were on the inside of my arm. I squinted and tried to lift my arm again. It wouldn't move. It wouldn't move because there was pressure on it, holding it down, face-up, on the bed. The pressure squeezed my wrist when I tried to lift it. There was someone holding my arm down by my wrist. I was hurting. I had to get up and make it stop. I tried to sit up.

"No! Keep still! I almost have it," a female voice yelled at me. She took her hand off my wrist and violently pushed me back down on the bed.

When my eyes focused, I noticed that there was a tall woman hovering over me. She had a needle in her hand. I watched her as she brought the needle down to my inner arm and stuck me again. It felt like she had stuck me in the same spot she had tried previously.

The pain was terrible. She was having a hard time drawing my blood. She snatched the needle out of my arm, sending an excruciating pain up my arm to my head.

"Ouch! Please… Stop it…!" I cried helplessly. Blood squirted from my arm out onto the bed sheet. My arm felt like she had been sticking me with needles while I had been asleep all morning.

"Hold still, child!" she demanded.

"No! Stop!" I cried louder.

The woman held my wrist down, pressed to the bed. She squeezed it tight. The pressure was so intense, and it felt like my stitches were going to break. I was growing scared. Tears were falling out of my eyes.

"Stop fighting me," she growled. "If you hold still, I will get your blood without all of this difficulty. But if you keep moving, it's going to keep hurting some more. Do you want that?"

I shook my head with tears drenching my face. She felt the need to squeeze my wrist some more. I wondered if she was doing that on purpose. I held as still as I could. It took her four more agonizing sticks to get all of the blood she needed. If I felt the need to hurt myself at that moment, I wouldn't have to, for she was doing a fine job. She filled six tubes of blood. When she was finished, I sat up and felt light-headed. She laughed when I fell back and laid my head on my pillow.

"You shouldn't sit up right away," she tardily said. She began putting labels on the tubes that held my blood.

"I have to get your vitals this morning. Take your shirt off, and if you have a bra, take that off too," she said while not looking at me.

When I had my shirt off and she had put away the tubes, she pulled out a stethoscope and a blood pressure tester. While checking my blood pressure, she yanked on my bandaged wrists and pulled my arm to straighten my posture. She then shoved the thermometer into my mouth roughly, which almost made me choke. She laughed when I coughed. It occurred to me that I was not dealing with a nice nurse at all. She was brutal, rough, and seemingly careless.

I didn't hear Janine moving around. I looked over at her side of the room, and she was still asleep. I wondered where Ms. Mosley was. The nurse told me to put my shirt back on and gather my personal items. She said that she was going to assist me in getting cleaned up.

I wanted to tell her "no, thank you" because she didn't seem like the kind of nurse I wanted touching my private areas. She was not like the nurse at the other hospital at all. Hesitating, I got up out of the bed and grabbed my underwear and a menstrual pad. When she saw me grab the pad, the look on her face changed from simply mean to terrifyingly angry.

"Don't *even* tell me that you are on your period, child," she said.

I nodded, afraid of what she was going to do to me.

The nurse shook her head with a grimace on her face. She turned away from me, grabbed the tubes and her bag, and stormed out of the room. Confused, I went to the door. Anxiety washed over me, and I couldn't make myself go out the door. I looked down at my arm as it ached in pain. I could see the spots where she'd stuck me with the needle. My skin color turned black and blue. I grew afraid that she wouldn't come back. If she wasn't going to help me, then I had no way to clean up. She was the only nurse who was apparently going to help me. I didn't mean to make her leave.

I forced myself to walk out the door and try to catch her. I was hoping that I could at least get her to give me new bandages for my wrists. I walked out the double doors that separated the Girl's Unit from the main area, and stopped when I saw Ms. Mosley and the nurse talking.

Ms. Mosley was upset. "Why didn't you help her get a bath?"

The nurse responded, "I am not about to clean her while she is on her period, Karen. This is not even my area. I work with the adults, not pediatrics. I don't appreciate you leaving messages on my voicemail like the one you left last night, either. I didn't know that you all had a new female patient on the Adolescent Unit who needed her blood drawn. I came to draw blood for you because your unit's nurse has not been showing up for her shifts. If you have a problem, you need to talk to Dr. Pelchat because I have nothing to do with what goes on over here. Don't *ever* call me with that kind of business again!"

Ms. Mosley stayed silent as the nurse stormed off. Geoffrey had been watching from behind the counselor's desk. He asked her if she was all right, and she nodded.

I hurried back to my room feeling embarrassed and dismayed. When I entered, Janine was coming out of the bathroom. She looked at me. Her hair looked soft and it flowed down her back. She smiled at me, flashing her cute pink dimple.

"What are you doing up so early?" Janine asked. She threw herself down on her bed and covered up with her treasured, pink blanket. She looked warm.

"The nurse came to take my blood," I confessed. I went back over to my bed, and covered myself with the thin, white blanket. It hardly did any good for me because I was still cold.

"Wasn't she supposed to be here yesterday?" Janine asked.

"Yes."

"I hate this place," she complained. "Wait. Didn't you say that the nurse is supposed to help you get cleaned up, too?"

I nodded.

"This place *really* sucks." Janine frowned at me. "I'm sorry," she said.

She tried to smile at me, but I couldn't smile back. I looked away from her. She must have drifted off into her own place. I turned back to her when I heard her giggle. She looked pretty when she smiled. Her eyes sparkled.

I looked down at my hands. I didn't want to see her face. I touched my face. It felt oily. I looked at my fingers. They were shiny. I touched my face again and felt my nose. There was a mild pain. I felt the spot where the pain grew stronger, a spot between my nose and my cheek, right on the crease of my nose, where it felt like a pimple was growing. I felt like crying. I looked up at Janine. She was lying down, and her eyes were closed. Her pink skin looked soft and clear.

Angrily I lay back down on the bed. I touched the pimple on my nose. I went from touching to digging. I dug the nail on my index finger into my skin and went as deep as I could into the pimple. Then I ripped as hard as I could. I felt the pressure of the pimple release as blood spilled down my nose. I could taste it on my lips.

"Hold still, Lexus," I fussed as squeezed the small, barely noticeable pimple on her chin.

Lexus tried to lie as still as she could on her back as I sat on top of her and hovered over her to try to kill the evil pimple.

"Oh, but it hurts," she whined.

"Then squeeze my hips or scratch my back. Just hold still," I told her.

Lexus wrapped her arms around my back and, as I squeezed her pimple, she dug her nails into my back. The pain was amazing. I felt too much adrenaline go to my head. I couldn't stop squeezing. I had to make the puss come out. One long, hard squeeze and Lexus dug her nails into my back even harder.

The puss shot out. She screamed, and I screamed. Well, my scream was more like a moan, as she had run her nails down my back. With the way things looked, if one of our parents had walked in, they would have gotten the wrong idea.

"Well, that was fun," I said jokingly, as I sat on top of her.

She looked beautiful, lying on her back. She looked up at me and laughed. "Get off of me," she giggled.

I got off her and grabbed a Kleenex from a tissue box. When I gave her the tissue, she wiped her chin. She looked at the bloody paper.

"Eww…this is nasty," she said. "I hate it when I get pimples."

"I couldn't even see it. It was so small," I said.

I looked into the mirror as I spoke to her. I frowned. I had oily skin with too many dark spots. I was ugly. I turned away from the mirror angrily. Lexus looked at me, and put a hand on my shoulder. I shoved her away from me. She sighed. She silently forgave me for shoving her, and tried to smile.

"You look so cute in your new outfit. I think we did a good job picking our new outfits for the picnic. Don't you think?"

She wanted me to respond. I looked at her mini-skirt and corset tank top. She was wearing nail polish and make-up. Then I looked at my denim jeans and long-sleeved sweater I wore to cover up my cuts. I didn't want to respond.

Still trying to be cheerful, she grabbed some lipstick. "Come on, just this once. Let me put some lipstick on you."

I stared at the lipstick, almost afraid. Lexus laughed and shoved me into a chair next to the dresser.

"Look, you will like this color," she said as she hovered over me and began to put the lipstick on my lips. Then she pulled out her blush. I tried to get up, but she pushed me back down.

"No," she said. "You made me sit still while I let you torture me, and now it's your turn." After the blush came the eye shadow. I sat still without a fight until she went for the liquid eyeliner. "Now, you will have to trust me," she warned.

I stayed quiet and stared at her. She laughed. "Don't worry. It's not like you're going to die."

"Yes, I am," I said.

"Shut up, no you won't. Now, look up at the ceiling." She ran that liner pen on the line of my bottom lashes, then along the top, without poking my eyes out, as I feared she would. "You don't need mascara," she complimented. "You've got nice, long eyelashes like your Mom."

I smiled at her.

She stood in front of me with her hands on her hips. She cocked her head as she studied her work of art. "You look nice," she finally said. "Look for yourself." She pulled me up out of the chair.

"No," I told her. "Lexus, I don't really want to look at myself in the mirror."

"Shut up," she said. "Look."

I stood in front of the mirror. I felt emotionless. I didn't look different. I just had color.

"What's the difference?" I asked her.

"What's the difference?" she repeated. "It's color!" She laughed at me. "Besides, I did a really good job on you. I could be your personal make-up artist."

"What would I need one of those for?"

"You know, when you grow up and you become a famous poet and publish books, you'll need someone to make you look good for TV talk shows and book signings."

I was shocked. I said, "You really think I'll get my poems published?"

She shoved me playfully. "You have enough of them! Why not?"

I smiled at her, overjoyed that she believed in me.

"So is it good, even though it's different?"

I thought for a moment. "I don't know if it's good-different or just me-looking-like–me-different."

"It had better be good-different because I did a really good job," she proclaimed. Then suddenly, "Oh, my goodness!"

"What?" I asked.

"I have a great idea! Come on!"

She grabbed my arm and pulled me out of the room. I had no idea where she was taking me until I saw our parents and John's parents on the back porch, watching the food barbeque. John and his little brother were with Nick. The three of them were sitting on a blanket in the grass. The parents looked at me. Mom was drinking a beer, and as soon as she saw me, she started choking.

I froze.

John's mom asked, "Did you do that yourself?"

I felt like a two-year-old who had just used the potty all by herself for the first time.

"No," Lexus said. "I did her make-up."

"That looks lovely, honey," her dad praised her.

Lexus giggled happily.

Jack looked at me without expression. He sat his beer down on the table and walked away. I watched him go into the house. Mom looked like she wanted to follow him. I tried to smile.

"You should let Lexus do your make-up more often," her mother said.

"Okay, thanks," I said.

I quickly left them on the porch, but Lexus went after me. I didn't see Jack when I went back into the house. I went back to the bedroom.

Lexus closed the door. "Are you okay?" she asked.

"Yes," I lied. I smiled at her to make her believe me.

"Yay! We are so cute," she said.

I rolled my eyes playfully. *She was so cute*. We wrapped our arms around each other and hugged.

"You're my best friend," I said.

Knock. Knock.

I woke up suddenly at the sound of the knocks on the door. Janine opened her eyes. Ms. Mosley entered the room.

"Hey, it's not time to get up yet," Janine whined to Ms. Mosley. "It's Saturday."

Ms. Mosley ignored her and stood near me while I sat up in bed. Janine saw that Ms. Mosley had not come for her, so she turned over and went back to sleep. Ms. Mosley looked down at me.

"Do you want me to help you get cleaned up now, or do you need to sleep a little longer?" she asked kindly.

"Okay," I said as I hurried up and got out of the bed. "We can do it now, please."

She nodded and headed towards the bathroom. Relieved, I grabbed my towel and personal items and followed Ms. Mosley to the bathroom. As I got undressed, Ms. Mosley prepared the shower. I felt nervous, like I had in the other hospital the first time the nurse had helped me get clean. Ms. Mosley could tell that I was nervous. She gently took my hand and led me to the shower. She had me stick my foot in the shower to test the water. I had to make sure it wasn't too hot or too cold. It was lukewarm, just right.

Ms. Mosley didn't remove the bandages before she cleaned me. I had to hold my arms out of the shower so that they wouldn't get wet. She didn't seem to be bothered by my menstrual flow. She seemed like she was trying to be careful and professional. She washed my hair and everywhere that was most necessary, all the while humming a song that I had heard once when I was child. It was comforting and it made me feel calm. When she finished, I could smell myself. But it wasn't like when I smelled myself before. This time I could smell the sweet apple shampoo and the Ivory soap. At that moment, those were the best scents that I had ever smelled in my entire life.

Ms. Mosley wrapped a towel around me. I stepped out of the shower. She looked at me. "Kristen, I have to remove your bandages now, okay?"

I nodded.

She took my arm into her hands. She started to unwrap the bandages and then stopped. "What happened to your arm?"

"The nurse," I said. "She was having a hard time taking my blood this morning." I looked at the damage. My arm had been badly bruised.

Ms. Mosley frowned. She didn't say anything in response, but just continued unwrapping the bandages from my wrists. I looked away. I couldn't look at what I had done to myself. Instead, I looked at the pale paint that was chipping off the walls. When the bandages were completely off, I felt the air hit my wrists. They felt cold. I tried to keep my focus on the chipped paint. That bathroom could have used a new paint job. There was suddenly a strange smell. I scrunched up my face. I couldn't move my hands to cover my nose, because Ms. Mosley was putting something on my wrists. It felt like water, but it couldn't have been, because it smelled too bad and it stung when it touched my skin.

"I'm sorry," she said. "It smells like that because it is a liquid ointment for your stitches. It is supposed to help them heal faster. It also keeps the wounds from infection."

I had to force myself not to look down. I watched her grab new bandages from her bag. The she started wrapping my wrists back up.

"There you go," she said with a sigh. "You are all done. Go ahead and get dressed. Do you need help?"

I shook my head as I walked back into the bedroom. Ms. Mosley walked to the door to exit the room. Before she left, she said, "I will be back at eight-thirty to get you and Janine up."

I went over to my side of the room and started getting dressed. I didn't see that Janine was awake.

"I bet you feel a lot better," she said, startling me.

"Yes I do," I replied.

"Did the nurse help you?"

"No. Ms. Mosley helped me."

She scrunched up her face. "Eww. Did she hurt you?"

"Why would she do that?" I asked.

Janine looked at me as if I should know the answer to that question.

"Because she's an evil wench," she answered.

I looked away from her. I didn't believe that anymore. Ms. Mosley seemed like the best person in this place besides Dr. Cuvo. I finished getting dressed and then sat down on the bed. I looked over at Janine. She was peeking out at me from under her pink blanket.

"Do you remember when you first got your period?" she suddenly asked. That question seemed to come unexpectedly.

Not really knowing if I should respond, I pushed myself to answer. "Sure," I said.

"I do, too," she told me. "I don't think that's something we forget."

"No," I agreed. "That's not something girls forget."

"Where were you when you found out you had it?"

"I was at home." Even though I answered her, I wasn't too comfortable going on about it, but I kept quiet to let her speak.

"You were lucky," she went on. "I was at school. But no one knew about me. I felt so scared that everyone would find out, though. Back when I was in fifth grade, a girl in our class got her period before all of the other girls. Her name was Kristen, just like you. She was the first girl in our class to get her period. I felt so bad for her because she didn't have any privacy. Every time she raised her hand to ask the teacher if she could use a bathroom pass, the other girls in the classroom would say that they had to go, too. Only three could go at a time, so the teacher sent two other girls off with her. Then, when she had to go again, the other girls who hadn't gotten a chance asked to go. It was like they all were taking turns going whenever Kristen would go, so that they could watch her or something."

"That's really sad." I felt devastated, and this wasn't even my story.

"Yeah, I know." Janine sat up and continued. "I feel guilty because I let curiosity get to me too. One day I went to the bathroom with Kristen and another girl named Cassie. Cassie had already followed Kristen to the bathroom a few times before. Since I hadn't had a turn, the other girls agreed that I should go to see what it looked like. When we were in the bathroom, Cassie told me to wait until Kristen went into the stall, and then she made me go into the one next to Kristen. When we could hear Kristen opening the plastic wrapper, we climbed up on top of the toilet and then leaned over the stall."

I stayed silent and listened in revulsion.

"Kristen saw me looking down at her while she changed her tampon. It was bloody and gross, and the look on her face was frightful. She looked like she was going to cry."

It did not amaze me to hear how cruel these girls were to this pitiable Kristen. Nor was it shocking to hear that Janine had been sucked into it herself. The girls had been curious, mean, and selfish. They were just like the girls I had gone to school with. That Kristen hadn't stood a chance if she had told someone. Perhaps she'd told a best friend in confidence that she had gotten her period, with hope that her friend would keep her secret. That Kristen obviously had been betrayed.

Not wanting to hear any more of the torturous menstruation stories about this other Kristen, I looked away from Janine and lay down on my back. Staring up at the ceiling, I tried to divert my thoughts away from the topic by searching for Mr. Sharp in my head.

"Are you going back to sleep?" she asked.

Annoyed, I said, "I don't know."

I could not reach him without my butterfly. I began to feel lonely, and the thought of poor Kristen in that bathroom stall would not go away. All I could picture was a little girl's face looking up from a bathroom stall and crying. I imagined her to look like what I used to look like in the fifth grade. We had the same sad eyes and frown.

"You should know that Saturdays are the best day here. We get to sleep until eight-thirty, and we all get to have breakfast on the unit with everyone. We can watch TV and talk on the phone longer. It's kind of like a free day. If you get to Level Three, you can leave the unit, do your laundry, and go outside. The only thing that sucks is that we still have group meetings."

I nodded. A few minutes of complete silence went by until Janine finally started speaking again. I was just getting comfortable and was trying to fall back to sleep.

"Is your Mom coming to visit today?"

"I don't know."

Janine sighed. "My dad is coming. He's going to bring my little brother."

"That's nice," I said.

"Daniel might be going home because he has a family session," she said. "That is going to suck if he leaves." Janine rolled over on her side, turning away from me.

I closed my eyes, remembering the way he had looked at her when he wiped the caramel from her chin. Then I pictured Lexus and John. I had to open my eyes quickly to stop myself. When I opened my eyes, Janine turned on her side, faced me, and stared at me strangely.

"Are you okay?"

"I am fine," I told her.

She frowned and said, "Do you like Daniel?"

I didn't answer.

"Can you believe he doesn't have a girlfriend? He used to have a girlfriend, but she like killed herself or something. It was stupid. If I was with Daniel, I wouldn't feel the need to kill myself."

"Do you have a boyfriend?" I asked.

She smiled and looked up at the ceiling.

"Sometimes," she said while still smiling.

Of course, you do, I thought to myself.

"I am really glad we get to sleep late on Saturdays."

Janine closed her eyes. She turned away from me, and this time she didn't open her mouth again. Getting that last hour of sleep wasn't hard for me. I couldn't stop thinking, but I was able to drift off in my thoughts. It felt good to be clean on the outside, but I still felt sick inside.

CHAPTER 16

Eight-thirty came faster than the minute I had closed my eyes and fallen asleep. It felt like only two minutes had passed since I had closed my eyes when Ms. Mosley came in to wake us up. She gently tugged at my fingers, and I heard her calling my name. I opened my eyes and saw her deep brown eyes looking down at me.

When she saw that I was awake, she smiled and said, "It's time to get up."

I lifted myself out of bed. I looked down at my body, remembering earlier this morning when Ms. Mosley had helped me clean up. I saw the black and blue bruises on my arms, and quickly threw a sweater over them. It was a normal habit to cover my bruises and scars since Mr. Sharp had come into my life. I looked over and noticed that Janine was not in the room. She wasn't in the bathroom either.

"Come on," Ms. Mosley hurried.

I had gotten the impression from Janine that Saturdays were laid back at Bent Creek. So it confused me when, immediately after breakfast, we had Group Therapy. This Group Therapy meeting was for the whole Adolescent Unit. We weren't broken into small groups. Instead, Geoffrey set up a bunch of chairs in the main room to make a circle. The room was full of other patients from the Adolescent Unit. Our groups were mixed together for this meeting.

Cadence seemed tired of picking on the new guy named Rocky. She'd moved on to someone else. Rocky was sitting next to the small guy that hated Janine. The small guy was still gaunt-looking. He and Rocky were talking about smoking marijuana and popping all kinds of pills. There was an open seat next to them, but I didn't feel comfortable enough to sit there. Janine and Tai wanted to sit on the love seat, but Geoffrey made them get up and join the circle.

Janine sat next to Daniel, and Tai sat next to Janine. Feeling left out, I sat next to Geoffrey. Most everyone was sitting in the circle next to their friends and chatting when a large, redheaded man walked into the room and sat down next to Geoffrey. When he sat down and looked up, most everyone quieted down.

"Hello," said the man. "It's nice to see you again, Kristen."

He remembered my name. I couldn't remember his name. I did remember Geoffrey being in awe of this man.

"You remember Dr. Pelchat, don't you?" Geoffrey asked me quietly. "He's the head of Bent Creek, and he's also a doctor here."

"I need everyone to please be quiet," the man demanded. "I'm Dr. Pelchat, for those of you who do not know me. I hope everyone is having a good morning. I know it is Saturday, and most of you want to get on with your day and do your thing, but as you know, we have to get through your group meeting with *me* for today."

There were random moans and sighs throughout the room.

"Today we are going to discuss drugs and alcohol."

A kid from Chris' group hooted and got some of the other kids in the room to cheer with him. "Did you bring enough for everybody, Doc?" asked Chris, who I assumed was Jake at that moment.

Dr. Pelchat waved a hand at him. "All right, sit down. Let's get down to business."

The room quieted back down. Dr. Pelchat looked at Geoffrey, and they both laughed.

At least he has a sense of humor, I thought.

"This is Alcohol and Drug Abuse Counseling Group. Here we will talk about good drugs, bad drugs, drugs that you take home, drugs that you sniff, drugs that you eat, and drugs that you drink. It'll be a real party in here."

I laughed along with everyone else.

Dr. Pelchat smiled at us. He looked at Rocky and said, "Hey man."

"Hey," Rocky said.

"Weren't you just about to tell me what you took two nights ago?" Dr. Pelchat suddenly asked him.

Rocky looked around, confused. "Uh, no, I wasn't."

"Oh, yes, yes, you were. I heard you over there talking, and I heard you say something about what you'd taken the night before you came here, and didn't you say something about being able to score any kind of drugs for anybody in here?"

Rocky's face went from pink to pale. He rubbed his palms together roughly and stared down at the floor with his face twisted in anger. He stayed silent and didn't say a word to Dr. Pelchat.

"I listened to every word you said when I was walking into this room. I heard you talk about how you have pot and acid, and I even think I heard you say something about heroin. Is that right?"

"Come on, man," Rocky whined.

"No, you listen to me." Dr. Pelchat stood up and went over to Rocky.

Everyone stared at Dr. Pelchat as he made Rocky look up at him. He was so tall that Rocky had to back his chair up to look at him. Or he could have just done that because he was afraid that Dr. Pelchat was going to hurt him.

"Let's get something straight. It is okay to talk about drugs here. In fact, I encourage it. Talk about it with your counselors, talk about it with your doctors. Hell, go ahead and talk about it with your peers, but *do not talk about dealing drugs in this hospital*. Do you understand?"

"Okay, get out of my face!" Rocky yelled.

Tai covered her mouth and closed her eyes, as if she was afraid for Rocky.

Dr. Pelchat bent down and put his face and his index finger in Rocky's face.

Dr. Pelchat said, "Now I am in your face! I want you to get it! I want you to know that you can't do that in here! If you want to brag and impress everyone in here, come up with something better. Okay? Now, listen to me. If I catch you using, dealing, or even offering to get drugs for anybody in here again, I will see to it that you are out of here and sent to jail. You can mess up your own life out there, but you are not going to do it in here to yourself or anybody else. Now, do you understand me?"

Rocky had his face turned with his arms folded across his chest. His eyes were focused away from Dr. Pelchat's, which were burning holes through him.

"Do you understand?" Dr. Pelchat repeated, this time yelling at the poor kid.

Rocky bravely turned his face slowly to Dr. Pelchat's and looked him in the eyes. "Yes," Rocky finally said through clenched teeth.

Dr. Pelchat suddenly smiled. "Good."

He stood up straight, turned around, and sat back down in his seat next to Geoffrey. Rocky let out a sigh of relief when Dr. Pelchat sat down. We all sighed in relief for Rocky. I even felt afraid for him. Tai's face was flushed white. She looked like she was the one who had been scolded.

"Did you ever really try any of those drugs?" Dr. Pelchat asked.

Rocky looked up from his sweaty hands. We'd all thought that Dr. Pelchat had gotten off his back.

"Well? Have you?" Dr. Pelchat asked, looking away from Rocky and turning his head to someone else. "Tai?" he called out to her.

Tai took a deep breath and nodded at him. "Uh- yes, just not- I mean, I haven't tried heroin, but you know. It was some bad stuff. I mean, I don't really know- it was kind of-"

Dr. Pelchat cut her off. "What did doing those drugs do to you? Why did you feel like you had to do it?"

This question proved easier to answer. When he asked her that question, his tone had softened, and he looked deep into her eyes. She thought for a moment and then responded.

"Well, it took me away. For those moments when I was high, it was, well, it was exhilarating. I couldn't cry. I couldn't get angry. I couldn't feel those things that made me human. I didn't want to be human if I had to feel those things. The people that I did drugs with would just let me be. They wouldn't bother me or make me talk about anything."

The thin boy sitting next to Rocky pulled his shirt over his mouth, and I could tell that he was laughing. He was trying to use the top of his shirt to cover it up. Dr. Pelchat and everyone else ignored him.

"When I came down," Tai continued with deep thought. "When I came down, all those problems that I was trying to smoke away were right there with me, except they felt ten times as worse." Tears were falling from her eyes. "So I tried to make that feeling stop. I did take that heroin, Dr. Pelchat. They gave it to me, and they left me alone. When I tried to tell them that I needed them to call my dad, they just laughed. I got so scared. I felt my lungs swell up like balloons, and they put all this pressure on my chest. I thought my lungs were going to explode.

"I don't remember much after I passed out, but the doctor said that my liver had collapsed, and that my right lung had stopped working. I have to get surgery, and I am not sure if I will be able to, since this will be my second time getting a new liver. The first time was when I was a baby. I was born with a bad liver, not because of drugs or anything. So, I was given another liver to save my life. The doctor said that I might have a hard time getting another liver because I had already been given one to save my life. It's like I just didn't care, and I wanted to mess up or something, but that's not it. It was because I couldn't get rid of it, not even by doing more. I just couldn't make it stop. There seems like there's just no way to make it stop. I'm a coward. That is why I did it."

"Tai," Dr. Pelchat said. "Honestly, I think that you are the bravest person in this room right now."

"Why?" she asked.

"You know why," he told her.

"Tell me why," she pleaded.

"No, Tai," he said softly, "Tell us why."

"Because I lived through it," she said. "And because I am here."

Dr. Pelchat said, "You said it. Not me, not Dr. Bent, not anyone else. You said it, Tai."

Geoffrey passed Tai a box of tissues. Tai wiped her eyes and smiled at Dr. Pelchat. Janine smiled and gave her a warm hug.

Dr. Pelchat looked over at Rocky and said, "Are you impressed? Does she have a better story?"

Rocky didn't look at Dr. Pelchat. He kept his eyes down, looking at his hands as he rubbed them together.

Geoffrey cleared his throat and leaned forward. He saw that Rocky was not going to respond, so he said, "Hey Rocky, I know that it seems like we're busting your chops here. The thing is that we don't encourage illegal drug use. You can't come in here and use drugs or offer them to other people. If you are caught doing either of those things, you will be sent to jail. We don't want that. We want you here so that you can actually get some help."

Rocky sat still, looking at Geoffrey as he spoke. When Geoffrey finished, Rocky's hard expression had slightly disappeared. He seemed humbled. It was probably because Geoffrey was being nice about it.

After that episode, Dr. Pelchat turned his attention to me. When he looked at me, I felt my insides squirm uncomfortably. He had this look. It was a different look than earlier. It was more stern and intimidating. I didn't like it.

"You're Kristen," he said. He must have been going through a Cadence syndrome. He seemed to like messing with the new people. "What drugs do you take?"

I looked at him, confused. "I'm sorry, I don't do drugs," I said.

"Sure you do," he said with a weird smile. "Every patient in here does drugs."

"I don't know what you-"

He cut me off from talking. "What drugs, as in medications, do you take, Kristen?" he clarified.

"Risperdol."

"Oh, okay," he said. "Impressive."

Rocky rolled his eyes.

"Very impressive," Dr. Pelchat continued. "Is it for schizophrenia?"

"*No!*" I almost shouted, but said with an angry tone.

"Why did you say it like that?" Cadence asked me. "You're not better than me!"

"Calm down, Cadence," Geoffrey said.

"Okay, so what about that?" Dr. Pelchat pressed on. "Why are you on Risperdol?"

I looked around the room. Everyone was staring at me. I guess it was Dr. Pelchat's turn to gang up on me now.

"I didn't mean anything by saying-"

"Risperdol is used to treat paranoia. It can also help with its symptoms, such as racing thoughts, delusions, and other symptoms depending on the dosage," Dr. Pelchat said. "If you think that you're just using Risperdol to get a good night's sleep, then that's far off. Moreover, if your doctor is letting you believe that that's all you need it for, then he's not giving you the right information. Kristen, I'm not that kind of doctor. I am going to give you the whole truth of it all."

He's right, I thought. He's not that kind of doctor. He's a jerk.

"Before being put on medicine - an anti-psychotic, like Risperdol - symptoms of schizophrenia may be obviously present in someone," he concluded. "I'm not telling you that you are schizophrenic, Kristen. I'm not your doctor, and we haven't spent enough counseling sessions together for me to know that about you. I can't diagnose you. My point to you and everyone in here is that it is important that you know and understand your drugs. You need to know what your doctors are giving you. I know that there's a nurse behind that counter with a big medication dictionary, and she'll let you read it, but that's not enough. You have to become educated.

"If you want real answers, you need to ask real questions. Talk to your doctors about what they are shoving down your throat, and why you have to take it. Don't be afraid. Because I'll tell you this, if you mess around and don't ask questions, you can get on the wrong medicine and can end up with some long–term, damaging effects. The wrong medicine can do the wrong job. For many people it only makes life worse. Most of the people that you hear about are in long–term, psychiatric facilities. These are places where they lock them up and sometimes throw away the key. Some of them are there because people have given up on them.

"A few of these people are there because their brains are so fried from drugs. Not just the illegal drugs, but drugs prescribed by their doctors, right along with countless numbers of misdiagnoses. These people sit in these hospitals with no chance at a real life. They are there until the day that they die. Most of them are already dead.

So, you think that most of you want to die now, use illegal drugs, and abuse your current medications that your doctors give you. Just mess up one time and see what happens. There are worse things than death, and there are worse things than living with the problems that you have now. One of those things is being alive while you are already dead, just like those people."

CHAPTER 17

Visiting hours were after lunch on Saturdays. Janine's father and little brother came to visit her, as she had said they would. Daniel's mother and grandmother came to visit him. Cadence had an older sister visit her. She brought with her new clothes for Cadence. Chris' mother and his big brother came to visit him.

No one came to visit Rocky, because his doctor had not approved visitors for him yet. Rocky went to his room, angry and wiping at his tears, when everyone's visitors arrived. I sat at a table in the main room with Tai. Tai didn't have any visitors, either, and she didn't seem too surprised.

She told me, "Why should I expect him to come visit me on his only day off of work? It's the only day that he has to spend time with *her*."

Someone called out to me. I turned around in my seat, and I saw a beautiful woman standing by the counselor's desk, leaning over and looking back at me. My insides felt like my skin, and my bones wouldn't hold. Tears came out of my eyes before my arms were around Lexus. My mother grabbed me and hugged me before I was out of Lexus' arms. I tried to wipe the tears away before we all pulled apart.

"Hi," Lexus said with a smile. "It's good to see you."

She probably didn't know what to say in a situation like this. Yes, she was visiting a friend in a hospital, but under the circumstances, "I hope you get well soon" wasn't quite fitting for the occasion. A nice, "Hi, it's good to see you" did just fine.

"It's good to see you too, Lexus," I said.

My mother looked at me and grabbed my arm, nearly knocking Lexus out of her way. She gave my arm a pinch and smiled so much that it seemed fake. It scared me a little because I had never seen her try so hard to seem pleasant.

"Where do we sit?" she asked me.

I led them over to the sitting area in the main room. It seemed like, when Lexus entered the room, it lit up. Everyone was staring at her. She was so beautiful. Chris offered his chair to Lexus, even though there were plenty of empty ones around. She said, "No, thank you," and we settled for the table in the far corner of the room, where Tai and I had been sitting together.

Tai rose up out of her chair as we approached the table. She looked at Lexus strangely and said, "Who's this?"

"This is my mother and my best friend," I told her.

Still looking at Lexus, Tai raised her eyebrows. Her expression made her look like she was shocked by what I had said. She quickly readjusted this expression, and smiled slightly, curling her lip up on one side.

"Nice to meet you," Tai said to Lexus. Then she turned away from us and walked to the Girls' Unit.

Lexus frowned and said, "I can't stay too long. I have to help my mom and dad out with party planning. I just wanted to come see you today."

"I'm glad you came," I told her.

"My mom and dad say hello, and they said that they will try to come visit you soon."

"How's your man doing?" my Mom asked.

I silently looked down at my hands that were resting in my lap to avoid eye contact with Lexus.

She smiled and, with a small giggle, she said, "He is fine."

My mother flashed that fake smile again and said, "That's wonderful." Then she turned her attention to me. "How are they treating you in here? Is it prison, like you thought it was?"

"No," I said. "It's okay."

"Do you see a doctor?" Lexus asked.

"Yes, I see Dr. Cuvo every day," I told her.

"Oh, yes, it's Dr. Cuvo. How is he?" Mom asked.

"I guess he's okay. He seems fine when I see him," I said.

I was waiting for more questions when I noticed Chris leaning over his table, staring at Lexus. He blushed when she turned to him and said hello. He waved to her and looked away. Lexus turned back to us, and rolled her eyes, annoyed.

I could tell the change from Chris to Jake by the sudden way he went from being coy to being assertive, and making vulgar gestures at her. Lexus didn't understand the transition, and she almost got up out of her seat, but his older brother explained to her Chris' condition. Chris sat, silently confused, because he couldn't recall what had happened. His brother didn't want to tell him, but Chris apologized anyway. Chris and his brother went to the other side of the room so that Lexus wouldn't feel too uncomfortable.

The damage was done already.

Lexus looked at me and said, "Is it always like this in here?"

"Well, Lexus," I responded, "This is a mental hospital."

"Yes, it is," she said in a snobbish tone.

My mother kept her gaze on me. I could tell that she was uncomfortable too, but she was trying to stay poised. She was probably waiting for Lexus to leave so that she could get whatever she needed to say to me off her chest.

Lexus' cell phone rang, and she reached into her purse. She answered, "This is Lexus. Hey, you! Of course, I won't be late. I was just finishing up at the hospital."

She turned to me and smiled. Then she excused herself and walked away from the table to the other side of the room to have more privacy.

Feeling alone, I turned to my mother. I wondered whom Lexus was speaking with. Almost sure of whom it was, wanting to be sure of whom it was, and worried about being alone with Mom after Lexus left me, I felt completely empty and overwhelmed at the same time. I hated when I felt that way.

"Nicholas and Alison both miss you," Mom said.

"I miss them," I said as I nervously pulled at my sleeves.

The silence came back. We stared at each other when the other person was not looking. I thought that we'd go on like that until Lexus came back, but I was wrong. It wasn't too long before Mom unleashed her true emotions.

"Just tell me. Why the hell did you do it?" She was stern and mean, but kept her voice low so that no one else could hear.

I shuddered when she spoke.

"What are you trying to do to me?" She blinked a lot when she got angry. "Are you mad at me about something? Is this some cry for attention? Jesus! You are almost eighteen years old, Kristen. You are almost an adult. This is not the way adults behave. Children do stupid things for attention."

I felt so alone and stupid. I wanted to say, *No, Mom, it was not a cry for help or attention. I want to die. Just let me die.* I couldn't say anything. I stayed silent, and I listened to her talk. I tried not to cry, but I couldn't help it. Mom just wouldn't understand.

"Talk to me!" She caught herself before she got too loud.

I opened my mouth, but only a cry came out. I covered my face with both of my hands when I saw Geoffrey look over from the desk.

Mom sighed heavily. "I can't do this," she said as she threw her hands up into the air. "I don't understand. Help me understand. What is your problem? I believe that you knew what you were doing. How did you think this would affect us? What about Nick and Alison? Do you think they need a sister who they learn what *not* to do from? Do you think they know how to feel when their big sister, who they are told to look up to, goes and does something completely selfish and stupid like what you did? Huh? Answer that for me, Kristen."

The tears did not stop running down my face. I never wanted to hurt my Nickyroo or Alison. They both had been through enough already, especially Nick. I couldn't breathe because I was trying not to cry aloud. I had to hold my breath. It was almost as if my mother and I were the only ones here. No one seemed to hear her scolding me, not even the ever-watchful Geoffrey.

Mom wasn't loud or yelling, but she was piercing me with her words. She made my insides rattle. I felt my chest burning and my cramps tightening. My heart was cracking from the core. I was a huge mess.

If only I had been able to cut deeper, I thought to myself.

Lexus returned to the table with a big smile on her face. "My parents say hello to both of you," she said. "They hope you feel better soon, Kristen. John says hello too."

I looked up as soon as she said his name. The metal ball in my chest wanted to turn. I smacked myself on the chest, not thinking.

"Kristen," my mother said. "Don't hit yourself."

I wiped my eyes. "Sorry."

Lexus sat down next to me and looked deep into my eyes. "Have you been crying?" she asked me.

I looked at my mother, and she shook her head at me. I forced a smile to Lexus. "I am just so happy to see you!" I told her. "I got a little teary-eyed."

"I'm so happy to see you," she said as she wrapped her arms around me.

"Ouch." My arm was between us. She squeezed me, and it hurt my wrist.

Lexus looked down. "Oh, no, I am so sorry. Are you okay?" She looked at the bandages and touched them.

I snatched my arms away and hid them in my lap. "I'm fine. It's okay, Lexus."

"Okay," she said in her sincere voice. "I have to go now. I told my mom that I would be back in thirty minutes. I will try to come visit you again next week. Get better soon, Kristen. See you later."

She gave me one last hug and then she said goodbye to Mom. Geoffrey walked her out. When Lexus was gone, I couldn't look at Mom.

"Hopefully you will be out of here in no more than two weeks," she said. "Your boss knows that you are in the hospital. She called because you hadn't shown up for work. I told her that you are in the hospital, and she said that she hopes you get better. Thank goodness, you still have a job. I brought you some deodorant, some clothes, and," she paused and reached into her purse and pulled out two small folded pieces of paper, "Nicholas and Alison wrote you letters."

She placed the two folded sheets of paper on the table, and I quickly grabbed them.

"I'll be back on Monday," she told me. "Do you need me to bring you anything else when I come?"

I shook my head, but then I thought about it. "Will you bring me a blanket?" I made myself ask her.

"Okay," she said. "And I'll bring your school work so that you can finish getting that done. I want you to graduate from that home schooling program." She gathered up her belongings and began to leave.

Before she got completely out of her chair, I stopped her by touching her arm. "I'm sorry I messed up," I said.

She looked at me with the most serious eyes. She said, "Whatever it is that you are going through, I can honestly say I do not understand. I guess that's why I am so upset. Just get better and get out of here. We need you at home."

I stood up and we hugged.

"I will bring you a hair brush, too," she said as we pulled away.

We said goodbye, and she walked to the exit, waved to me, and then disappeared with Geoffrey. It was like I wasn't even there. Mr. Sharp screamed loudly to get out, but there was nowhere for me to go and let him out. The earth seemed to be shaking in my head. I felt exhausted, alone, angry, sad, confused, and empty-everything but dead.

CHAPTER 18

When Dr. Cuvo came for me, I was alone in my bedroom with my head buried in my pillow. I heard Dr. Cuvo calling out my name from the hallway. I was able to dry my tears and pull my hair back into a ponytail before he entered my room. He knocked and then entered. When he came in, I pretended I was asleep in case my eyes were red from crying. He would think that they were red because I was tired.

I felt a tender hand brush my back. His touch made me open my eyes suddenly.

"Did I scare you, Kristen?" he asked in a gentle voice.

I wiped my eyes and sat up, shaking my head.

"Sorry to wake you up," he said as he pulled a chair over beside my bed. "It's time for your session."

"Are we going to your office?" I asked him.

Dr. Cuvo looked around, and then he looked back at me. His eyes sparkled. He said with a smile, "This can be my office for now."

Irritated, I tried to smile back at him because I knew he was trying to be funny.

"It's good to see you. You look good today." He smiled at me kindly.

I tried not to blush. I knew he was thinking about our last session and my huge embarrassment. Still embarrassed, I thanked him for the compliment.

"So, you had some visitors today. Was it nice to see your family?"

"Yes." I wasn't feeling chatty.

Dr. Cuvo crossed his legs in the chair and rested my chart on his knee. "Was it your Mom and a cousin of yours?"

"Mom and my—Lexus," I said.

"Who is Lexus?" he asked.

"She's a friend of our family."

"A visit from a friend is always good," Dr. Cuvo said with a smile.

"I thought that the order was only for my Mom to come here and visit me."

"I wrote an order for adult visitors. Meaning you can only have visitors who are over the age of eighteen. Which, in most cases, are only parental visits, but in your case, your Mom brought your friend. Besides, wasn't it nice to see your friend?"

I hesitated and stuttered out, "Yes."

The look on his face told me that he wasn't buying it.

"Are you sure about that?" he asked.

I was tired. I didn't feel like talking. I felt like I was being badgered.

"What do you know?" I snapped at him.

Being Dr. Cuvo, he didn't get angry with me for yelling at him.

He leaned forward and said, "I don't know anything unless you talk to me, Kristen."

I hated when he did that. I was already in a bad mood when he'd come in. Now, he wouldn't leave me alone. I couldn't hold the tears back any longer. Dr. Cuvo got up out of his chair and sat my chart down on the seat. He sat down next to me on my bed and placed his hands on my shoulders to make me face him. I buried my face in my hands.

"Kristen, what's going on? Please talk to me," he said. "Let me help you."

I closed my eyes and tried to breathe. My chest was pounding in pain, and breathing became heavy.

"Please calm down, Kristen. Breathe slowly," Dr. Cuvo said as he squeezed my shoulders.

My insides felt like they were trying to pour out of my eyes. My heart was racing as fast as my mind. My mind filled with thoughts of what had brought me here, the pills, when I'd picked up that knife, and what had made me cut deeper. I had seen Mr. Sharp so clear that night. I knew why I had done it, and I knew what had made me cut deeper. I wanted to tell him. I wanted to tell him so badly. That was the hardest thing I that I had to do, and I tried.

I opened my mouth and cried, "She shut it off! She didn't pick it up! I thought that I could—but no! No! And Mr. Sharp—she didn't do it! I…" My words were just mumbles and rants. I saw Dr. Cuvo looking into my eyes helplessly, trying to understand what I was trying to say.

"He said, 'You're a loser! Loser! Cut *deeper*!' I cut *deep*!"

"Kristen," said Dr. Cuvo. "Who's calling you a loser?"

"Sharp! Sharp!" I screamed while crying, wishing he could understand.

"Yes, I know. Who called you a loser, and told you to cut deep?" He sighed heavily as he squeezed my shoulders.

He didn't understand what I was trying to say. I needed him to understand, so I kept trying through the tears.

"It was Sh...Sh...Sharp," I cried as I struggled to breathe.

Dr. Cuvo gave up and he pressed his finger to my lips to hush me. "Please, Kristen, just try to breathe." He made me look into his eyes.

I felt myself get light-headed as I panted and sobbed. I closed my eyes so that the room would stop spinning.

"If you don't calm down and breathe more slowly, you are going to hyperventilate. Please, Kristen," he begged.

I opened my eyes, and his eyes caught mine. His eyes were very gentle. I tried to look away from him.

"No!" I cried.

The pain of the metal ball beginning to turn in my chest made it harder for me to breathe. The pain grew sharper with each pant. "I'm going to die," I admitted to Dr. Cuvo. My eyes rolled back and I shut them.

Dr. Cuvo grabbed my hands. My head jerked back. He caught my head in his left hand and he placed his right hand on my cheek. He turned my face towards his. I tried to turn away, but he wouldn't let me.

"Open your eyes, Kristen," he said in a gentle voice.

I was afraid to open my eyes, because I still felt his warm hand caressing my face. I felt his breath on my skin.

I slowly opened my eyes, confused. I wanted him to let me go. When my eyes were open, I saw his deep, dark eyes still staring at me.

"Kristen," he said softly. "Breathe."

My breathing and the spinning, metal ball in my chest began to slow down.

"No," he said. "You're not going to die."

"But it hurts," I cried softly.

He said, "I know. That's the only way we can get through the pain. It's going to hurt before it gets better. You have to get it out of you."

I sighed.

"Come here," he said as he suddenly pulled me closer towards him. His hand went from my cheek to my shoulder down to my back. Then his arms wrapped around me, and he squeezed me gently. I realized he was hugging me. "It is okay, Kristen. Put your arms around me."

Confused, and suddenly feeling awkward, I did as he told me to. When my arms were wrapped around him, he pulled me even closer, making our torsos touch. Dr. Cuvo stroked my back with his hands. This quickly began to calm me, but when I realized I was breathing normally again, I began to feel awkward.

Scared, I called out to him softly, "Dr. Cuvo?"

"Kristen," he moaned in a soft and deep voice. "It's okay."

"Dr. Cuvo, I am sorry to interrupt, but I was looking for you because--" the familiar voice burst through the door.

Suddenly there was complete silence. Dr. Cuvo and I were not wrapped in each other's arms any longer. Dr. Cuvo was now standing with his back turned to Geoffrey and me. He stood up and walked over to the window. He shuffled around with his clothes and wiped his face.

"What? What is it?" Dr. Cuvo asked Geoffrey without looking at him.

Geoffrey cocked his head and looked at Dr. Cuvo's backside, then looked at me, and then back at Dr. Cuvo. He stared at Dr. Cuvo suspiciously and said, "I'm sorry I didn't knock. Karen told me that you were going to bring Kristen to your office for her session. I went to your office, and you weren't there, so I came here to see if by chance we'd catch up with each other." Geoffrey paused and looked at me. "Uh—I just wanted to let you know that Kristen needs to come to the gym when she's finished. That's where everyone is. Sorry to disturb you."

"Thank you, Geoffrey," Dr. Cuvo said. "We were just finishing up. I'll bring her."

Geoffrey nodded. He turned away, but he spun back around and looked at me. "Are you okay, Kristen?"

I nodded and looked away from him.

He looked over at Dr. Cuvo, who still seemed to be pretending to look out of the window. "Okay," Geoffrey said. He exited the room.

Dr. Cuvo turned around and looked at me. He hurried over to the door, opened it, and stuck his head out. He came back inside and closed the door. He picked up my chart and sat down in the chair facing me. He began writing in my chart.

I sat still, not knowing what to do. I was confused, and I felt awkward. I looked down at my hands and tried to concentrate on picking at my nails.

"Kristen," Dr. Cuvo called out to me.

I looked up at him.

"I'm going to increase your Risperdol to two milligrams. You'll start that dosage tonight. I am going to keep a close watch with this increase. I want to eventually get you up to three milligrams to stabilize your mood swings."

He wrote a few more things in my chart, and then he closed it, stood up, and stretched his hand out. It was the end of the session, and it was time for the end-of-session handshake.

I shook his hand. With my hand in his, he tightened his grip and helped me get up and off the bed by giving me a yank.

He smiled and said, "Come on. I'll take you to the gym."

"I thought I had to be Level Three to go to the gym," I said as we left the room.

"If the whole unit is in the gym, those who are not Level Three may go to the gym, too."

"When can I go to Level Three?" I asked.

"We'll see. I need to see more improvement in your session with me and in your group therapy. Do you see this chart? Your counselors and the other doctors who run the groups write notes on your behavior and your participation after every group."

Dr. Cuvo stuck his key in the door that led us out of the Adolescent Unit. He opened the door for me and let me out first. He followed behind.

"They write in all of our charts?" I asked.

"Yes, everyone's charts," he assured me.

"That's a lot of work," I said.

"And it takes a lot of time," he admitted to me.

"Why don't you moderate any groups?" I asked.

"This is the gym," he said as we came to a stop at a large, wooden door with a sign that read GYM. "Goodbye, Kristen."

"Bye, Dr. Cuvo," I said.

He started to walk away, but he stopped and came back over to me. He kept walking closer to me, and I backed up and hit the wall. He shocked me with how close he was standing to me. He put his hand on my shoulder and squeezed it hard, practically pinning me to the wall. He looked around and then turned his attention to me. He leaned his face close to mine. "Whatever we do and whatever we say in our sessions together are to be kept confidential, Kristen. Remember that. Okay?"

He was so close to my face that looking up at him almost made me cross-eyed. "Okay," I said nervously.

"Okay," he said. He backed off, looking around while straightening his tie. "I'll see you later." He walked away, leaving me alone in the hallway.

I leaned against the wall, trying to make sense of what had just happened. I closed my eyes and tried to get my thoughts together before I went inside. I didn't really want to go, but I had to.

Suddenly there was a hard thud on the doors to the gym. It scared me. I stepped forward, away from the wall. There was another hard thud. I opened the door to the gymnasium, and a huge, red ball flew towards me. I was like a deer in headlights--stunned. I couldn't move. The ball hit me straight in the face. I fell to the floor, and hit the back of my head. I faintly heard Ms. Mosley yelling. I saw Janine, Tai, and Ms. Mosley looking down at me before I blacked out.

CHAPTER 19

When John and I had been in high school together, I'd been amazed at how tall he had grown to be. He'd had to have been at least six feet tall by the time he was Junior. When I had first met him at Mom and Jack's wedding, he had been only eight years old, and we'd been about the same height.

The night when I'd started to notice John, he and his family had come over to my family's home for dinner. Jack's brother, Jonathan Sr., had been there, along with his wife, Mariah, John Jr., and James, who was John's little brother, and about the same age as the twins. Lexus had been there, too, spending the night over at my house.

After dinner, our parents had gone out on the back porch to drink beer and talk about adult stuff. The twins and James Jr. had gone to the den to watch cartoons. Lexus, John, and I stayed in the dining room. No one except John seemed to have room for dessert. He'd eaten the most out of all of us, helping himself to two slices of pecan pie and three scoops of chocolate ice cream. As Lexus and I watched him, I wondered what he would think if he knew that I had made that pie that he seemed to be enjoying very much. I stayed quiet, even though I longed to tell him. Lexus laughed at him while he stuffed his face with pie and ice cream.

"What's so funny?" John asked Lexus.

"Nothing," she said. "Is it good?"

"Why don't you have some and see for yourself," he teased her.

I blushed. I was flattered that John was enjoying my pie.

"Stop it," I whispered to Lexus.

She nudged me playfully.

Lexus turned to John and said, "So, what school are you going to after graduation?"

"I'm going to State," he told Lexus with a convincingly handsome smile. "Where are you going?" he asked her as he took another bite of pie.

"After my graduation, I'm going to State, too," Lexus said.

"I guess it's a good thing I am only a sophomore. I don't have to think that far ahead yet," I forced out. I didn't want to feel left out. After all, I had made the pie.

As they laughed, I noticed Lexus trying to get cute like she always did with boys. She pushed her long hair out of her face and leaned her chin on the palm of her left hand as she tilted her face towards John. His eyes followed her movement.

"Kristen's going to the school where all of the best writers go. Aren't you Kristen?" She turned her face to me, smiling.

"You write?" John asked me with surprise.

I took a bite of my pie and nodded nervously as his eyes ripped through me.

"I only write a little," I said.

"Kristen, stop," Lexus said as she shoved me playfully. "She has so many notebooks of poems waiting to be published."

I rolled my eyes at her.

John asked, "Do you write stories too?"

"No. I only write poetry."

"Have you ever tried to write a story?"

John seemed more interested in me than in his dessert. I felt a pain in my chest. This nervous and strange pain made me confused. I couldn't comprehend why he asked me questions and why he was interested in me. Lexus watched us as we talked. She kept pushing her hair out of her face and smiling at John.

"Kristen did get two of her poems published," Lexus tattled.

"It was only the school paper. I won a contest. It was one of those stupid contests where they make you write a poem using fifteen lines or less on a stupid topic, like the weather. It was nothing," I said.

John had nodded at me. He'd finished his pie and ice cream in one last bite. Then he'd looked at me.

John said, "I write, too."

John smiled at me with a beautiful, convincing smile. His eyes sparkled. Looking at him had made me tingle. His eyes were gentle, and when he smiled, it made him even more attractive. As I gazed at him, I began to feel my heart beat faster. It was the first time I could feel that heavy drumming beat inside of me. It hurt, but it felt nice. That was the moment when I realized that I was in love with John.

CHAPTER 20

I remembered that I had left the letters that Nick and Alison had written me in the bedroom. Unfortunately, when I woke up, the nurse saw me on the main unit. She said that I had a slight concussion. I had to stay awake and hold an ice pack on my head to keep the swelling down.

Ms. Mosley did not let me leave the main unit. She said that she wanted me to stay by the counselor's desk so that she could keep an eye on me. I felt the bump on my head swell. I glared at that little runt who had kicked the ball at me. He laughed as he passed me by and walked onto the Boys' Unit with his tongue sticking out. I wanted to get up and slam his head into something so he could know how it felt. But I remained still and looked over at Ms. Mosley. She sat behind the counselor's desk, and she caught me looking at her. She furrowed her eyebrows at me and then got back to reading a book.

Bored, I looked around the room. Daniel was sitting alone at a table, drawing on a sketchpad. I went over and joined him. He looked up from his drawing and caught me looking at him. I looked away.

"Are you okay?" I heard him say.

I turned back toward him. He wasn't looking at me. He was concentrating on his drawing.

"I guess," I responded. I liked that he seemed to be concerned about me.

He said, "I missed all of the excitement earlier. I always do."

"Where were you?" I asked.

He erased an error he'd caught in his drawing. When he was finished erasing, he blew away the eraser debris.

"I was in my session with Dr. Finch," he replied.

I remembered Janine saying that Daniel might get to go home soon.

"Did your family session go well?" I asked.

Daniel's eyes suddenly shot up at me. He seemed upset that I had asked. Daniel looked at me as if I had dared to cross a line that I had no business crossing. Feeling stupid, I lowered my face and stared at my fingers.

"It *went*," he finally replied.

I looked back up at him. I hadn't expected him to respond.

"Are you going home?" I asked him.

He stopped drawing and threw his pencil down on the table, frustrated. He looked down at his shaking hands.

"I need a cigarette!" he shouted angrily.

"Settle down," Geoffrey said from behind the counselor's desk.

"I'm sick of this place!" Daniel yelled back.

"That's enough, Daniel," Ms. Mosley warned him.

I felt bad because I had asked him if he was going home, and that question had seemed to trigger his anger. He apparently was not going to be able to go home. I'd only made him feel worse. I didn't want to say anything else that would make him upset. If I had just kept to myself, he probably would have been fine.

I got up to leave the table so that I wouldn't cause any more trouble for him. His eyes followed me as I started to leave. He picked up his pencil and started drawing again.

"Why are you leaving?" he asked.

"I thought I'd let you finish your drawing in peace," I answered.

He frowned at the drawing. Apparently unsatisfied with it, he crumpled the sheet of paper into a ball and threw it down on the table. I reached out for the paper ball, but he quickly snatched it up and shook his head at me.

"No, it's stupid," he said, not smiling. "I don't want you to see it."

I pulled my hand back, flattered. He didn't want me to see it because he wanted me to like his drawing if I saw it. I smiled, and he noticed.

"I can't believe it. There's a smile."

"What?"

"You're smiling."

"So," I said.

"So? You're always walking around here with this frown on your face. Or you're in a daze, somewhere in your own world," he observed.

I felt myself blush. "Wow," I said, "I didn't think anyone was paying that much attention to me in here."

"I wasn't," he said. "But if I was, I would say that the smile looks much better than those frowns."

"Well, look at where I am," I said, referring to Bent Creek.

He smiled too and leaned back in the chair. He started tossing the balled-up sheet of paper into the air and catching it. "So, what's your talent?" he asked.

"My talent?"

"Yeah, your talent. What's the special thing that you do?"

"I don't have any talents," I lied.

"Everyone has something exceptional that they do," he pressed on.

"You draw."

"I don't really draw. I mean, I'm *not* Picasso. I guess I just sketch a little."

I nodded at him. "Okay, since you only sketch, I guess I just jot stuff every now and then."

"Jot stuff?"

"Yes. I mean, I haven't written anything in a long time. Not since— anyways, that was my talent."

Daniel looked at me strangely. He opened his mouth to say something, but I looked away from him. When I turned back around, he was looking down at his hands. There was the silence that I hated. Just when I thought that he might like me. He probably had grown bored with me.

"Where's Janine?" he finally asked.

I looked around. "I don't know where she is."

He shrugged it off. "Rocky is my roommate," he said in an awkward voice.

Then, I looked at him strangely and asked, "Why did you say it like that? What's wrong?"

"He's weird," Daniel said. "He's usually quiet, but he has these moments. He talks to himself and randomly starts biting his arms. He just does some off-the-wall stuff. Last night, when I was trying to get to sleep, he was making creepy, choking noises. I looked up to see if he was okay. When I looked over at him, he stopped making noises. He was just staring at me. It was really disturbing."

"Did you tell on him? Maybe you can get a new roommate."

"Janine!" Daniel suddenly stood up to greet her.

Janine had come in from the Girls' Unit. She didn't look happy.

"Hi," Janine said to Daniel.

"Sit down, Janine," I invited her.

She ignored me and looked at Daniel. "Have you seen Dr. Cuvo anywhere?"

Daniel shrugged. "No," he said. "I haven't seen your doctor."

"I didn't see him yet," Janine whined.

"Are you serious? It's almost the end of the day," I said.

"Yeah, I know," she responded, "but he's seen *you*." She seemed mad at me.

I looked at her, not knowing what to say. She rolled her eyes at me.

She said, "I'm going to go talk to someone."

Janine stormed to the counselor's desk, and she loudly made clear that she hadn't seen Dr. Cuvo yet. Geoffrey told her that Dr. Pelchat would see her before the day was over.

Janine questioned him, "Why? Is Dr. Cuvo not coming to see me?" "Please go sit down and wait for Dr. Pelchat," Geoffrey pleaded with her.

Janine stared at Geoffrey. Geoffrey looked up at her from his chair. Janine asked, "Is something wrong with Dr. Cuvo?"

Ms. Mosley got up from her chair and walked over next to Geoffrey. She put her hand on Geoffrey's shoulder. He stayed quiet.

I got up from where I was sitting and went over to the desk. I was concerned and wanted to know, too.

"Is Dr. Cuvo okay?" I asked.

Geoffrey frowned at me. "Janine and Kristen, please sit down."

Ms. Mosley kept a calm demeanor, but strongly urged us to step away from the counselor's desk. She said, "If you both don't do as you are asked, you will go to your room."

Janine angrily stomped off to the Girls' Unit. I started to follow her, but Ms. Mosley called out to me. I had forgotten about my head injury. She wanted me to stay in the main room so that she could monitor my concussion.

I looked over at the table where Daniel and I had been sitting. Daniel had already disappeared to the Boys' Unit. Looking at the table, I noticed something. Just underneath it, on the floor, was a crumpled-up sheet of paper. I rushed over to the table and grabbed the paper. I smiled at my prize, and then looked around to make sure Daniel wasn't coming back for it.

Ms. Mosley whispered something to Geoffrey that made him squirm uncomfortably in his chair. When she said all that she needed to say, he nodded at her and picked up the telephone and started dialing a number. Ms. Mosley said goodbye to Geoffrey, and she left the unit. Without looking back, I ran to my room.

CHAPTER 21

Dear Kristen,

I miss you so much. Mom said that you would be home soon. I hope you feel better. What made you sick and why can't me and Nicholas come see you? Are the doctors being mean to you? Did they stick you with a needle? I hate needles. Hurry up and get better so that you can come back home.

Love,

Alison

She signed the letter with a heart next to her name. I was glad to know that Alison didn't know why I was in the hospital. I knew my mother wouldn't tell her. I thought that Nick might, but my mother probably told him not to tell her what happened.

I heard it in my mind so clearly: Mom may have said to Alison, "Don't worry. Your sister will be home. She's just sick. That's why she had to go to the hospital." To her friends (John's parents and Lexus' parents), she probably said, "You know Kristen, such a drama queen. She is calling out for attention, and it's a good thing she *is* in the hospital. Maybe it will do her some good to be locked up."

Then, of course, they would all smile, shrug it off, comfort Mom, and feel sorry for her having to deal with a "sick" child in the hospital. I dreaded the day I had to get out of the hospital. I hadn't really thought that far ahead. Who knew how long it was going to take to get better in Bent Creek? I didn't know. Dr. Cuvo didn't know. I didn't even know if Dr. Cuvo was okay. He was acting strange, and it made me feel strange.

I looked over at Janine. She was lying on her bed, reading a magazine. She seemed to be deep into what she was reading. She was a lot calmer than she'd been in the main area. I wanted to ask her what she thought may have happened to Dr. Cuvo, but I didn't want to get her upset again. At the counselor's desk, she'd seemed like she suspected something terrible. The fear and anger that had been in her voice made me wonder.

"What?" Janine asked, noticing that I was staring at her.

She smoothed out her magazine so it lay flat on the bed in front of her. As soon as she smoothed the magazine's pages out, I saw what she was interested in. She wasn't reading an article. Posing in the magazine were four super-models barely covered up in two-piece bikinis. Their faces were glamorously painted in make-up. They had perfectly tanned skin. Their bodies were perfectly thin. The bikinis were bright, provocative, and expensive. They looked like live-action Barbie dolls.

I said, "Janine, summer is almost over. Are you thinking about getting one of those swimsuits?"

Janine scoffed.

"If I could fit in one," she said.

"I'm sure they come in different sizes," I told her.

She raised her eyes slightly and said, "I don't want one unless I can look like that in it. If I looked like that, I would be perfect."

She looked almost crazed. Her eyes were sharp as she stared at the pictures. I didn't know whether I should to tell someone that she had that magazine. It couldn't be helping her. She turned the page, and there was a picture of a handsome, teen pop singer. He was very famous for his sensational dance moves and chart-topping albums. I remembered Alison screaming over the boy when she'd seen him on television accepting a Grammy Award. Janine's attention seemed to be focused on the cute and popular star instead of the anorexic quadruplets on the previous page. I let it go, and went back to minding my own business.

I looked beside me and saw Daniel's crumpled-up artwork. I smiled as I grabbed it, remembering our conversation. I opened the paper, and inside was a drawing of a mysterious girl. She didn't appear to be smiling. Her hair was long, and it went down her shoulders. She had a swoop bang that covered one eye. She was beautiful. She looked like she didn't smile much. She probably didn't need to. Her perfectly sculpted, heart-shaped lips made her expressions without moving. I noticed that she actually was smiling, even though her lips weren't curled up enough at the corners to show it. Her eyes gave a hint that she may have been in love.

A sick feeling came over me. It wasn't nausea. It was the sickness that came with love. When you loved someone and they didn't know that you loved them, it was sickening. Who was this girl? Whom did she love? Where was she? Maybe she was gone because she'd loved him. She'd realized that it wasn't what she thought it would be. Maybe he'd told her that he loved her, and maybe he'd let her down. I leaned back on my pillow.

Dear Kristen,

Are you okay? Why did you do that? You scared me so bad. How could you do something like that? I am mad at you. Didn't we say that we would always be there for each other? Mom said that we would start over and get better as a family. Why did you mess everything up? Mom is mad. She closed your door and said that no one can go in there. I don't want you to die. There is hope for you.

Love,

Nick

I folded his letter in two, and closed myself up inside. The pain was deep. I couldn't do anything locked in Bent Creek. I couldn't do anything to make him understand. I didn't want him to understand. Nick was the one who'd gotten the support after Jack had been sent to prison. Everyone had said that Nick was the one who'd needed treatment because he'd been the one hurt. Alison and I hadn't been hurt. No, we hadn't been hurt at all. Everyone had listened to Nick because he'd been Jack's victim. He'd been small and helpless. He had been heard. Mom had made sure of it. Nick had received treatment. He'd gone through years of psychiatric help and support. And I had begun cutting myself. Mr. Sharp had become my only real friend. He'd showed me how to deal with the pain. I'd tried to kill myself, but I hadn't succeeded. *That* was what Nick couldn't understand.

I balled up his letter in anger. The feeling of sickness and death swelled back up inside of me. If my heart could just stop right now, if it could just go with the rotting feeling that I had inside, if it would just stop on my command, I would be free, I thought.

In anger, I tore the letter into pieces. I couldn't hold the rage inside of me in any longer. I bit into the shredded pieces of paper and chewed them. While chewing, I grabbed my pillow and repeatedly punched it as hard as I could.

I screamed, "I'm sorry! I'm sorry! I'm sorry!"

I screamed until my throat burned. Janine rushed over to my side and tried to grab my arm. I pushed her away, still screaming. She flew back and hit the wall. I wasn't aware of my own strength. I fell back on my bed and started biting the sheets, having swallowed the paper in my mouth.

Janine ran out of the room. I couldn't stop her. I was too busy trying to eat my bed sheets in a fit of rage. I tried to focus my mind, but I was too far gone. Mr. Sharp stared at me from across the room. Nodding his head and smiling, he told me to bleed. I bit hard into the sheet, and let it cut my lip. Blood pinched out. It wasn't satisfying enough, so I tried harder so that the blood would spill. My teeth ground into the sheets, and I heard myself grunting and snarling like an animal. This madness was wonderful, and it made Mr. Sharp excited.

"That's right," he said. "Do them all a favor. You're hopeless. That's why things are the way they are. It's because you are hopeless, Kristen. Hopeless."

I hadn't always been... hopeless...

Hope had risen out of my fingertips and onto the paper when I used to write. I'd loved writing poems. Dad used to be my biggest fan. He used to ask to read some of my poetry whenever I was writing and he'd knock on my bedroom door and just come in without an answer. He used to hover over me in curiosity. He used to be interested in me.

"Is my girl writing again?" he asked.

"Yes, Daddy, but it's not ready yet. You can't read it," I told him with a shy giggle.

He wouldn't let up. He kept pressing me until I gave in and read to him what I had written so far.

"Okay, fine. Are you ready?" I gave in.

"Yeah," he said with a smile. "I don't think I can wait any longer to hear what future award-winning poet, Kristen Elliott, has written."

"All right," I said. I looked into his eyes and my heart fluttered. "Happiness and Hope, by Kristen Elliott. There are no real words to describe what happens when I look into your eyes. Is it happiness? It makes hope rise. Hope that I always make you smile. Hope that your smile will never disappear. Convincing, charming, sweet, and always there for me. I hope that we will always be."

"Who was that for?" he asked.

"Dad," I said, feeling shy.

"Okay. It's beautiful," he said. He leaned in and kissed me. He walked over to the door. He winked with one last sweet smile, and he left.

There was no more hope. There were no more smiles.

I didn't think about what I was doing when I swung as hard as I could. I had to keep them away from me. The counselors were pulling on me. Three of them grabbed me off the bed and carried me from the bedroom. I continued to scream with blood dripping from my mouth. They carried me to a room and laid me down on a bed. I kicked and screamed harder when I saw that the nurse had a needle.

Geoffrey told her to stick me. He was probably angry that I had knocked his glasses off his face while I'd been having the tantrum. The nurse and another counselor locked me down in restraints. The nurse stuck the long needle in my neck and pushed all of the liquid inside that needle into my veins. It burned.

I screamed out to them hoarsely that I hated them and that I needed to die. My throat burned. I felt myself start to move in slow motion. My mouth slowed down. Screaming became hard to do, so I stopped.

Exhausted tears fell out of my eyes. I closed my eyes and tried to ignore the bright lights and the dizziness that came over me. My mind stopped racing. Thoughts slowed down. Warmness came over me.

I heard them talking over me. I couldn't move. I couldn't open my eyelids to see them. The lids felt too heavy.

"She will be okay. Give her a few hours," I heard the nurse say. "Are you all right, Geoffrey?"

The door shut.

"No," I tried to scream out. It was just a whisper.

I heard my heart pounding in my brain. It was loud, and it made my head hurt. I knew this was prison. I knew it. Where was Dr. Cuvo? He'd said that I could tell him if something terrible happened. Something terrible was happening. I tried one last time to yell out, but my mouth wouldn't open. My teeth weighed down my jaws. I felt a loss of control over my body. Every part of me was too heavy to move. Even my brain felt weighed down. Exhausted and without hope, I decided to give up. I took a deep breath and let go.

PART 2

The Mirror

By Kristen Elliott

The mirror

Made of shattered glass and full of veins

Disfiguring her maimed beautiful image.

Inside and out

A reflection bears the burden

Of who she is

What she has become

And what will forever be.

One side Her-self

The other side just

Her.

CHAPTER 22

When you are heavily sedated, it is almost like being awake, but you are so deep in sleep that you don't even realize it. When I slept, I often dreamed. As I laid in the BCR, I had very vivid dreams of the past that felt real.

John and I used to sit together after school and read our poetry to each other. I was just a freshman, and he was a junior. He played on the basketball team, swam for the swim team, made Honor Roll Society, and was in our high school's writing club. He was a celebrity in my eyes, and he had many admirers at our school. They were mostly girls. What kind of interest did he have in a loser like me? I wondered every time a pretty girl walked by and smiled, but he looked right through her and continued to talk to me and show me attention.

John's smile reminded me of my dad's. John's father was my dad's brother, after all. Did that make us cousins? Well, technically John had no blood relation to me. John's father and my dad weren't really close to each other, as most siblings were. Our families were acquainted, and we lived close by, no matter what. In spite of it all, I still could not force myself look at John as a relative. I liked him too much. I loved him less like a relative, and more like what I wanted him to be: a boyfriend.

My dreams carried me into a deep sleep filled with vivid images and heavy thoughts of sadness and nothing. Suppressed feelings arose in my dreams to haunt me, turning these dreams into the most awful, realistic nightmares. Mr. Sharp always found a way to work himself into my thoughts while I slept. His voice seemed louder in my dreams than it did when I was awake.

"How many times have you been kissed, Kristen?" he taunted me. "Come on, and tell me how many. Have you ever been kissed?"

I told Mr. Sharp, "He might kiss me. He might, if I look at him in the way those girls do when they want boys to kiss them. He'll know, and he'll want to." Mr. Sharp cut me deep with a knife, so that I wouldn't feel the pain of what I knew would never be.

"John will never do that," Mr. Sharp said as my blood dripped down my arms. "John won't kiss you because he does not love you that way. No one can ever love you like that."

I wanted to wake from this dream. I didn't want to be pulled back into the past. I didn't want to see John smiling as he looked at my writings and read them aloud. This entity pulled me in. I was fourteen years old again, sitting in the room where the writing club met after school. John and I were the only ones in the room. I wasn't in the writing club. I just wanted to let him read some of my writings, and I wanted to read some of his. I was sincerely interested in his writing as well as spending more time with him. It was nice to know that John was interested in my work. He was interested in something about me. That fact was hard to believe at first, but when he and I sat in the room together, just the two of us, and he smiled at me with genuine affection, I could not deny it. The feeling of being close to him was how I imagined being in love felt. I was nervous, but I was calm and excited all at the same time. This dream felt as real as when it had actually happened.

The day was warm, and the sun was out in a partly cloudy sky. I felt my skin tingling like it always did when John smiled at me. He looked beautiful as he parted his lips slightly, smiled, and started to pass the sheet of notebook paper back to me that contained a piece of my soul in the form of words. He held the paper out to me and softly said, "Kristen." It was just simply, "Kristen." The sound of my name from his lips and the way he said it made me blush.

"What do you think?" I asked nervously.

"I think that you should join our writing club," he admitted.

As I reached out to grab my paper from his hand, I shook my head and said, "No, thanks. That's okay."

His smile disappeared, and what looked like disappointment took its place. He snatched the paper back towards him.

"Oh, you're scared," he said.

"Scared of what? I'm not scared," I defended.

A grin appeared on his face.

He said, "Yes, you are. You're safe in this little world you've created for yourself. You write your poems and you keep them on a shelf. I'm the first person you've let actually read something because you're afraid of letting your work out for other people to see and criticize."

"*I'm* scared? What about you? You haven't put any writings of yours in my hands yet. I've already shared three of my poems with you, John."

He laughed, "You know what? You're right."

He reached into his notebook and, without looking at what he was selecting, ripped out a single sheet of paper. He slid it across the desk to me.

I cleared my throat and began to read aloud. The poem did not have a title, nor did it have many lines. However, the emotion that it made me feel almost crushed me. I felt everything in those few lines that he wrote.

I began, "Disappointment is like grinding your teeth ten times and then ten thousand times over."

John stopped me by calling out to me. I looked up from the paper, and saw that he was reaching his hand out to me.

"I gave you the wrong one," he said. "Don't read that one."

"Now who's scared?" I got up from the table and continued reading while pacing around the room.

"I swear that I try to make you proud. I try to make you agree. Why is it that everyone else gets it, but you just cannot see? You said, 'Fly that kite, son! Fly it, and you will see how high you can get it!' It was almost like that kite was my life, and if I didn't make it fly, you would be disappointed in me. Am I flying now? Is it enough? Or do you need more from me? Tell me how it should fly. Tell me which direction to get it into flight. Tell me how high. I don't want to disappoint you, Dad, because I want to fly this kite. For you."

I looked over at John. He was silently staring at me. The look on his face was unreadable.

I asked, "When did you write this?"

"It's old. It's from middle school or something. I don't know. Can I have it back now?" He seemed annoyed and anxious.

Before handing him the paper, I sat down in the empty chair next to him.

"If no one else sees how beautiful and great you are, I believe that he does. John, you are incredible. You know that, right?"

John's eyes stayed fixed upon me. His lips were shivering. He bit down on his bottom lip to control it. Of course, he couldn't let me see him so emotional, but I had already felt the emotion in his poem.

"John," I called out to him.

John nodded his head, and I watched his beautiful eyes as tears fell out of each one.

"You know," he whispered to me, "I wrote that after we had tried to fly a kite together. I had made Honor Roll for the first time, and Mom suggested that we celebrate at the park. My dad had this whole speech for me. He said that life was only going to move up from there. Since I made Honor Roll, he said that I could join the basketball team, and that I should keep making Honor Roll. He told me to keep doing exceptionally well so that I could have everything that I wanted in life when I got out of school. We got ready to fly the kite after the talk he gave me. It seemed like he wanted perfection from that moment on. It was as if he immediately expected it! But he wasn't going to get it on that day, because I screwed it up."

"What happened?"

"He hit me."

"What?" I almost laughed because of how he sounded. So what? His father hit him. We got a lot worse at home. What was one hit? I couldn't laugh, though, because he looked up at me with hurt in his face. I could see how much it had upset him to recall that painful memory.

"He hit me because I couldn't get the kite to fly on my first try. He was there, giving me orders and dictating to me, as I tried to follow everything he said on my own. He got so frustrated with me. I don't know, I guess I wasn't moving fast enough or doing it exactly how he wanted me to. So he took the hard, wooden handle that held the end of the kite, and he whacked me right across the face with it."

The metal ball in my chest felt like it was going to turn. I swallowed to make it stop.

I asked, "What did your mom do?"

"My mom only saw me fall to the ground. She didn't see him hit me. I lied to her and told her that I accidentally hit myself. I didn't want her to be upset. But I told Dad that if he ever hit me like that again, I would tell her, without hesitation," he said.

"Did he ever hit you like that again?"

"No," John said. "I think he was sorry for doing that. It was as if it wasn't even my dad out there. He became someone else. I don't know, but he hasn't been like that again. Temporary insanity or something. Anyways, that's what made me write that. Everything is fine now."

He snatched his paper out of my hand and put the paper containing my poem in my empty hand. I almost wanted to tell John that I knew how he felt. I wanted to tell him about when my Dad had become the monster, but I didn't. Besides, John wouldn't have really understood because his dad did not seem to be anything like Jack. It would have been nice to tell someone, though. I was too scared to say anything, so I stayed silent about it.

John started packing up his notebook and putting his jacket on. I assumed that he was ready to leave, so I put on my jacket and put my notebook in my backpack. As we were preparing to leave, I asked, "So, can you a fly kite now?"

He looked at me strangely. "What made you ask me that?"

"Curiosity? To break the awkward silence? I don't know."

"The truth is, I haven't tried to fly a kite since then," he admitted. "It's in a box under my bed."

"You should take your kite out and fly it," I said.

"What would that accomplish?"

"I get it," I said. "So *you're* scared." I threw my backpack over my shoulder and left John in the room, alone.

CHAPTER 23

There were only two good things about being locked up in the Behavioral Control Room. One was that I was not expected to go to any group meetings that seemed to take forever, followed by the doctor saying, "Time's up!" The other was that I was able to catch up on much needed sleep without Ms. Mosley bursting into the room, screaming for me to "Get up! Get up! Up! Up! Up!"

The bad definitely outweighed the good, though. When they came in to wake me up, I felt like I was going to be taken to judgment and then sent to the gallows. Three counselors, a nurse, and a doctor, whom I hadn't met before then, came into the room. It was overwhelming to see those many people around me as I was just waking up.

Before anyone released me from the restraints, the doctor had to poke me. He pushed back my eyelids and flashed light from a penlight into my eyes. He lifted my shirt and tickled my stomach. I tried not to laugh, but I couldn't help it. When he heard me laugh, a smile appeared on his face. He pressed the hard and cold stethoscope to my chest and listened to my heart. The nurse checked my blood pressure and my temperature after the doctor asked her to check my vitals. Then he wrote everything down in my chart and nodded at the counselors.

One counselor held my arms down, another held my feet, and then the other hovered over me and began to unlock the restraints with his key. I watched as the nurse held the needle full of the medicine that made me fall asleep. She looked ready. I kept my eyes on her as the counselor set me free. I didn't like the nurses too much at Bent Creek. It was hard to trust them when they held needles in their hands.

I closed my eyes as the doctor unwrapped the bandages around my wrists. I did not expect him to examine my wrists. It seemed like he was taking a long time. I had to keep my eyes closed because I did not want to see the damage that I had caused. It had to have looked worse than the little cuts on my arms and legs from Mr. Sharp. I felt the nurse wrapping the bandages around my wrists. I opened my eyes. The doctor was writing.

When I thought that my arms and legs were mine again, two of the counselors grabbed my arms. I felt bombarded. I didn't understand why they had to hold me until my feet touched the floor. My legs were like rubber. They wouldn't go straight.

"Easy there, Kristen," a counselor kindly said. "Let us help you get back to the unit."

My voice was hoarse. I said, "Thank you."

"Don't worry about it," he said. "Just try to move one foot in front of the other like you normally do. We will hold you up."

The nurse and the doctor led the way as two of the counselors held on to me and aided me to the unit. The other counselor followed behind us. Once we were on the unit, the doctor took my chart to the counselor's desk and started talking with Dr. Pelchat, who was sitting there with Ms. Mosley and Geoffrey. I turned away when Geoffrey made eye contact with me. I felt sorry for hitting him earlier.

The kind counselor walked me over to the empty couch on the main unit. He asked me if I was all right and if I needed anything. I told him that my throat was dry, and I asked if I could get a drink of water. He smiled and went to get some water for me.

When he moved, I saw Daniel sitting at one of the tables with Janine and a few other kids. Janine did not look good at all. Her hair was wet, she was in mismatched pajamas, and she didn't have any of her make-up on. She looked like she had been sleeping all day and had just woken up. It wasn't like Janine to step out of the room without her make-up on and her hair fixed up nicely.

The counselor came back and gave me a cup of lukewarm water. I almost spit it back out, because it tasted disgusting. I heard him chuckling from above me. "I'm Mr. Anton. If you need anything, let me know."

"Thanks, Mr. Anton," I said.

"Just sit tight. Your doctor wants to see you in a few minutes," he said. He started to walk away.

"Dr. Cuvo?" I asked.

"No," he said. "Dr. Pelchat wants to see you," he clarified.

Disappointed and scared, I looked over at Dr. Pelchat. He was talking to the medical doctor, and didn't even look at me when I entered the room. It was just as I thought. I was going to be sent to the judge. I was going to be sentenced. Then, I was going to be sent to the gallows.

CHAPTER 24

Dr. Pelchat didn't look my way when he walked off the unit with my chart. He didn't have any other charts in his hands, either. That made me nervous. Before he left, he said something to Ms. Mosley that made her eyes widen. She tried to straighten her expression when she saw me looking over at her. Then she looked away when she caught me looking at her and Dr. Pelchat.

When he left the unit, I stood up. My legs felt a lot better. I started walking over to the counselor's desk, but Geoffrey got in my path.

"Kristen, I don't think it's a good idea for you to be walking around right now," he said.

"I'm sorry," I said.

"What?"

"I didn't mean to hit you," I explained. I felt a tear slide down my left cheek. The metal ball burned in my chest as the events of that day played back in my mind.

Geoffrey's warm smile told me that it was all right. He patted my shoulder gently.

"Kristen, I am made of bricks. Really, I am."

We both laughed.

"You feel like you can walk?" Geoffrey asked.

"Yes, I think so." I said.

"All right," he said. "Don't go too far, though. Dr. Pelchat will be right back."

I ground my teeth unintentionally when I heard Dr. Pelchat's name. There was no time for me to worry, though--I had to get to the bathroom, and quick!

CHAPTER 25

I walked back onto the main unit feeling refreshed and relieved. I heard laughter coming from the table where Janine and Daniel were sitting.

I walked over, and Rocky said to me, "You have to see this."

It was a shock to see him smiling. Rocky always seemed depressed or angry whenever I saw him. When I looked down at the table, there were sheets of paper scattered around. There were drawings on the papers that looked like comic strips. Daniel was drawing fast. He pushed the papers out of his way when he finished one drawing, so that he could start another.

One of the pictures caught my eye. It was a caricature of Janine. She had a big head and a little body. It was funny because the big head had a cowboy hat on it, and the little body had a skimpy mini-skirt that hardly looked like it fit her waist, with a little tube top over a pair of exaggerated breasts that bulged with cleavage. The cowgirl boots were drawn as big as the breasts. The smile on the caricature's face was overly dramatic and silly.

What made the picture even funnier was how Daniel drew his own face on a donkey's body with an embellished smile. His ears were really eye-catching on his huge head. The little body was comedic, along with a tiny tail. Janine's caricature had Daniel the Donkey on a rope leash. I didn't bother to look at the other drawings. That was the one that everyone was looking at.

Daniel laughed as he pushed his latest drawing towards Janine. She looked at it and smiled. Everyone just laughed harder. I did not. I watched her to see if she'd laugh, as he wanted her to. The drawing was of Janine's caricature bent over a fence, and her butt was in the air, as if she were falling. Instead of the donkey trying to catch her, he just ogled at her large and excessively-drawn rear end that was up in the air. Daniel drew little hearts around the stupid, love-struck donkey's face.

Janine pushed the drawing back towards Daniel.

She said, "Is my ass really that big?"

Everyone laughed. They must have thought that she was joking.

Daniel said, "Of course not, Janine. It's a caricature! Oh, come on, you don't like my cartoon?"

Janine let a huge smile take over the frown on her face. She shoved Daniel playfully. Daniel smiled back at her.

"I thought so," he said.

He started gathering up his drawings, and then passed them around the table because everyone was asking to see them. I looked at Janine from across the table. She wouldn't look at me.

"Janine," I called out to her.

She ignored me.

Dr. Finch walked into the room then and called out for Daniel. Daniel gave Janine the drawing of the first picture I had seen.

"That's for you to look at and laugh at when you start to feel that way again," he said to her.

Janine kept her eyes on the paper and didn't say a word to him. Daniel said bye to everyone and then he left the unit with Dr. Finch for his session. Janine held onto her drawing with a weak smile on her face. She really was a pretty girl. Her hair had dried and her cheeks were naturally pink, like she was already wearing blush. I wanted to say something to her, but I was afraid she'd just ignore me again.

Tai went off with Dr. Bent for her session. Rocky wasn't laughing anymore. He'd gotten into a conversation with another boy. Everyone seemed to be off in his or her own world, including Janine. She held onto her drawing and she seemed sad. I don't know what came over me when I reached across the table and gently grabbed her hand.

She didn't pull away from me. She just raised her eyes and looked at me. She seemed like she was split in two. I saw a sad Janine on one side, and on the other side I saw the fun and sweet Janine from a few weeks ago. This sad Janine seemed like she was barely holding herself together. I knew the feeling, like you are about to fall off the edge of the earth.

"Janine? Have you seen a doctor yet?" I asked.

"I saw Dr. Pelchat earlier when you were in the BCR," Janine said.

"What did he say?"

Janine said, "You'll get to talk to him. I don't think Dr. Cuvo is coming back."

"Why don't you think he's coming back?"

I saw that I was upsetting her more. She lay her head down on the table and started sobbing. I squeezed her hand gently.

"Okay. I'm sorry," I said. "Please don't cry. Janine. Please. I'm sorry."

Janine sat up straight and wiped her wet cheeks. She picked up the drawing that Daniel had given to her, and laughed at it.

"He's so crazy," she said with a giggle.

I looked down at the drawing. I expected to laugh with her, not scowl at it. But I felt that ball wanting to turn in my chest.

"Are you all right, Kristen?"

I snapped out of it and nodded my head to Janine.

"What's wrong?"

I faked a smile.

"Nothing. I like that. He can really draw."

She shrugged and said, "Yeah, he *can* draw. I'm going to go put this in the bedroom. Are you coming?" The fun and sweet Janine seemed to have come back.

"No," I said. "I have to wait for Dr. Pelchat."

Janine waved to me and ran off with her drawing. I looked down at the table and saw the other drawings. Rocky grabbed the one of the donkey looking at Janine's butt, and he walked off to his room.

CHAPTER 26

Since the afternoon that John and I had talked together in the classroom, I felt like John was avoiding me. I hardly saw him around anymore. When Lexus came over to visit one weekend when Jack was out of town, she told me that John had transferred to her school and that she had seen him around. That explained why I hadn't seen him at my school. That day, Lexus suggested that we call him and see if John would bring his little brother, James, over to play with Nicholas, since he did come over quite often for sleepovers, mostly when Jack had to go out of town on job assignments.

Lexus shoved the cordless telephone into my hand.

"Call him and tell him to come over and play with us," she excitedly requested.

I shrugged, dialed John's number, and waited for an answer while the phone rang. When the ringing stopped, I spoke into the phone.

"Hello?"

"Yes? Who is this?" The squeaky voice on the other end answered. It was John's little brother, James.

"This is Kristen. Is John there?"

"Hold on. John, pick up the phone!"

"Hello," John's voice greeted me, from the other end of the line.

I felt a chill creep up my spine. He'd caught me by surprise.

I shook it off and said, "Hey John. It's me, Kristen."

"Hey! Kristen, I haven't talked to you in a while."

"Where have you been?"

"Well, since I transferred schools, I haven't really talked to anybody."

"Yeah? Why did you leave?"

"We're moving soon. My mom wanted me to get a jump on the school up there, so that I won't be too behind. But we aren't moving for a few more weeks, so I have to drive every day."

"That sucks."

"I know. Doesn't matter. It just sucks not getting to see everyone. James isn't going to like leaving his friends when we move."

"Well, then, you should bring James over to hang out with Nicholas. They probably won't be able to see each other too often after you all move."

John sighed, and then silence took over.

"Jack is out of town, working," I added.

"I'll ask James if he wants to hang out with Nick. We'll see," John said.

"Wait," I said. "Maybe we can all hang out too. My friend Lexus is here."

"See you guys in about an hour."

He hung up. I hung up, too, and looked over at Lexus, who had a pair of earbuds on, covering her ears. The earbuds blasted the tune of a familiar, upbeat melody. Lexus was lip-syncing to her favorite song. When she saw that I wasn't on the phone anymore, she removed the earbuds from her ears and smiled at me.

"So?" she inquired.

"So, what?" I asked.

"So... is he coming?"

I nodded with a wide smile.

"Oh! Look at you! You're all happy," she teased.

I shrugged my shoulders, trying to appear nonchalant.

She raised one eyebrow at me and nudged me.

"Isn't he, like, your *cousin*, or something?" Lexus asked with a devious look on her face.

"No," I said sternly. "Jack is *not* my dad."

Bitterness rose up in my nostrils and came out in a frustrated sigh.

Lexus noticed and said, "Whatever! No time for grudges against your mom and dad just because you got grounded last week. Cute boy is coming over!"

"Yeah," I sighed. I tried to brighten my mood and not let Lexus see me upset.

"When he went to your school, did you guys spend a lot of time together?"

"Not really," I said. "We talked about writing sometimes after school."

"Did you and John talk alone?"

I blushed.

"Yes. We were alone," I admitted.

Lexus gasped and her eyes grew big.

She suddenly asked, "How does he kiss?"

That question caught me off guard. I froze up. Inside, I knew that if I had ever been kissed, I would have told her. Outside, I tried not to let it show that I had never come close to kissing anyone. Not even once. The only kiss I'd ever gotten from someone that I loved other than my mother was when I'd let Jack kiss me at their wedding. My mind drifted to that happy time.

This wasn't real. This had to be one of Lexus' tests. The smile on her face was fake. It was like she was enjoying it. She knew I had never been kissed.

No. Lexus isn't like that, I told myself. She was just hoping that I might have stepped up to that level that she was way beyond. I had to convince myself that Lexus was not doing that to me.

"Are you okay?" she asked.

"He's good," I said, giving her a fake smile.

For a quick second, I saw her mouth drop. She shut her mouth quickly enough to try to cover up her shock. She gasped wildly and shoved me playfully.

"Are you serious? You skank! Why didn't you tell me?" Lexus asked.

I shrugged my shoulders. I didn't know what to say. The look on her face was different from any look I'd ever seen before. She was slightly smiling, and nervously pushing her hair out of her face. She looked like she wasn't breathing.

"Are you okay, Lexus?"

Her smile grew wider.

"I'm fine. Come on. What are you going to wear?"

"This," I said, gesturing to my outfit that was made up of simply blue jeans and a t-shirt.

"Uh, no," Lexus said as she grabbed my arm and pulled me to my closet.

When James and John arrived, Lexus and I were in the living room, flipping through channels on the television. Nick ran to me and hugged me tightly.

"What's that for?" I asked him.

Without him having to say a word, James and John walked into the living room. Lexus stood up and walked over to John. She tugged his arm and said hello. Nickyroo still had his tiny arms around my waist. I gently pushed him away and then kissed him on the forehead.

"Have fun," I told him before he and James ran off to play together.

"Hey, John," I greeted.

"Hey," he said. "Have I been away that long? You look different."

"No kidding. Is that my lipstick?" a voice said from the other side of the living room.

I looked over and saw my mom with her hands on her hips.

"No," Lexus put in. "It's *my* lipstick."

"Mom, we were just messing around. I'll go wash it off."

"No. Keep it on," she said. "You look nice, for once. Thank you, Lexus."

Lexus smiled and looked over at me.

"See! I told you," she boasted. "You look great. I don't know why she didn't even want to look in the mirror to see for herself."

I looked away from them, embarrassed. I didn't want them there. I didn't even want to be there.

"Is something special going on?" John asked.

"No," Lexus said. "I think she looks nice."

My mom said goodbye to us and then walked out of the living room.

"It's *different*," John said.

"I'm going to my-" Without thinking, I started to leave.

Lexus grabbed my arm and hit John on his arm.

"So, are we hanging out? What do you guys want to do?" Lexus asked.

John's eyes lit up.

"I've got something to show you," he said to me. "Come on."

He headed out the front door.

"Great!" Lexus grabbed my arm and pulled me along.

When we were outside, John pointed to a shiny, black, 1967 Ford Mustang that was parked in our driveway. Lexus gasped and let out a scream.

"Sexy!" she commented. "Is that yours, John?"

"That's your dad's. Right, John?" I said to take the attention off Lexus.

"Yeah," John told me. "He said I can drive it and see if it grows on me. I might get to keep it after I graduate."

"That would make a hot graduation present," Lexus charmingly expressed. She walked over to the classic vehicle and stared at it admiringly. As we checked out the exterior of the car, I could feel John's eyes beaming towards me. Lexus didn't seem to notice. She seemed to be enamored with John's car. She ohhed and aahed and rubbed it like it was a kitten. I thought the car was going to start purring because of how she was fawning all over it.

"Can I?" she asked John with her hand on the door.

"Sure, but watch the interior," John warned. "My dad had it detailed."

Lexus hopped into the front seat. John laughed. He looked away from Lexus and back over at me. I was smiling on the outside and nervous on the inside. I could see that he liked Lexus. Everybody liked Lexus. She had that kind of effect on people, especially guys. Why would John be any different? I wanted to disappear.

"Kristen," he called out to me. "Come here. I want to show you something."

I followed John to the trunk of the car, which he opened with a big, convincing smile on his face. When he pulled out the large and bright kite, I had to cover up my huge smile. He rubbed his hands gently over the red, white, and blue, American Flag-designed kite. Then, he turned to me. His eyes were bright and gleaming with the sun beaming down on him. He looked like some kind of beautiful creature that had fallen from heaven.

With sweet eyes and that wonderful smile he asked, "Kristen, will you fly this kite with me?"

I knew something had changed for the better. Uncontrollable feelings of fear, love, strength, and want spilled inside of me. I felt a little bit of those overwhelming emotions squeeze out of one tear from my left eye. I couldn't speak. I just nodded.

He stepped in close to me and whispered in my ear.

"Thank you for what you said to me, Kristen. You reminded me of something really important."

I remained closed to him, and whispered back, "What, John?"

He chuckled, and said, "You reminded me of what's most important. Not to be afraid, and just do it."

I turned my head slowly towards him. He didn't move. Our foreheads touched and our eyes met. It felt like we were magnets. There was an invisible force keeping us close together. We were so close that, if I moved half of an inch, our lips would touch.

"Sometimes I feel," he whispered, "that I can do anything. No matter if I'm scared, I know that I can do this. I don't know why I suddenly felt that after we spoke that day."

"It's just simply, because you're wonderful," I reminded him.

He closed his eyes and lowered his head with a smile. I kept my eyes open and moved my lips close to his ear. I whispered, "You can move. I dare you to move. Don't be afraid, John. Just do it." I couldn't believe I said it. I couldn't imagine what he might have been thinking, but I was not thinking at that moment. I was only feeling the emotions of love and want. I wanted John to kiss me so badly.

He looked up at me with eyes so gentle. He bit down on his bottom lip and squinted his eyes lusciously. The magnetic force started to pull me in. Even though John did not move, I knew it was all right, so I moved, but the force was only moving one way. When I moved in, he pulled back.

"Kristen," I heard Lexus call out to me.

I looked around, confused and embarrassed. Lexus tugged on my arm. She was standing with one hand on her hip and with the other scratching her head. She laughed, broke in between John and me, and grabbed the kite out of John's hands.

"*You* like kites?" she asked in a snobbish tone.

John laughed and grabbed the kite back from her playfully.

"Yes, I do. You got a problem with that?" John joked around with Lexus.

Lexus laughed along with him and hit him on his arm.

She said, "No. I never flew a kite before. Show me how to fly it, John."

"Let's do it!" John said.

"Okay!" Lexus exclaimed as she kept smiling and standing close to him. She made John blush so easily.

"Come on, Kristen. We're going to fly this thing, right?" John asked as he ran off with Lexus to the backyard.

"Yeah, sure." I said as I slowly walked after them.

Mr. Sharp said, "Kristen, I told you". He liked taunting me.

"I'll be there in a minute," I told John and Lexus.

I went into the house and into the bathroom. I locked the door as Mr. Sharp called out to me.

"Cut! Come on! Don't be afraid. Do it! Let *me* kiss you!"

CHAPTER 27

Geoffrey escorted me to Dr. Pelchat's office. Dr. Pelchat looked the same as when I'd first met him. He was tall, heavy, and had a head full of red, curly hair. He smiled like a jolly Santa Claus when Geoffrey greeted him. When Geoffrey was gone, I stood in Dr. Pelchat's office, silent and nervous.

Dr. Pelchat opened my chart and looked through the pages. After a moment of silence, he finally looked up at me. The jolly Santa Claus had left the room with Geoffrey. Dr. Pelchat didn't seem anything like Dr. Cuvo, judging from his demeanor.

"Will you please take a seat?" he asked me. I sat down and kept my eyes on him. "Let's get right to it. I'm taking you off of the Effexor and the Risperdol."

"What? I don't understand," I said.

"The medication that Dr. Cuvo put you on, I'm taking you off, starting today," he said.

"Why?"

"Do you know why Dr. Cuvo put you on those medications?"

"I don't know. I mean, I wasn't sleeping well at night."

Dr. Pelchat seemed upset. He said, "Kristen, do you know anything about Effexor or Risperdol? Do you know what they are?"

"No," I admitted.

"Effexor is an anti-depressant, and Risperdol is an anti-psychotic. Now, I'm not taking you off these medications because I don't think that there isn't anything going on with you. The truth is, from the notes that Dr. Cuvo left in your chart, I don't know what you need. My job as your doctor is to find out what the problem is and find out how to help you so that we can get you feeling better. I don't have any information in this chart that can help me do that. So now, we are going to have to start from scratch. Starting with what brought you here to Bent Creek."

I flushed. Disappointed and overwhelmed, I put my face in my hands. Tears fell into the palms of my hands. He was so harsh and stern when he spoke. Start from scratch? What did he mean by that? I started to panic, but fought hard not to let the metal ball turn in my chest.

"What I am going to do is arrange for a test. It is a clinical test to measure your level of anxiety and depression so that I can provide the best treatment for you. I am not going to put you on some random medication and hope that it works. I think we've had this conversation before about the long-term effects that certain medicines can have when they're not administered properly. Before the test, though, I am going to meet with you every day, and next time we meet, I want you to be prepared to tell me the whole reason of why you are in Bent Creek."

"Isn't it obvious? Can't you see?" I felt that same anger creeping back inside of me that I'd had when I had first met Dr. Cuvo.

"I don't believe everything I first see," he replied.

I had nothing more to say because I was shocked by his reply.

"Good," Dr. Pelchat responded to my silence. "I will take you back to the unit."

Walking back to the unit was awkward. Dr. Pelchat stayed close and made me walk ahead of him. I felt his eyes burning holes in me. It was the beginning all over again. I didn't like it, and it only made me angry. I felt like I couldn't really trust anyone.

When we were back on the unit, Dr. Pelchat said that he'd see me later. He didn't stick his hand out for a handshake as Dr. Cuvo had done.

What had happened to Dr. Cuvo? Why had he left us?

CHAPTER 28

Dr. Cuvo never came back. I couldn't think straight right after the sudden change. The rest of the day seemed empty. I tried not to think about Dr. Cuvo, and I tried not to wonder what it was that had caused him to go away. Dr. Pelchat was definitely not like Dr. Cuvo. He was stern and seemed all about business and getting things done. Dr. Cuvo at least had seemed like he cared. He'd hugged me. He'd been gentle and patient.

I grew scared as I continued to dwell on the days to come. Why did I have to take a test? What was this test going to tell Dr. Pelchat about me? What were my nights going to be like without the Risperdol? Would I go back to not being able to rest again? What was it going to be like to have Dr. Pelchat as my doctor? When would I get out of Bent Creek? All kinds of disturbing thoughts and questions filled my mind.

When the head nurse called everyone to take their medications, I stayed seated. Janine didn't seem like herself. She didn't get up to take her medication, either. Staring off into a daze, she held on tight to her pink blanket.

We were sitting on the sofa, out on the main unit, in front of the television. Geoffrey was giving out granola bars and graham crackers with apple juice. The counselors called it "snack time." Snack time reminded me of when I was a little kid in Kindergarten.

Janine's eyes were slightly puffy because she hadn't been sleeping well. I could tell that Dr. Cuvo's absence was having a huge effect on her. She had so many thoughts going on in her head, but she just wouldn't talk to me when we were alone. I knew she was hiding something. It was eating her up because she looked terrible. She didn't brush her hair, her lips were chapped, she wasn't wearing her make-up as often as she used to, and she was running to the bathroom a lot more than before.

Janine took a sip of her apple juice. She sat her cup on the table beside the sofa and picked up the granola bar that Geoffrey had given her. She stared at it like it was a foreign object. Tai came back from taking her medicine and looked at Janine.

Janine said out of nowhere, "They said that they'd let us see a doctor, even if Dr. Cuvo isn't here."

Tai rolled her eyes coldly.

"Janine. What is your deal with Dr. Cuvo, anyway? Why can't you just let it go?"

Janine threw the granola bar onto the floor, causing it to break into crumbs and make a mess on the carpet. At that moment Daniel, Chris, and a few others from our group walked over to sit in front of the television with their snacks.

"I would have eaten that if you didn't want it," Daniel said to Janine as he approached. He didn't notice that she was angry.

Rocky leaned towards me and asked, "What's wrong with her?"

"She's gotten too attached to her doctor," Tai said in a mean voice.

"Leave her alone, Tai," Daniel stood up for Janine.

"Maybe he's sick," Chris said, trying to comfort Janine.

Janine leaned forward and forced a smile towards Chris. "Maybe you're right, Chris."

Daniel's facial expression showed worry.

"Did you get to see another doctor?"

"I talked to Dr. Pelchat. He won't tell me where Dr. Cuvo is. He keeps asking me all these questions like I did something to..." Her voice trailed off.

Everyone stayed silent. Even Tai didn't have anything to say after that. Chris started tapping his fingers on the side table. This tapping turned into an offbeat drumming, and it became very annoying. Daniel looked at Chris, who stopped drumming his fingers and turned away, embarrassed. He looked around at all of us, except Daniel. Then, out of nowhere, a big smile appeared on his face.

He said, "I have some good news."

We looked at him attentively, eager to hear the good news. We all needed some uplifting.

"I'm going home tomorrow," Chris announced proudly.

His smile was bright and handsome, but at that moment, no one cared about his smile. Chris had only meant to replace the melancholy silence with cheer, but he had only made everyone sadder. Even I felt a hint of envy, and I wasn't even close to Chris. It was just the fact that he was getting out of Bent Creek and we were staying in. We forced our smiles and congratulated him. We told him we'd miss him and that we hoped he would do better. Deep down inside, we hated him.

"Are you afraid to use the word hate?" Dr. Bent asked a short while later, in our Anger Management session.

She was sitting in the middle of a circle that our group had made. We'd all joined our chairs together, trapping Dr. Bent and Daniel in the middle, where they both sat in two separate chairs facing each other. We watched as Dr. Bent worked her Anger Management Therapy skills on Daniel. As he usually seemed to do when he was in his own world, Daniel fiddled with his shoelaces.

"No," Daniel admitted. "I'll use the word hate. Like I hate that I am still here."

"No," Dr. Bent corrected him. "I meant hate towards another person. Would you say that you hate your mother?"

Daniel looked as if he had to think about that question before he answered. He could have been sure to answer in the negative. Of course, he didn't hate his mother. No one can hate their mother. No matter what has happened. Right?

"No," he finally said. "I just don't get how she could take my step-dad back after all that mess he put us through. Here I am, stuck in this stupid hospital, and she goes to *him*."

Dr. Bent nodded her head and stayed focused on Daniel. She waved her hand to make him keep talking.

"Go on, Daniel," she encouraged.

"When she's with him, she's always so sad. She thinks that he's just going to make everything better, and he only makes her miserable. When he left, she started to work and buy food and take care of everything. She took care of herself. She took care of... me..." His voice faded off.

Dr. Bent said, "You have to find a better way to cope, Daniel. Your mother is a grown woman, and no matter how irresponsible or wrong her choices may be, you are still her child. You have to open up to her and be honest."

"What if she doesn't listen to me?" Daniel let out his fear.

"Then, are you prepared to find a new way to cope that's better than what you did before?" Dr. Bent said.

"No. And that's why I'm still here. I'm afraid that she won't listen to me. I'll get angry again and..." Daniel said.

Daniel did not seem to find any comfort in this. He shook his head with glassy eyes. He gasped and let out a deep and depressed-sounding sigh.

Janine was staring off somewhere else, looking dazed and distant. She sat, slumped down in her chair, and she was still. I worried about her. I didn't know what to say to her to make her feel better. I didn't know any more about Dr. Cuvo than she did. I'd thought that maybe she'd feel better after she had a visit from her father, but I guessed I was wrong.

I didn't volunteer to get in the middle of the circle after Daniel. Dr. Bent liked it when we volunteered to participate in her exercises. I could tell that she didn't like calling on people and making them feel awkward. After Group ended, we were allowed to go back to the main unit. Dr. Pelchat and Dr. Finch were on the unit, calling patients into their offices for their one-on-one.

Today there was a new girl. She looked different with her light brown eyes and a seemingly cold stare. She had dyed, black hair with a red streak down her bangs. Her lip was pierced. She had a lot of dark make-up on, and her eyes were puffy and red. She was somewhat heavy, and she wore a torn, brown jacket, blue jeans, and a t-shirt that had a cartoon drawing on it. The cartoon was of an innocent-looking, white bunny rabbit that had a thought bubble above its head. Inside the bubble, it read: YOU SMELL LIKE BUTT.

When I saw her, I had a feeling that she was Dr. Pelchat's patient. He seemed to get the hard cases. And she had a mean look to her. Rocky, who'd been talking to the new girl, was being pulled into the office with Dr. Pelchat for his one-on-one session. I watched as Rocky dragged himself behind Dr. Pelchat, his expression stubborn and miserable. I could tell by his body language that he was dreading it.

I dreaded Dr. Cuvo not coming back. I remembered how angry I had been when I had first met him. I had been so mean to him. Now I wanted him to know that he wasn't the one I was mad at.

I just didn't know how to talk to Dr. Cuvo when I'd had a chance. I didn't know how to respond to someone who looked at me with so much tenderness and care. I didn't know how to get out what I really needed to say to someone who I didn't know really wanted to listen to me. It wasn't pride. It was shame for the life that I lived and for who I was. I felt, at that moment, that if Dr. Cuvo had been there, I would have let out everything. I could have just poured my heart out to him about everything. I would have told him about that night I'd taken all of those pills, and he would have known why I'd finally picked up that knife and had tried to cut as deep as I could to make the pain go away and to finally get to sleep. I wanted to sleep. I wished he were here.

"Excuse you!" screamed a harsh voice into my ear while delivering me a rough shove to get me out of her way.

I looked up, and the hazel-eyed, new girl was giving me a cold stare as she walked off with Geoffrey. Wondering what her problem was, I walked over to one of the tables and sat down. The room seemed empty without Janine and the rest of my group. Most of the other kids who were here were ones I didn't really know. I folded my arms on top of the table and lay my head down.

When I looked up, Daniel was suddenly hovering over me, staring down. This made me bury my head quickly in my arms. Maybe he was just daydreaming, I thought to myself. But when I peeked from under my arms, his eyes were aware and they were gazing at me.

"What?" I shot at him.

He shuddered in shock from the harsh tone of my voice.

"You're moody," he noticed.

I told him, "I just don't like when people stare at me."

He looked down at my bandaged wrists. "Are those coming off anytime soon?" he asked.

"I don't know, probably," I answered.

"Have you seen what your wrists look like yet?"

This question shocked me because I didn't expect Daniel to ask me something like that.

"Yes! Of course," I lied to him.

He was staring at me again. He probably didn't believe me.

"How long has it been since you decided to try to hack yourself to death?" Daniel asked.

I wanted to kick him hard from underneath the table where we were sitting. I lifted my head from my arms and held up three fingers. "It's been three weeks. Three weeks since I tried to hack myself to death," I told him as calmly as possible. I didn't want him to see that he had gotten to me.

"Three weeks? That's it?" he asked.

He pushed his arms out to me and turned them over to show me his wrists. He had big, bulging scars from where he had once self-injured. The scars were pure white. There were faded lines through some of the scars where he had had stitches.

"When I had cut my wrists, I was in the regular hospital for a long time before they put me into a place like Bent Creek. See, I had cut so deep that I had almost hit the artery. That was my goal. Instead, I nicked my vein. And, well, all that did was make a big mess. But it was deep enough, I guess, for the time." He left his wrists out and stared down at them as if he were reminiscing. "Man," he said. "If I had hit that artery, there would have been no turning back. They would not have been able to save me. Would they?"

My eyes softened to his. I don't know what came over me. Somehow, I was affected by everything he had said. I slowly reached out and let the tips of my fingers touch the scars. I ran my fingers over his painful-looking scars. He jumped as if I had shocked him, but he didn't snatch his arms away. I traced his scars with my fingers, and I almost felt like crying. He sighed deeply. I had hoped he had realized that I wasn't going to hurt him.

"Were you serious?" I asked him as I stared down at his wrists and gently caressed them.

"I guess," he said. "I don't know." His voice sounded different, like it had gotten deeper.

I looked up at him. Our eyes locked. He quickly snatched his arms away and put his hands in his lap. I wanted to hug him.

"How old were you?" I asked, even though he wasn't even looking at me anymore.

"I was thirteen. My dad had just been locked up, and my mom had gone into this deep depression. She wouldn't go to work. She wouldn't even get up to go to the store to get food. I didn't know what to do to make her happy again. So I just..."

Daniel seemed choked up. He took a deep breath and held it like he was holding back his tears. I held back my own tears for him.

"You were so young," I said.

"How old were you when you started cutting?" he asked me suddenly.

"I don't really remember," I admitted to him. "I may have been about thirteen or fourteen. It's like there's a big gap in my memory around that time."

"Why?" he asked.

"I don't know," I said. "I remember bits and pieces from that time. I can recall scenes like a movie, but some things I just can't see too clearly. It's like it was just taken away from me. I don't know."

Daniel leaned and put his cheek into the palm of his hand while his elbow rested on top of the table.

"I remember everything," he said.

"When I do cut," I heard myself say, "It's almost like it's not even me doing it."

"Who is it?" he asked, as if we were just having a normal conversation.

I wanted to tell him about Mr. Sharp, but that didn't seem right. It might have scared him. Therefore, I just shrugged my shoulders and looked away from his deep eyes.

"Kristen?" He called out when I looked away from him.

The sound of my name coming from his lips made me feel strange. It was something about his voice. He made it sound so delicate. It made me feel like something I had missed a long time ago.

Daniel continued, "What do you first notice about a person when you meet them?"

I smiled, almost wanting to laugh. It seemed like something random at the time. "Their smile," I answered honestly.

He smiled and said, "You like smiles."

I nodded. "What about you, Daniel?" I asked him.

"I notice," he said, thinking about his answer, "the eyes." I noticed he was staring into mine as he said this.

What was he doing? I wondered.

I asked, "Who was that girl in that picture you drew?"

"Who?"

"Remember, you were drawing the other day and you didn't want me to see it." I smiled, remembering how he'd been behaving.

He was not smiling now. "Do you have my drawing?"

I didn't want to answer, seeing how he seemed a little irritated.

"No," I lied. "I just saw it on the floor, and I glanced at it. It's probably in the trash now."

"Oh," he sighed. He looked down and started playing with his shoelaces.

I didn't know how to take that. Was he disappointed or relieved?

"So," I pressed on, "who was that?"

"It was my girlfriend," he said in a low voice.

"I thought you didn't have a girlfriend," I told him.

He looked up, shocked. "Where did you hear that?"

I thought about Janine and her big mouth.

"No one. I guess I just..." I didn't know what to say.

He shrugged it off.

"She's at home. She's probably writing me another letter," he laughed. "She was always bad at reading and writing. She hated talking on the phone. She was so complicated." He was blushing for some reason. "She definitely doesn't smile. But under her runny mascara, which she never could put on right, she did. Only, she did it with her eyes. Smiles and eyes. That's all she was." He took a deep breath. "Is," he corrected himself.

I felt my heart melt. Then envy crept inside, and I shook it off quickly.

"Will she come visit you?" I forced myself to say.

He chuckled. "Probably not," he admitted. "She hates hospitals. I mean she *really* hates them. Once we were walking back to my house when we were coming home from the movies, and it just started raining outside. It was thundering and lightning. The only place that we could go to try to wait the storm out was a hospital that we were passing by. She was more scared of the hospital than the storm. She said that she would rather be struck by lightning than wait inside of a hospital. We ran all the way to my place in the storm."

He kept laughing as though it was his happiest memory, and he never wanted to let go. He seemed to be holding on firm to it. I tried to smile back at him, but it was too hard. His story seemed too sad, for some reason. There was something else about his story. It made me sad, and I wanted to deny it.

My insides began to tremble, and I felt my skin grow cold. I looked at the clock. Visiting hours were coming soon. I could feel the temperature in the room dropping.

My mother came a half-hour after visiting hours began. As soon as she gave me my blanket, I wrapped it around me.

"Thanks, Mom," I said, hugging her. I allowed myself to warm up to her.

She smiled and said, "You must be feeling better."

"It stays cold in here," I told her. "And they only give you these really thin, white blankets. It's kind of creepy."

She laughed.

"What?"

"Nothing," she said. "It's just nice to see you smiling again. You must be getting better. Are they treating you well?"

"Yes," I said. "I'm fine." I smelled my blanket. It smelled like wild orchids.

"I brought your school books so that you can get your homework done while you are in here. You're home schooling, so you have to keep up with that."

I shoved the books aside and continued to snuggle my blanket.

"Here's your brush," she said as she started removing items from a plastic bag. "Make sure you use that, Kristen. Your hair is a mess."

My smile disappeared. Just when I thought that it was okay to start smiling around her again, she reminded me why I couldn't.

"Here's a new toothbrush. They took the toothpaste. I guess you can't have that on your own. She said that they will give it to you in the morning. There's some extra underwear that I got out of your drawers at home." She sat the bag down on the floor next to my chair.

"Thanks, Mom." I said.

"Sure. You needed that stuff, right? So, I brought it."

Afraid that there would be awkward silence, I spoke quickly. "How are Nicky and Ally?"

"They are fine," she said. "They are with John's mother. Mariah is going to watch them until I get home. Nick is getting on my nerves about coming to visit you. But even if he could come see you, I wouldn't let them come here." She shook her head at me.

I understood why.

"I don't want them to see me here," I told her.

"Think about it," she said. "You want to set an example for them. "What kind of example is this supposed to be? Do you want to be the big sister who they learn what *not* to do from?"

I shook my head.

She continued. "I really need you to get yourself together, Kristen. All of this teenage depression stuff has to stop. You are getting too old for this. I know that you have been through a lot, but you don't see Nick pulling this kind of crap. Besides, I don't want him to look at you and think that, just because you are doing these bad things, it's okay for him to deal with his anger like this. He has had it a lot worse than you have, and he doesn't go around cutting himself with knives and swallowing pills for attention. It doesn't help anyone when you're like this."

It took every part of me not to cry. I felt a tear dangling in the corner of my eye. I blinked, and unfortunately, it fell. The first tear ran down my cheek, and I sniffed. Other tears followed. This made Mom angry.

"Get a hold of yourself," she said. "I'm not yelling at you. For God's sake, Kristen. Why are you crying? You see? This is your problem. I just can't have a normal conversation with you. You just start crying, and then won't say anything. Will you just tell me why you did it? Will you, please?"

I put my hands to my face. I hid behind them and sobbed harder.

She growled angrily, "Kristen, what the hell is your problem? I am your mother. You should be able to talk to me. What is it? How can I help you?"

I uncovered my face. I was stunned. She wanted to help me.

"What can *you* do to help *me*?" I said to her with red eyes and a tear-drenched face.

"Yes," she said in a frustrated tone.

I stared into her eyes. "Don't make me go with you to Jack's parole hearing," I forced out.

She gasped in shock.

Then, the awkward silence came. I grabbed my bag, my blanket, and my school books and walked off to my room without saying another word. She didn't even call out to me. She didn't try to stop me from walking away. She just sat there, staring at nothing in silence. I don't know what happened after that. I don't know how long she sat there or how long it took her to leave, but when I came back out after putting my things down and realizing I had been too hard on her, she was gone.

I went to Mr. Anton and asked him if my mom had said anything to him before she'd left, and he said no. I asked Ms. Mosley if my mom had said anything to her. She said no. Then, finally, I went to Geoffrey, who was sitting near the end of the counselor's desk, and I asked if my mother had said anything to him.

He said, "Your mom told me to tell you she'll see you later on this week."

CHAPTER 29

It was almost time for the lights to go out. I was reading my chemistry book because I wasn't feeling tired. Janine walked out of the bathroom in her matching cotton pajamas. Her hair was neatly brushed and pushed behind her ears. She looked clean and pretty. Her eyes were heavy and sad. Janine threw herself down on her bed and snuggled under her pink blanket.

"I'm so tired," she whispered as she placed her head down on her pillow and closed her eyes.

"Are you all right?" I asked her. I was sure she could hear the worry in my voice.

"I feel so strange," she said. "Dr. Pelchat took me off of my Depakote."

"Why did he do that?" I asked her. I sat my textbook on my night table next to my bed.

"He made me take a test. He said that my emotions weren't balancing out, and that it wouldn't balance out if I stayed on Depakote." She pushed her face into her pillow and screamed, "Nothing ever balances out! Dr. Cuvo would never let him do this to me! He put me on some other medicine. What am I going to do?"

"I don't know, Janine," I said, feeling helpless. "Maybe it will help you."

"No!" she yelled, lifting her head up and punching her pillow. Her eyes were red and she was angry. "I need my medicine! I need *my* doctor. Dr. Cuvo!"

I went over to her quickly and carefully put my hand on her shoulder.

"Janine. It's okay. You have to stop yelling, or Ms. Mosley is going to come in here and say something. You don't want her to put you in the BCR for yelling." I tried to warn her in a calm voice. I was afraid for her.

Janine calmed down when she realized how she was behaving. She scooted herself closer to me and held on tight to her blanket.

"I saw my daddy today," she whispered, softly.

I almost couldn't hear her.

"Do you know what he said when he saw me?" she asked.

"What did he say?"

"He told me that he didn't want to talk to me while I was sad. He said that it wasn't pleasing to see me this way, and that he couldn't stay around me. He said I should have been feeling better by now since I've been here for a few weeks now. He always said that I looked pretty when I smile. I can't be sad, Kristen. I have to be perfect. But perfect is just too hard without my medicine and Dr. Cuvo. And I gained so much weight. I'm fat!"

"Shh, Janine," I said as I squeezed her shoulder gently. "You're not fat. You *are* perfect. I wish I looked as pretty as you."

She ignored me and continued, "Daddy hates it when I'm a mess. He said that if I'm not better soon, he's going to let them send me to long-term treatment. You go after four weeks here to that place. They can't keep you at Bent Creek longer than four weeks. I don't want to go to that kind of hospital."

Janine grabbed my waist, put her head in my lap, and hugged me tightly. I let her cry on my lap and I stayed quiet. Nothing I could say would have made her feel better. It all made sense. She was pretty, and she could have it all, including her father's love. If only she could be perfect.

I don't know if I could have been anything close to perfect for my dad. I was his loving daughter. He was my Prince Charming daddy. My daddy made me feel like I was perfect just the way I was. I didn't feel like I had to go the extra mile to please him. When the monster swallowed my dad, I didn't want to accept it. There were times when I did test Jack's patience just to see if I could catch a glimpse of my daddy staring out from those eyes that the monster may have trapped him in. There was no sign of him. He was dead.

The worst day of our lives was approaching, and I remembered the last time I had tested Jack, that horrible monster, to see if my dad was still alive. It was a rainy day, and I had missed the bus to school. Mom had the flu and she could hardly get out of bed. Jack was on his way to work, and I asked him if he could give me a ride to school.

"Go ahead and get in the truck," he demanded. "I'll be out there in a minute."

I looked up at him, pleading with my eyes. *Daddy? Are you there?*

"What the hell are you staring at?" he yelled. "Do you want a ride to school or not?"

Without a word, I turned away from the monster, hating him, and I went out to the truck. Shortly after settling into the truck, Jack came out the front door and into the pouring rain. He hurried to get out of the stormy weather.

When he finally settled into the truck, he said, "Wow, it is really pouring down out there. Isn't it, Kristen?"

I looked over at him with hope. He'd said my name so sweetly. Was it my dad? I watched as he put the keys into the ignition and started up the car. He turned the heater on.

"Are you cold?" he asked me.

I smiled. It had to have been Daddy. Only he would be concerned about me. Right?

"All right," he said. "There we go. And now we are off to school."

He pulled out of the driveway. I smiled as I stared at him. I pondered the memories of him in my mind as I kept searching. I wanted to see more of him if I could. I wanted Dad to defeat Jack and come back. It couldn't be too late! He looked at me and didn't return my smile.

"I got all A's on my report card yesterday. Did Mom show it to you?" I asked my dad.

Jack answered, "Yes. I saw that. How the hell did you miss the bus to school?"

My dad would have congratulated me. My dad would have said that he was proud of me. If I had done badly, Jack, that monster, would have found some way to hurt me. He didn't let me see much of Lexus. He said that I was getting too close to her, and that I needed to be with my own family. He was afraid that I was telling her things.

"Whatever happens in our home is our business," he would say to me. "It's none of theirs! If I hear that you've been saying things, you'll never see Lexus again."

I took his threats seriously.

"What?" Jack asked me as he drove me to school. "Did you turn deaf and dumb on me in the last few minutes? I asked you a question. How did you miss the damn school bus?"

I hated when he yelled at me. I squeezed my book bag close to my chest.

I forced out, "I accidentally woke up late."

He snarled at me, "I hope you don't think I'm going to do this for you every time you miss the bus."

What was he talking about? This was the first time I had ever woken up late for school. It was the first time he had ever had to drive me to school. It would certainly be the last.

"If you do this again, you're just going to have to miss school. I have a job. I can't afford to be late!"

"I know," I said. "I'm sorry."

Jack kept silent and concentrated on the road. It was raining so hard that I hardly recognized what street we were on. The rain drenched the windows. Jack turned the windshield wipers up full-speed.

"I earned first place in our Writing Club's writing competition last week," I said. "I get to advance to our State's writing competition. They even pinned up my poem to the Honors Wall at school. That's good. Right, Dad? I mean...um... my counselor said that it's good for me, since I want to be a writer. I'll get to put on my college application that my poem went to our State's writing competition, even if I don't win. What do you think, Dad?"

I was speaking to him, but he wasn't there. Therefore, he didn't answer me. Jack concentrated on the road. I could tell that he was frustrated and shutting me out. He was determined to keep me away from my daddy. That monster wanted to kill him completely and take him away from me. On that day the monster ripped Dad completely from my heart. Jack pulled up to the driveway that led to my school, and he stopped. The rain seemed to pour down heavier.

"I don't think you can stop right here," I told him. "Can you drive me to the front of the school, since it's raining really hard?"

"It's not a long walk. Just get out and walk the rest of the way so that I don't have to go past the security at your school. I can just go straight to work from here."

"But Dad," I called out to him. "There's lightning out there. Please? Will you drive me up to the door?" I pleaded. "I'm scared."

He sat still, holding onto the steering wheel. He gripped the wheel so tightly that his knuckles turned white. Jack kept his jaws clenched tight. I sat there beside him and didn't move. I waited.

He looked at me and pierced me with his eyes. I looked to see if my Dad was in there somewhere, but I saw nothing but pure evil. That monster was a demon. Through that demon's eyes, I didn't see my daddy, or even a soul. His eyes looked black and hollow.

It seemed too late to escape. My heart felt like it nearly jumped out of my chest. I knew that I had to try to get away from the monster. I reached for the door handle, but I was not quick enough. The demon grabbed the back of my neck and yanked me over to him. When he raised his fist into the air, I knew that I should not have been afraid of the harmless storm. I should have been afraid of the demon. He brought his fist down, and it went to my chest. I grabbed my chest in shock and in pain. He didn't stop. He punched me more and more, harder and harder. The blows came at me faster and faster. He grunted. He snarled and growled like something not human.

It took a minute for the shock to pass and for me to realize that this demon was beating me. I was on my back in the truck, helpless and trapped. I reached my hands into the air, trying to block his blows. The pain was excruciating. I tried to block him out. I tried to see my daddy's face again. He was gone. He wasn't coming back.

I cried out, "Daddy! No! Daddy! Help! Help me, Daddy!" My dad wasn't coming to rescue me. He wasn't going to come back ever again.

When I screamed out, the demon stopped pummeling me. I grabbed my book bag and dashed out of the truck, causing myself to fall onto the pavement and scrape my hands. I scrambled up and ran as fast as I could without looking back.

I ran down the school driveway and let the rain take me. The lightning crashed through the sky as fast as it went through my heart. The thunder roared, and it didn't make me shudder because I had just gone through the scariest thing that I could ever imagine at that time. I ran past security. I went inside of the building as the security guards called out to me. I ignored them and ran past the school office, where I knew I was supposed to check in and get a pass because I was late. I didn't care. I ran to my savior. I ran to the bathroom, into the stall, and locked the door. Opening my book bag made me so desperate and anxious that I was drooling, grunting, crying, and screaming loudly.

"Mr. Sharp! Mr. Sharp!" I cried out to him.

"*Here I am,*" he answered.

I pulled the knife out quickly and let his smiles make me feel better.

Janine and I fell asleep. Her head was in my lap and her arms stayed wrapped around my waist. Janine had her warm, pink blanket over her legs. I was in a sitting position with my back against the headboard. If Ms. Mosley had come in to do night checks, we would have been in trouble for falling asleep that way.

I woke up when I heard the door rush open. I thought we had been caught. The lamp on Janine's table was still on. When I saw who it was, I knew something was wrong. The clock on the wall read 2:27 a.m. What was Tai doing in our room? She was shaking badly and she was talking in jumbles.

"What's wrong, Tai?" I asked her, jumping up quickly and accidentally pushing Janine off me.

Poor Janine sat up, startled out of her sleep.

Tai didn't make any sense. She was speaking excessively fast for her words to be coherent. Janine was so drowsy that she could hardly sit up straight. She looked around, confused, and with red puffy eyes.

"What's wrong with Tai?" she asked.

"Come on, Janine!" Tai said to her. "Come on, Kristen!"

"What?" I asked her again. Her excitement was making me nervous.

"He's going crazy!" she exclaimed. Without another word, she grabbed Janine's hand and pulled her out of the bed. Janine grabbed my hand, and we rushed out of the room.

As Tai led us down the hallway to exit the Girls' Unit, she tried explaining again. "I was at the water fountain just a few minutes ago when I heard a boy screaming. I don't know what Ms. Mosley saw, but she jumped over the counselor's desk and she ran so fast. I walked out of the door, and I saw Daniel in the hallway in his shorts, and he was going crazy. He was just screaming like he was losing his mind."

"Is he all right?" I asked.

"I don't know," Tai said. "Let's go see."

As we walked up closer to the door that led to the main unit, I heard someone crying and screaming. A crowd was growing because more girls were coming out of their rooms to see what all the commotion was about. The new girl pushed past us, and she was the first one out of the doors. We followed behind her.

When we walked out onto the main unit, Geoffrey ran past us, jumped over the counter, and picked up the telephone. Instead of yelling at us, he screamed profanity at whoever was on the other end of that phone. The doors to the Boys' Unit were wide open. I saw Daniel sitting on the floor, rocking back and forth, crying and screaming. I could only see part of Ms. Mosley. She was bending over something, hovering. I couldn't see what it was. I knew that Daniel wasn't the problem, since no one was consoling him.

Ms. Mosley looked up and turned towards us. She yelled, "Tell them to hurry, Geoffrey! Get the ambulance!"

Geoffrey screamed louder into the phone, "You need to get them here now! I don't know! Just hurry!"

Daniel scrambled up off the floor as Ms. Mosley tried to soothe him. When she moved towards Daniel, we saw what it was that was causing the trouble. Daniel cried louder. Ms. Mosley tried to put her arms around him, but he pushed her away and turned away from her.

Tai said, "Oh, my God! Look!"

She pointed to Rocky. He was on the floor with a bed sheet tied around his neck. Rocky's face and arms were the same shade of purplish blue as the late evening sky. His tongue was hanging out of his mouth, and his eyes were rolled back and almost bulging out of his head. He was not moving at all.

Janine let out a blood-curdling and horrifying scream. That's when Ms. Mosley and Geoffrey noticed that we were standing here. Ms. Mosley called out to Geoffrey as she tried to block us from seeing what we had already seen.

Geoffrey quickly hung up the phone and ran from behind the counter over to us.

"Get back on the Girls' Unit, now!" He yelled as he shooed us off.

The girls scuttled back through the doors. Janine fell to the floor before we could get moving. Tai and I grabbed her arms and tried to carry her back with us. Geoffrey told us to take her to our room. She was crying and shaking badly.

We could only carry Janine so far. She was too heavy to carry all the way, so we tried to make her stand up and walk. She just fell to the floor, crying. Tai bent down beside her.

She said, "Come on, Janine. You have to get down the hallway. He's all right. Rocky will be okay."

"No, he's not," the new girl said. "He's dead."

"Shut the hell up, Mena! Nobody asked you!" Tai yelled.

Mena shook her head.

She looked down at Janine and said to her, "Did you see his neck? I bet it's broken. He probably crushed his windpipe too. He can't breathe."

"No! No!" Janine cried as she started to pull her hair. I grabbed her hands to make her stop.

"Shut the hell up!" Tai jumped up and screamed into Mena's face.

"Make me," Mena dared her.

The girls were throat to throat, and I knew that, in a second, Tai was going to take that dare. I jumped up from beside Janine and stood between the two of them.

Facing Tai, I said, "Tai, you have to help me carry Janine. She's not going to make it down the hallway."

Tai rolled her eyes and went over to Janine. We both got a hold of her and lifted her up. It took all of my strength to get Janine down the hallway and back to our room. I could tell that it took all of Tai's strength to ignore Mena. When we reached the room and guided Janine to her bed, she crawled underneath her blanket and continued to cry.

"Tai," I said, "please stay with Janine. I'll be right back."

"Sure, okay. Tell me what's going on when you get back," she requested.

I nodded and then ran out the door. The hallway was empty. The other girls had gone back to their rooms. I crept up to the door that went back to the main unit and carefully peeked out. I didn't know that Mena was out there until I saw her when I stuck my head out. She looked at me and didn't say a word. She just pointed.

The EMTs pulled a stretcher down the boys' hallway. One of the EMTs yelled into a radio and two others hovered over Rocky for a minute. Then they lifted him onto the stretcher. Another EMT held up an IV drip that she had attached to Rocky. The EMTs worked fast. As they rushed Rocky out, the stretcher rolled by us, and never before in my life had I ever seen a person hanging on one strand of life. His head was in something that looked like a glass box. It was morbid. His eyelids were shut, and someone must have put his tongue back in his mouth. But his face was still blue and his cheeks were swollen. Another girl had come from the unit and was standing beside me.

She said, "Oh God, I'll pray for him. God, please let Rocky be all right."

Mena replied on behalf of God, "He's dead." She pushed past the girl and me without excusing herself and went back to the Girls' Unit and down the hallway towards her bedroom.

I had to hold my anger inside. Mena obviously had serious problems. For her to just assume that Rocky was dead was just cruel. She didn't even show any emotion, nor did it seem as if she cared. Ms. Mosley and Geoffrey brought Daniel out to the main unit. He was crying and saying that he was sorry for falling asleep. The girl beside me called out to Daniel. That made Geoffrey and Ms. Mosley notice us. Geoffrey came over and told us to go back to bed. He walked us onto the unit and stood in the hallway until we were in our rooms.

When I entered my room, Tai immediately asked me what I saw. Janine was still shaking and crying. I sat down on Janine's bed next to Tai. Janine snuggled close to me and put her arms around my waist and her head in my lap. I rubbed her back like she was a baby.

"He's all right," I lied. "They took him to the hospital."

Tai sighed in relief. She leaned her head on my shoulder and closed her eyes. Janine stopped shaking and closed her eyes, too. I was afraid to close my eyes. I was thinking about Rocky. He could be dead by morning. He could be dead in just a few minutes. I looked down at my bandaged wrists. I closed my eyes, trying not to think about that day. Then, I heard Tai's voice.

She said, "Are you all right?"

I opened my eyes. I couldn't speak. I only nodded my head.

"Okay," she said. She closed her eyes and placed her head on my shoulder. "I'm not leaving," she assured me.

Gently I rested my head on top of Tai's head. We stayed like that until morning.

CHAPTER 20

We slept in late the next morning. I opened my eyes when I heard Geoffrey come into our bedroom. My arm had fallen asleep while it had been under Tai's head.

Calmly, he said, "Girls, wake up. Come on. Dr. Pelchat wants everyone for the group meeting."

Tai and Janine woke up. Tai saw Geoffrey in the room. She asked him if she was in trouble for sleeping in the room with us.

Geoffrey said, "Don't worry about it, Tai. Girls, don't worry about getting your day clothes on. Just throw on your robes and your socks and come on out on the main unit."

When Geoffrey left the room, Tai got up and stretched.

"I'm going to get my shoes on and rinse my mouth out. I'll see you out there," Tai said as she left our room.

Janine looked up at me as I put my shoes on. She started to say something.

"Are you all right, Janine?" I asked her.

She looked at me strangely and then she covered her mouth and ran to the bathroom. I heard her retching.

"Janine!" I called out to her. I knocked on the bathroom door. I did not want to burst in on her throwing up, but I was afraid not to.

"Go away!" she cried. "Please go."

"I can't leave you like this, Janine," I said.

"I will be okay. I'm just a little sick. I can't -" she started throwing up again while she was trying to talk. I knew she wasn't making herself throw up, so I left her alone.

When I got out to the main unit, I saw chairs scattered everywhere. Ms. Mosley put her coat on like she was getting ready to leave. Geoffrey was helping Mr. Anton get the room straightened up. I didn't see Dr. Pelchat anywhere. Daniel was sitting on the sofa by himself. I went over to it and sat down next to him. Mena came over and sat in a chair near us, and a few others also came over.

Mena looked at Daniel.

"Did you see the corpse?" she asked him.

Daniel didn't say anything.

I snapped at her, "He tried to break his neck. Have some sympathy."

Mena's eyes grew dark in her devious stare.

She said, "He doesn't want sympathy."

Daniel said, "You need to shut the hell up, Mena."

Mena started to say something, but Dr. Pelchat walked onto the unit then. Janine also appeared and sat down on the sofa between Daniel and me. She leaned her head on my shoulder. It was strange to see her being clingy. I couldn't believe that she was clinging to me.

Daniel leaned and whispered in her ear. She nodded at him, and then she leaned her head on his shoulder. I started to ask her if she was all right, but Dr. Pelchat called for everyone to gather around and take a seat. Tai came in and sat as far away from Mena as possible. Others had been asleep during all of the commotion with Rocky last night, and they seemed confused.

Dr. Pelchat took a seat with Geoffrey and the other staff members. Ms. Mosley looked like she was about to leave, but Dr. Pelchat told her to sit down with them. She looked tired, angry, and ready to go home.

Dr. Pelchat began, "I know that this day is starting off a little different.

Some of you know what's going on and some of you don't. There was an incident last night that occurred on our unit."

Daniel shifted uncomfortably. Janine wrapped her arms around him. I watched as Daniel tried to smile at her. Mena grinned at me as if she knew something I didn't know. I looked back at Dr. Pelchat.

He continued, "One of your peers is in the hospital right now. He's in critical condition and he is going to be in that hospital for a while."

"What happened?" someone asked.

"I'm going to be honest with you," Dr. Pelchat began.

Ms. Mosley wasn't going to let him finish. She leaned forward in her chair with her coat on and her purse attached to her shoulder.

"We are not getting into that right now," she said, speaking to Dr. Pelchat.

We all read Dr. Pelchat's facial expression quite clearly. He did not seem in the mood for any confrontation.

He said to Ms. Mosley, "Yes we are, Ms. Mosley. We are going to talk about this."

"I don't think that's a very good idea, Dr. Pelchat," she voiced. "It could give these children ideas."

I could tell that this was not going to go well between Dr. Pelchat and Ms. Mosley.

"Yeah!" he exclaimed sarcastically. "Let's talk about giving them ideas! Here's the idea that your friend Rocky had last night," he said to all of us.

Ms. Mosley stood up. "No! Don't do this, Dr. Pelchat."

"Rocky took the bed sheet from his bed and tied it as tight as he could around the door knob," Dr. Pelchat explained.

I heard gasps and sighs around the room. Daniel covered his face with his hands.

"Please, Dr. Pelchat," Ms. Mosley pleaded.

Ignoring her, he continued, "And then he tied it around his neck. Then he got the idea that, if he ran down the hallway as fast as he could, he could break his neck and kill himself. That's what he did. He ran until that door slammed shut and he could not run any farther, and it snapped his neck. It broke his windpipe and he stopped breathing. You know what? He failed. He's not dead. He's lying in a hospital with needles and all kinds of tubes stuck in him so that he can breathe, get nourishment, and so that he can be a vegetable."

Ms. Mosley started to leave. "That's it," she said. "I'm not staying here while you do this to them."

"You will sit here and you will listen with everyone else," Dr. Pelchat commanded. You need to hear everything I have to say, just like the rest of the doctors, nurses, and counselors in here. If you walk out that door, you better not ever walk back in here," he warned.

She scowled at him. "How could you sit here and talk like this in front of them!"

"More than half of them are in here in for trying to do what Rocky tried last night! They are here because they can't kill themselves right, just like Rocky couldn't. But you see," he said, now turning his attention back to us, "all of you are here, alive, and are able to feed yourselves, dress yourselves, and say what you want and need. Rocky will never be able to do that again. He is going to have to live the rest of his life in a wheelchair as a paraplegic. His mother is going to have to feed him through a tube, and wash and dress him, and when he has to use the bathroom -"

Everyone made noises and looked around at each other.

"That's right," he said. "She's going to have to change his diaper like he's a baby."

We all looked at each other with grossed-out faces.

Ms. Mosley sat back down and looked devastated, as though she was just realizing what was going on. She put her hand over her mouth and started to sob. Daniel stared down at the floor with tears in his eyes. He didn't have shoes on, so he couldn't play with shoelaces, so instead he tugged on his socks and stretched them out.

I looked at Janine, who was still laying her head on Daniel's shoulder, and her arms were still wrapped around him. A feeling came inside of me that made me want to push Janine away from him. I slowly stretched out my arm and placed my hand on Daniel's shoulder. Janine looked at my hand and then looked at me. I pretended not to notice her looking at me. I gave Daniel's shoulder a gentle squeeze, and then pulled my hand away. He didn't move. He kept looking down at his socks. Janine took her arms from around his waist and just kept her head on his shoulder. Tai looked at me and shook her head.

Dr. Pelchat said to Ms. Mosley, "I know you were on watch last night, and I know you feel responsible. You are not responsible for this."

She was crying. She began, "Yes, I know, but I can't help -"

"Don't," Dr. Pelchat stopped her. "We will talk about this later in my office, but right now I want to talk to them."

Ms. Mosley wiped her face and nodded. She tried to straighten up.

Dr. Pelchat turned his attention back to us. "I called this meeting because I want you all to hear me. I want the words that are coming out of my mouth to be the first thing you hear today, so that you can take it in, think about it, and keep it from here on out. What Rocky tried to do last night, you know, the whole suicide attempt, is not an option. Let's just get it out there. *It is not an option.* It's not an option out *there*." He pointed to a window. "And it is most certainly not an option in *here*."

He paused and looked around the room at all of us.

"If you feel like whatever is going on in your life is so bad that you cannot get through it, I'm just going to tell you right now that is not possible. Every problem has a solution. Suicide is not it. It's just not. Because that attempt to take your own life can make life so much worse than that little problem that you thought you could never get out of. Instead of getting out of a problem, suicide will only add more problems, both to your life and to everyone else's around you."

His words cut deep into my soul. He was speaking directly to me.

"I know some of you can't help your emotions. You get angry and you don't know why. You start crying for what seems like no reason at all. Some of you blame everything on yourself, and you feel like the whole world is ending. Nobody can understand it. Nobody knows how this feels. Do they? No. They don't know what it is like when you feel like God has put a two-ton bag of bricks on your shoulders and He tells you that you have to stand up straight with your head erect, and you have to point your chin to the sky and keep a big smile on your face. Then you feel like you're being forced to walk like that with those bricks strapped to your back for the rest of your life. They can't even imagine how that feels! You feel like you are so alone and that there is nobody who can relate or understand. They all think you're crazy! That's why *you* are here, right?

Wrong! *We* are here. The people who understand you and who do not think that you are crazy are right here. It's me. It's Dr. Finch. It's Dr. Bent. It's Ms. Karen Mosley, Geoffrey, and Mr. Anton. It's all of us who come here every single day because we know exactly what is going on. Do you think we are here just because we have to collect a paycheck? If that's what you think, you are wrong. It might be that way in some places, but not here at Bent Creek. Do you know why all of us are here for you every day? Because we know what it's like to be where you are right now."

I looked at him, shocked. Everyone seemed to be listening intently.

"Everyone you see here knows exactly how you feel, and some of us have been in the same place as you. You *do* have people to talk to here. There are people who care about you and who will be there for you twenty-four hours a day. If any of you want to talk about what happened last night, don't hold back. You talk about it. Talk about it to each other, your families, and talk to your doctors and the counselors. Those are your options. Suicide is *not* an option."

CHAPTER 31

"I think Dr. Pelchat took it personally when Rocky tried to kill himself," said Tai as we ate our breakfast in the cafeteria.

Tai, Janine, Daniel, Mena, and two others sat at a table together. I sat next to Daniel after grabbing a bowl of cereal. Mena had a smirk on her face. I watched her as she buttered her toast. She had too much attitude. It was as if she thought that she knew everything. I felt like I would not get along with her.

"Rocky was his patient," Tai told us.

"Can we not talk about this?" Daniel said as he tried to eat his toast.

"It's more than that," Mena commented.

Tai narrowed her eyes at her. "How do you figure?"

Mena chuckled.

She shook her head saying, "Don't you know anything?"

She looked at all of us. Our silence showed that we had no idea what she was talking about. Tai seemed very irritated and aggravated. Mena snickered. She looked at Tai.

Mena said, "I'm sorry. This must be your first time in a place like this."

"You don't know me!" Tai snapped back at her.

I felt the tension rise between Tai and Mena.

Daniel said, "This is not about you! This is about what happened to our friend last night. Rocky is lying in a hospital with his head in a box, and he is fighting for his life! Did you think about that?"

The girls looked away from each other with shame. At least Tai looked like she was ashamed. Mena just kept a straight face and remained quiet. She picked up her breakfast tray and walked away from the table.

When she was gone, Tai seemed to be relieved.

She said, "That girl is seriously asking for a beat down."

As we sat at the table, I wondered what Mena had meant. I should have just ignored her like everyone else did, but the thought only lingered.

Our first group meeting with Dr. Bent took place after breakfast. We all sat around a long table, and Dr. Bent wanted to discuss our thoughts and feelings about what had happened to Rocky. At first, there weren't any volunteers who wanted to share. Dr. Bent seemed to like it when she had volunteers to speak. Daniel, who was more open than the rest of us, was in his own world this morning. He sat in his chair, silently staring down at his shoes. He wasn't even picking at his shoelaces. It was the most silent I had ever seen him.

When I closed my eyes, I still saw Rocky lying on the stretcher with his head barely attached to his body. His face was stone-blue, and he looked dead. I shuddered as I flashed back to that scene. Daniel must have been seeing the whole thing repeatedly in his mind.

"I keep hearing the door slam when he did it, and it woke me up. He was on the floor," Daniel sobbed to Dr. Bent. "If I hadn't fallen asleep while he was talking to me, maybe I could have stopped him."

"It's not your fault, Daniel," Dr. Bent said. "You know it's not your fault. Don't do that to yourself."

Daniel shook his head and said, "I know it's not my fault. I just wish I had been awake. He had been saying stuff, and I didn't know what he was talking about. I thought he was just trying to bother me like he always did at night. He never liked to sleep. He'd just lie there and make weird noises or talk to himself. I swear, I didn't know."

"Oh, God! I need a cigarette," Tai said as she slapped herself in the forehead miserably.

Daniel raised his head to that.

"Rocky was thirteen, and he smoked, too," he said. "He was thirteen and he wanted to die. I know what that's like. I was the same way. Why didn't I catch that? Why didn't I see it coming?"

Daniel's voice faded out, and his sobs turned to heavy cries. He cried so hard that he made tears come out of my eyes. Janine shook her head and started to get up and go to him, but Dr. Bent reached him first. While she stood next to him, she picked up the telephone and called someone to come get Daniel, because she didn't think that he needed to be in Group. Within a minute, Dr. Finch came into the room without knocking. He told Daniel to come with him. Daniel seemed relieved to be leaving with his doctor. Rocky's suicide attempt may have been too much for him to talk about in Group Therapy.

When Daniel and Dr. Finch were gone, Dr. Bent moved in on Mena, who was sitting cross-legged on the end of the long table. She was leaning back and had her arms folded across her chest. She was staring up at the ceiling, letting the bright hospital lights burn into her eyes. She didn't blink once. Dr. Bent called out to her. Mena moved her head slowly and fixed her eyes on Dr. Bent, who was at the opposite end of the table.

"How old are you, Mena?" Dr. Bent asked.

"I'm seventeen," she said.

Dr. Bent boldly asked, "Would you care to share with us what brought you here?"

Mena shook her head while keeping her eyes on Dr. Bent, as if she didn't trust her.

Dr. Bent leaned forward. She said in a calm voice, "No one here will judge you, Mena."

"Everything I say can stay in this room, and no one will judge me or hold it against me because we are all in this together...blah...blah...blah...blah.

I know all of this," Mena said to Dr. Bent.

Dr. Bent was sitting back in her seat with her arms folded across her chest, silently staring at Mena.

Mena looked away from Dr. Bent. She said, "I have 'anger problems', or so they say."

"So who say?" asked Dr. Bent.

Mena sighed. "The judge who put me here for four weeks," she said. "I guess four weeks is the longest I can be here at this place."

Dr. Bent nodded. "Yes, four weeks is the longest any patient can be here. This is a short-term hospital. If you don't show any progress as it gets closer to four weeks' time, then arrangements are made with a long-term facility."

"Well, I don't plan on being here that long," Mena made clear. "I'm just here because that judge thinks I have these 'anger problems,' and I don't. So..."

"Well, what happened to make the judge say that you had anger problems?" Dr. Bent kept pressing the subject.

Mena was getting frustrated. "Don't you have suicidal people to talk to? Didn't you just have a kid kill himself last night, right here in this hospital?"

"Dr. Pelchat's your doctor, right?"

Mena nodded.

"Dr. Pelchat is a wonderful doctor. I'm sure you will get the treatment you need so that you don't have to go to a long-term hospital."

Mena didn't respond. She looked back up at the ceiling and stared into the bright light. Dr. Bent left Mena alone and started talking to Tai, who said that it wasn't fair that, after a situation like what had happened the night before, they all couldn't have a cigarette. Dr. Bent laughed, and other people joined in, I guess because they wanted cigarettes too.

After Dr. Bent's Group Therapy meeting, and on the way back to the

Adolescent Unit, Mena kept staring at me. She looked down at me, and I thought she was trying to intimidate me. I didn't like her. I didn't like to be stared at, and she could tell that it was making me upset, but she kept on staring.

"Are you worried about your boyfriend?" she asked me suddenly.

I looked at her, shocked. I must have had a stupid expression on my face, because she smirked. I didn't respond to her. I tried to ignore her to make her feel like she was talking to herself.

"You know who I'm talking about," she carried on. "The little baby that was crying back there. You know, the one who let his roommate break his neck."

I turned to her. I almost opened my mouth. Something told me to hold it in and not say anything back to her. Instead of giving in, I walked past her to the counselor's desk. I stayed there to avoid her. Where there was authority, I noticed she'd try to stay as far away as possible. Mena went to the Girls' Unit. I sighed in relief.

Suddenly a feeling inside of me that I had not felt in a long time took over me. Mr. Anton was behind the counter, and I asked him for a blank sheet of paper and a pencil. He asked me if I was going to write a letter, and I told him that I didn't know what I was going to write. I just felt like writing.

He handed over the paper and pencil and, while he handed it to me, he said, "Most writers make masterpieces while they are in a place like Bent Creek."

I nodded my head. "Maybe," I responded.

I quickly sat down at the table and started writing. I didn't stop until my fingers cramped up and my mind stopped spilling. When I was done, I scanned the paper, and realized that none of it seemed to make sense. They were just words on paper that had responded to a strong feeling inside of me. It didn't matter if it made sense, because I'd just had to write it out.

I folded the sheet of paper, stuck it in my back pocket, and returned the pencil to Mr. Anton. I went to the bedroom, and Janine was not in there. My silver butterfly sat peacefully on the table next to my bed. My heart was pounding as I stared at the sharp, shiny wings. I picked the butterfly up off the table. Mr. Sharp always made it okay. I didn't need to understand anything else. I didn't need to write again. I didn't need to find a cure, or an answer, and I didn't feel like I needed to cry. That's why Mr. Sharp was there.

I lifted my pant leg and pressed the cold, silver wing to my leg, and it made me shudder. The pain reminded me of the last time I had pressed something sharp to my skin. I wasn't used to the pain again. I couldn't do it. I took the butterfly in my fist and I squeezed it in anger.

No! No! Don't you dare cry, Kristen! No! I threw the butterfly down onto the table and cried. Why did I let Mena get to me? Why did I do it?

Mr. Sharp was sitting on the table, holding my butterfly in his hand. He shoved it towards me, but I just lay there, staring at him. He shook his head in disappointment. I closed my eyes and let him disappear from my mind as I tried not to think of my upcoming meeting with Dr. Pelchat.

CHAPTER 32

Dr. Pelchat did not come right out and ask me to talk about what had brought me to Bent Creek. When we were in his office, he sat behind his desk, as usual, with my chart open. He scanned through the chart and kept the same calm, but stern, look on his face. He looked up at me and sighed deeply.

"What?" I asked nervously.

He shrugged his shoulders and said, "I don't know, Kristen."

He seemed very strange to me. I shook my head. "I don't know, either," I said with a sigh.

Dr. Pelchat said, "I think that I'm starting to have an idea about you from your behavioral pattern. The notes that were left for me are very vague, kind of like Dr. Cuvo himself, but I can learn something from what was written. Is it true that, while you were in the hospital, right after meeting with Dr. Cuvo for the first time, you started banging your wrists on the side of your bed?"

I turned red in embarrassment. I felt my cheeks get hot.

"Does it say that?" I asked him.

"Yes, it does," he said. "You expressed this rage, and had to be sedated to control your behavior. This has happened twice since your hospitalization."

"Yes, that one time after I met Dr. Cuvo at the main hospital, and then when I was put in the BCR," I admitted.

I felt like some kind of criminal who had to tell the truth in front of a judge in court. If you lied, you could be sent to jail for life. Dr. Pelchat had that way about him that made you feel like you had to tell the truth.

"It also says here that you expressed some worry when you first arrived here at Bent Creek. You were worried that it would be like a prison, and that you would be sort of an outcast from your peers and that they would ridicule you. Then your attitude seemed to change very quickly. You began to show a nurturing attitude towards your peers as you grew comfortable. Even so, I'm concerned about your mood swings. We had to put you in the BCR because of your outburst. In addition, when you were in the hospital, you first appeared calm to Dr. Cuvo, but when he left, your emotions and your mood changed very quickly. You became violent."

"I'm not going to hurt anyone, if you are thinking that. I don't want to hurt anyone. I don't know what came over me that day when they put me in the BCR and had to stick me with the needle. I was just...I mean, I was..."

"You were angry," he said.

"Yes," I replied.

"What about when you first met Dr. Cuvo?"

I didn't know what to say except the truth. "When I was angry in the hospital, it wasn't at Dr. Cuvo."

"You were not angry with him at all?"

"I was mean to him, and I was mad because I didn't want to deal with a doctor. I didn't want to be there."

"Where did you want to be?"

"I don't know. Not in the hospital," I said.

Then, there was silence. All I could do was stare down at my bandaged wrists and not say a word. I had no idea what he was getting at, but he was scaring me. I tried to hold back the tears.

He said, "I just need to ask you a few questions that will help me administer the right test for you."

"All right," I agreed.

"Do you ever get the feeling that the people you love or trust will leave you or abandon you?"

"What do you mean?" I asked.

"Do you ever feel like, when you do something that you know may not be so pleasing to, say, your mother, that she'll leave you or abandon you somehow?"

I thought about her signing me away to Bent Creek. And I thought about the times when we'd have our talks. She always made me feel like I had to go along with what she wanted, and that what she said was the only way, even if it didn't feel right. If I didn't go along with her, I knew she'd be angry enough to get rid of me if she had a chance. That's what she'd done when she'd made me go to Bent Creek. I nodded positively to Dr. Pelchat.

He scribbled in my chart and then asked, "Do you ever feel like something always has to be happening in your life, and if it's not, you get a feeling of emptiness?"

I could tell that he was reading the questions from a sheet, but he was trying to put the questions into his own words so that I could understand. That question made me think.

"When it was quiet and I was alone, I would get scared," I told him. "It felt like the world was ending sometimes, and it just scared me, like there was no one that existed but me."

Dr. Pelchat looked into my eyes. That made me nervous, and I looked away.

He said, "You're a cutter, right?"

I nodded.

"Who am I here with?"

Shocked, I turned back towards him. My heart jumped inside of my chest. I could feel something else pulling inside of me.

"What do you mean?" I asked.

"Do you ever feel like you're not yourself? Like, when you get these wild ideas in your head, does it feel like someone else is putting those thoughts in there? Maybe an influence, like a voice, or maybe you see other people whom others cannot see?"

Mr. Sharp suddenly appeared. He was just itching to come out. Up to now, I had been able to keep him locked inside, but Dr. Pelchat was pushing his buttons. I didn't want to end up in the BCR again. I tried to hold back.

I answered, "I don't know what you mean by wild ideas. I do think that things can happen, and will happen, if I make certain choices. Maybe feeling like the world is ending when I feel empty is a little wild, but-"

"How about this," he asked. "How about I put it in a different way? Answer this as honestly as you can. If your mom comes over to you, and she starts hugging you and smiling, and giving you gifts because she says that you are doing an amazing job in school by making good grades, attending all of your classes, and doing all those things, how do you take that behavior?"

I said, "I'd think that she was proud of me and that she was happy."

"Okay," he said. "Now how about if, the next day, after she was hugging you and smiling, and giving you all of those gifts, she just storms over to you and starts yelling at you, and she tells you that she needs you to help out more around the house, like cleaning your room, helping with chores, and trying to put more effort into the upkeep of your home than you do at school? How would you take that behavior?"

"Honestly, I'd probably cut," I admitted.

"Why do you feel that you have to punish yourself?"

"It's like it's too much. I don't understand how she can be happy with me one day and then just be mad at me the next because I didn't clean the kitchen. I'd think that she didn't care about the good job I did in school. All she would care about is how I didn't clean the kitchen or do a good job in the house. It wouldn't even matter anymore that I did well in school. She'd just want to be mad at me and punish me."

Dr. Pelchat didn't say a word. The look on his face was genuinely sincere with concern. He scribbled in my chart. As he did, I began to wonder if I had done the right thing by answering honestly.

Dr. Pelchat looked up when he was finished writing, and he said, "You will be taking the test this week. I'm writing an order to have this done no later than Wednesday, and I'm writing an order for you to see a physician about your stitches."

My heart began to race. "Why did you ask me all of those questions?"

"Like I said, it will help me determine what kind of psychological test I need to administer. It also helps with me with your diagnosis."

"What's my diagnosis?"

"I'm not going to mark it officially until after you take the test," he said.

"Do you have any idea?"

"Kristen," he said.

"Please, Dr. Pelchat," I begged. "As hard as it was for me, I sat here and I was completely honest with you, and I answered your questions. Could you please tell me something?"

He looked at me with sincere eyes. He opened my chart back up and scanned through his notes. "I'm not making this official," he said. "You have symptoms of what is called Borderline Personality Disorder."

I sat back in my chair. "A personality disorder?" I asked. "You mean, like I split into different personalities like Chris and Jake? What do you mean?"

"No," he said. "Not like that. It's Borderline. It means that a person with BPD is suffering from a split in their personality that borders them on psychosis and neurosis. Do you understand?"

I shook my head.

"On the borderline of psychosis and neurosis. Psychosis is an impaired state of mind. There are the delusions, the twisted perceptions, and personality changes that you have displayed here. And then there's neurosis, which is a mental imbalance that can cause you to be stressed, and it often causes depression, but it does not prevent you from making rash decisions and functioning normally in everyday life."

"So, I'm just a confused person?" I was certainly confused now. "That doesn't make any sense, Dr. Pelchat. It has to be one or the other."

He looked worried. "I shouldn't have said anything. I apologize, Kristen. This is not your official diagnosis. But now that I've told you about this disorder, and just in case, I feel that you should educate yourself."

He reached into his desk drawer and pulled out a thick, paperback book. He placed the book in my hands. The cover of the book was black and white. There was a picture of a woman on the front cover. She was staring into a mirror. The mirror was split in two. One side of the mirror the woman was smiling and wearing all black and on the other side of the mirror, she was wearing all white, and she was frowning. It reminded me of a yin-yang symbol, and the comedy and tragedy theatrical sign.

He said, "Read this book. It may not be the best book on the subject, but it will give you a better understanding of Borderline Personality Disorder. When you read it, please do not take everything in it personally. It doesn't all pertain to every BPD sufferer. It's more of a general textbook on the disorder. I would like for you to read it to gain some understanding of BPD."

I took the book and tried not to look scared. I didn't want to have Borderline Personality Disorder. I wanted to go home. Scared, I stood up when Dr. Pelchat stood up.

He said to me, "I'm going to speak with you and your mother tomorrow during your session."

"It's going to be a family session?" This didn't comfort me at all.

Dr. Pelchat said, "It's not going to be a family session. You probably won't have one of those until you are ready to leave Bent Creek. We are just going to touch basis with your mom on your progress and let her know about the testing. It will be all right."

I nodded, trusting him.

"Come on. I'll take you back to the unit. Please read that book when you get a chance."

I knew I should have trusted Dr. Pelchat, but the thoughts in my mind were racing. I could just picture how this meeting was going to go with Mom, Dr. Pelchat, and me. I could see Mom angry and fighting to remain calm while Dr. Pelchat told her what was going on. Then, when she had her chance, she'd pounce on me with her harsh words and anger, and blame me for causing all of this trouble. I was useless. She told me what she needed and expected of me, and I seemed only to make things worse.

CHAPTER 33

That night, after our group meeting with Ms. Mosley, we all sat around and waited for Geoffrey to tell us it was time to go to bed. I was sitting on the sofa with the book that Dr. Pelchat had given me. Nervousness prevented me from opening it. I just kept looking at the cover and reading the back of the book over and over again.

Everyone who had to take medication had lined up at the nurse's station and were waiting for their pills. Janine was in line, and she was standing behind Mena and in front of Daniel. I noticed Daniel staring at her. His eyes were low, and he hung back like he was checking her out. I sat the book down on the occasional table near the sofa. Then I got up, walked over to Janine, and touched her shoulder. She looked at me and smiled. Daniel smiled at me as if he was happy to see me.

"Do you have to take nighttime medication?" Janine asked.

"It was boring, sitting over there by myself," I told them.

Daniel laughed. He said, "Yeah, we need a game system in here, like an Xbox...or *something*."

I laughed, and stumbled back. Stumbling caused a chain reaction. I bumped into Janine, and Janine accidentally bumped into Mena. Janine jumped back and scooted next to Daniel, which made it look, from Mena's point of view, like I had hit her. When she turned around, she saw me standing there.

"I apologize, Mena," I said to her.

She moved in close to me and stung me with her eyes. She got so close that I thought she was going to hit me.

Mena said, "It's not business. It's personal."

"What?" I asked.

"Mena Suarez!" the nurse called out to her.

Mena turned to the nurse and realized just then that it was her turn to get her medicine. The nurse placed the cup of water and the small cup with the medicine in it on the table.

"It's time for your medicine," the nurse said in a sweet voice.

Mena gulped down the medicine. When the nurse was finished checking her mouth, Mena turned around and brushed past us without saying a word. She went straight to the Girls' Unit. Janine looked at me and shook her head as she walked up to the nurse to receive her medicine. I looked at Daniel, who was chuckling to himself.

He said, "That girl is crazy. I thought Tai was messed up. Looks like Tai has met her match."

I kept an eye on Janine. She was sorting out her medication with the nurse. I used that opportunity to talk with Daniel.

I said, "Are you feeling okay?"

He stopped chuckling and his smile disappeared. He nodded and looked away from me.

I smiled and said, "Okay."

The nurse called Daniel up to the counter. I moved out of his way, and, as he stepped up, Janine walked up to me and said, "Come on, let's go to the room. They are going to tell us to go to bed soon anyway."

I grabbed the book off the table and caught up with Janine. As we walked off to the Girls' Unit, I looked back at Daniel. He swallowed his pills without the water, and the nurse checked his mouth. When he was finished, he stepped out of line. Janine and I were about to go through the doors to the Girls' Unit when Daniel looked over at us. I knew I wouldn't see Daniel for the rest of the night. Yet, I didn't want to let him go without knowing that he was okay for sure. When he looked at me, our eyes locked. I gave him a warm smile. He took a deep breath, making his chest rise fast. Then, as he exhaled, he let it slowly fall. Before I followed Janine out of the room, I saw him return a smile to me.

CHAPTER 34

During visiting hours the next day, there was a lot of talk about Rocky. Everyone seemed to have different versions of Rocky's suicide attempt. They made up stories of how it happened, and what the counselors had been doing while he had hurt himself. The truth was, no one really knew exactly what had happened, and how it had happened, except Dr. Pelchat, because it was his job to know.

Daniel was in counseling with his mother and Dr. Finch. A lot of the parents who were visiting seemed to be upset and concerned over Rocky and about their kids' safety. My mother in particular was very upset.

Dr. Pelchat led us to his office, which was across from Dr. Cuvo's old office. Mom and I sat down in the chairs that faced Dr. Pelchat's desk. He didn't bother to open my chart as he normally did, but he seemed to want to get right down to business. Mom was determined, too.

Mom began, "What is going on around here? Is it true that a child committed suicide? How are we supposed to trust our children in your care if you don't have people working here that can prevent these things from happening?"

Dr. Pelchat sat back in his chair. He didn't look upset or bothered. He crossed his left leg over his right and leaned back with his chin up and his right hand rubbing his stubble.

"I understand your concern. Please let me assure you that Kristen, as well as the other patients here, are in the best care of our counselors, nurses, and doctors. What happened to the patient the other night was an unforeseen event. My counselors were on task and keeping watch. You must understand that there are thirty-eight beds in total on the Adolescent Ward. More than half of those beds are filled right now. We don't keep eyes on them when they are in their beds, asleep, every single minute. We do night checks, and we keep watch at night. The patients in the Adolescent Ward are responsible enough, once admitted to their rooms and are moved from Level One, to be trusted on their own at night. Unfortunately, the patient that was hurt was an exception. If it serves as comfort to you, the young man is not dead. The staff that was on duty that night was able to get him medical attention before his condition worsened."

My mother looked at me, and then coldly turned to Dr. Pelchat. "How can I be assured that Kristen will not be in any danger of trying to commit suicide again?"

"Mom," I pleaded.

"That's up to Kristen," Dr. Pelchat said. He looked at me. "Kristen makes her own choices, just like Rocky did. We will, however, move her back to Level One, take away her privileges, and that limits her freedom on the ward, if we feel that she is in danger or in need of that extra attention. But Kristen seems to be progressing fine. I don't think that we have anything to worry about." He smiled at me slightly.

I turned to my mother and sighed. Mom kept her eyes on Dr. Pelchat. She seemed satisfied to hear his assurance.

She said, "So, what happened to Dr. Cuvo? I thought that he was Kristen's doctor."

Finally! I thought to myself.

"That is one of the things I wanted to discuss with you today," Dr. Pelchat told her. "Dr. Cuvo is no longer a part of our staff. His contract with us has ended. I am Kristen's doctor now. I meet with her every day, just as Dr. Cuvo did. I will prescribe and monitor her medications. First, I have ordered a psychological test for Kristen so that I can give her a proper diagnosis. Then I will be able to prescribe the right kind of medications that will help her. I don't want to just put her on something and hope that it works. I would really like her to get the right help so that she can recover and leave Bent Creek, and hopefully not have to come back here for in-patient treatment again."

"I would like that, too," Mom said.

"Kristen has been doing very well in her meetings with me, and with her groups and the counselors. The transition from her treatment with Dr. Cuvo to me has progressed well. Transitioning can be a bit difficult for most patients because they form trusting relationships with their doctors, and this trust takes time to build. I want all of us - you, me and Kristen - to be able to work together at some point in opening the communication up between the two of you, and eventually in a family meeting that will include Kristen's siblings."

My heart jumped.

Dr. Pelchat continued, "Because once you are out of here, Kristen, you may only see me once a week for out-patient treatment. You will need to be able to open up to your mother."

"And you," he said, turning to Mom again, "should be able to be there for her when she needs to come to you. Kristen is not in a normal situation. If she were, she wouldn't be here. Right?"

"Yes, well," Mom began. "I hope we can do *something* to help her. Why do you have to give her a test? Is it for any particular mental health disorder or illness?"

Without hesitation, Dr. Pelchat said, "I'm going to test her for Borderline Personality Disorder."

"What is Borderline Personality Disorder? Is it some kind of disease?" Mom asked.

"It's not a disease. It's not something that you can catch, like a cold," Dr. Pelchat said with a little aggravation in his tone. "BPD has to do with emotional irregularities, meaning that something that may affect you and me, in what would be considered a normal way, might not necessarily effect a person with BPD in that way. The emotion becomes so much more intense than it should be, or we could see a major *lack* of emotion compared to what is considered normal. BPD is a complicated and sensitive disorder that requires treatment, and patients need careful monitoring of medication. That is why I want to give Kristen this test so that I can properly diagnose her and give her the right treatment."

Mom sighed and shook her head in disbelief. She said, "How did this happen? How did she get this Borderline Personality Disorder?"

"Honestly, right now I can't pinpoint exactly what caused it in Kristen. If the test shows that she should be diagnosed with BPD, then I will find out why so that we can conquer it. But most studies have shown that BPD usually develops around her age, and it is common in women who have suffered abuse as a child, and also patients who have parents who have the disorder."

When Mom heard that, she gasped and sat back in the chair. She shook her head.

"I see," Mom said. "Well, you know, Kristen seems to have so many problems. I mean, look at her arms! You see how she started cutting herself up and doing all of these self-destructive things. I want her to get some kind of help that will make her stop this. I feel like it's my fault because she doesn't talk to me. She's mad at me or something. That's why she did this!" She gestured to my wrists.

I hid my wrists in my lap and looked down, trying to hold back tears. I hated when she blamed herself for the mess I caused. She probably didn't really feel like it was her fault, but she sounded convincing. She wanted Dr. Pelchat to feel sorry for her and see what she had to go through and deal with. What she had to deal with was me. Her problem child. Her disturbed and sick daughter. The daughter that should have been dead weeks ago.

Mom went on. "And my son. He watches everything Kristen does. He looks up to her. I'm sure she's told you what happened to our family, and what happened to my son, Nicholas."

"Mom, no, please," I said. I couldn't hold my tears back any longer.

"Nicholas and Alison are my two youngest children. They are twins. Nicholas was molested by my husband, Jack. Jack's not Kristen's father. He's the twins' father."

I reached out and tried to grab my mother's arm, and I begged her to stop, but she grabbed my hand and squeezed affectionately, which made my tears come out even harder. Listening to Mom talk about our family was heart-wrenching. The metal ball turned in my chest so hard that I felt as though my heart was going to explode. I wanted her to stop it, but she only made it worse.

"No one knew what was going on. But when everything was brought out into the open, and my husband was locked up, the judge ordered that I send Nicholas to a doctor for counseling. It has helped him so much. I wish that I had thought to get Kristen into counseling as well, because then we probably wouldn't even be here. Nicholas would never try anything like this. But if he sees his big sister, whom he looks up to so much, doing this, then I'm afraid that he's going to get all kinds of thoughts in his head."

No, I thought. Not Nick. He knows that he has people who are there for him. He was the one who was hurt. He was the one who needed counseling after what had happened to him. Not me.

Why was I behaving this way? Why did I feel this way? Why did I want to die? Sitting inside that office, listening to Mom spill all of our secrets, I was reminded of that feeling that I had felt weeks before, when I had picked up the bottle of pills and had washed as many down as I could before I'd started feeling nauseated. I'd stood over the bathroom sink with Nick's face fresh in my mind.

One pill for Nick. Another pill for each tear Nick had shed while Jack had thrust his disgusting genitals inside of him. I had a hard time swallowing those pills down because of the fear that rose up inside me from knowing what I was about to do. The bitter taste and chalkiness of the pills made me sick. I finally chewed and swallowed the pills down, along with the fear. "This has to be done", I told myself. Then I started over.

One pill for losing my Daddy. Two pills for me standing there and watching everything happen. Three pills for not screaming. Four pills for not moving. Five pills for finally having the proof and not running to the phone right away. Six pills for my stupid mouth dropping wide open and not making a sound. Seven pills for knowing what was going on all along. Eight pills for not doing a damn thing about it. Nine pills for crying about it every night since that day, and not being able to sleep. Ten pills for hating Lexus and John. After ten pills, I tilted my head back and emptied the rest of the bottle into my throat. I choked and chewed those chalky pills down. I thought that last one was for Nick.

As I felt myself fading away after taking the pills, I saw clearly in my mind the day everything fell apart. The day Nick was sick and had to stay home from school. The day Mom asked me to stay with him, but I told her that I had to go to school because I was too concerned about a stupid test that I didn't want to miss. When the truth was, I didn't want to be home in that horrible house full of monsters. I could feel it every day and every night. Besides, Nick was old enough to stay home from school by himself for a few hours. He could take care of himself until three o'clock, when Alison and I got home from school. Being stupid and selfish, I went to school, and there wasn't any test. I convinced Mom, though, and she finally agreed that Nick would be all right.

I didn't expect to see Jack's truck in the yard when the school bus brought me home from school. He usually didn't get home from work until a little before Mom got home from work. Alison and I should have gotten home first. When I went to unlock the front door, I saw that the door was already slightly open. I pushed the door open quietly and entered the house. After I closed the door, I tried to stay quiet as I headed towards Nicholas' bedroom.

As I moved closer, I heard strange noises--smothered cries, hard grunting, and growling, like an angry dog. The noises grew louder as I got closer to Nick's bedroom door. My heart nearly jumped out of my chest when I heard those smothered cries. Nicky was crying. He was hurt. Naturally, I rushed over to his door, but before I could put my hand on the doorknob and push the door open, I was stunned and paralyzed by what I could see through the crack.

"Nick!" I screamed.

I thought I screamed. I opened my mouth, but nothing came out. I couldn't move. I couldn't speak. I couldn't do anything but watch Jack push himself into Nick while he buried Nick's head in the pillow, face down. Nick was smothering in his own tears and the pillow. Jack pushed and pushed. With each push, Nick screamed and cried harder. He couldn't breathe! His face was in the pillow to smother his cries.

I heard him. I could have stopped him, but I didn't. I didn't stop Jack. Jack stopped himself when he came. He fell, exhausted, on top of Nick's little body. Nick stopped screaming and laid limp, face-down, in the pillow. That's when I moved. That's when I screamed. That's when I was sure that the demon had killed my little brother.

"Nick!" I screamed and screamed his name at the top of my lungs, afraid that he was dead.

When Jack heard me, he looked up. He saw me standing in the doorway, screaming and scared out of my mind. Jack jumped up from on top of Nick, and he pulled himself out of him. His private parts were swinging everywhere. Frightened, I ran into the kitchen and picked up the phone. I didn't hear the phone ring, but when I picked up, Mom was on the line.

"Kristen?" she called out to me. "The phone didn't even ring once. How did you know I was calling?"

"Mom," I cried. "Mom, please come home! Mom, please!"

She heard the panic in my voice. "Kristen, I'm in the car right now. I'm right around the corner. I was just calling to let you know I was coming home early to bring Nick his medicine."

"Kristen!" I then heard Jack yelling at me. He was stumbling down the hallway as he tried to put his clothes back on.

Afraid, I dropped the phone without even hanging up. Then I ran over quickly to the sink and grabbed Mom's chef knife. I grabbed the biggest one that I knew would do the most damage.

At that moment, Alison came through the front door and called out to me. With the knife in hand I ran to the living room, to the front door, and Jack met me there. Alison stood at the door, seeing the knife in my hand. Jack didn't say a word, nor did he hesitate. He ran past me and pushed Alison out of his way, and then rushed out of the front door. Alison called out to her daddy and ran out after him. I followed her and grabbed her when we got outside so that she wouldn't try to run too far after him. Jack ran down the street and then disappeared around the corner.

Alison snatched away from me angrily. She looked up at me, afraid.

"Why did Daddy run away? Why do you have a knife in your hand? Kristen, I'm scared." She was only eight years old, but she'd known that something was wrong.

"Alison, everything is okay," I told her. "Right now I need you to be a big girl for me."

"But Kristen," she whined.

"Please, Alison," I pleaded. "I need you to go into your room and close the door. You know our favorite movie?"

"Yes," she said. "Peter Pan."

"That's right," I said. "Peter Pan, because you've got a crush on Peter, don't you?"

I was trying to distract her and make her forget about what had just happened. I forced a convincing smile.

She giggled and nodded. "Peter's cute, and he can fly."

"Yes, he sure can! Tinkerbelle, too!"

Her innocent eyes began to sparkle, and she laughed. I knew that she was starting to become distracted. Her mind was on Peter Pan. She wasn't worried about what had been going on. We walked back into the house and I moved her along towards her bedroom. As we walked by, I sat the knife down on an occasional table in the living room. I shoved Alison along so that she wouldn't notice as we passed by.

She said, "I love Tinkerbelle."

"Me too," I told her. "So, I need you to go into your room and close your door. Like a big girl, I want you to put your Peter Pan movie in the DVD player, like I showed you before. You remember?"

She nodded with the same smile on her face.

"Okay. That's my big girl. Can you go do that for me, right now?"

"I sure can," she said as we went back into the house. "Are you and Nick going to watch Peter Pan with me?"

"Why don't you go ahead and get it started? I will go check on Nick. Remember, he's sick. Stay in your room while I check on him. Don't come out until I come in there to watch the movie with you."

"Kristen, what if I have to go pee?"

"If you have to go pee, just yell out the door first," I told her.

She looked up at me dubiously and tilted her head.

"Go ahead!" I forced while tickling her.

She laughed and struggled to get me to stop tickling her. I kept tickling until I saw that she was amused and not suspicious anymore. She then dropped her book bag on the floor and wiggled away from me, still laughing.

I let her go. As she ran down the hallway that led to the bedrooms, I said, "And don't bother Nick, because he's not feeling well."

"Okay," she said. She ran off to her room without stopping, and she shut her door just as had I asked her to.

When I heard Alison's bedroom door shut, I shuddered. I closed my eyes and took a deep breath. *Mom? Where are you?* I wondered.

I looked out the window to see if, by chance, Mom was pulling in. There was no sign of her. She had said that she was right around the corner. She must have just been leaving her job.

I quickly grabbed the knife off the table and put it back in the kitchen sink. I knew that I had to go to Nick, even if Mom wasn't here. He could still be alive. He could probably be saved. Maybe it wasn't too late.

I was afraid to go in there. I didn't want to see my little brother dead. I didn't want to see him naked and hurt. I slowly approached his bedroom door. Earlier, Jack had shut the door, which made it even harder for me. I slowly turned the knob and pushed the door open.

To my surprise, Nick was on the floor. He was not on the bed with his face down in the pillow anymore. He was lying on the cold, hardwood floor, wrapped in his blanket. He was whimpering softly with sticky tears and drying mucus on his face. He had probably been crying so hard and for so long that he didn't have enough strength to cry anymore. He was just whimpering, looking weak and sick.

I knelt down on the floor beside him, and I smelled Jack's overbearing scent on him. No wonder Jack had made him take showers with him before Mom got home.

I placed my hand on Nicholas' forehead. He was burning up. I wrapped him tighter in the blanket, in the hopes that he would sweat the fever out.

I felt him shivering violently under the blanket.

"Kristen?" he cried out. "I don't feel so well."

I felt a chunk rise in my throat, but I swallowed it back down. "I know, Nickyroo," I said. "I know, baby. Just lie here in my arms."

His large brown eyes looked up at me, pleading. "Did you see Daddy?"

"I'm sorry, baby," I said. It felt like tears were going to fall, but they didn't. There was only hate and anger. But I held onto Nick and looked into his eyes. "He is never going to hurt you again. I won't let him, ever again."

Nick closed his eyes and let his head fall back into my arms. I held him like he was a little baby.

"I'm sorry, Kristen," he said.

"No, baby, no. It's not your fault. It's that monster's fault. Jack is a monster. He hurt you, and now he's going to go where bad people go when they hurt people. You understand?"

Nick tried to nod. That's when Mom ran into the bedroom and, before she could ask what was going on, she saw with her own eyes. I didn't say a word, and everything that she had already suspected, and possibly had already known in the back of her mind, was finally exposed.

Mom shook her head in what seemed like disbelief. It didn't take long for her tears to start falling. She called out to Nick, and he looked over at her. Alison must have heard Mom come through the door, because she came out of her room, ran over to Mom, and hugged her. Mom was still crying and staring at Nick.

I acted quickly and went over to Alison. I took her hand and led her back to her bedroom while Mom tended to Nick. Alison whined that she wanted to see Mom, but I told her that Mom needed to give Nick his medicine, and that she needed to stay in her room until she was told to come out. I sat with her and watched one scene of Peter Pan with her until she felt she'd had enough attention, and I could then leave without a fuss. All the while, it hurt me inside to have to be strong and not cry. The anger was overwhelming me. I wanted to confront Mom with what I had seen.

When I went back into Nick's room, Mom was helping Nick to the bathroom to get him cleaned up and dressed.

"Where is he?" she asked me.

"He ran away," I said. "He ran down the street and around the corner."

"Well, he couldn't have gone far," she said.

"He may have gone to John's house," I added.

"Call Jonathan and Mariah for me," Mom demanded.

I shook my head. "We need to call the police."

"Kristen! Do as I say! Call John's parents right now, and tell them to get over here!"

When John's parents, Jonathan Sr. and Mariah, arrived, they all went into the living room to sit down and talk. John and his little brother, James, were here as well. Nick sat down next to Mom and leaned on her shoulder. Mom wanted to ask that James be excused, but Nick insisted that James needed to stay.

When Mariah asked him why, James admitted that Jack had tried to get him to take a shower with him once when he'd stayed over to play with Nick. James had said no, and Jack hadn't pressed him any more about it. James and John had been very upset then, and now Mariah looked like she was going to cry.

Mom then told them that, according to Nick, Jack had been molesting him, too, and she didn't know how long it had been going on, or that it had even been going on. It was *then* that they all decided to call the police. I opened my mouth to say what I had seen. I wanted to tell Jonathan and Mariah everything, since it was now all out in the open. I felt that I owed it to Nick because I hadn't stopped Jack. I wanted to tell the police too, if it would help.

I began, "When the police get here, I can tell them what-"

Mom immediately shot me down with her cold eyes. She didn't say a word, and it made me shut my mouth.

Jonathan Sr. looked at Mom, and then at me.

"What is it, Kristen? Go on, say it," Jonathan encouraged.

Mom stood up and grabbed my arm. She yanked me off the couch where I was sitting next to her and Nick.

She said, "No. Kristen, go and check on your sister. We can finish up here with Nick. The police will be here soon. I will need you to stay with Alison."

"It seemed like she had something to say," Jonathan pressed.

My mother shoved me off and, when she thought that I was out of earshot, she said to them, "I'm sorry. I don't think it's a good idea to have Kristen around while we do this. She tends to get a bit over-dramatic about things, and she doesn't really know anything about what's going on. It's best to keep her out of this, for her and Alison's sake."

Dr. Pelchat sat back in his chair with a changed expression. At first, he had been calm and seemed emotionally detached to the conversation, but as Mom spoke and told him everything, he seemed to grow concerned.

"Why would you do that?" he asked my mother. "Kristen had seen everything that had happened to her little brother, and you would not give her a chance to speak about it?"

"I was thinking of my son at the time. Everyone was already upset. We didn't need Kristen making things worse and getting us even more upset. She can be a little over-dramatic at times. It's true. Just look at us, sitting here in this place. And she's the cause of it. It's always been this way with her. So, I didn't know what else to do but just send her away."

"Mom, no!" I cried. "It's my entire fault. It's my fault."

"No, Kristen. It isn't your fault," I heard Dr. Pelchat say. "None of it is your fault. You had every right to speak about what you saw."

Dr. Pelchat seemed to make sense, but my head was a stuffed-up mess. I put my face in my hands and cried until I was sure blood was going to gush out. The pain in my chest from the metal ball shot up and down as I gasped for air.

My head was full of the cries of pain, and the cries of betrayal of trust.

"How could you? How could you hurt us, you bastard?" My mother screamed to Jack as the police shoved him, handcuffed at the wrists and feet, into the patrol car.

I silently watched from the living room window. Jonathan Sr. and Mariah stood beside Mom and Nick as the police prepared to take them down to the station to make their statements. Jonathan Sr., Jack's brother, watched in silent anger. I guessed he didn't have anything to say to Jack, or he was too angry to speak.

John was still at school, and I was glad that he hadn't been here to see all of this happening. I would not have been able to face him.

My whole body felt like pudding when, for the first time in my life, I ever saw a man cry. Jack pressed his forehead to the glass window of the squad car, and I saw tears falling from his face. I felt like I was going to break too, but I didn't. I thought that it would feel good to see Jack arrested and punished, but my heart didn't let me rejoice, nor did it let me cry.

While Mom and Nick were with the police, I had to stay home with Alison. I wanted to go with Nick. Mom insisted that it was unnecessary for me to go. She told me to watch over Alison while they were gone, and to keep her calm. Alison didn't know what was going on. She never know the truth because we weren't allowed to tell her. All she knew was that her father had done something bad enough to get him in jail, and that one day he was going to get out, and she would be able to see him again.

Alison asked Mom why her dad was not coming home for a long time.

Mom said, "Daddy did a bad thing. When people do bad things, they are sent to jail. Like, when you misbehave, I make you go to your room for a while. Well, Daddy has to go, sit, and think about what he did. And when his punishment is over, you will be able to see him again."

"No! I never want to see him again. I will kill myself if I ever have to see him again," I told Mom, right in front of Alison.

Mom snapped, "Kristen!"

Alison didn't understand what I said. She didn't really hear me, either, because she didn't look shocked or scared, like I expected. She was still staring up at Mom and waiting for her to finish explaining.

Instead of responding to me, Mom kissed Alison goodbye and told me to keep an eye on her, and she and Nick left with the police. Alison cried in my arms. She cried because the man that she loved and never thought would ever leave her was gone. I felt the same way. But it wasn't Jack I was crying for. It was my Daddy. I already cried for Jack. To see Jack put away did not made me cry.

When the commotion finished, and it was only Alison and me, I sat with her in her bedroom until she fell asleep, crying in my arms. I laid her down on her bed and kissed her cheek. She looked distressed in her sleep, with dry and sticky tears staining her face. Alison and Nick were too young for all of it.

I left Alison alone in her room. When I went into the hallway and shut the door behind me, I felt a sudden cold draft. It was the demons. The walls, the paint, and the floor that creaked beneath my feet were the demons. They held everything. I had to walk past Nick's room to get to the bathroom. Why did it feel like one of the hardest things I'd ever have to do?

I tried to run past the room without looking in. But, when I darted past, I couldn't help but turn my head toward the open doorway. I saw the blanket Nick had been wrapped in on the floor, and I saw Jack's underwear on Nick's bed. I went into the bathroom and slammed the door shut behind me.

My neck itched badly, and I felt like I couldn't breathe. I closed my eyes, and all I saw was Nick being smothered, his naked body, and the monster devouring him. I then opened my eyes, afraid to close them ever again. I tried to tell myself to keep it together. I didn't want to call for Mr. Sharp. Instead, I had to make myself breathe. I had to kill the itch.

I sat on the floor in front of the toilet, and tried to push the tears out. The tears didn't come out. Instead, a burst of emotion bubbled up in laughter. I started laughing hysterically and I couldn't stop. I beat my chest, confused, angry, and laughing. My head screamed at me to stop, but I couldn't obey it. I had no control over this sudden outpour of emotion. It felt like someone else was inside of me. I could only sit here and let them control me, as if I were a puppet.

My stomach then tightened and cramped in pain as I laughed uncontrollably. I felt my chest grow warm, unable to laugh anymore. I hovered over the toilet and set my mouth free from the puppet strings. I began to throw up the tears that I could not squeeze out of my eyes. No more laughing. No crying. I stayed over the toilet, throwing up everything that came up. When there was nothing else to vomit, I heaved in pain. It hurt, but I had experienced pain much worse than that. When I couldn't retch anymore, I lay on the floor with my head pressed to the cold tile. I slowly took deep breaths and tried not to see Nick's face. I tried not to see Jack. I tried not to think about the experience of seeing the worst thing I had ever seen. It couldn't be unseen. I knew this, and it frightened me.

It seemed like hours before Mom and Nick came home. I was still in the bathroom, but I had fallen asleep and didn't hear them come through the door. Mom must have been home for a while before she found me in the bathroom on the floor. When she came into the bathroom, Nick followed behind her in his pajamas. When she opened the door, I sat up immediately, startled and confused.

Mom pushed Nick away and told him to go to sleep in the room with Alison and not to look in the bathroom. Nick, naturally curious, called out to me. He must have seen me on the floor. Mom then came into the bathroom with me and shut the door, after shooing him away.

I felt dazed. It was almost like a dream. Mom stood over me with her hands on her hips. She stared down at me with a disappointed look on her face. I covered my face with my hands. I was hoping that it was all a nightmare, but seeing Mom standing there with her face hard and angry, I knew it wasn't. Everything I'd seen was real. Everything Nick had just been through was real. The monster was gone, but our family was now broken. In realizing this, I began to feel dizzy again. I placed my head back down on the floor.

"Get up, right now," Mom demanded.

I shook my head and rolled onto my side. I didn't ever want to move from that cold, tile floor.

"Do you just want to lie there and die?" she screamed.

I didn't answer, and this made her even more irritated.

"Get the hell up, Kristen!"

She bent over me and grabbed my arm tightly. I groaned in pain. She yanked me up off the floor and threw me against the wall. I hit my head, hard. She was angry, and I knew what was coming next. Mom pointed her finger at my face. Her face was so close to mine that I could almost taste the two-to-eight cups of coffee that she must have drank at the hospital while she'd talked to the police, and while the doctors had examined Nick.

"Before this depression crap even starts, I'm going to tell you right now that I will not stand for it. You will not put me through this kind of hell while we go through this. After everything that we have been through today and before everything that we are about to go through, I want to get this one thing straight with you: *You are not allowed to break down like this.* I need you to be strong. *We* need you to be strong. While I am going to have to go to that courthouse with Nick and get through this divorce and conviction, I need you to look out for Alison. And the only way you can do that is if you have it together. If you can't stand up and get your act together, Kristen, then I don't know what to do with you. You are not a child. The attention cannot be on you right now. You have to be my equal and help me through this."

She stared at me for a response, but I didn't make a sound. In frustration and anger, a reflex must have triggered. She raised her hand and slapped me hard across my face.

"Is this the only way to get through to you? Is this how I get a response from you?"

I held onto my face in pain, and I stared up at her, shocked. The blow had come unexpectedly. This made a single tear come out of my eye. She took a step back from me and shook her head.

"Mom," I cried. "Why?"

She said, "I don't know what came over me, Kristen. I don't want it to be this way. I just need you to understand that we have to stick together now. We have to start a whole new life. It's a whole new beginning." She paused. "Listen, Jack is gone. He's gone now. I know that he hurt us as a family, not just Nicholas."

"How do you know?" I asked.

"He's not coming back to hurt us. He's taking a plea deal. He's admitted to his wrong, so he's going to jail and staying there."

"I won't have to see him again?"

"No," she said, relieved that I was talking to her. "Nick and I are going to have to go to court, but it's just to give testimony and for Jack's sentencing. You won't have to be there." She seemed excited while telling me this. "We will be all right, Kristen. I need you to help us. We are going to move out of this place, and we are going to get a new everything. It will be a new beginning for us. Okay?"

I nodded, trusting her. I thought that maybe I could just let it go. That maybe it would be easy.

"Okay, Mom," I said as she reached her arms out to me. "A new beginning." I fell into her arms, where I knew it was safe.

Dr. Pelchat stared at my mother as she finished explaining Jack's sentencing and Nick's testimony.

When she was finished, he asked, "So, Kristen did not get to give her testimony about what she had seen? I mean, after all, she was the one who'd walked in on your ex-husband abusing your son."

Mom shook her head and said, "Because of Jack admitting his wrong–doing, we did not need Kristen getting involved. I wanted to keep her out of it."

"Why?" Dr. Pelchat asked. "Wouldn't it have been good for Kristen to be able to talk to someone about what she had seen?"

"I thought I was doing right by her. I didn't want her to get involved if she didn't need to. She was just a child. The toll it was taking on Nick, all the pressure, and the attorney's questioning. The judge and courts, it would have all taken such a toll on her. I wanted to avoid putting any more stress on the rest of my family if I could help it."

Dr. Pelchat didn't look as though he was satisfied with that answer. He closed his eyes and rubbed his forehead. Sighing, I could see him trying to hold back judgment.

He finally said, "You see that the pain that Kristen is going through now is a result of your neglect. She should have been allowed to talk to someone. Maybe not the judge, because he had all the evidence and confessions needed to convict and sentence your ex-husband, but Kristen should have been allowed to see a counselor, just like your son did. In fact, all of you - the entire family - should have seen a counselor together, as well as individually."

Mom sat in silence. She looked at me as I sobbed in the chair. I glanced at her, and she rolled her eyes coldly at me. She turned back to Dr. Pelchat.

"How's your son?" he asked Mom. "Does he show any signs of depression, or has he had any suicide attempts?"

Defensively Mom immediately replied, "No! He would never do anything like *this girl* did!"

The way she said "this girl" made me flinch, as though she had raised her hand to hit me in the head with a blunt object. Mom was upset and getting defensive. Dr. Pelchat must have sensed an argument approaching.

"That's good to hear," he told her. "And now we have to make sure that Kristen gets through this and doesn't do anything like this again."

"I hope so," she said, turning to me again. "We can't go through this again." Her eyes pierced me fiercely.

Dr. Pelchat leaned towards me with a box of tissues. I grabbed them, blew my nose, and cleaned up my face. Dr. Pelchat looked as if he couldn't let something go.

He finally asked Mom, "I'm going to go ahead and take a shot in the dark and ask if you have any idea what may have made Kristen go as far as she did?"

"You mean when she tried to-"

"Yes," Dr. Pelchat responded immediately.

Mom looked at me. Her stern and piercing eyes dared me to speak. She knew what I knew, and she was not going to say it.

She shook her head and said, "It just had to be a lot of things built up inside of her. I'm just glad that she is alive, and now she is getting the helps she needs."

She was still staring at me, piercing me with her eyes. Her act was so good. I knew the truth behind it. She didn't tell him, and she didn't want me to tell him.

Why, Mom? Why?

He opened his mouth to speak, but suddenly his phone rang. He answered, "Dr. Pelchat."

Whoever was on the other end was giving him an earful, because he didn't say a word. He just nodded and sighed. He looked at me and uncrossed his legs impatiently.

Finally, he said, "All right. No worries. See you then." He hung up the phone. He looked at Mom and said, "I'm afraid I'm going to have to say that our time is up for the day."

Mom stood up and started gathering her belongings to leave. Dr. Pelchat assured her that this would not be our last meeting. He said that, before I was discharged, a final family meeting was required.

Mom seemed relieved to be leaving. Before Dr. Pelchat opened the door, she asked if she could be left alone with me for a moment. Dr. Pelchat looked at me to make sure that I would be all right. I wiped the last of my tears away and nodded at him.

He looked at Mom and said, "I will be right outside the door." He opened the door, and when he stepped out, he shut it behind him.

Mom turned to me and smiled. She said, "You feel better?"

Not knowing how to respond, I just nodded silently.

This frustrated her. She hated when I was not vocal in my responses to her. She moved in closer to me and raised her hand. I flinched, not knowing what to expect.

She laughed. "Relax," she said. She touched my sorry attempt at making a neat ponytail. "You need to use your hair brush." She twiddled my hair and tried to fix the dead ponytail. "Do you need me to bring you anything else when I come back?"

I shook my head, still refusing to speak. It wasn't because I was trying to vex her, because I wasn't. I was just ashamed and felt terrible. She was trying to help me, and she worked so hard, alone, and I only made it harder for her.

"Well, I have to go, Kristen. I have to go and take care of Alison and Nicholas. They need me. You know," she said, with a smile that I didn't quite understand, "in less than a month, you will be eighteen. You will be all grown up, and you will have to be able to take care of yourself."

It somehow felt like she was letting go of me, but I didn't know for sure. She was getting at something. My heart began to race in anticipation of what she was going to say.

"Kristen," she said kindly. "It's nothing to be afraid of. You have to grow up. You have to turn eighteen. When you get out of here, you will be fine. I believe that Dr. Pelchat is here to help you, and he said that you are doing well. I know you will be just fine. Just concentrate on getting better and getting out of here. Finish your homework and get those last few lessons out of the way so that you can graduate from home school and you can move on with your life. That's what we want, right? We want a new and better life. It will be a new beginning for you when you are out of here."

She looked at me with so much hope. I couldn't let her down.

I nodded and said, "I'm sorry, Mom."

She smiled and closed her eyes. She spread her arms out and let me fall into them. That was where I felt safe.

"You'll make it up to me. Just get better and get out of here so that we can have you home. Get whatever it is out of your system, now that you have the chance. Lingering over things will just make you sicker. Be strong and be a good example to Nicholas and Alison."

I pulled away and looked at her. She put my face between her hands by placing a palm on each cheek. She said, with that confusing smile, "You don't want to be the example of what they learn what *not to do* from.

You want to be a good, big sister. Okay?"

"Yes," I said. It was true. I did want to be a good, big sister.

She gently pushed me away. Her smile was warm and less confusing now. She was satisfied. Or so I thought. I started to open the door, but she stopped me. She looked into my eyes.

"Kristen," she said. "One last thing. Do you want to tell me *why* you did this to yourself?" She gestured to my wrists.

Didn't she know? I thought she knew. "I want to tell you," I said. I felt the tears begin to well up again.

"Then tell me," she said warmly and trustingly.

I took a deep breath and thought back to when I'd swallowed the pills and when I'd picked up the knife. I shook my head. Mr. Sharp wanted me to stop. He wanted to grab me and cover my mouth, but I pushed him away as hard as I could.

"Jack's letter," I pushed out.

Mom gasped. She shook her head in disbelief. "No," she said.

"I read it," I admitted.

"Kristen, that has nothing to do with you."

"What about Nick? Mom? Are you going to be there for Jack? I know that he wants you there."

Mom's smile was nowhere to be found. Her eyes were big and her mouth was open.

"I knew it. I knew you had read it. Kristen, is this why? Is this why you are putting us through this crap? You should know me better than this. Why would I even..." she took a deep breath to calm herself. "You should have come to me so we could have talked about it."

"Why didn't you tell me about the hearing, Mom?" I asked.

She was stunned in disbelief. "How dare you? I was trying to protect you. Is this the way you treat me? I don't appreciate your tone, either. I have been here for you every single day. I have come here and I have taken care of you. I could just go and not come back until it's time for you to get out of here. Or, if they decide to leave you in here until you are eighteen, then I won't have to come back. Maybe that would make it easier. How would you feel if I did that?"

Fear grew inside me. I shouldn't have spoken up. I should have just nodded my head and agreed with her. It would make it easier on her if they did leave me here or send me to a long-term hospital.

Afraid that was what she was going to let happen, I pleaded, "I'm sorry, Mom. I *am* sorry. I won't say anything about it to Dr. Pelchat. That's not why I did it. I don't know why I did it. I was scared, or I was just not thinking. I am so sorry. I will make it up to you. I promise."

"Yes, you will," she said to me. She seemed to calm down after my apology. "Just get out of here so that you can come home. Do what you have to do in your groups, take your test, and take your medicine. And, if you do have a Borderline Personality Disorder thing he was talking about, just get through it. Be strong."

"Yes, Mom. I will never do this again and wind up in here again," I told her.

"I know you won't, Kristen," she said. "Because next time you will only have *yourself* to deal with."

CHAPTER 35

I knew that there was something inside of me that I wanted to let go of and let die, so that I could move on with my life. I wanted my mother to see that I was not going to cause any more problems, and that I was going to be a good example for Nick and Alison. I had my mind set to do everything I had to do to get out of Bent Creek and not let my family down.

During Morning Group the next day, I volunteered to speak first.

"My name is Kristen. I am in Group Two. Ms. Mosley is our group leader. Our group goal for the day is to respect our peers' opinions in Groups today. And my personal goal for today is to talk more in my Groups."

Dr. Finch looked amazed. He smiled and thanked me for volunteering to speak first.

"It seems like you are doing very well so far with your personal goal."

I smiled, proud of myself. I knew I was doing what I had to do.

Daniel spoke next. "I'm Daniel. I'm in the same group as Kristen, so we have the same group goal. We have to respect each other's opinions. My personal goal is to try to have a good family session today. This is the second try, so I really hope it goes well."

I smiled at him, silently wishing him good luck. He smiled and winked at me before looking down at his shoelaces, but not touching them like he used to. I wished I knew how to wink back. But, if I had tried, Daniel probably would have thought I had gotten something caught in my eye.

I looked over at Janine. Dr. Finch wanted her to speak next. She was in our group, too, so she stated our group goal. Her personal goal was to find out what had happened to Dr. Cuvo. No one commented on that. Dr. Finch seemed as if he wanted to say something to her, but he saw that she was angry and not like her usual self. He moved on to a more interesting piece of work.

"What do I have to say again?" Mena slouched back in her seat with her arms folded across her chest.

Her camouflage, hooded sweater was zipped up, and the hood was pulled over her head.

"Tell us your name, your group goal, and your personal goal for the day," Dr. Finch told her patiently.

She sighed heavily. She seemed sad. "I'm Mena." She looked up at Dr. Finch.

"Now, tell us your goals please, Mena," he requested.

"Daniel already said our group goal, and I don't have a personal goal."

She rolled her eyes away from us. We were all staring at her because she was talking. She must not have liked everyone looking at her so intently.

"That is unacceptable," Dr. Finch said. "Why don't you sit there and think about how you can help improve your situation here. While you think about it, try to figure out what you need to do to accomplish it. Then you will have yourself a personal goal. Just remember, you don't have to try to do it all in one day. You can take it step by step, and day by day. That is why we have personal goals every single day. This is to build us up and get us closer to accomplishing that bigger goal."

"Yeah, the bigger goal. Getting the hell out of here," Tai commented.

Everyone laughed, including Dr. Finch. Mena sat still with no expression on her face. She didn't even look annoyed.

When we were finished laughing, Dr. Finch said, "We will come back to you, Mena."

"Whatever," she said.

Dr. Finch's patience had apparently run out with Mena. He pointed towards the door and said, "Go to Ms. Mosley, right now."

"For what?"

"Mena, get out!" he yelled at her.

Mena got up angrily. She shoved her chair back and made it hit the wall behind her. This caused a loud bang that made my ears ring. Janine and I shuddered. Dr. Finch seemed like a calm man, but Mena seemed to have pushed his buttons. She stormed out of the room, muttering curses at Dr. Finch.

I already didn't like her.

After breakfast, Dr. Pelchat called me to his office. I sat down with a smile on my face. I was going to keep this up for as long as I could until I got out of here. I could lay it on as thick as believing could make it. He smiled back at me. He was buying it. His cherry, Santa-like cheeks squished under his tiny, blue eyes.

"Are you feeling better today?" he asked me.

I nodded. "Yes. Yesterday was kind of weird. But after that talk we had with my mother, I really feel like things are going to be okay."

"I'm glad you feel that way," he said. "You did very well."

"I did? How?"

"When I left you and your mother alone, you took the time to open up to her, which is what I was hoping you would do," he admitted.

I was dismayed. "Is that why you asked if my mother knew why I hurt myself?"

He sighed. "Yes. I wanted to open the communication up between you and your mother. You did very well, Kristen. I know it was hard, but you were very brave throughout the entire time."

"I don't feel very brave."

"I know, but you are. You'll see."

I felt a pain go through my chest. "It helped, knowing that you were near the whole time. Even though it hurt to talk that much about what had happened, I feel like it helped. You were the first person I ever got a chance to talk to about it. It was hard, and I couldn't stop crying, but if you and Mom hadn't pushed, I may have never had a chance to talk to anyone."

That much honesty hurt me inside. It was hard to let out, but Dr. Pelchat didn't seem to mind.

Dr. Pelchat replied, "That's what we need to do. We need you to open up more and talk about it."

I nodded at him. Still nervous and feeling strange, I said, "It hurts, but I'm going to try."

"Good. So, Kristen, did you get a chance to look at the book I loaned you?"

I thought back to the day he'd told me about Borderline Personality Disorder. I was too afraid. I did want to know about it. But...

"No," I admitted, "not yet."

"I recommend that you do. When you have time to yourself, you should read it."

"I haven't even taken the test yet," I argued. My heart began to beat fast. "How do we even know if this is my diagnosis?" I tried to smile so that I wouldn't seem too scared.

Dr. Pelchat sighed. He shook his head. "We don't know for sure. Not yet. But I have seen a lot of warning signs for disorders dealing with psychosis. You, Kristen, have major signs of Borderline Personality Disorder."

"What *exactly* am I doing?"

Almost yelling, I was giving away how scared I was. I couldn't have this disorder. Not if I was supposed to be a good example for Nicky and Alison.

"Read the book, Kristen. Please." He was sincere, and his eyes were very gentle.

I nodded, and promised to read the book. I had to read the book because I wanted to know what it was that I was doing that made me such an obvious candidate for this Borderline Personality Disorder. I needed to know so that I could fix it and not cause any more problems for my family.

"How are you sleeping at night?" he asked.

"I don't know," I said. "I get to sleep, and I wake up sometimes. I guess it's okay."

"Do you feel different since we stopped the medication?"

"I feel..." I didn't know how to answer these questions. Everything was mixed up, and I felt confused. I should have known how I was sleeping. I should have known if I felt different without the medicine. I just shook my head. I started to feel hopeless.

Dr. Pelchat looked up from my chart towards me. He stopped writing and put my chart on top of his desk.

"I know how hard this is for you," he said. "You know, I had a pretty weird day yesterday. After your mother left, I went into the lunchroom to grab a bite to eat with Geoffrey. Well, he told me something that just completely blew my mind."

"What did he say?" I asked.

"He said that he wanted to be a doctor, just like me. He wanted to go to medical school and really go all the way. He told me that he admired me, and that he looked up to me, like I was his father or something."

Dr. Pelchat seemed amused and relaxed. He was smiling and happy.

I felt calm, and I smiled back at him. "He really does look up to you, Dr. Pelchat. He told me that one day when we were talking."

"Really?" He seemed surprised. "I wouldn't have known it if he hadn't said it."

I looked around and realized the sudden change of mood. The sun was shining through the blinds that hung over the wide, glass windows. The room was warm, and the tension lifted.

"I like this," I admitted.

"What?" Dr. Pelchat asked.

"I like us having a conversation, instead of you asking me a million questions. It feels normal," I said.

"What's normal?" Dr. Pelchat asked.

I thought about that question before answering. I couldn't come up with a single response that made sense.

"I don't know," I said with a giggle.

"Exactly. That's why I don't like normal," Dr. Pelchat responded. "There's no explanation for it."

I laughed. "Well, that's obvious, Dr. Pelchat. Look at where you work."

He looked around as though shocked. And he put his hand to his chest, like I had offended him.

"What do you mean, Kristen? There is absolutely nothing wrong with anyone here. We are *all* normal in here. "

We both laughed. I hadn't laughed that hard in a while. When that moment between us had passed, Dr. Pelchat kept a calming smile on his face.

"Let's try something, Kristen. Let's try to have a 'normal' conversation."

"What's a normal conversation?"

"We will talk to each other. I ask a question, and you answer, and then you'll ask me a question, and I'll answer. We will just talk. What do you think?"

I wasn't sure how I felt about it. It seemed different from my other sessions with him and from ones I'd had with Dr. Cuvo. I nodded at him.

"Why do you do what you do?" I asked first.

"Do you mean, why am I a psychiatrist?"

"Yes."

"For the money," he said.

Shocked, and in partial disbelief, I laughed.

"What's so funny?" He looked so serious.

"Aren't you supposed to say something like you had always wanted to help people since you were a child, or since you went through this when you were younger, you wanted to help people who are going through this, too? It just doesn't seem..."

"It doesn't seem like a 'normal' thing for a doctor to say, does it?" Dr. Pelchat asked.

"No," I said. "It doesn't."

His smile appeared again. "I do want to help. That's why I'm here," he laughed.

"But the money isn't bad, either."

We laughed together.

"Where are you from?" Dr. Pelchat asked.

"I was born in California," I told him. I suddenly started to miss California and our little apartment. I started to miss microwave-cooked hot dogs and cold cuts sandwiches.

"How did you get here?"

"My mom decided to get married, and Jack moved us here. Now we're stuck in Atlanta." Realizing that he had asked me two questions, and afraid that he was going to ask me more questions that would lead to something, I caught him before he could ask another question. "Where are *you* from?"

"I'm from here," he said. "I was born and raised here. I went to college in New York, and I worked at Bellevue for about ten years. Then I moved back here some years ago."

"Why did you come back?" I asked.

"I came back to take care of my mother," he told me. "I started working here at Bent Creek under Dr. Bent, who I've known since we were teenagers. She took a chance on a young kid like me." He laughed at himself. "I can appreciate being here so much more than when I was working in New York. I'm home. I am passionate about our work here. Besides, I used to work with Alzheimer's patients. Trust me, you kids are so much easier."

He made a face that was supposed to be funny.

I wanted to laugh, but it made me uncomfortable. Was it okay to laugh about that?

His large hands moved across the desk, making me nervous. "Your mother said that you will be graduating high school soon."

"Right," I said with a sigh.

"Do you have any plans for what you would like to do after graduation?"

I shrugged my shoulders. "I like to write. I don't know. I'm not that good. I just write what I feel. I am passionate about writing. It's the only thing I can't stop doing, no matter how bad I am at it."

"Then don't stop," he said.

I saw in his eyes that he really meant it. Perhaps he was feeling something at that moment. Maybe it was for Rocky. I didn't know what to say next. Talking about the future made me feel sick inside. What could I ever do? What was I useful for? Dr. Pelchat was a good doctor. I'd just talked to him, we had a normal conversation, and he hadn't even yelled or been frustrated. Not once.

Dr. Pelchat reached for my chart and grabbed a pen.

"My father," I said. "He's still in California."

Dr. Pelchat looked up from my chart. "Does he know that you are here?"

"No," I said. "Not unless my mother told him."

"What do you think he'd do if he knew that you were in the hospital?"

"That's two questions in a row, Dr. Pelchat. I thought we were having a conversation." I called him out on it that time.

Dr. Pelchat began writing again. Without looking at me, he said, "This is a conversation, Kristen. This is not a question game. We are adults."

I didn't reply. I was turning eighteen in less than a month. Was I an adult? Was I ready to be an adult? I didn't know if I was, or even if I wanted to be an adult. Mom certainly wanted me to grow up. I had to grow up soon. I knew that. I looked away from Dr. Pelchat. He was probably already writing something that would set me back from getting out of Bent Creek. The sad and pathetic feeling crept back inside of me.

"I'm nervous about the test," I admitted to Dr. Pelchat. "What if I...what if I have Borderline Personality Disorder?"

I looked down at my bandaged wrists and wished I hadn't admitted that I was afraid.

"There is no need to be nervous," Dr. Pelchat assured me. "All you have to do is be honest. The results depend on how open and honest you are about things that are going on with you. That's all. There are no tricks in this test. The test is not designed to make you look good or bad. It's just a test to help us to know how we can help you. That's the only way you're going to get the help you need and get better."

I wished it were that easy.

CHAPTER 36

Daniel sat with our group at the lunch table, silent but with a smile on his face. He was being very mysterious, the way he was smiling and staring off into space. I could only assume that his family session had gone well that day. He didn't volunteer any information.

Tai spoke up. "What's with you?"

Daniel shrugged. "Where's Janine?" he asked, to change the subject.

Janine wasn't at lunch with us. In fact, after breakfast and our morning Group, no one had seen her.

"Maybe she's asleep in the bedroom," I said.

"Maybe," Daniel agreed.

He seemed worried about her. His smile disappeared. Daniel took a bite of his food. When he chewed, his cheeks squinched, and he looked like a chipmunk. I couldn't help but smile at him. When he looked up at me and saw me smiling at him, I wanted to turn away, but I couldn't. He returned a smile. It was the best smile he had ever given me.

Suddenly, I began to see John's face. His smiles were kind. When we'd flown the kite together - the day we'd almost kissed - all of us had been nothing but smiles.

Then I started to remember his face when he'd told his father that he didn't want to come to our house anymore. After his uncle Jack was arrested, he hadn't felt right coming over to help us move into our new place. I had heard them talking outside while we had been moving our furniture out of the house. He hadn't smiled at me that day. When I'd gone to him to say hello, his eyes had been so confusing, and his tone cold. He hadn't looked me in the eyes when he'd spoken to me.

John's father had let him leave because John couldn't stand being there at the house. He'd said that he was disgusted. He'd never clarified exactly what it was that had disgusted him. Had it been my family? The situation? The house? Had it been Jack? Nick? Mom? Me? There was no doubt in my mind that things had changed between John and me. It hurt to think that he didn't look at my family and me the same anymore. I just wanted everything to be okay again.

"I think that everything *is* going to be okay," Daniel said to our group.

Our group was doing dialectical behavior therapy. Dr. Bent called it DBT Skills Group.

Dr. Bent smiled and nodded in approval. "What about your father?" she asked him.

Daniel continued to smile. He said, "Finally, he's moving away. My mother got their divorce settled."

I saw the happiness in his eyes. Dr. Bent put her hands together, as if she were praying. She smiled and said, "Good for you. Good for you and your mother."

"It is what's best for the both of us," he said. "Things are going to be better. She has a job now, and my father won't be there, making life harder for us. I told Mom that I will do my part, too. I'm going to finish school and get a job to help her. She is doing what she has to do to take care of us, so I have to do what I'm supposed to. All we can do is try."

"Good," Dr. Bent said. "That is very good, Daniel. Without trying, you would not have gotten this far. You have come a long way. Remember to use your DBT Skills modules and Coping Skills methods every day when you are out of here to stay on track. Do you remember what the DBT Skills modules include?"

Daniel answered, "Mindfulness, distress tolerance, emotion regulation, and interpersonal effectiveness."

"That's right," Dr. Bent commended Daniel. "Mindfulness is designed to teach you how to focus your mind and attention on everyday matters. Distress tolerance focuses on accepting your situations. It helps you find ways to survive and tolerate those stressful moments that arise, without involving yourself in difficult behaviors such as getting overly angry and acting out on it. Emotion regulation skills help you learn to identify and label your current emotions, identify your challenges to changing emotions, reduce emotional reactivity, and increase positive emotions. Of course, using your interpersonal effectiveness skills teaches you effective strategies when asking for what you need, and it helps you to cope with interpersonal conflict."

"I feel like I've done most of that," Daniel admitted. "It's going to be more challenging to put those skills into action when I'm at home. Now that I know what I have to do, it's going to be different to *see* the changes. It is easier in here with you all beside me."

"You're moving forward, Daniel," Dr. Bent assured him. "That's just how it is when you make great changes."

"I'll do my best," Daniel said.

"Good, Daniel. You've worked so hard, and have come such a long way. Do your best. You owe it to yourself, and you deserve it," Dr. Bent said with an encouraging smile. She seemed to be very impressed with Daniel. I knew that I was impressed with him.

Daniel was real. He was better, and it seemed like he would be getting out of here soon. I wanted to feel real. I wanted to be better. For Daniel, it had been three weeks of working it out in therapy at Bent Creek, and some work from his mother. She'd had to make a move that was best for the both of them so that things could get better. For me, it frightened me to think of what it would take, and how long, for me to get better.

Daniel's mother worked with him in therapy, and she must have listened to what Dr. Finch had told her to do to make things better for her and Daniel. That's why it was getting better for them. That's why Daniel was better. She was his mother, and she took care of him.

My mother wanted me to do this for her, Nick, and Alison. I was the one with the problem, and I had to fix it. It was all on me. *I* was the one with Borderline Personality Disorder. How could I fix it on my own?

"Why are you here?" I asked Daniel. We were alone after dinner, sitting across from each other on the main unit.

The main unit was calm. The only sounds I heard were from the television. Prime time dramas were on, and Tai was into the detective mysteries. She and a few others were watching a modernized Sherlock Holmes drama. Janine and Mena were out of sight. Everyone was in their own place and doing their own thing. Daniel and I were the only ones at the table together.

I wanted to take advantage of the privacy that Daniel and I had by talking to him and getting to know him better. I looked into Daniel's eyes. I wasn't afraid to talk to him anymore.

"Did you try to kill yourself?" I asked.

He was sketching on a notepad. He didn't pay me attention until I reached across the table and gently touched his arm. Daniel put his pencil down and stared at his sketch. The way his eyes suddenly shot up at me was intimidating and attractive.

He took a deep breath and said, "Are you sure you want to have this conversation?"

"I only asked a question," I said. "You don't have to -"

"No," he said, "I didn't try to kill myself. And I didn't do a cry-for-help kind of thing. I just had a nervous breakdown or something."

"Why? I mean..." I didn't know exactly what to say without sounding like an idiot. "What made you break down? Was it your father?"

"Everything just hit me all at one time," he admitted. "When my father was sent away to jail, my mother made promises that she didn't keep. She promised to take care of us. But when my father came back, she was sidetracked. Everything became about him. He hated me. Then my best friend and I were going to run away. She was having problems at home, too. It seemed like a perfect plan, but when it came time to go, I couldn't do it. I didn't want to leave my mom with him."

"Were you sad because you decided to stay?"

He shook his head and said, "It's good that I stayed. It's just…"

"It's just – what?"

"I miss her." His eyes welled with tears.

"Who? Your mom?" I asked.

"The girl in the drawing that you stole from me," he said. He smiled slightly. "Her name was Theresa. We were going to run away together. The day that we were going to leave, my father went crazy on my mom, and I knew I couldn't leave her with him. I decided to stay to help her. Theresa couldn't understand that. We got into a huge argument, and she just left. I didn't think that she would really leave without me, so I didn't try to stop her."

"You haven't seen her since?" I asked him.

A single tear fell out of his eye. He said, "They found her car off the side of the road with her in it. She wasn't breathing. So…"

"I'm so sorry, Daniel."

"Yeah," he sighed. "Me too. She didn't believe in what I believed. I blamed myself for everything. I felt like it was my fault, because I didn't stop her or run away with her. But I know now that it's not my fault. Even if I had run away, the problems would have still been there. My father would probably have killed my mother. Theresa probably would have still killed herself, and I probably would have done it, too."

"Were you scared?"

"At first I was. When I first got here, I thought I was being punished. Now I see what being a survivor really is. It's not giving up. It's not running away. It's getting through whatever it is you have to get through to make it. It is allowing you to grow stronger for whatever is coming next. It is being brave and choosing to live through it all so that you can share your story and help others. That's what a survivor does. I don't want to run away anymore. I just want to live and make things better. My mom wants to do the same. I tell you, Kristen, Bent Creek may seem like the worst place to be right now, but you'll see. It's not."

He looked straight into my eyes and said, "I've watched you."

My heart started beating fast. He grabbed my hand gently and looked down at my bandaged wrists. His fingers traced the fresh tape that Ms. Mosley had used for the bandages when she'd changed them this morning. I closed my eyes and let myself feel this moment between us.

"You seem so sad and regretful. You can't just let it out, can you?"

I shook my head. My eyes were still closed. I felt tears begin to well up in them. There were no words to describe that moment. His words and the feelings inside of me were just too much. The tears poured out from underneath my eyelids. He squeezed my hands. I jolted, not afraid, just feeling too much.

"Open your eyes," he said.

I did open my eyes, and his large, beautiful eyes stared into mine.

"You know how the old people in here always have something to say to us? And when they talk, they think they know everything. You know?" He chuckled a little. Then his smile disappeared.

"There are things I keep hearing over and over that I do believe, though. They sound old–fashioned, and they are definitely cliché. But remember this, Kristen," he told me with his seriously passionate stare. "This too shall pass, and what doesn't kill you *will* make you stronger." He paused. "If you let it. Keep your head up and your eyes open. That's how you will survive. If what you go through doesn't kill you, let it make you stronger."

CHAPTER 37

It was obvious that Daniel was going home. He didn't say anything to us about leaving during breakfast the next day, but I already knew he was leaving, since we'd talked the night before. Daniel had left me with a powerful feeling inside. It was a feeling that I wished to keep with me forever. I almost wanted to be him, just so that I could know what it was like to be that strong and be a survivor.

After our last group of the day, Daniel's mother and his grandmother came for him. Daniel didn't talk much in our group meetings that day. He didn't really say much to any of us. He may have felt bad for having to leave, while we were still stuck inside. However, I knew that he was happy to be leaving.

"Have a cigarette for the both of us. Okay?" Tai requested. She punched his chest playfully.

He rubbed the spot where she'd punched. "I'll have two as soon as I get out of here. One for you and one for me," he assured her.

When she smiled, he wrapped his arms around her, and they hugged. Tai was blushing as he pulled away from her. Moving on, Daniel said goodbye to a few other people.

When he came over to say goodbye to me, I looked away from his eyes. I put my head down, and closed my eyes. He gently placed his fingers under my chin, and lifted my head up so that I could look him in the eyes.

"Always keep your eyes open and head up," he told me.

His sweet smile made me feel warm inside. He leaned in slowly, and, for a moment, I didn't know what to do with my hands or my arms; my body wouldn't move. He wrapped both of his arms around me and squeezed me gently. I closed my eyes and hugged him back. Squeezing a little tighter, I took in that moment. I wanted to remember that good feeling for the rest of my life.

Daniel pulled away from me, and gave me one last smile before turning and walking away. He now stood between his grandmother and mother, who were waiting for him by the exit door with Dr. Finch.

I sighed, still holding onto our moment. Mena then walked onto the unit with Dr. Pelchat. They must have just had a session. Dr. Pelchat looked irritated and tired. Mena looked angry, like she always did. Janine suddenly appeared out of nowhere, running over to me. She asked me something, but I didn't understand her clearly.

"What did you say?" I asked her.

 Dr. Finch used his key to open the exit door. Hearing the door open, Janine turned to see what was going on. She saw Daniel about to leave, and quickly ran over to him. He saw her and dropped his bags without hesitation.

"Oh, my God! Janine!" he exclaimed. "I thought I'd miss you!"

Daniel grabbed her in his arms, and they squeezed each other tightly. Janine was crying.

"Daniel, we have to go," his mother pushed. She picked up the bags he had dropped.

Daniel didn't let go, because Janine wasn't letting go of him. She slipped a folded piece of paper into the back pocket of his jeans. She whispered in his ear. A pain went through my chest. What did she say to him to make him close his eyes and smile that way? He was smiling in that convincing way. When he pulled back to look her in the eyes, I noticed that his eyes were amazingly aglow. Daniel's eyes seemed to be radiating some kind of affection as he looked down at Janine. I did not understand that look.

She must have whispered to him her permission to move, because without hesitating, he had moved. Their lips were pressing so passionately together. First, it was a gentle peck. Then her tongue was in his mouth, and his lips were over her bottom lip.

My mind seemed to suck me back into a place where I couldn't get out.

Where was I?

I was in the doorway of my bedroom at our new home. This home was the place that we had moved to after Jack was arrested, and Mom had sold our old house. The house where the terrible things had happened was gone. It was no longer our nightmare since we had moved out of there and into our new house. This new home was a part of our family's new beginning.

Lexus came over to help me paint my new bedroom. She was staying over at my house for the weekend. John came over to help me paint, too, when he learned that Lexus was visiting. Lexus had that kind of effect on people. People liked to be around her. Lexus was beautiful. She was interesting. She wasn't complicated. She was likeable and lovable. She was...she was...nothing like me.

We decided to paint as much of my room as we could on the first day. The walls were originally a sickening shade of green. I wanted all of the walls painted black. Our goal was to try to finish painting by Saturday because we were going to celebrate Lexus' high school graduation on that Sunday. Lexus suggested that we include John because he was also graduating high school that year.

The whole weekend was fun with the three of us painting and celebrating. Lexus was helpful and kept the mood light with her cheerfulness. John was charming and fun to be around because he was just simply wonderful as is.

While we painted my bedroom, I listened to Lexus and John talk about what colleges they were going to attend in the upcoming year. They argued about the politics of going to a State University versus a College. I decided to step out of the room to grab sodas for the three of us. When I returned to the room, I was in high spirits. I wanted to hear more about their plans and ask them questions about what it was like to be finished with high school.

However, at that moment, I couldn't speak. I couldn't move. I couldn't understand anything.

John's arms were wrapped around Lexus' perfectly slim waist. Her hair was swept up in a high ponytail, and she had little drops of paint in it. His dried-paint-covered hands were greedily rubbing all over her neck, her shoulders, and her back. I heard Lexus moaning as John hungrily kissed her from her lips to her neck and shoulders. I just stood in the doorway of my bedroom, silent and still, while watching in disbelief and heartache. They didn't even notice that I was there.

I had backed away from the open doorway and stood in the hallway. I tried to get my thoughts together. I wiped away my tears. With a sick feeling still in my chest, I walked into the room and slammed the door behind me. I made sure I slammed it hard enough for the both of them to know I was there.

Lexus and John were startled. They backed away from each other. Lexus sighed in relief when she saw that it was only me. John looked at me and, when our eyes met, he blushed. I looked at Lexus.

She said with a smile, "Kristen, your room is coming along nicely. Don't you think?"

I walked toward them and looked around the room. With a forced smile, I nodded in agreement. Lexus was glowing, and so was John. They didn't look nervous at all. I couldn't understand it. I was sure that I would never understand.

"What? Did you want it to be you?" Mena said to me.

I looked up. I was back in Bent Creek, and standing on the main unit. Mena stood directly in front of me, blocking my view of Daniel and Janine. Then it hit me. She wasn't smiling, nor was she joking. She was serious.

She said, "Don't go cutting your wrists up over *that*," and walked away.

When Mena was out of my way, I saw that Daniel was gone. The exit door was closed, and Dr. Pelchat was coming towards me. I wanted to say something to Mena. Angrily, I started to walk towards her, but Dr. Pelchat called out to me. I stopped in place.

Approaching me, he said, "I just wanted to remind you to read over that book I gave you."

"I will, Dr. Pelchat," I assured him.

"Good," he said. "I've scheduled your test for Tuesday." He walked away.

I stood there, staring at the exit doors. Daniel was gone. Janine was gone. Mena was gone. She had asked if I wanted it to be me. That question felt like it could have destroyed me if I had an answer for it. Did I want it to be me? Did I want Daniel to kiss me?

I'd wanted *John* to kiss me. I'd wanted him to move towards me, but he'd never moved. Everyone had been happy when Lexus and John had announced that they were dating. Mom was happy for them, their parents were happy for them, and all of their friends were happy for them. Everyone was happy for them except me. It was okay for them to kiss in front of everyone, just like Daniel and Janine did. They didn't have to hide or keep it a secret. They were glowing, and they were free. I didn't know what that felt like. I didn't know what it was like to be kissed and set free.

When I returned to my bedroom, I felt relieved. I let my face hit my pillow, and I just lay on the bed, on my stomach. I stared at the silver butterfly pendant that I had sneaked into Bent Creek so that Mr. Sharp could stay with me. I twisted it between my fingertips. Mr. Sharp spoke to me through those sharp wings. He felt my pain. He liked it when I was this way, so that he could give me attention.

I couldn't do it. Not here. Not in the room on the bed where, at any moment, a counselor could walk in and see me, and then go write about it in my chart. That would set me back. So, I lay there in pain. I let the pain shoot from my mind, down my back, and to the metal ball that turned tirelessly in my chest.

My mind ran back and forth from Janine and Daniel to John and Lexus. Then to how useless, ugly, and terrible I was. Tears fell hard onto my pillow. All I could do was cry, because it hurt too badly to move. I wanted Mr. Sharp. He watched me with tears in his eyes.

It's so much better to cut. It feels less painful than this. One cut, that's all you need. You need to breathe. Bleed so that you can breathe.

He told me this repeatedly, but I wouldn't do it. I couldn't take a chance on being set back. I lay as still as possible, and let the metal ball turn in my chest. The pain made the tears fall harder. My mind would not stop. It wouldn't let me quit thinking about what a horrible person I was. Everything I was putting my family through, why John hated me so much, why Lexus didn't answer her phone the night that I had found the letter Jack had written, when I'd needed someone to talk to and only Mr. Sharp had been there, and what a useless person I was. I could never be a survivor the way that Daniel had described.

I put all my pain on other people. That was why he never moved. That was why I had all of that pain inside of me. I stared at Mr. Sharp, who was only my age, but made me call him Mister because he knew so much more about life than I did. He knew the past, and he knew the future. That's why he hated it when I denied him. I denied him, and let my tears fall until I couldn't feel or see him anymore.

CHAPTER 38

I woke up, startled by a loud thud that came from the other side of the room. I opened my eyes and all of the lights were out. I couldn't see what was going on. I called out for Janine, but she didn't answer. I sat up, feeling dizzy, and I turned on the lamp beside my bed. I had to let my eyes adjust for a minute. When I could see clearly, I didn't see Janine in her bed. Where was the noise coming from? I saw that the bathroom light was on.

The thuds, accompanied by a strange gurgling sound, were coming from the other side of the door. The gurgles were followed by heaving and groaning. I became frightened. It sounded like someone was inside of the bathroom, dying.

"Janine?" I called out to her from my bed.

When I didn't get an answer, I got up off the bed slowly and went over to the bathroom door. I scratched gently on the outside of the door.

"Janine," I called again. "Are you in there?"

My question was answered by another loud thud, followed by painful groaning sounds. I jumped back, afraid. I had to open the door, so I shook the fear away and yanked the door open. A strong and bitter smell suddenly filled the air. I covered my nose immediately, and I wanted to cover my eyes, too, from what I was seeing.

Janine was crouched over the toilet with her whole hand down her throat. Blood spilled out of her mouth. She fell backwards and hit her back against the wall behind her. There was the thud. She sat back up and tried to breathe, but only a gurgle came out. She grabbed her stomach in pain and groaned. More vomit and blood came up and spilled all over her ruined, pink pajamas. Blood caked in her matted hair. Vomit slopped on the floor and covered the toilet. She sat in her own blood and vomit as she struggled to sit back up and hover back over the toilet. I stood in the bathroom, terrified and disgusted.

"Janine!" I exclaimed.

She looked over at me, just now noticing I was here. She took her hand out of her throat and tried to speak, but a chunk of blood came out. She reached out to me with her bloody hand. It was like I was in the middle of a horror movie. She coughed up another chunk and spat it out. It flew at me and landed on my shirt. Still reaching out for me, she started moving towards me. Afraid, I ran out of the bathroom and onto the main unit, where Ms. Mosley and Mr. Anton were sitting at the counselor's desk. I called out to Ms. Mosley desperately. She stood up immediately.

"What's wrong, Kristen?" she asked.

I didn't tell her what I'd seen. I just told her that it was important that she came with me to our bedroom. I didn't want to make her panic.

She followed me quickly. When she saw Janine, she covered her mouth and nose. She almost gagged. The terrifying and sickening smell was overbearing. Ms. Mosley went over to Janine and grabbed her arms to keep her from putting her hands back in her mouth. Blood got all over Ms. Mosley's clothes and hands.

"It is okay, Janine," she said, as she seemed to try to be gentle.

However, Janine was not gentle. She fought back at Ms. Mosley and screamed, hoarsely.

Ms. Mosley yelled at me, "Go get Mr. Anton! Please, Kristen! Hurry! And tell Geoffrey to call the nurse and an ambulance!"

I did exactly what she said. I followed Mr. Anton back to our room. They both tried to get Janine to get up and move, but she wouldn't. She just cried and tried to scream. She didn't have enough strength to fight back. Blood got all over the two counselors. The on-call nurse came into the bathroom with a needle that I knew too well. I stood back.

She said to Ms. Mosley and Mr. Anton, "I didn't realize it was this bad. You have to get back. You are getting her blood all over you. The ambulance will be here soon."

"I can't," Ms. Mosley said. "She will keep it up if we don't hold her down."

"Hold her," the nurse said. "I've got a sedative." The nurse went over to Janine with that needle ready.

Janine tried to scream as she saw the nurse with the needle come closer to her. Mr. Anton told me to leave the room. I ran before the nurse stuck the needle into Janine. I couldn't stand the smell. Nor could I watch my friend suffer in pain.

The ambulance then came for Janine. I sat on the main unit with Geoffrey. It was amazing that no one had woken up during all of the commotion, as they had when Rocky had attempted suicide. I was glad that Mena was not awake. What if I hadn't woken up? Would Janine have been dead?

I watched as the EMTs rolled Janine away on a stretcher. I thought of Rocky. Janine didn't have her head in a box. She was just silent and still like he had been. Her eyes were open, and she was staring up at the ceiling in a daze. It hurt to see my friend that way. I wanted to run up to her and tell her that everything was going to be okay, but I couldn't do that. I didn't really know if anything was going to okay.

Ms. Mosley rubbed Janine's bloody hand and told her to be calm, and that she was going to be taken care of somewhere else. I wanted to go with Janine and be there for her, but I knew that wasn't going to happen.

I looked back at the Girls' Unit as they rolled her out of the exit doors. I felt Death creeping around us. He was waiting around. He was stalking us, waiting to capture us. I took it personally when Janine was taken away. It hurt too bad to turn away. I had to watch as they rolled her out the exit door. Death followed behind her. He turned and looked at me before the doors shut and he showed me a bony finger. That finger waved at me, and then he and Janine disappeared. That was the last time I saw Janine.

CHAPTER 39

It is one thing to be in a dilemma and another thing to be stuck. Dilemmas can be worked out with time and effort. There's usually a release somewhere that can be seen. But when you're stuck, you're in one place or situation without foresight. You wait until you can be free.

Here, at Bent Creek, I felt stuck.

After Janine was taken away, I found it hard to go back into our room. Her warm, pink blanket was lying on her bed. It was neatly spread out across the top. Her clothes were folded in each drawer of the dresser that she used. Her hair brush, toothbrush, comb, hair ribbons, deodorant, feminine products - everything - was still sitting in its place, waiting for her, as if she were coming back to use them.

Mr. Anton told me to go into the room to pack up my belongings. I couldn't stay in that room anymore. As I admired Janine's things, I saw her clearly in my mind. She was sweet and beautiful. I ran my hand over her pink blanket.

I remembered how she had cried on my lap that night, the same day when Dr. Cuvo hadn't come back and Rocky had attempted suicide. After Dr. Cuvo had left, Janine had become so upset. It was as though Dr. Cuvo had become a part of her. He had been like life support. Daniel had been the only one who had made her smile after Dr. Cuvo had left.

Then Daniel had left, too. Maybe Janine had felt like she didn't really have anyone. Maybe she'd felt abandoned. She had admitted that she'd felt that she couldn't please her father and make him happy. Maybe she'd been stuck. She'd been stuck by herself, clinging too much to people who couldn't carry her.

I quickly packed up my things so that I could leave the room. On my way out the door, I ran into the maintenance lady. She was a short woman with wrinkled skin. She pushed a large cart that had cleaning solutions, and she smelled strongly of cigarettes and ammonia.

"You want to get out of my way so that I can clean up that mess in the bathroom?" she asked me in an irritated tone.

I didn't respond. I slipped past her and kept walking with my bags. Mr. Anton met me in the hallway. He grabbed my bags for me and kindly smiled.

"Come with me, Kristen," he said in almost a whisper.

I followed him down the hallway quietly, because everyone on the unit was already in bed. I wasn't feeling very tired, but was interested to see who I was going to be rooming with. We came to the door of the new room. Mr. Anton knocked once. There was no answer. He knocked again.

"What?" shouted a familiar voice from the other side of the door.

"We are coming in. Are you decent?" Mr. Anton asked. He waited a few seconds for an answer. She didn't respond, so he opened the door.

The new room was a lot bigger than my old room.

"You can take that bed right over there near the bathroom, Kristen," Mr. Anton suggested. He sat my bags down on the bed.

I looked around to see whose familiar voice that had been. Mr. Anton knocked on the bathroom door.

He said to the door, "Don't be too long in there. Kristen's your new roommate. So be nice." He turned to me before walking out of the door. "Good night, Kristen." He left me in the bedroom, alone.

I sighed heavily, relieved that he was gone. I unfolded my blanket and pulled out Janine's blanket. I had hidden hers inside of mine so that Mr.

Anton wouldn't see it. I put Janine's blanket beside my pillow, folded up. I probably shouldn't have taken it, but it reminded me of the Janine I had first met when I had come to Bent Creek. She had helped me meet everyone, and she had been very friendly. She hadn't made fun of me or made me feel like a loser. She'd loved smiles, and she had just been beautiful to me.

I looked over at my new roommate's bed. She didn't have her own blanket. There was the hospital's thin, white blanket spread across her bed. I shivered, remembering my first night in Bent Creek. Then I thought about the familiar voice that I had heard when Mr. Anton had knocked on the door. I hoped that my new roommate was nice.

The bathroom door opened, and a grinning face appeared before me. Those large, dark brown eyes were menacingly sweet. She still had on her loose, black jeans, a camouflage t-shirt, and that tight ponytail. I imagined this as the full gear that she had slept in. That girl looked like she was always prepared for battle. She didn't strike me as the type of girl who wore nightgowns and matching, pink pajamas.

"Well, I guess we are roommates now," she observed aloud.

I kept my eyes on her as she walked past me, and over to her bed. When she lay down and turned her lamp off, I threw myself down on the bed and stuffed my face into Janine's blanket. I thought to myself, Mena? Mena! Of all people to be stuck with! Mena!

CHAPTER 40

I knew that my mother was getting restless with me being away. When she came to visit me the next day, she brought my schoolwork and my last paycheck from work.

"I received your paycheck in the mail. Here's your schoolwork. This is your last year, so you need to hurry and finish up. You want to get your diploma before you are nineteen, don't you?" she said as she stacked the books up on the table where we were sitting. She seemed like her normal self, but more anxious. "Do you need anything else?" she asked.

I shook my head. "Thank you, Mom," I said.

I looked down at my school books. Physics 2, Calculus, Civics... What had I gotten myself into?

"Kristen," Mom calmly called out to me.

I had drifted off into a daydream. I looked at her after setting my books aside. They started to give me a headache.

"Do me a favor. Why don't you go ahead, sign the back of your paycheck, and endorse it to me. I can take it to my bank and get it cashed for you." She smiled sincerely. It was almost frightening.

I twisted uncomfortably in my chair. "Why can't I just cash it when I get out of here? I have to mail a portion of it off for my school tuition. I have to pay for this semester at the end of the month, anyway."

"Well, endorse your check to me, and I will mail it off for you. Besides, we don't know when you are getting out of here. And I also need the portion that you are supposed to give me so that I can get a few things."

I looked down at my paycheck with a slight frown. It didn't feel right, but Mom was right. I showed it to her.

"My tuition is due by next Tuesday. That's the end of this month. If it is late, they only give me five days before they add a late fee. Can you cash it and mail it off for me tomorrow?"

I looked into her eyes. Her smile went from frightening to warm.

"Yes, Kristen, I will do that," she assured me.

I believed her. So, I endorsed the check to her, and handed it over. As soon as she took it, she seemed to calm down. But it seemed like something was on her mind.

"Are you okay?" I asked her. "What's going on?"

"Nothing. I'm just tired from work. So, you have to take that test tomorrow. Are you nervous?"

This was the most we'd talked without yelling or crying since I had been in Bent Creek.

"Not really," I said. "It's going to be pretty simple."

"Well, I hope you do well on it," she said kindly. "And if you *do* have that Borderline Personality Disorder, I want you to know that we will do what we have to do to help you. If that means coming to the doctor every week, then that's what we will have to do, and if you have to take medicine, then we'll get that taken care of, too. I just want you to become a normal adult and be able to function right on your own. You will be eighteen soon and graduating from home school. I know that you plan on going to college, and you will be working and on your own. So I want you to be able to take care of everything for yourself."

The sound of her voice made me sad. She was so sure about what she wanted for me. On the outside, it seemed like she was any other normal parent, just wanting the best for her child. But on the inside, I felt as though she just couldn't wait to get rid of her problem. Her problem was me, and having to take care of me.

"Do you know anything about Borderline Personality Disorder?" Mom asked.

I shook my head. I remembered the book that Dr. Pelchat had given me, but I hadn't had a chance to read it.

"Dr. Pelchat gave me a book to read," I told her. "It's about BPD."

"That's good," she said.

An awkward silence crept in.

Mom broke the silence. "Can you receive phone calls here? Are you at that level?"

"Yes," I told her, "but it has to be during visiting hours or scheduled."

"Good. Lexus has been asking if she could call the hospital to talk to you. I guess she doesn't really have much time to visit, with everything that's been going on with her and John."

I shrugged. I couldn't think about Lexus or John. I had to be strong and stay positive to get out of Bent Creek.

"I miss her," I heard slip from between my lips.

Mom nodded at me. "I will give her the hospital's number. Everyone has been asking about you. Of course, Alison and Nick want to come visit you. They miss you. They have written you other letters, but I must have forgotten those letters at home. Oh, well. I'll bring the letters to you next time."

"Will you hug them for me?"

"Of course I will."

"And please tell everyone who's been asking "hello" for me."

"I will do that."

"And Mom?"

"Yes?"

"I *will* be out of here soon. I feel different. I feel like I can beat this, and I won't be doing anything to get myself back in here again."

Mom smiled warmly. It was a real smile, not a forced one. She believed me. I believed me.

After visiting hours, I immediately wanted to go back to the room to get the book that Dr. Pelchat had given me on BPD. I remembered seeing Mena go to the Girls' Unit. I knew she'd be in the room, lying on her bed, probably listening to music that screamed she hated the world.

Against my feelings, I went to the room anyway. When I walked in, the room was empty. Mena wasn't there. Relieved, I went over to my bed and grabbed the book from the bedside table. I looked at the cover. There was a picture of a girl's reflection from inside of a broken mirror. The shards of the mirror remained in the center. Pieces had broken out from the center and had scattered, causing the girl's reflection to look distorted. Her face was misshapen and disoriented.

The cover was playing tricks on my eyes. It made me want to open it. So I did, and skipped through the pages. The titles of the chapters looked boring: *Borderline Personality Disorder, What is BPD? Who Am I? The Symptoms and the Root, The Borderline*. One chapter caught my attention: *Self-Injury and Suicide.*

I read on. I found a quote from a girl who had been suffering with Borderline Personality Disorder at the time she was interviewed for the book. She'd written:

"I tend to think about suicide quite often. When I think about it, it seems like the only welcoming solution. It's the only thing I seem to be able to think about, and it makes me feel as if I have something. I find it very hard to not self–mutilate, and I tell myself that this is what I deserve. When I hurt myself, the fear and the pain of everything that is going on in my life disappears."

It was as though I were reading my own words. Afraid, I threw the book down to the floor. I covered my eyes with my hands and tried not to see the girl's face on the front cover. I tried not to hear her voice speaking those words. It was easier to cut. It was so easy to cut so deep. Deep enough to get wire-sutured stitches, but not deep enough to die.

Mr. Sharp's angry eyes breathed cold air through my heart that pumped hate through my veins. His shining eyes begged. He was upset. How long could I deny him? How did I think that I could deny him? He whispered through those silver butterfly wings onto my skin, *If you deny me now, then you deny me forever. I will leave you. You will be alone.*

I was too scared. When the wings pressed to my skin, I jolted. The pain was not how I remembered it. It used to be so easy. But I couldn't do it. I put the butterfly pendant back into my pocket, and I didn't hear Mr. Sharp anymore. Instead, the pain got thicker and heavier. I got up off the bed quickly and I rushed onto the main unit. Geoffrey was sitting at the counselor's desk. I leaned on the desk and greeted him. He smiled up at me.

"Hey there! Do you need something?"

"May I have a pencil and a sheet of paper, please?" I asked him.

Geoffrey handed over two sheets of paper and a pencil. I took it, thanked him, and went to the sitting area. Most of the other patients were watching television or talking. I sat down at a table that faced away from the television, and I put the sheet down. I held the pencil between my fingers and sat, frozen, with the tip of the pencil touching the paper.

I remembered when it used to be so easy. Every feeling I had was so easy to write down and pour out of me onto the paper. They went from just mere thoughts and feelings to words and creative expression. They traveled from my mind and heart to my fingertips, to the pen, into the ink, and out onto the paper. It was hard, sitting here at Bent Creek with the pencil and the paper. Mr. Sharp kept screaming in my mind. What if he really did leave me? What would I be? Who would I be without him?

I was writing instead of cutting--was I the one abandoning him? Writing used to be so easy. Easier than cutting, anyway. But here in Bent Creek, neither came to me easily. I felt abandoned, in a way. I stared down at the paper. What was I feeling?

CHAPTER 41

The next day, Dr. Pelchat called for me after lunch. When we arrived in one of the Group Therapy rooms, he didn't waste any time.

There was a booklet on the table, and two No. 2 pencils. When he told me that I had sixty minutes to complete the test, I felt like I was back in public school. Dr. Pelchat looked down at his watch and nodded.

He said, "This is a yes-or-no choice test. You just have to answer as truthfully as possible. If you don't understand a question or you cannot answer it, then skip over it. Some questions may not seem to apply to you. Everyone who takes this test has different experiences. Just answer as best you can. Responding openly and honestly to all of the questions is the only way that we can accurately assess whether or not there is something we can do to help you. If you are not open and honest, the test measures will indicate that you are being defensive or suppressing information or simply lying to hide things you don't want us to know. This response attitude then prevents an accurate assessment of your situation, and then we may have to do this all over again. So, remember to be honest. Go ahead and start when I walk out of the room. If you need me, I will be across the hall. Good luck."

"Good luck" didn't seem like the right thing for a doctor to say, but I nodded at him anyway.

When I heard the door shut behind me, I opened the test booklet and began. The first question was simple: Do you feel that you worry excessively about too many things? Yes or No.

Second question: Do you have a fear of losing control of yourself? Yes or No.

Do you feel afraid that you will be in a place or a situation from which you feel that you will not be able to escape? Yes or No.

Do you find it difficult to let go of the past? Yes or No.

Do you find yourself constantly having to answer to a higher authority due to your actions? Yes or No.

Suddenly I was taken back to an earlier time, when I had been called to the principal's office at my last high school.

"This is the second time we have had to call you into our office," the principal said.

Mrs. Dickinson was always so sincere, and she spoke in such a calm voice. This time she wasn't so calm. She nervously stared down at the bloody kitchen knife that was sitting on her desk. She had it in a plastic bag, with paper towels wrapped around the blade. Mrs. Dickinson wasn't talking to me. She was talking to my mother, who was sitting next to me while we sat, face to face, with Mrs. Dickinson.

I sat quietly as she told my mom about what had happened. She only told her side of the story, about the girl who had been in the bathroom while I had been slicing myself with the kitchen knife. I'd made a mess on the floor, and the girl had been scared, so she'd run to get the school nurse.

When the school nurse had seen me, I had already put the knife away, but I couldn't hide the blood I'd spilled, or even the cuts on my arms. The nurse had pulled me into her office so that we could have a "nice talk" while she wrapped up my arms. Did she need to call the principal? Apparently she'd felt the need to after she'd found the bloody knife in my backpack. She hadn't even asked me why I'd done it. She was so quick to tell on me.

So that's how I wound up in Mrs. Dickinson's office, with my arms wrapped up and my mom sitting next to me, ready to snap my neck because she'd had to be pulled out of work to come to my school.

"This is very serious," Mrs. Dickinson continued. "Last time we caught her with razor blades in her locker. Now she has a real knife! Normally, in situations like this, we would have to call the police, and Kristen would be arrested for bringing a deadly weapon to school. From what I see, Kristen does not need to go to jail. I think she needs to see a psychiatrist."

Mom sat up straight and jumped in, "No! Excuse me. I don't think that you are certified to even make a suggestion like that. Is your degree in psychology?"

Mrs. Dickinson said, "No. but-"

"I didn't think so," Mom cut her off. "You can be assured that this will be handled. With our family's break–up and the divorce, things have just been a little rough, and Kristen is dealing with it in her own way. It's not necessarily the right way, but we are working on it."

"Have you even noticed Kristen's change?" Mrs. Dickinson ignored my mom. "The way her grades have been dropping? She pulled out of the Writing Club, which I thought was very important to her. She's been absent eighteen days this semester. Did you even notice?"

Mom looked at me while rubbing her neck, the way she did when she was nervous but trying not to let it show. She put on her intimidating face and stared at Mrs. Dickinson.

"You know it's hard on all of us right now. I will deal with her. This will not be a problem anymore. Believe that."

She turned and looked at me. She kept her eyes on me.

"I hope not," Mrs. Dickinson said. "Because next time this happens, not only am I going to have to get the police involved, but she will be kicked out."

Mom brought me home right after the meeting with Mrs. Dickinson. It was a good thing Nick and Alison were both still in school. When we got back home, Mom did not hesitate when we got through the front door. She slammed the door shut, and before I could put my backpack down, she slapped me across my face. I looked up at her, hurt and shocked.

"I work two jobs," she began, "to feed you and the twins. I put a roof over your heads. I clothe you. I am dealing with this, and trying to make it work for all of us, and this is the kind of mess that I have to deal with! All I ask of you is to help me out by trying to set an example for your brother and your sister. You don't want to be the example from which they learn what *not* to do. Just do what we talked about. What about our new beginning, Kristen? You have to stop this. If you keep this up, they will call Child Protective Services, and they will take you, Nick, and Ally away. You don't want that, do you?"

Anger seemed to be seeping out of her with each word she spoke. Afraid to say anything, I just looked at her. I did not react or answer her question. I just stayed silent and listened.

"I worry. I worry all the time. You don't think I cry and I get depressed? Sometimes I just want to punch my fists into the wall and just go crazy, too! But I don't, because I think about you and the twins, and I know that's not what you need to see. I know that I need to keep it together for all of you. I can't just act the way that I feel. You can't act like this! Now I want you to stop. Stop right now!"

I let the tears fall as she scolded me. She was right. Somewhere I needed to feel that she was right and not just know it in my mind. I just couldn't feel it. I thought about what Mrs. Dickinson had suggested, and I dared to bring it up.

"Mom," I said, while wiping my eyes. "Maybe I need help. Maybe I should go see the doctor that the judge ordered you to take Nick to after Jack's trial was over."

Her shoulders tensed up, and she looked away from me. "What would you say to a doctor that you can't say to me?"

I shrugged, afraid to answer. I tried anyway.

"I could talk about the things I saw. I could talk about Jack and what he did. I can't keep letting it play in my mind. It's like a movie that won't stop playing. I can't hit pause sometimes, Mom. I can't make it go away. I feel so sick when I think about how I knew what was going on when Jack would take showers with Nick, and when he would hurt him so bad, and I knew what was going on, Mom! I knew! And I just want to die sometimes, because it happened, and I knew! And then when I saw Jack, and he had Nick in the-"

She put her hands up and covered her ears. She shook her head with tears in her eyes. I looked at her, confused and hurting deep inside. I was crying so hard that my breathing became shallow and rough. The metal ball in my chest was turning at about a hundred miles an hour.

"Mom!" I cried. "Mom, please. Just let me talk to Nick's doctor. Maybe I can get help, too. Maybe I can stop-"

Mom uncovered her ears and grabbed my shoulders. She shook me hard.

"No! No! No! You do *not* need a doctor. Don't do this, Kristen. The only reason you want to see a doctor is because you want attention, just like Nick. Nick was the one who was hurt. That's why the judge said *he* should see a doctor. You are always so dramatic and seeking attention! That therapy is for your brother. Think of his future if he did not get that treatment. What do you think his life is going to be like? All you will do when you get in there is complain about the past, and nothing has really happened to you. You're going to tell the doctor that you knew what was happening? Well, if you knew and you were so sure, why didn't you help your brother? Why did you let it continue? Why didn't you come to me? Tell me, Kristen. Why?"

The feeling of death seeped into my soul. I had never wanted to be dead as much as I did at that moment. She was right, I thought. I should have said something. But I wasn't sure until I'd finally seen Jack doing what he'd done to Nick. It wasn't until that last day when I'd seen him, hovered over Nick and having sex with him, that I really knew for sure. Didn't I try to tell her? Didn't I show her the mess in the bathroom? Didn't I try to call the police when he'd gone out of control on Nick? I had.

I realized why Mom did not want me to see the doctor. She was afraid for herself. I bit down on my lip so hard that I could taste blood. Mom took her hands off my shoulders, and she backed away from me, almost looking like she was drained of her energy. She placed her hand on her forehead, like she was checking to see if she had a fever.

She looked away from me and said, "If you need to talk to keep from doing that mess you've been doing, then come to *me*. Don't go into the kitchen and touch my knives. And those knives and little swords that you like to collect are to stay in the boxes that you keep them in. Do you understand, Kristen?"

I didn't answer because I was not all there. I was still in a daze from the realization that had come over me.

She yelled, "Do you understand me?"

I snapped out of the daze and looked at her with wet eyes. I nodded.

"Let me hear you say it."

"Yes. I understand now," I said.

She nodded and came over to me. She wrapped her arms around me to try to make me feel safe again. I tried not to let it affect me, but I needed her arms so badly. I closed my eyes and gave in. I allowed myself to believe that she was right. If I did go to the doctor, I would be calling attention to myself, and then I could get her in trouble. I didn't want the people to come and take us away. I didn't want to have to cut. At that moment, I told myself that I would try to stop.

"Mom," I said.

She pulled away from me and looked into my eyes.

"If I get a job, could I check into doing home schooling?"

Mom thought for a moment. A smile appeared on her face. She said, "That doesn't sound like a bad idea. Let me think about it some more. Meanwhile, you should look into finding an after-school job or a weekend job. I think that will help you. You won't have time to sit and think about things that are supposed to be behind us."

"And it could help, because then you won't have to work two jobs," I added.

She nodded and started to walk away. "Let me think about it," she said.

Question number 59: Do you constantly find yourself feeling bad about yourself, and that you are a failure because you have let yourself or your family down? Yes or No.

Yes.

Final question: Do you have constant thoughts of death or being dead? Yes or No.

Yes.

CHAPTER 42

The next part of the day was filled with poking and prodding. But it wasn't as bad as I'd expected. After the test, Dr. Pelchat told me that my results would be back no later than a week. Then he took me to another part of Bent Creek. We had to walk through the Adult Ward to get there. I grew nervous passing through there. There were a lot of elderly people sitting alone and in corners. A few other patients who looked younger, but who actually were a lot older than me, were watching television or sitting alone as well. The atmosphere was different from the Adolescent Ward. At least, in the Adolescent Ward, we talked, even if it was to make fun of someone. Like when Tai made fun of me for not being able to take a bath. I cringed as I thought back on that.

"This is the Adult Ward, Kristen. We've had a few kids in the Adolescent Ward actually turn eighteen and graduate to the Adult Ward while they were here in Bent Creek. I've seen some adolescents leave Bent Creek, only to come back, old enough to go straight to the Adult Ward. It doesn't look too fun, does it?"

Dr. Pelchat always had a way of reaching me. Though his words did scare me, I tried to listen and take it all in.

When we got to the other side of the hospital, we entered the medical clinic. The waiting room was empty. A nurse came out of the back, and she took Dr. Pelchat to the side. He handed her my chart and they began talking. They were talking about me. I heard her say that the doctor, whose name was Dr. Mitsen, was going to look at my stitches and determine if it was time for them to be removed. Shortly after they spoke, the nurse came over to me with a sweet smile and, in a tiny voice, invited me to the back, where I assumed the doctor was waiting. Dr. Pelchat assured me that he'd be back to escort me back to the Adolescent Ward.

I followed the nurse, and she led me to an examination room. I had to get changed into the hospital gown, so the nurse left me in the room alone. After I was changed, I looked around and studied the room. It was a normal examination room, with the examining table that reclined back, the doctor's rolling chair, a sink, and some cabinets. But what was different about this room from others I had been in was that this room had locks on the cabinets. And there were no cotton balls in small jars, or those sticks that the doctor put on your tongue to make you say "Ahhhh!" There weren't even any lollipops that the doctor was supposed hand out when a patient was well behaved.

Dr. Mitsen entered the room. He was a tall and thin, friendly-looking kind of man. Even when he unwrapped the bandages and saw the sad scars and the wires and stringed stitches, he still remained smiling. While he examined me, he asked me questions about school.

It was as though this was a normal check-up at a regular, family clinic. After examining my wrists, he determined that the stitches would need to be in for another two weeks because of the vein damage. He said that they needed to heal properly. Therefore, he told me to keep cleaning the stitches and not to get them wet. He kept the bandages off my wrists. It made me feel a little uneasy. I looked down at my wrists and saw the lines and rows of the damage I had done. Mr. Sharp smiled from somewhere inside of me. I felt almost safe, but, without the bandages, I felt somewhat scared.

I asked, "Dr. Mitsen? Are you going to put the bandages back on?"

His warm smile was kind and gentle. He said, "I think it's best to leave them off since the stitches will be coming out soon. Let them air off a bit." He chuckled.

I tried to smile back.

When the doctor was finished with my examination, he sat down in the rolling chair and wrote in my chart. Naturally, I was curious. I tried to look at what he was writing. He laughed when he looked up and caught me peeking.

"Don't worry, Kristen. I'm not writing anything terrible. Everything I just told you is what I'm writing in here." He was so warm when he spoke. "Okay, Kristen Elliott. If you are not here in Bent Creek in two weeks, when it's time to take those stitches out, I'm going to see to it that you get back here to see me. And don't worry, because it won't hurt taking them out as much as it did putting them in."

"I guess I was lucky. I was sleeping the whole time," I told him. I let out a snicker.

Dr. Mitsen didn't find it funny. He ignored my sick humor and opened the door to leave. He said goodbye and left so that I could get dressed. After I was dressed, I walked back out to the front where Dr. Pelchat was waiting. Dr. Pelchat was reading over my chart.

"Two more weeks in those chains," he said. "Don't worry, Kristen. Two weeks will go by as fast as the past four weeks has for you."

CHAPTER 43

Friday was exactly four weeks to the day since I had taken the pills and had cut my wrists. Four weeks ago, I had almost died.

I opened my eyes and saw the sun shining through the windows. Ms. Mosley never failed. I looked at my bare wrists. No bandages. I held them up to the sunlight. Then I pressed my arms to my chest and kept them there, as if I was hugging them. I closed my eyes and let the sunshine warm me.

Ms. Mosley crept into the room. I heard her shoes squeak on the floor. I opened my eyes and saw her standing at the foot of my bed. I sat up.

"Are you ready?" she asked me.

I nodded and got out of bed. I tried to gather my things for my bath quietly. I didn't want Mena to wake up and see Ms. Mosley helping me. I could hear all of her smart remarks in my head. She would shove it in my face as much as she could, and as loud as possible.

"So, how did it go with the doctor?" Ms. Mosley asked.

"The doctor said two more weeks," I told her.

I knew she could have read about it in my chart. She was trying to make conversation because of the awkward silence while she helped me clean up. After I was drying off, she put the treatment for my stitches on my wrists. The smell was strong.

I thought back to the day I had woken up in the hospital. I'd had no idea where I was, or that I had been asleep for a week. From looking at my stitches, I couldn't really tell that I had done that much damage. I had waited so long to look at what I had done. Now that the bandages were off, I had no choice. When I looked down, it didn't really feel like the wrists I was looking at were mine.

"How long have the stitches been in?" she asked as I started to dress.

I frowned, remembering how angry I had been when I had woken up. How angry I had been at Dr. Cuvo! He had only been doing his job, trying to help me. I had been so harsh in the beginning. I had been asleep for a whole week before I realized that I was still alive.

"It's been a month," I told her.

"Seems like a long time?" she asked as she stared down at my wrists. She looked like she wanted to touch them. I wouldn't have minded, but she didn't.

"No," I honestly replied. "It doesn't seem that long ago at all."

Ms. Mosley nodded and seemed to be forcing herself to look away from me.

I admired Ms. Mosley for her honesty and her influence on me to want to be honest not only with her, but with myself as well. I was scared, but I began to feel something change within myself each time she and I were together. She didn't make these moments awkward, because I felt that she really did care each time she helped me.

"Do you think that Janine is okay?" I asked her.

Ms. Mosley looked back up at me as if she was not expecting me to say anything else.

She smiled at me and she said, "I'm sure Janine is going to be fine. She's getting the help that she needs."

"What if she's like Rocky? What if she dies?"

"She didn't do enough damage. Thank God for that," she told me.

She was right. Ms. Mosley wouldn't have said that just to make me feel comfortable.

With my mind still aching and worried inside, I held back what I really wanted to ask her. However, Ms. Mosley wasn't the type of counselor to let something like that go. She used her gift of deep perception, and she saw right through me.

"If there is something bothering you, I'm here to listen," Ms. Mosley assured me.

"Sometimes I wonder if..." I hesitated. I took a deep breath and continued. "I wonder if, I mean, when I get out of here, will I do it again?"

"Do what again?"

"Will I hurt myself?"

She gave me a look of deep concern, and the words she spoke were earnest.

"It is true that there are people who leave the hospital, and they do fall back into deep depression, self-injuring, and some try and even succeed in committing suicide. Some people leave the hospital still feeling a little weak. If the doctors notice that these people are not better, they have to be placed in a long-term facility so that they can take more time to heal. But some people come here because they had suffered a moment of weakness, as you did. As they begin to heal here at Bent Creek, they begin to grow stronger, and then they build up enough strength to be able to survive outside of the hospital. You, Kristen, I believe, will be a survivor."

"How do you know? Maybe I'm like Rocky. Or I'll be like Janine, and have to go to a long-term hospital."

"Don't you dare do that to yourself," Ms. Mosley said. "I know that you're not going to be weak when you leave here, because I can already see you healing. You're a fast healer, Kristen. You're strong. You don't see it, but you are. You ask these questions, not because you're scared, though you think you are. You're not scared of what the answer's going to be, because you already know that what I'm going to tell you is the truth. You'll take that truth to heart and you'll remember it. Then you'll use it. That's how you learn to heal. That's how you will learn to survive."

I was scared because I wasn't completely sure. I knew that she wouldn't lie to me, but how could she be certain that I was strong enough to be a survivor once I left Bent Creek? She seemed positive of what she spoke, but I was unsure and confused. I didn't want to talk about it anymore.

"Thank you," I said to her with a forced smile.

Ms. Mosley nodded at me. I could tell that she did not want to drop the conversation by the way she stared at me intensely, but she did close the subject anyway.

"You'll understand when the time comes," she said. "I'll let you finish getting dressed."

She left me alone in the bathroom.

After I was completely dressed, I went back into the bedroom. Mena was fast asleep in her own bed. I tiptoed quietly to my bed so that I wouldn't wake her.

At eight o'clock Ms. Mosley came into the room to wake us up. "Vitals! Come on! Get up, girls! You need to come get your vitals checked! Let's start the day!"

Mena growled with her head under her pillow. "I hate you!" she complained as Ms. Mosley continued her way down the hallway towards the other girls' rooms.

"I hate it when she does that!" she kept on.

I ignored her as I slid my shoes onto my feet. Mena kept the pillow over her head and snuggled up under the thin, white blanket. I folded Janine's blanket and laid it neatly on top of mine. I walked past Mena to get out of the door. As I walked out, I passed Ms. Mosley. She was coming back into our room to make sure we were up. As I got down to the double doors that led to the main unit, I could hear Ms. Mosley nagging at Mena to get out of the bed. I could picture Mena's angry face all scrunched up and her evil eyes rolling as she tensed up under Ms. Mosley's stern morning breath and intimidating motherly scold.

I smiled at the thought.

Geoffrey smiled at me. I realized I was on the unit and unintentionally looking his way. He was checking vital signs on the patients. He must have thought that I was smiling at him. But he didn't greet me as he normally did. He shooed the other kid who was sitting in the chair away when he was finished, and I took the empty seat. Geoffrey began checking my blood pressure. I stayed silent, but I kept the smile on my face.

When Geoffrey was finished checking my vital signs, I went over and sat down at an empty table. Other patients started filling the room. Mena walked in, sleepy-eyed. She got in line to get her vitals checked.

For some reason I couldn't take my eyes off her. There was something different about her. She didn't have the same evil look that she seemed to have had permanently engraved on her face. She seemed calm and almost humbled. When she was finished with her vitals, she looked over at me. She started heading my way, as if she was going to sit at the table with me, but Tai cut her off, sitting down at the table with me instead. Mena walked the opposite way and sat down in a chair near the corner of the room by herself.

Tai smiled at me wearily. "Morning, sunshine," she said in a flat tone.

"Good morning," I said with just as much excitement.

"Are you ready for another day in hell?"

I shook my head and leaned back in the chair.

"Did you hear about Rocky?" Tai leaned back too. Then she rolled up a piece of paper and stuck it in her mouth. She sucked on it as if it was a cigarette.

I looked at her strangely. "What are you doing?"

"Hey! Give me a break," she pleaded. "I asked you a question. Did you hear about Rocky?"

I shook my head. My body felt numb all of a sudden. I couldn't move until she told me and relieved my mind. I was expecting what was coming next, but I was sure I was wrong. I had to be wrong.

"He's dead," she assured me. She spit the piece of paper out of her mouth onto the table. Then she lay her head down on her arms as they lay folded across the table.

My head felt stuffy. The numbness seeped in.

"How do you know?" I asked.

"*Please,*" Tai scoffed. "I hear these people talk in here all the time. The only thing is, Dr. Pelchat doesn't know. He doesn't know because no one wants to call him and tell him. They probably won't tell him until he comes in to work. I wonder if we'll get another group speech, or if he and Ms. Mosley will get into a *real* boxing match." She seemed a little too excited at the thought.

I tried to move my fingers. I tried to move my head. Nothing wanted to work. Nothing felt real on my body. Everyone seemed too normal for this to be true. When Ms. Mosley came in to help me clean up, she seemed like everything was fine. She didn't behave as though a former patient had just died. Geoffrey was smiling. He seemed all right.

I scanned the room with my eyes. This time I tried to look closer. Geoffrey was smiling, but he wasn't talking to anyone. Usually he made jokes or tried to make conversation while checking vitals. Ms. Mosley seemed like her usual self, but she wasn't saying much, either. Except when Ms. Mosley and I had been alone in the bathroom, when I had asked her those questions, she had seemed to be more concerned. She'd pressed me so hard to talk to her and to tell her what was wrong. When I had told her, she'd seemed determined to get me to understand how I needed to be a survivor.

"Oh, that's cool!" Tai exclaimed. "You got your bandages off! Oh, yeah! You really cut yourself!" She was too amused.

I hid my arms under the table. I ignored her. "Does anyone else know about Rocky besides the counselors?" I asked.

She shrugged. "I overheard Ms. Mosley talking to Geoffrey a few hours ago when I was going to the water fountain to get a drink. They were the only ones I heard talking about it. You're the only one I've told besides Jesse, over there. Jesse told me that he didn't like Rocky anyway. I didn't either, but still, he shouldn't have died. That sucks."

"Time for Group!" Dr. Finch came through the main unit doors that led to freedom. "Let's just go ahead and circle up in the living room there. Come on, everyone!" Dr. Finch seemed like his normal self.

As everyone began to gather around the circle, I noticed that there seemed to be more people here than before Daniel had left. I sat down when I got to the circle. When everyone was settled, Dr. Finch began as he normally did in Morning Group. He noticed that there were new faces, and said that we'd introduce ourselves and go over goals. I was hoping he wouldn't call on me first. I was still trying to figure out if what Tai had said about Rocky was true. It couldn't have been. My mind was completely consumed with it.

"Kristen?" Dr. Finch called out to me.

I looked up, startled. I shuddered when I saw that all eyes were on me.

"Yes?" I answered, a bit confused.

"It's your turn," Tai told me.

I heard a few people laugh at me. I must have been the first person to speak. Dr. Finch always went first, but everyone knew that he didn't really count.

I took a deep breath and tried to gather my thoughts. Don't think about Rocky! Don't think about death! I kept trying to tell myself this.

"I'm Kristen," I said.

Then I paused. Mena was staring right at me. Her eyes were completely blank. I looked away from her.

"I'm seventeen," I said. I swallowed. *My birthday is in a few weeks*, I thought to myself. *No. That's not right*, I told myself. *Wait. I'm in Group. Think, Kristen, think.* But I couldn't think. "I'm seventeen."

"Yeah! You already said that," said another patient whom I had never seen before. Others began to laugh at me. Even Tai laughed.

Dr. Finch put his hand up. "Quiet!" he said.

The room fell to a hush.

"Kristen," Dr. Finch said. "Are you all right?"

I should have said yes and moved on, but my mind wouldn't let me. I was feeling too much all at once, and I couldn't get control. My head felt like it was full of helium and the only things weighing it down were my eyeballs. My eyes felt like they weighed a ton. I shook my head and touched my temples.

"My head is hurting really bad," I told Dr. Finch.

"Do you need to see the nurse?"

"Yes, I think so," I told him.

"Go ahead," he said.

As I walked away from the circle, I watched Tai's jaw drop. She rolled her eyes coldly at me and looked away. She was upset because I was leaving. Maybe she thought I was faking my headache. Mena's eyes followed me out of the sitting area. But there was still no real expression on her face. She was just blank.

I exited the sitting area and went over to the nurse's station that was near the counselor's desk. I approached the nurse who was busy gathering medication and getting the pills ready for morning medication. I told her I had a bad headache. She looked at my chart to make sure the doctor didn't order that I not have pain killers. She put my chart down, gathered up two little blue pills, and put them in a cup. Then she brought me a cup of water.

"That's Aleve," she said. "That should help your headache."

I swallowed the Aleve and the water down quickly. When I was finished, she took my garbage and threw it away. I thanked her. As I started to walk away, Geoffrey looked up at me from behind the counselor's desk. He was on the telephone. He waved to me to come to him. I walked over.

"Kristen," he said. "I don't normally do this, because phone calls are limited to a certain time. But since you are here, I will let you take this call if you want."

I was frustrated because of my headache. Geoffrey seemed to be talking too loudly. I was confused as to who could be calling me. Then I remembered Mom had said that Lexus had wanted to call me. Geoffrey stretched his arm out to me with the phone in his hand. I took a deep breath as I took the phone from him.

"Keep it short, please," he said. "Dr. Pelchat will be here soon."

I had to take the phone call. The phone was already in my hand.

"Hello," I greeted into the phone.

"Kristen!" a familiar, sweet voice exclaimed.

"Lexus," I said.

Her voice was completely calm and sweet. It didn't sound like morning where she was. "How are you?"

I tried to smile, but there was too much going on inside of my head. I coughed a little.

"Are you okay?" she asked.

"Yes," I said. "So, what's going on?"

"Nothing," she said. "I just wanted to hear your voice." Her voice was sincere. Did she miss me? I didn't want to allow myself to think that. "*We* miss you," she continued. "I tried to call you before, but they said that you couldn't receive calls yet. I guess I called when you were at lunch or something. I want to come see you again, but everything has been so crazy. But I will try to come see you tomorrow. I have some time off."

I smiled. I said in a low voice, "I miss you." It was almost a whisper.

I saw Geoffrey look at me. He tapped his index finger on his watch and nodded at the door to remind me of Dr. Pelchat coming in at any moment. I tried to stay focused on Lexus. She loved me. She really did miss me.

"Do you really miss me, Lexus?" I asked her.

"Yes," she whispered. "I miss you."

I closed my eyes and let myself feel her words. I kept letting them play in my mind exactly the way she'd said it. My eyes began to water. I heard a voice in the background on Lexus' end.

Her voice was louder when she said, "*We all* miss you!" She seemed a little too eager and over-dramatic when she spoke. "Yes, *we all* miss you over here." I could just picture her. She was smiling, playing with her hair, and she was doing what she always did when someone else was watching her. She was putting on a show.

I clenched my jaws. My thoughts were ruined. She wasn't for real. A sharp pain went through my chest.

"Kristen!" Geoffrey frantically called out to me.

I looked over at him.

"Kristen, give me the phone! Now!" He reached out for it.

I looked at the door, and Dr. Pelchat was coming in. He was putting his key in the door.

Lexus continued, "John is here. He wants to..."

I quickly handed Geoffrey the phone. He hung it up just in time. Dr. Pelchat entered and he closed the door behind him. I could already see in his face that he had to know about Rocky. He was the only one in here who looked affected, except for me. I was obviously not okay. His face was red, his shoulders were slumped, and he didn't smile. He didn't greet Geoffrey or any of us. Geoffrey tried to approach him, but he just put his hand up. Geoffrey shut his mouth, and then Dr. Pelchat grabbed a chart and walked away.

Geoffrey told me to go back to my group. When I returned, Morning Group was letting out to take morning medication, and then go to breakfast. Tai ran up to me.

She asked, "Do you think they will tell us?"

I didn't want to disappoint her. I shrugged, unsure. She walked on ahead of me and didn't say anything more. Mena pushed past me. When she got ahead, she looked back at me. It was a long and hard stare. What did she want to say? I hated her eyes. When she saw that I wasn't going to say anything to her, she turned away from me and kept walking forward.

I didn't have anything to say. I felt completely lost at that moment. I looked down at my wrists. If Rocky really was dead, why had he died later on? Could they not have saved him? Had he tried to kill himself again after getting better?

I didn't really understand what had happened. Dr. Pelchat had every reason to be upset. He probably didn't want us to know about it, because he thought that we'd get ideas from Rocky's behavior. Maybe he thought we'd try to get away with it ourselves while we were in Bent Creek, or even when we got out. We were supposed to be protected. He'd told us that suicide was not an option.

Dr. Pelchat hadn't protected Rocky. Rocky hadn't wanted to be protected. Maybe he hadn't thought that he could be protected from what had been going on inside of himself. We didn't feel protected. I didn't feel like I could be protected. Not from everything that had happened and what was going to happen. Maybe that's how Rocky had felt, I thought to myself. Most of us would end up envying Rocky.

As the day went on, everything just seemed too normal. I hadn't seen Dr. Pelchat yet for my session. I hadn't seen him since the morning when he had come through the doors to our ward. Knowing what we knew made things seem a little too normal. Tai said that she could tell in our group meetings that the counselors were worried, and were trying to be calm.

Finally, after lunch, Dr. Bent called us into Anger Management. The only people I recognized in my group were Tai and Mena. There were only nine of us. I sat on the end seat, far away from Mena. Dr. Bent let everyone introduce themselves with just first names. We didn't go through the regular routine of stating our name, age, and reason for being at Bent Creek. Mena still didn't seem like herself. She was quiet and distant, and she didn't have any expression on her face.

When it was her turn to speak, she wearily told everyone her name, and it passed on. I was the last one to speak.

Dr. Bent leaned forward in her seat. She began to explain what AngerManagement was about, and what we were going to discuss. Mena unexpectedly raised her hand, as if she had something to say. Dr. Bent looked shocked.

She said, "Yes, Mena? Do you have a question?"

Mena stared down at her fingernails.

"Yes?" Dr. Bent pressed.

Mena raised her eyes with her head still low, giving her an intimidating look. She looked angry. She took a deep breath and looked back down at her fingernails. They looked clean, but she picked at them as if they were dirty. Finally, she opened her mouth to speak.

"Is it true?" Mena asked.

Dr. Bent shook her head. "I'm sorry. Is what true?"

"You know what I'm talking about," Mena growled.

Now she was looking straight into Dr. Bent's eyes. Her jaws were tight and her fists were clenched.

"You'll have to tell me what it is you are talking about," Dr. Bent told her.

"Fine," Mena said. "You want to do it this way?" She was getting upset, but she seemed to be trying to stay calm.

"Mena, please calm down," said Dr. Bent. "Listen to me. Maybe you should wait to talk to your doctor if it's something that is making you this upset."

"This is Anger Management, isn't it?" Mena yelled. I could sense that she was going to lose her temper. "Is Rocky dead?"

Dr. Bent closed her eyes. She nodded her head. "I'm not going to lie to you. He did suffer with some complications, and he passed away yesterday morning."

Everyone in the room gasped except Tai, Mena, Dr. Bent, and me. We were the only ones in the room who had actually known who Rocky was. Dr. Bent kept on speaking. She went on about sadness, grief, anger. She told us that we needed to learn how to cope with death because it was a part of life. Her words did not seem to be getting through, because Rocky was young like us. He wasn't supposed to be dead. Not yet.

As Dr. Bent went on, I watched Mena's face turn red. She bit down on her bottom lip and she shuffled her body around. She looked like she was holding something inside and was trying her best to keep it inside of her. It seemed almost like it was going to burst out of her.

"Today," Dr. Bent said, "we will talk about how to cope with suicide. When someone you know, like a close friend, commits suicide, we need to know how to cope with it."

"How?" Mena screamed. "How do you people sit here and say these stupid things? You don't know us! You don't even care about us! You think that you know everything! He had a life! A life! And he saw beyond what any of you blind-folded idiots could ever see! It was the truth, and you made him feel like he was crazy! That's why he did it! That's why he got away. He's freer than all of you! And you know it! Tell the truth! I hate you! I hate all of you!"

At that point, it was obvious that Dr. Bent had enough of Mena. She pointed towards the door and said, "Mena, get out."

"Fine!" Mena said as she stormed towards the door. When she exited, she slammed the door behind her.

Dr. Bent called Geoffrey on the telephone. She told him what had happened and asked him to meet Mena on the unit and to deal with her. I had a feeling it meant that Mena was going to the BCR.

"Are you okay?" Tai asked Dr. Bent.

Dr. Bent nodded. "Yes. Thank you," she said to Tai.

Dr. Bent looked angry, but she remained calm. She shook herself off calmly and said, "We have something effective to talk about. We are going to talk about this."

We stayed silent. I was shocked. By the looks of everyone else, it seemed as though they didn't expect her to want to talk about it, either.

"We have to finish talking about this and how we deal with situations like this," she said as tears began to fall from her eyes. Her voice remained calm and vigorous. "I hope that you know, without a doubt, that we are here to help you. We will always do our best as long as you are in our care. You have someone to talk to here, and you have people who really do care about you. We will do our best to guide you and show you the right way to cope and contend with life. Everything you go through and everything that you feel affects your life. *This is your life!* You only have one. No matter what you suffer with, every day that you wake up, and every minute that you are breathing air, is another chance for you to make the choice to do what is right to help yourself. We can only do so much. We can only take you by the hand and show you, but you have to let go and move on your own towards making the right choices."

She wiped her tears away and continued, "If you want help, we are here, and you are going to get it. You will receive the help that you came here for. The truth is that some people, no matter how hard you try, just can't be helped. With some people, no matter how far along in life they are, there's just nothing that can be done."

My thoughts went from hopeful to hopeless. What did she mean by that? I thought that she was going to say that we all could be helped, and that there was hope for all of us, but she didn't. Her words were precise. That scared me.

After Dr. Bent's coping skills group, I went back to the main unit feeling worse than I had when I'd woken up that morning. My mind stayed on the book. I wanted to go back to the room to get the book and continue to read more about Borderline Personality Disorder, but I was too scared to go back there alone. Mr. Sharp rang in my ears. He begged for my veins. Why?

Rocky's death was affecting me more that I knew. Everyone's fascination with how he'd done it. All of the details. The visions of his head in that box. His tongue extended from his mouth. Daniel's cries.

Before the tears could even begin to fall, I went to the counselor's desk where Geoffrey was sitting, keeping an eye on the unit. I asked for a pen and a sheet of paper. Without hesitation, Geoffrey handed me one sheet and a pencil, but demanded that I return the pencil when I was finished with it.

"Yes," I said. "So that I won't try to stick it in my eye. Right?" I sarcastically replied.

"Hey now, Kristen!" He seemed shocked.

The mood was not good in this place. I sat at a table where I was sure Geoffrey could see me. When I sat down, I waved at him because he was still staring. He rolled his eyes and looked away from me.

When Mr. Sharp had called out to me while I had been in public school, it had usually been easy to slip into the girls' bathroom and get those feelings out. The blood would soak in and decorate the soft, white toilet paper. I used to like to watch the quilted pattern's white, floral motif get painted red with the rouge lineage that spilled from my veins.

When I had been in a class like AP Chemistry or College Literature, it had been too difficult to escape. These classes had been taught by authority figures that were supposed to make us feel privileged and special, just because we could read a chapter or two ahead of the required assignment quicker than others in our class. They had decided that we were gifted, and put us there with teachers that had been hard asses and quick to knock us down to make us feel not so special and stupid because of their own insecurities. When I couldn't escape, I had pulled out a random sheet of paper and had used my pencil, not to jam my own eye out with, but instead I'd bleed my thoughts onto the paper. I had decorated the white, less soft, college ruled, blue lined, motif paper with speckles of grey with words.

This time it was Geoffrey watching, instead of an uptight teacher.

I began:

What is it when you try?
Get to the end.
Succeed and die.
What is it when you fail?
Was it all just a fake?
A real way out?
An easy bail?
Carrying a heavy load upon my chest,
Without a helpful trailer.
Feeling sorry for myself?
A disastrous and complete...

I swear that it was the worst thing I had ever written. However, it had come from somewhere that needed to kick it out. Rocky's face appeared in my mind. I remembered when Cadence had been obsessed with pestering him when he had first come to Bent Creek. I remembered when I had first spoken to him. The very first thing I had said directly to him was, "How did you do it?" or something like that. I had asked him how he'd tried to kill himself. Why had I asked him that, the exact day I had met him? What had I been thinking? He hadn't answered me.

I read the last four lines of the poem again:
Carrying a heavy load upon my chest,
Without a helpful trailer.
Feeling sorry for myself?
A disastrous and complete...

Disgusted, I did not want to continue. Nevertheless, I pressed the pencil to the paper again to decorate the rest. Bleed in the gray.

...failure.

I read the poem silently to myself. I read it again. Then I read it once more. That made three times I read that horrible poem before I broke the pencil in half and threw it across the room. Both parts of the pencil hit the metal legs of the table across the way, and it made a loud clang. This made Geoffrey look up at me.

"Kristen!" he exclaimed.

I aggressively pushed the paper away from myself, and it slid off of the table. Geoffrey shook his head and looked away from me. He didn't even ask me what was wrong. He didn't tell me to pick up the broken pencil pieces. He just looked away. For some reason, this made me angrier. I got up from the table and stormed off to my room. I wished the doors had locks on them. I'd keep everyone out, just like at home. I could go in my room and just lock the door. Keep it shut and stay in there for hours. Mom didn't care. I was out of her way. I sat on the edge of my bed and saw the BPD book sitting on the edge of the occasional table. I picked it up without hesitation.

"Tell me! Tell me what's wrong with me! Tell me now!" I screamed at the book.

Of course it didn't answer me back verbally. But Mr. Sharp was sure there. He was shining through those sharp butterfly wings that rested between the pages. I forgot I had left him in there. I shook the book to see what page he would fall out. He fell out of page 136 and landed on my lap. I kept the book open and looked at the page. Oh yes, I thought as I began to read page 136. It was on the chapter of symptoms of

Borderline Personality Disorder:

The constant feeling and fear of abandonment and being alone.
Frequent and sometimes extreme mood swings.
A changing and unsure sense of identity.
Over-sensitivity to criticism and real or imagined rejection.
The constant feelings of worthlessness that quickly alters to belief that
one is deserving of better treatment and recognition than what is given.
Do you feel that everyone is ignoring you? Do you feel that no one
cares? Do you feel that you are the one who goes out of your way for
everyone else, but that no one is there for you? Is that what you feel you
deserve? And at times do you feel that you are being wronged?

"This doesn't make sense," I said to the book. "What are you talking
about?"

The need for attention.
The fear of being alone.
Pushing family and friends away and avoiding new contact in fear of
being abandoned.
"What? I want her attention? But then I push her away? *I* called her!"

Impulsive behavior.
Depression.
Constant mood changes.
Violent outbursts.
Self injury and other self-destructive behavior such as the abuse of
alcohol and drugs.
Suicidal hints and behavior.
Suicidal attempts that may be just to call for attention. Which sometimes
leads to accidental suicide without the intention of succeeding.

I had nothing to say back to the book.

When it was time to meet with Dr. Pelchat, I didn't speak about Rocky.
Dr. Pelchat didn't seem to be all the way there with me. I knew that it
was because of Rocky's death. I wanted to ask him, just to make sure it
was true. Dr. Bent wouldn't have said it was true if it actually wasn't. I
didn't want to upset Dr. Pelchat anymore.

I told him that I had started to read the book on BPD. He was glad to
hear that. He suggested that I read more. There was no talk about
medication because he didn't have a diagnosis for me yet. He assured me

that the test results would be back in a few days. I didn't know whether to be glad about that, because I didn't want to worry for a while, or if I should be anxious and upset because I'd be finding out very soon if I did have Borderline Personality Disorder. From what I had read, it seemed like I understood too well some of the words written down in that book.

"How are you feeling today, Kristen?" he asked.

I looked around the room and shook my head. "I don't know. It's been a weird day. How are you?"

"Is how I'm doing really what concerns you right now?"

"I'm curious."

"You know, Kristen, I'm curious about something too."

My heart began to beat fast. I waited to hear what he had to say.

"Did you hear about Rocky's death?"

"Yes, I did," I responded.

I could feel him staring at me. I still was not looking at him. Instead, I let my eyes roam around the room.

"How did it make you feel to hear that one of your peers actually succeeded in taking his life?"

I couldn't believe he was asking me this. He'd caught me off guard. I didn't say anything in response.

"Is it hard for you to talk about?"

"How did it make you feel, Dr. Pelchat? He was one of your patients."

"My concern right now is you, Kristen."

"Why is Rocky's suicide your concern for me? That doesn't make any sense."

"It makes perfect sense, Kristen."

"How is that?"

"Look at your wrists."

Anger began to well inside of me. I locked eyes with him. And when I did, I knew he had me. I couldn't look away when he began to speak.

"You tried to kill yourself a little less than a month and a half ago. Your heart stopped beating, and you could have died. Do you realize that, Kristen?"

"Do you feel like you failed? Kristen?"

"I failed? Is that what this is about? I failed! And Rocky succeeded. He got out!" The anger and the tears flowed out of me.

"That's how you see it? Rocky got out? And you failed because you didn't?"

"Why do you say that? Why do you keep saying 'failed'?"

"Isn't that what you mean? Those were your words. You said 'failed'."

"What? No. You just said. You said, 'You failed.'"

"I'm just repeating what you wrote."

"What I wrote?"

Dr. Pelchat opened my chart and pulled out a wrinkled, sheet of paper. He reached out and handed it to me. I looked at it.

"My crappy poem."

I had never seen Dr. Pelchat look so shocked. "Is that what you call it, Kristen?" he asked.

"Yes," I said.

"It doesn't look like a crappy poem to me. It looks like a very deep piece of work created from an expression of serious emotion."

I tried not to let his compliment affect the anger I was feeling inside.

"How did you get this?" I asked.

"I found it on the floor of the main unit right next to a broken pencil. The sitting area was being cleared out, and I asked Geoffrey who had taken paper and pencil from the counselor's desk, and hadn't returned the pencil. Your name was mentioned."

"Right."

"Why are you so angry, Kristen?"

"What makes you think I'm angry, Dr. Pelchat?" I only said his name because he kept saying mine every time he asked me a question.

"You are responding to me with some anger in your voice. Are you angry?"

"I'm upset."

"What is that poem about?"

"It's about the Devil," I snapped. I was annoyed at him for asking me so many questions.

"The Devil? Help me understand, Kristen. How does the Devil tie into that?"

"It's about how the Devil is evil. And we are evil. And we do evil things that the Devil likes. Like hurting people. Like hurting children. Like killing ourselves. And when we do this, we may not necessarily be trying to kill ourselves, but maybe we are trying to do something else."

"Are you speaking about yourself?"

"I don't know. Rocky killed himself. He got put in here because he had tried to kill himself. But then when he got in here, the place that was supposed to help him, well, he succeeded in killing himself."

Dr. Pelchat did not respond. He just kept looking at me.

So I continued, "I tried to kill myself. I failed. But now I feel..." I stopped myself. "I mean, I feel confused."

"About what?"

"I thought that I wanted to die."

"Do you not feel like you want to die?"

"Sometimes."

"How about right now?"

"Frustrated. Confused."

"I see. Does Rocky's suicide make you feel frustrated and confused about your own feelings towards what you had tried to do to yourself?"

I thought about his question. Rocky seemed to really want to die. He had tried it and even when he was brought in to Bent Creek, the feeling seemed not to leave him. Maybe he was in the wrong place. Maybe he needed to be somewhere long term, like Janine. Was he hopeless, as Dr. Bent had said that some people are? Was I hopeless too?

"Yes," I answered Dr. Pelchat. "It does change my feelings. I do sometimes feel like I would be better off gone, but then I feel like..."

"Yes? Like what, Kristen?"

"Like it can't all be hopeless. Right?"

"No," Dr. Pelchat assured me. "You're not hopeless. If you are hopeless, then, what are we both doing here?"

I don't know, I thought to myself. I sank back in my seat feeling calm, but still a bit frustrated. I wanted to understand what it felt like to be hopeful and actually want to get through all of this. I needed to know what it meant to cope, survive, and not feel like I wanted to die.

Dr. Pelchat opened my chart and began to write. I tried to sit up to see what he was writing. Doctors were good at scribbling so that no one could understand what they were writing except other doctors and nurses. It seemed like a secret code only doctors used.

Finally, Dr. Pelchat looked back up at me. He said, "You are making great progress. You should know that, Kristen."

Even more confused, I said with a sarcastic smile, "That's good to know, *Dr. Pelchat.*"

Going to bed that night was lonesome. Even though I didn't really like Mena, it felt strange not having her there in the bed next to mine. Mr. Sharp wasn't creeping around me. He always appeared in my lonely and empty times. He hadn't bothered me since that day I'd denied him. He'd said he wouldn't come back, and that scared me. I snuggled under Janine's blanket. I started thinking about if Mr. Sharp really had left me. I felt my heart jump. How lonely would I really be if he actually had left?

I'd be lost and empty.

I closed my eyes and tried to stop thinking. But the more I tried not to think, the faster my mind raced. Too many thoughts, and no pen or paper to write. No Mr. Sharp to bleed it away. No relief. Just myself, alone, in the dark, underneath the blanket, in a cold and empty room. Scared, I lay still and let my mind take over.

I thought back to when I'd picked up the pills and had swallowed them down. I ran my fingers over the stitches and felt them. I felt the scars. I thought of when I'd picked up the knife. I thought of when I'd begun to slice. I thought of when I'd dialed Lexus on the phone and it had rung with no answer. I'd hung up and tried again. That time it had gone straight to voice mail.

Lexus had said that she missed me. She had said that she was coming to visit me the next day. I tried to smile and focus on the next day. I felt a tear come out of my eye. If only she had known...

CHAPTER 44

Keeping true to what she had said, Lexus was the first person to show up for visiting hours the next day. I was surprised that she was the first, because she was a very busy person. She showed up with a sweet smile, and presented me with a warm embrace. She smelled sweet, like wild cherries. Her hair was down and sweeping over her shoulders. Her gorgeous smile made me feel like old times when we were really friends, and nothing was fake. Not even our smiles and hugs.

After we hugged each other, Lexus removed her sweater, commenting that it was too warm inside the main unit. Then we sat down at a table together. We gave each other awkward smiles, not really knowing what to say or where to begin our conversation.

I finally said, "Thank you for coming to visit me." Then I smiled again.

She returned the smile, even warmer than before. "Of course," she said. "I told you that I was coming. We hung up kind of weird yesterday."

"Yeah," I laughed nervously. "I had to go. I didn't really get to say goodbye, because my doctor was coming and I wasn't really supposed to be on the phone."

"Oh!" she chuckled. "That's a shame. John wanted to say hi to you."

I rolled my eyes coldly at her.

She noticed. Changing the subject, she suddenly asked, "Are you comfortable?"

I had to think about it for a second before I answered. "Well," I replied, "It's okay. I am as comfortable as I'm going to be in a mental hospital."

"I guess so," she said, with her fake smile.

"How's your family?" I asked, because I wanted to change the subject.

She smiled what seemed like a genuine smile while looking down at her hands as they rested in her lap underneath the table.

"Everyone is doing great," she said. "My mom just bought a new SUV. Yeah, so that's cool. Dad's happy about it, because he doesn't have to share the truck with her anymore." She laughed to herself, seemingly amused.

I tried to smile back at her. "That's nice," I told her.

The mood was too awkward. I wasn't feeling cheerful and chatty. There was something eating at me from the inside. I didn't want it to come out, because I knew that if it did, it would ruin the whole visit. It was something about her smile. It was the way she looked nice and smelled so good. It was making me angry inside. I wanted to tell her to stop faking her smiles with me, and let's be real. But I didn't want to mess things up.

"How's John?" I asked without thinking.

A look of surprise came over her face. She seemed like she had to think before she answered. She looked me in the eyes, like she was searching me to make sure I had really meant to ask that question.

"We are great!" Lexus said happily.

I looked down at my hands, because she kept looking down at hers. I felt sick inside again. The silence was making it worse. Whatever was gnawing at me wanted to burst out and just bite Lexus' head off. I swallowed until that ball in my chest slowed down. It was spinning too fast.

"Kristen, there is something that's been bothering me. We are supposed to be real friends, right? Well, I feel like we should talk and be real with each other."

"What is it?" I asked her. I somehow already knew. I had a feeling that inquiring further would damage our short visit, but I had to hear her. I wanted to know what she was really thinking.

"Why did you do it?"

I'd known she was going to ask eventually. I just hadn't known that she would ask me while I was still at Bent Creek. I didn't look up at her. I just kept staring down at my hands as they rested on my lap.

"Was it because of that night?" she prodded on.

I didn't answer. To vex her, I raised my arms to pretend I was stretching, and I rolled up my sleeves. Her eyes grew big when she saw the exposed stitches and the scars on my arms. She looked down at the table and shook her head. It was all too real for her perfect world, I thought.

"Kristen, please," she pleaded. "I need to know. I need you to tell me, because I've been beating myself up over this. I don't want to think that you did this, and that it's my fault. If it could have been prevented because I-"

"So you think it's about you?" I growled at her. "You think this is all about you."

"No," she pleaded. "I didn't say that. That's not what I meant, Kristen."

"Yes, it is what you meant," I told her. "It's always about you, Lexus. Isn't it? That's why you didn't answer your phone. That's why you didn't want to talk to me."

"Kristen, the reason I didn't answer my phone was not because of you. John didn't want us to answer our phones that night. There was a good reason for us not to answer our phones. John, he-"

"What did he tell you?" I asked her. "Did he tell you not to answer the phone because he didn't want you to be burdened with all of my problems? Did he tell you not to talk to me because all I do is talk about depressing things and make you depressed and sad, too?"

"No," she said. Lexus sounded like she was going to cry. "It was not like that. If you would just listen, I will tell you. We were trying to plan our future together. You are right. We didn't want to be burdened with any problems. *Not that night.*"

My eyes shot up from my hands to her fake, sympathetic frowning face. I was gazing at her, hard. I kept silent as she continued to speak.

"I love you, Kristen. I really do. You are like a sister to me. I mean, we have been through a lot together, especially when your family went through all of that mess. I could never just let you hurt. If I had have known that you had hurt yourself, I would have been there for you. But that night, I just wanted to be happy and enjoy that night with him. Everything was perfect. I didn't want to ruin that."

"Then it's a good thing you didn't answer your phone," I said to her in a calm, but stern, voice.

"It wasn't like that," she pleaded.

"Yes, it was!"

"Kristen, no..."

I shook my head. "Yes, it was. It's okay, Lexus. You, your Prince Charming, and your perfect family were having the perfect evening together. Your phone rings and you guys see that it's me trying to call. You think to yourself, 'Oh, God, I don't want to ruin this night by answering Kristen's call, because I already know it's going to be depressing and sad, and Kristen will ruin everything. That girl, Kristen, she's just full of problems. She's nothing but a burden!'"

I was breathing hard. The metal ball in my chest was turning so hard that I could hardly get the air in and out of my lungs fast enough to catch my breath.

I looked at Lexus as tears fell from her eyes. She shook her head angrily.

"That's not fair, Kristen. Not after everything that I have done for you. Not after all this time I've been your friend."

"Fine," I said coldly.

"I can't be like you!" she screamed. "I like being happy. I like being in love with a man who loves *me*! I like *living*! Being *alive*!"

"I said it's fine!" I screamed back at her. "Maybe you should stay away from me. I make you so unhappy. I make everyone feel so burdened and disgusted. Everything is so depressing with me. Maybe I'll even drive you to want to kill yourself. Go on! You deserve to be happy. Why don't you let the doctors deal with me? You don't have to worry about being my friend and being there for me anymore. It's not your responsibility. I shouldn't have real friends anyway. I'll ruin them, just like I'm ruining you. I'll make them check their caller I.D. every time the phone rings. And when they see my number, they won't pick up the phone. Just like you. Just go! Go before I ruin your happiness and your perfect life!"

I had never seen Lexus' face so sour. It felt rather good to see that hurt look on her face. For the first time in a long time, Lexus and I were being real. I knew that this sadness would not last too long for her. All she had to do was run into John's arms. Then she would tell him everything. That would make him hate me even more. John would comfort Lexus. She'd forget about our argument, and everything about me. She'd move on and never look back. She wouldn't remember that terrible, sick, and depressing friend who'd burdened her.

Truth be told, I wasn't angry with her for not answering her phone that night. I wouldn't have answered my call, either. It would have ruined her night if she had answered the phone, because I had already taken the pills. I had gotten scared, and I could only think to call her. When she hadn't answered, I'd grabbed the knife and had run it across my wrists to finish. I didn't want to be scared anymore.

Lexus gathered her purse and grabbed her sweater off the back of the chair where she was sitting.

"I don't know why I thought I could come here and talk to you," she said to me as she dug into her purse to find her keys.

She was very upset. I started to feel bad, but it was too late to stop her or to take back anything I had said.

"I thought I could come here and tell you the good news," she said.

"What good news?" I asked.

Lexus stayed silent as she swung her sweater over her shoulders. She slipped her left arm through the sleeve. As her hand slid out of the other end, I saw the diamond on her ring finger. I took a deep breath. I couldn't move.

"I'm leaving," she said. "I have nothing more to say to you. Call me when you are out of here. Maybe you will learn to listen to yourself when you speak. Right now, I don't think you do. Bye!" She left.

I sat, stuck to my seat. When she'd said that she wanted to tell me the good news, I'd had no idea what it could be until I'd seen the engagement ring that had not been on her finger when I had last seen her. Lexus hadn't had to say a word. That terrible metal ball turned tirelessly in my chest, making it get tighter and tighter. I squeezed my eyes shut. It hurt too badly. Tears began to fall out of my eyes.

I heard Geoffrey call out to me. I looked back at him. He called for me to come over to him because he was concerned. He asked me what was wrong. Without answering him, I got up and ran to my room before he could ask any more questions.

CHAPTER 45

Mena looked up at me, startled. She was lounging back on her bed, twisting the wings of my sterling silver butterfly pendant between her fingertips, and playing with Mr. Sharp. At first, I was shocked to see her because of what had happened in Anger Management yesterday, and because she was touching my butterfly.

I stood in front of her bed and looked down to make sure it was my pendant. I saw the silver wings shimmer in the sunlight that was coming through the blinds hanging from the window.

"What are you doing?" I scolded her.

Mena silently smiled at me while she teased me with the pendant.

"Don't smile at me," I said to her. "I am so sick of you." I leaned in close to her, not scared if she tried to hit me.

Mena took me by the hand and yanked me down. I flopped down on the bed next to her. She leaned over to me and pushed my hair out of my face. She kept her grip on my hand. She wasn't hurting me, but she was confusing me. Then she lifted my sleeve on the arm of the hand that she was holding.

"Did you know," she said, "that more than forty percent of people who attempt suicide become a statistic when they are released from a psychiatric hospital?"

"No," I told her as I tried to shove her away. She kept a tight grip.

"They become a statistic of people who succeed in killing themselves when they get out. They attempt suicide again, and then they actually die."

Scared, I tried to push her away again, but she held on tighter.

"Mena!" I cried out. "Please. I don't know what you're talking about. Let me go."

She shoved my hand away from rejecting her. I tried to pull away, but she had a good grip on my hand. She got my sleeve up to my elbow, and we both looked down at the stitches on my wrists. I began to calm down as I stared at the reality written in my skin. I saw the red stitches rooted in my skin. I saw the ugliness that I had created.

Mena loosened her grip on my hand as she saw me begin to accept it.

"It is really sad, isn't it?" she asked me.

"What do you mean?"

"You're born into this screwed-up world, and this is the place you end up. Or you end up in your grave." She shook her head as she continued to look down at my wrist. "Rocky knew what to do. He knew exactly what to do to make it happen. He knew he wanted to be free and never turn back."

"What are you talking about?"

She looked seriously into my eyes. "If you really want to die, there are ways to make it happen, whether they come to try to save you or not. There are ways that make it impossible to turn back, even when you're scared. Rocky snapped his neck. He cut his lifeline. He was dead when those losers got here to try to save him. It's like jumping off of a bridge onto a highway, shooting yourself in the head, or cutting your wrists the right way."

She gestured up and down with her fingers, running them down my exposed wrist. I watched her. She then ran her fingers across my wrist where I had cut the wrong way, and she shook her head at me.

"You didn't do it right."

I couldn't take my eyes off her. I didn't want to. What she said made sense to me. I looked down at my wrist again, then back up at her.

"No repair," she said. "No tears, no time for regret. Just die."

"I *was* serious about it," I told her.

She nodded her head. "Maybe," she said. "But you knew you could be saved. You probably even got scared. Rocky didn't want to be saved, and he wasn't scared. He wasn't scared because he did not leave his edge, even after they locked him up in this mind-bending place. They just want to pump us up full of pills that blind us to reality. They want the sun to keep shining, and they want us to like it.

They want us to be like your pretty, little friend out there. The one that came to visit you today."

I looked at her, shocked.

"Don't look at me like that," she said. "It's obvious how different the two of you are. You were getting so loud. I thought you were going to really let her have it. You should have. Let me guess, she's the pretty and successful one that your mom tells you to look up to, and you're the one that reminds her every day of how great she is. Man, she's lucky to have a friend like *you*."

I swallowed hard at what she said. As the silver butterfly wings twisted between her fingertips, I could see Mr. Sharp's smile. He hadn't left me.

"Don't take it the wrong way," Mena said. "I'm not trying to make you feel bad. You just need to know the truth. You need to think openly with the gift that you have. You are so much smarter than she is. She's blind. You are not in here because you did something bad. You are here because you know what other people can't accept. So they make us feel like we need to be alive and ignore the truth that is inside of us because they don't want us to know it. They want to keep being blinded from everything. You already know, don't you?"

Mr. Sharp was there. He nodded through me. "Yes, I know," he said through my lips.

"Don't let your edge go," she said to me. "Don't let it go for them. When you can finally move, that's when you will make them see that this is all you have." She held up the butterfly.

The silver, sharp wings made Mr. Sharp excited.

I knew what they wanted me to do. I took the butterfly from between her fingers.

"Don't worry," she said. "I won't say anything. I have my own." She reached into her pillowcase and pulled out a thin, naked razor blade. "I broke the plastic part from around one of those razors you buy from the grocery store and took this out. It's amazing how the cheaper ones are so much sharper than the more expensive shavers are. It's not as cute as yours, but it does do the job."

She lifted her pant leg, and I saw the fresh bruises on her legs.

"When did you do that to your legs?"

"My arms would have been too obvious. Last night they put me in that dark room. It's a good thing they didn't tie me down. They left me in there all night, after what had happened with Dr. Bent. I hate the dark. I needed to stay calm, so my razor saw to it." She pressed the razor to her lips roughly and kissed it.

"What happened yesterday?" I asked her. "You just went crazy."

"I didn't go crazy," she said with serious eyes. "I didn't do anything to that woman that she couldn't go home and drink off. It's like I said before. They want to blind us. Dr. Bent's no different. Why would they want to hide that Rocky *did* kill himself? Think about it."

I could see that she was beginning to get upset again, so I didn't say anything else. I began to get up, but she grabbed my hand again. I sat back down next to her.

She smiled deviously. "Do you want to?"

She held up her razor and gestured to my butterfly pendant. Mr. Sharp smiled back at her through my face. I tried to push back through. I shook my head, but she wasn't buying it. I knew that she could see Mr. Sharp clearly.

Mena calmly took the butterfly pendant out of my hand. She pressed the tip of the wing to my arm gently. My heart began to race. She pressed it hard onto my skin, and a sharp pain went through my veins.

"No," I moaned, but Mr. Sharp wouldn't let me pull away.

She continued to press. "Shhh," she shushed me. "We're almost there."

Mena pressed the wings harder to my skin until it broke though. The pain pushed through, and a rush of adrenaline flushed out of me. She dragged the wing down and made a bloody line on my arm. The warm redness gushed out from the wound as she pressed the wing deeply into my skin and dragged it down my arm. When the blood came through, Mr. Sharp burst inside of me in relief. He sighed softly with my breath and he let a moan out of my throat.

A tear came out of my eye while the tingling sensation ran through my skin. I looked down at the blood. It was exhilarating. Breathing heavily, and with that amazing feeling that I missed, I looked at Mena wide-eyed. I was amazed at what she had just done to me.

Mr. Sharp made me take the butterfly pendant from out of her hand.

"No one has ever done that to me before," I told her.

I looked down at my arm again. I saw the blood and remained calm. Mr. Sharp embraced me warmly through the blood. The anger caused by Lexus seeped out from the fresh wound.

Mena was smiling. She leaned in close to me. "That's good," she said. You're satisfied." She touched my hair again. This time she moved my bangs completely from my face.

I started to feel too strange. I moved slightly away from her.

"You're okay," she said. She scooted closer once more.

"Yes," I said. "I'm fine." I was a little confused.

"Kristen," she said as she gently touched my face with the left palm of her hand. "Have you ever…"

"Kristen?" A man's voice called out to me with a knock on the door.

I jumped up off Mena's bed, startled and still a little confused. I pulled my sleeve down and shoved the butterfly pendant into my pocket.

"Yes? Come in!" I called out.

Mr. Anton entered the room. If Mr. Anton hadn't knocked, I wondered, what would have happened?

Mr. Anton stood halfway through the door and said, "Kristen, come with me. I am going to take you to Dr. Pelchat's office. It is time for your session."

The pain in my chest swelled back up.

CHAPTER 46

When I entered Dr. Pelchat's office, he was already sitting behind his desk with his legs crossed and my chart open with his pen in hand. As soon as Mr. Anton left me and shut the door, Dr. Pelchat insisted that I take a seat. He was completely serious and used a professional tone. His demeanor worried me.

"Is there something the matter?" I asked.

Dr. Pelchat leaned back in his chair, realizing that I had caught on that there was something going on. He took off his glasses and looked at me.

Wiping the sweat from his brow, he said to me, "The matter is your test results. They came in this morning."

I gasped. I felt my heart jump.

"Don't be alarmed," he assured me. "Everything is going to be alright."

"What did the test tell you? Was it able to tell you anything?"

My heart would not stop racing. What if the test didn't say anything? What if I was completely lost and hopeless? What if I couldn't be helped?

"Yes. The test did return results, but it was not what we were hoping."

"No? What did it say?"

"First off, I want to ask you something."

"What do you want to ask me?"

The delay from him stalling was bothering me. I wanted to know what was going on with me, and what the test had told him.

"How is your new roommate situation coming along?"

I thought back to earlier when I had let Mena cut me with the butterfly wing pendant.

"It's okay," I told him.

"I understand that you were the one to find your former roommate, Janine, in the bathroom of your old bedroom. That must have been really scary."

I shook my head, remembering the screams and the look on Janine's face as they were trying to hold her down and keep her from hurting herself. I could almost smell the blood again.

"Yes," I said. "It was really scary. Do you know how she is doing?"

"She is doing a lot better. It's thanks to you, Kristen. If you hadn't called for help for her, she could have been seriously injured. Now she's somewhere where she will get the full attention she needs. Bent Creek is not the best place for someone with extremes like Janine has. She has to be somewhere where they can watch her constantly."

"You mean an institution?" I asked him.

Dr. Pelchat nodded softly. "Janine's not necessarily in an institution. She's in a long-term care facility where the doctors and staff are a little less lenient and are more watchful."

"They won't hurt her, right?"

"No," Dr. Pelchat assured me with a strong tone. "They will see to it that Janine gets the full attention and help that she needs to get her to full recovery. She will get the care that we here at Bent Creek are not fully equipped to handle here. We are just a short–term, in-patient facility. We only keep patients up to a maximum of four to five weeks, if that. If, at the end of that time, we don't see progress, then we make the necessary arrangements for you to go to a long-term facility, like Janine."

I thought back to when I had been in the room with Mena. She had said something about people who had gotten out of the hospital and attempted suicide again, and then succeeded. I grew scared thinking about Janine.

I asked, "Is it true that there are people who become statistics?"

"What kind of a statistic?"

"I heard that forty percent of the people who are hospitalized for attempted suicide get released, and then do it again. But then they succeed and die because of it."

"Where did you hear that?"

"I just heard some people talking," I lied.

He shook his head and said, "I don't think that forty percent is quite the accurate number. It is true that *some* patients are released from psychiatric care when their condition has not gotten better, even though it may seem that way. Some of them do carry out their original plans and succeed. That's why most doctors do their best to make sure that, if extended care is needed for these patients, they'll get it by staying longer in treatment, or they are sent to a facility that can provide the care they need. In Janine's case, she was sent to a long-term care hospital."

Scared, I held back my tears the best I could.

"Am I going to have to go there, too?"

Dr. Pelchat leaned forward in his chair and unfolded his hands. He looked deeply into my eyes.

"Kristen, your condition is serious. However, I don't believe that you need to go to a long-term inpatient facility. I do not think that it is so severe that I cannot help you now, or even after you are released from here. You will need long-term treatment, but the kind of treatment that I can provide for you once you are out of here will not require barred windows and padded walls."

"What are you saying?" I couldn't take it much longer.

"Your test results were very clear. You do have Borderline Personality Disorder."

I don't know why - it wasn't as if I wasn't expecting it but tears immediately shot out of my eyes. Soft sobs filled my chest. It was like finding out my favorite pet had died. I was realizing that I was losing my mind, and a doctor was confirming it. Everything I'd read in that book he had given me had hit too close to home for it not to be true.

"Kristen, this is not the end. This is not a definitive label. This is the beginning of your healing. This is getting what needs to be out in the open so that we can start your healing process. I want to help you during the time that you have left here and thereafter. Borderline Personality Disorder does not make you who you are. It is just a diagnosis. It's what is causing you to behave the way you do and think the way you do. It's not you. It's a disorder. And we are going to work together to help you cope, deal, and eventually heal with medication, out-patient individual therapy, and even family group therapy. You will not suffer with this forever."

"I know," I told him through mumbles and tears. I grabbed a tissue from the Kleenex box on his desk and blew my nose. "I was just hoping that there was a chance that I didn't have to suffer with this."

"To be honest," Dr. Pelchat began, "I'm relieved."

"Why?"

"Because it could have been a lot worse. I'm glad that we took the time to get the test done and wait for the results before putting you on any other medications. I didn't want to diagnose you with BPD without being completely sure, and you know that I'm not going to just give you any random medication based off a hunch. I didn't agree to it when Dr. Cuvo first came to me with your case. That's why I wanted to see you myself."

"Was I that complicated?"

"Not complicated. We wanted to be sure," he told me sincerely. "And now you and I are going to get you onto the path of healing, together. Not everyone with BPD suffers forever. It's going to take a lot of work. I will do my part, and I know that you will do yours."

"Sometimes I don't feel that I'm even strong enough to do anything," I told him.

"You were not strong when you tried to kill yourself. But you were strong enough to stick it out here in Bent Creek, and you were strong enough to start to open up in group therapy. You were even strong enough to take the test. It wasn't just because you felt you had to, but because somewhere deep down inside, you wanted to know exactly what was going on with you. You want to know if you can heal. You want help. To sit there, listen to all of this, and take it in as well as you are doing, I have to say, makes you even stronger than I am giving you credit for. You are already healing. Kristen, give yourself some credit."

"No," I said through my last few tears. "I'm crying like a baby."

"Crying is okay," he said. "If you weren't crying, and if you were just sitting there with no reaction, then I'd be worried about you. You are handling this very well. Tell me, do you feel that this diagnosis is accurate, based on what you read in the book I gave you, what you understand about BPD, and what you've noticed within yourself?"

I nodded my head in full honesty.

"Based on what you understand about Borderline Personality Disorder, can you tell me what you notice within yourself that makes you feel this is an accurate diagnosis for you?"

I took a deep breath and tried to pull myself together enough to talk about this. It was harder than it seemed. It wasn't easy to pour myself out to Dr. Pelchat, but it was what he wanted from me. He was trying to be my doctor and help me.

"I don't know how to explain it. The way I think about certain situations and the way I feel that I have to handle them, it doesn't seem like it's the right way, but I don't know any other way. Today, my best friend came to see me, and she wanted to tell me about her engagement. All I could think about was how terrible I felt and how angry I was. She tried to be nice to me, and she had come all the way out here to see me. I was angry with her for not answering the phone on the night I had hurt myself. I blamed her for what I had done, but I knew that it wasn't her fault. She didn't know at the time I had called what I had done. I just kept thinking that if I kept pushing her buttons, I could make her upset and hurt her. I thought that if I hurt her I would feel better somehow. I thought that it would relieve my guilt and pain. It only made me feel worse, because now I know she hates me. I'm such a mess. Why do I do this? Every time! Why do I feel that I have to be like this? I push everyone away before anyone can hurt me or leave me. Why do I do this?"

"Kristen, you just said it."

"There's something rotten inside of me that makes me rotten," I told him. "I'm rotten, and I can't see it, like everyone else, but I know I am because of these thoughts and these feelings. They can see it. My mother, my father, Jack, John, and now Lexus--everyone. I was even afraid that Dr. Cuvo would see it."

"What happens when they see it, Kristen?"

"They hate me. They try to get rid of me. They stop talking to me. They show me what a real burden I am. They all hate me."

"Do you really think that your mother hates you?"

I stayed silent for a moment and kept my gaze on the snotty tissue in my hand. Did I really think that my mother hated me? She did make sure that I was brought to the hospital. She was there for me when I needed help. I did realize this even before Dr. Pelchat asked me that question. I threw the tissue in the wastebasket beside Dr. Pelchat's desk. Then, I finally shook my head.

"She doesn't hate me," I said. "She just wants me to be away from her so that she won't have to deal with me. She can't wait for me to turn eighteen so that she can have a reason to make me leave. It's because of that..."

"That rotten thing that is inside of you," Dr. Pelchat said. He seemed to understand what I was trying to say.

"Right." The sharp metal ball turned slowly in my chest. I held back my pathetic tears.

"Now you know what that rotten thing is, Kristen."

"It is me."

"It's not you," he said. "It's the illness. It's BPD. Now that you know what it is that is causing these thinking errors, you can do whatever it takes to get rid of this rotten disorder. It's very important that you know this and accept that it is not you. *BPD is not you!* You are not rotten. I know that this is going to be hard for you to get right away, because you are so used to the way your mind is conditioned. Your mom, your family, and your friends do not hate you. They will not leave you. We are going to start getting rid of those thinking errors that cause you to feel otherwise. You are going to get into your mind the right way of thinking. We are going to start with the fact that BPD is a serious disorder, and you will not be ignored or abandoned. It's time to re-shape your mind and get rid of these thoughts that are trying to destroy you."

I thought back to Mena and what she'd said about how I should open my mind to the fact that there may be nothing wrong with me. That I may be smarter than Lexus, and how the doctors want to use medicine and mind-bending therapy to blind us. I didn't know what to believe. I wanted to be rid of this Borderline Personality Disorder. I really did not want to feel the way I felt and think the way I thought. However, how was I to be sure that that's what the problem was? How was I to be sure that I wasn't the problem?

I was very scared. I was scared to think of what it would be like to be normal, like Lexus, and not have that rotten thing inside of me. I couldn't see myself without seeing and knowing how terrible I was and I couldn't see myself without Mr. Sharp. What would I be like without cutting? I'd be oblivious. I'd be blinded.

"You can survive this," Dr. Pelchat said.

"I could be a survivor?" I asked.

"Yes, a survivor," he assured me.

What would it take to survive BPD? It scared me to think about what that would mean. Suddenly I didn't want to be in the room with Dr. Pelchat anymore, and I regretted speaking so openly and crying to him. I tried to tell myself that he'd take it as me making progress, and it would get me closer to getting out of Bent Creek. What then, when I got out? I tried not to think too much about it, because I didn't want to make Dr. Pelchat think that I had begun to worry. I wiped my eyes and looked up at him. I noticed that he hadn't written in my chart - not even once - since we had begun. He was staring at me, waiting to see if I was going to open up anymore.

I folded my arms across my chest the way I saw Mena do when she was in group meetings. It seemed to make the doctors back off of her, except for Dr. Bent. However, I had the feeling that Dr. Bent would not be pressing Mena's buttons so hard anymore.

Dr. Pelchat took the hint, and decided to take the initiative to get conversation going again. "Now that we've got your diagnosis out there, it's time we make plans on getting your treatment started."

"I'm going have to take medication?"

"Yes," he said. "I am going to get you back on anti-depressants, and eventually a mood stabilizer. I want to reach out to you with what is going to be most effective at this time. Right now I believe what we need to do is continue your individual therapy sessions with me, even after your discharge. I will see to it that you to continue to see me at the clinic in outpatient treatment, once a week. But before we begin your discharge, we must have your family session."

"Dr. Pelchat, I don't want to go through that again," I said.

I thought back to that painful session with Mom and Dr. Pelchat.

Dr. Pelchat knew. He said, "This family session will be nothing like that last one. The last one served its purpose, and we were able to get everything out on the table. You won't have to go through that again. I know that, with your brother and sister here this time, it will not be as it was when it was just us and your mother."

The look on my face had to have matched everything I was feeling. I was almost angry, but was surprised and in disbelief at the same time.

"Did you say that my brother and sister are coming to this session?"

"It's a family session. Everyone in the household should be there. Yes, your brother and your sister have to live with you, and it's fair for them to get an understanding of what is going on with you. They know that you are in the hospital. I'm sure that they are very concerned. And they are going to need to know how they can cope and deal with this situation, because they are old enough to understand. So, yes, this Saturday we are having a family session with me, you, your mom, and your little brother and sister."

He made it sound so definite, as if I had no choice or say in the matter. It was clear that I didn't. He opened my chart after making his point, and I watched him write in capital letters on a yellow sheet:

FAMILY SESSION: SATURDAY AT 3:00PM.

There it was, set in stone. I was going to have to face all of them. I was going to have to face Mom again. What was even worse than facing Mom, I was going to have to face Nicholas. I hadn't seen him since he'd found me on that horrible night. I hadn't wanted him to be the one. I felt sad and angry inside again. Nevertheless, I wasn't going to cry this time. I couldn't let Dr. Pelchat see me upset about the family session. It was required to get out of Bent Creek.

CHAPTER 47

Morning came. It was Friday. There was only one more day until my family session. I tried not to think about it, but it was too hard. Every hour that passed by seemed to go by faster than a minute. The clock read 8:00am and we were at breakfast. Then it was time for Coping Skills with Dr. Bent, and it was already 2:00pm. I felt like I had just left the cafeteria for breakfast. Maybe I was getting it confused with lunch. I was almost like a zombie.

"Kristen!"

I looked up, startled at the tone of her voice when she called out to me. Dr. Bent and everyone in the room was looking at me and waiting for me to speak. I had been lost in my own thoughts and in my own space, not really paying any attention to my group. Group Therapy was important, especially with Dr. Bent. Nothing got past her. Mena was in our group. She was sitting next to me, looking at me, and right along with everyone else.

"Kristen? Are you all right?" Dr. Bent asked.

"Yes," I assured her.

"It's your turn," she said.

I sat up straight in my seat and cleared my throat. I was halfway there before I had completely zoned out, so I knew the last person to speak was Tai. I didn't want to ask Dr. Bent to fill me in on what we were talking about, so I assumed it was something related to what Tai was speaking of. She was talking about her family. She had mentioned that her father and stepmother were coming for a family visit the following Monday.

I spoke up, "I haven't had a family session yet, but I will tomorrow. So..."

"What do you expect to accomplish?" Dr. Bent inquired.

I shrugged and replied, "I don't know. I guess it could go either way." That was not a good way to respond, I thought, only after I had said it.

"Why do you say that?" Dr. Bent really liked to press on an issue.

Hell, I'd dug myself in the hole. Time to try and climb back out. "I didn't mean it like that," I tried to clean up. "What I mean is, I could try to do better and help my family see that I am making an effort to try to get better. I want to show them that I can continue to keep getting better. Then, they can accept it and help me by supporting me, or I could show them that this time here has done nothing for me by being negative and not really trying. Nevertheless, of course, my time here has been very good. I can say that I do feel different in my attitude towards my life. I actually want to do better."

"That is absolutely wonderful, Kristen," she said.

Relief rushed through me. I saved myself.

"I'm very glad that you feel the progress that you have made. I must say that you have come a long way since you first came in here. I'm proud of you." Her smile was so convincing.

I smiled back, but hoped that my smile could have been just as convincing as hers could.

The main unit was almost empty after visiting hours. I didn't have any visitors, nor did Mena. She sat at the table in the living room, alone, staring at a blank screen on the television. The television was not on, and she was not indulging in any other kind of entertainment. She was just sitting and staring like she was almost catatonic. I began to worry, so I started walking towards her, but a voice called out to me before I could get close enough to grab her attention.

A gentle hand squeezed my shoulder. I turned around. It was Geoffrey. I hadn't expected it to be him. I calmly and almost unnoticeably pulled my long sleeve down over my arm to make sure it was down far enough so that he wouldn't see my fresh cuts. He didn't notice, because he smiled as if happy to see me. I returned the smile. He had one of those jolly smiles that made you want to smile back, even if you were in a bad mood.

"Come over here with me, Kristen. Let's talk." He sat down at one of the tables on the main unit. I joined him.

My heart started beating a little faster when we sat down, because he looked me in the eyes immediately, and the smile disappeared from his face. He seemed serious. I hadn't seen him serious since that night with Rocky. I wondered what this could be about.

"How are you holding up?" he asked.

"I'm okay," I said.

"I mean, with everything that's happened in here the last few weeks you've been here. It's been a lot for you. First with Rocky, and then with Janine. How are you really doing?"

"I guess I'm just like everyone else," I told him.

"Hmm," he said.

It was that "hmm" the way Jack used to say. It made my heart jump.

"Why?" I asked. "Is there something I should be feeling?"

"No," he said. "Your feelings are yours. I can't tell you how to feel. It's just that, if there is something more that you are feeling, and you may be too embarrassed or too ashamed to say, I want to let you know that it's all right."

"Thanks, Geoffrey. I know."

"Because I know when I saw Janine, I got a little scared. I mean, it really frightened me to see that. I hadn't known Janine that long, but I did get to know her through the Group Therapy sessions I sat in on, and whenever we'd pass each other on the unit. I guess I figured, since you were her roommate and you were around her a lot more than me, that it would be a little hard on you too."

I sighed. He was right. "I was scared," I admitted. "When I saw her down on the floor and sick the way she was, it felt like I wasn't even seeing the Janine that I remembered. It had been like that for a while since Dr. Cuvo left. She had just been so different. It hurt to see her so down, because the Janine that I remember is the one that I really admired. She was so pretty and nice. She was funny. She helped me feel more like I fit in here with everyone. But then she just started to drift away."

Geoffrey looked me in the eyes as I spoke, and that old feeling of discomfort filled me. I wanted to ask him to stop staring at me, but then I realized that he wasn't staring at me. He was really listening to me. It seemed like he actually cared because he empathized with me.

"I miss Janine," I said. I felt tears begin to well up. He opened his mouth to speak, but I continued, "I miss Dr. Cuvo. I miss Daniel and Rocky. I didn't even really know Rocky."

"I know, Kristen," Geoffrey said sincerely. "I miss them, too. It's amazing how, when we make a choice and do something to ourselves. It affects everyone else around us, whether it's positive or negative. Daniel made progress well enough for him to get out of here. So he made it out without needing extended care. We all miss him. Dr. Cuvo's resignation affected his patients. Janine's actions affected you and everyone who was trying to help her. You didn't even know Rocky, and his choice and actions have affected not only you, but also everyone else. Even Dr. Pelchat has to find a way to cope with all of this."

"Wow," I said as I wiped my eyes with my sleeve. "How?"

"We know that we can influence a change and do our best to help you, but we can't make you change. It lies within you. You are the one who has to put forth the effort to get better. It gets hard, especially when you get out of the comforting walls of Bent Creek. You won't have your doctor coming to visit you every day. You won't have Ms. Mosley or me there to scream at you in the morning and motivate you to get on with your life every day. You have to begin to see and do for yourself as you receive treatment and continue therapy while you're out there. Just take the advice from your doctor and us: take your medicine, and maintain yourself. That's very important. No matter what you go through, you have to remember that you must always maintain who you are. If you can maintain and not let yourself get lost in the troubles, then you will become a survivor."

Everything he said sank deep inside of me. I wanted to maintain a stable mind so that, when I got out of Bent Creek, I would be able to survive.

"You are so right," I responded. "Thank you, Geoffrey."

"Sure thing," he said with a big smile.

I couldn't help but smile back.

"Don't hold things inside like that," he said. "If you want to say something, say it. Especially when someone shows concern and gives you a chance to express yourself."

"Okay," I said.

CHAPTER 48

I blinked once after I got up from the table with Tai to get ready for dinner, and time seemed to skip with that one blink. I was lying in bed with a full stomach. I was all cleaned up and in my pajamas. How had night come so fast? I rolled over on the bed and found my silver butterfly pendant outside of the pillowcase. I gently tucked it back in. Mr. Sharp winked at me as the luster on the wings shined.

I heard Mena enter the room. She came out of the bathroom wearing an open robe. Her long hair fell down her back and over her shoulders. She only had on panties underneath that robe, and I could see everything else. She walked over to her bed and sat down. She started to put lotion on, but before she could rub it on herself, she caught me looking at her. I quickly looked back down at my pillow. I heard her chuckle.

"It sucks," she said in a calm voice. "We can't have our own bathrobe belts." Even though I wasn't looking at her, I could tell she was smiling.

I slowly looked back up. She wasn't looking at me anymore, but I was certainly looking at her. She had taken her robe completely off. She gently rubbed the lotion on her body. Her long black locks were curly from the water in the shower, and she let them hang down her back and drape her shoulders. Her beautiful skin was like caramel. She didn't look like Mena, but it was her. I made myself turn away. I played with my pendant while it was inside of the pillowcase to keep myself occupied.

"Okay," she said, "I'm dressed. You can look up now. Not that I had stopped you from looking."

I ignored her and stayed turned away. When I heard the bed creak, I turned towards her because I knew she'd be under the sheets and the thin, white blanket. She was telling the truth; she was completely dressed and her hair was pulled back in her usual ponytail. Her ponytails were always so tight that she looked like she'd had a face lift. This made her look even meaner. Now she looked like Mena again. I was strangely comforted by this.

"Why are you grinning?" she asked me.

"No reason," I said, and then I stopped smiling.

"Good night," she said as she tried to snuggle under the thin, white blanket.

I felt bad for her. No one had come to visit her, so she couldn't even ask for a thicker blanket. The nights were so cold in the hospital, no matter how warm it got outside. It seemed like they cranked the AC up higher at nighttime. Poor Mena wrapped herself in the blanket, like she was in a cocoon, just to keep warm. I lay comfortably under Janine's blanket and mine.

The comfort didn't last long. I woke up in the hallway again. This time it was daytime instead of night, and I was in front of Nicholas' old bedroom again. The door was completely closed this time, and I didn't hear anything coming from the other side. If only I could just wake up. I shook my head, pulled my hair, and even bit myself, but I did all of this in the hallway. Nothing would get me back to Bent Creek. I didn't want to be in this place. Not again.

Feeling hopeless, I started to turn away, but before I could move an inch, I heard a low moan from the other side of the door. It was a painful moan followed by another. I put my ear to the door, and the painful moans were mixed with low cries. I had heard these cries before. The cries had played in my mind until that night when I'd tried to make them stop. The night I'd taken the pills and had taken the knife to make myself rest. The night I'd let Nick see me weak.

I reached out for the door, and this scene suddenly started to move in slow motion. Every move I made and every sound I heard was dramatically played out. I couldn't hit a button to make it play faster.

I turned the knob to Nick's door, which seemed to take an eternity. The door opened slowly, without a creak. Jack was naked on top of Nick. He was hurting him all over again, but this time I could see everything a lot clearer, since time had slowed down. I opened my mouth to scream, but nothing came out. I wanted to move. I wanted to go over and grab him and kill him, but I couldn't move. Jack raped Nicholas until I thought he was dead. That's when I screamed, and Jack saw me watching. I got scared and I turned away, sure that Nick was dead. I ran for the kitchen, but before I could get down the hallway, Dr. Cuvo and Dr. Pelchat were there, waiting for me. Dr. Pelchat had my chart open in his hand and held a pen, ready to write. Dr. Cuvo had something shiny in his hands, and he held it out to me.

I looked at what it was before I took it. I'd grabbed the knife out of the drawer. He had it ready for me, because he knew I was going to need it. Dr. Pelchat nodded at me when I looked at him. I took the knife from Dr. Cuvo and quickly turned back towards Nick's room down the hallway. I tried to make time go faster, but it wouldn't. I could only take slow, angry steps. As I got closer to the door, I let the anger rise inside of me so that I would have enough strength to make the knife go all the way through him and make it hurt and make him cry worse than the way he made Nick cry. Tears fell out of my eyes, and that's when the anger took over.

I was two steps away from Nick's door when the door flew open at a normal speed, while I was still in slow motion, and Jack ran from the doors, faster than time was allowing me to go. He ran past me quickly before I had time to register that he'd made time to work for him and I hadn't. I was still moving towards the door. When I got to Nick's door, I opened it immediately. Time sucked me back into normal speed as soon as I saw my brother, wrapped in his blanket and lying on the floor. Jack was gone. The knife slipped from my hand and fell to the floor.

Nick lay on the floor and didn't move. He didn't make a sound. I turned to Dr. Pelchat and Dr. Cuvo, who were standing at the end of the hallway. They seemed to be moving in slow time. I saw Dr. Pelchat writing in my chart, and Dr. Cuvo was looking over his shoulder. I knew what was coming next. I looked in at Nick as he lay motionless and probably dead. I looked back at the doctors desperately.

"No, please..." I pleaded with them.

Dr. Pelchat kept writing.

"No..." I cried in a whisper. "Please don't do this."

"Kriiiisstenn," Dr. Cuvo bellowed out in a scary, deep, slow-motion voice.

"Please..." I pleaded. "What did you write?"

"Whaaaat did I wriiiite?" Dr. Pelchat's voice was even more demonic.

He threw his head back and laughed with the voice of a monster. While lost in his laughter, he let Dr. Cuvo take my chart from his hands before he dropped it. As Dr. Pelchat laughed and amused himself, it only made me even more frightened. The sounds of the deep and horrific laughs were making bumps form on my skin. Dr. Cuvo turned the chart to me slowly.

I squinted my eyes to see. Dr. Cuvo took one step closer. I squinted harder. Dr. Cuvo turned to Dr. Pelchat, annoyed at the laughter. As he turned his head back to me, his eyes started to roll to the back of his head, where I could only see white. His arms took on a super-fast speed of motion and stretched out to me. The chart was up close and suddenly in my face.

KRISTEN FAILED!!!!!!

The terrorizing laughs grew louder as I pulled my hair in fear and anger. "No! No! No!" I screamed. I tried to run into the room with Nick so that I could hide from them and protect Nick.

"No! No! No!" I continued to scream.

Suddenly strong arms were wrapped around me, and they were holding me back.

"No! Let me! No! Stop! No!" I swung my arms wildly at whatever was holding me back from getting to him.

"Kristen. It's okay. It's all right, Kristen." This sweet voice that spoke to me was like an angel coming to rescue me from the terror.

I didn't feel completely safe yet, and I was sure that Nick wasn't safe. I tried to swing a little more, but suddenly I didn't have as much strength as I'd had in my dream. I felt tired and my head was heavy, like I had just woken up.

"Come on. Calm down, sweetie. It's okay. It's me. Kristen. It's Ms. Mosley."

I opened my eyes and saw the angel's face. It really was Ms. Mosley sitting beside me. And I was in Bent Creek. I was in my bed, sitting up, and Ms. Mosley had one arm wrapped around me while she used her other hand to hold both of my arms from swinging. When I saw the gleam of the softly lit night light on the wall, I realized that I was not dreaming anymore.

I pressed my face against Ms. Mosley's shoulder, where I let my tears fall. I didn't care if Mena woke up and saw me crying. I didn't even care that I was crying on Ms. Mosley, and, from what I could feel, I could tell she didn't mind, either. Her hand went from her tight death grip holding my arms to softly holding my hands to comfort me. We stayed like that until I finished letting out my tears.

I finally stopped crying and sobbing. I pulled away from Ms. Mosley.

"What happened?" I asked her.

"I was going to ask you the same question," she said.

"I think I was dreaming."

"It must have been something awful, Kristen. I could hear you screaming from the main unit. I'm surprised you didn't wake up your roommate." She looked over at Mena, who was motionless and still wrapped in her cocoon.

Ms. Mosley turned back to me and asked, "Did you have a nightmare?"

"Yes," I told her.

She asked, "Well, do you want to talk about it?"

"I don't really know how to say it. It was just really scary. I couldn't control anything. It was too evil."

"Did you say your prayers before you went to sleep?"

I shook my head. I didn't want to admit that I didn't normally say a prayer before I went to sleep.

"I find that whispering a little prayer before I go to sleep helps me get to sleep faster, and it comforts me in knowing that God is watching over me."

"Okay," I said.

"And whenever I find myself stuck in a nightmare that I can't seem to get out of, I call out to Him. I even get on my knees inside of my dream and start praying. Sometimes I have to do that. And he sends his angel and pulls me right out."

"I guess He sent you to me again," I said. I wanted to make her feel like her words were having an effect on me. In actuality, I had begun to ponder. When she said that she felt the comfort of knowing that God was watching over her, I thought of something else.

"I hear everything," she said. "And what I don't hear, I take it as God telling me I don't need to hear it." She smiled warmly.

I couldn't smile back. The thought stuck out in my mind.

"What's going on there? You still troubled by that dream?"

"A little," I said. "Ms. Mosley? I have to ask you something."

"Yes? You can ask me anything," she assured me, with a touch of her hand to my shoulder and a gentle squeeze.

"If someone dies, do you believe that they go to heaven if they are good, and if they are bad, they go to hell?"

"I believe that God passes judgment on everyone when they are called home and, yes, they are sent on to their eternal resting place. Though hell doesn't really seem like a place for rest."

"If someone kills himself, does God pass judgment on that person to go to hell?"

"I've heard that in Sunday school, listed among grave sins that will send a person straight to hell, but I heard a lot of other things, lists of reasons. It used to scare me because I knew that I wasn't perfect. I was bound to make a mistake or two in my life. One being my bad habit of smoking. I know God doesn't like that. But you know something? I learned a lot more about God and his great justice as I studied more and started to understand. Through the teachings, I heard many different reasons from different preachers growing up about the things that God sends people to hell for, and what He finds acceptable enough to let us into heaven. And what I found was that all of these preachers were saying that what was going to get us into heaven were deeds that *they* were all doing so that *they* could appear to be more righteous. What they were teaching us were their own opinions of how righteous they thought they were, and they tried to tell us that, if we were like them, then we would be able to go to heaven, no matter what. It was a different one each time. As I learned more about our Heavenly Father and what kind of God he is, I came to appreciate something that the preachers never told me."

"What?"

"I learned and came to appreciate that no man - not the preacher, not you, or me, or any other man or woman - can judge a person and say that what they do or how they live their life, or even how their life ends, it is what is going to get any of us into heaven. That is God's job because He is the reader of our hearts. It's not fair for me to say that anyone who kills themselves is going to hell, because I don't know that person's heart, their reverence with God, or their complete state of mind. There are illnesses that can drive a person completely insane. Some don't even know what they are doing if they do commit suicide, because they are unstable. Then, there are people who sacrifice themselves to save others, and they do it, knowing that they will have to die. Does that mean that they've given up on life and God? So Kristen, I can't answer you with a straight yes or no. I can only say that God would be the one to ask when you get there, because He is the one who can read your heart and who will finally judge you."

"What if your preachers were right? What if God does send a person to hell for committing suicide, no matter what? Then what will that be like?"

"Hell? What is hell like?"

"Yes," I said, with a bit of desperation in my tone.

"Well," she began. I could tell that she now felt obligated to answer, since she had said so much already. "From what I've been taught, if you are judged to go to hell, all of the sins that God has not forgiven that you have committed are laid before you, and you are tormented and punished in those sins to remind you of your wickedness. This continues on for eternity."

I was now staring at her. She was cutting deep into me. I spoke up. "These were the things that I had learned. If you are good, you go to heaven, and if you are bad, you go to hell. If a person commits suicide and God judges them to hell, they have to be tormented by their sins forever. Then, that person would be jumping off a building or shooting themselves in the head, or whatever they did to get sent to hell, all over again. Forever!"

The thought of restless torment frightened me. Then I thought of Rocky being stuck in hell. I thought of him having to run down the hallway of the Boys' Unit in Bent Creek, being forced to haunt it so that he could be tormented by his eternal sin.

Ms. Mosley saw that I was scared, and she wrapped her arms around me. She gave me a gentle hug. As she leaned into me she said, "Remember what I told you. God is the reader of your heart, and He is the only one who can judge you. He will always take care of you."

CHAPTER 49

The next morning I woke up from only two hours of sleep. After Ms. Mosley had left me, I couldn't get back to sleep. Mr. Sharp had hidden inside my pillowcase. I'd been afraid that Ms. Mosley would come back in and find us. She had comforted me enough to make me calm. I wasn't afraid, because she'd helped me appreciate that I had a chance to have a peaceful, eternal rest someday, and that God was really taking care of me. I believed that He had to have been, in order for Ms. Mosley to be there to pull me from that horrible dream. It wasn't the first time she had been there for me.

I knew that my family session was going to come faster than the previous day had gone by. I tried to think positively and think about all that Geoffrey and Ms. Mosley had said to me. I thought of what Dr. Pelchat had told me about BPD and how Borderline Personality Disorder was not me. We were going to work hard to treat it and cure me. Knowing these possibilities made me feel more hopeful. I was only afraid of seeing Nick again after that night. I told myself not to think about it, so that I wouldn't make myself feel badly again. I knew the time was coming, but I didn't have to think about it.

Before Ms. Mosley came into our room to make sure we were up to get our vitals checked, Mena and I dressed for the day. Mena looked at me while I dressed, and I felt her eyes on me. It was a bit uncomfortable, because she was really staring.

Exasperated, I finally said, "What?"

She asked, "Are you okay?"

"Yes. Why?"

"Wake up! Vitals! Come on, girls!" Ms. Mosley's loud voice filled the hallway of the Girls' Unit.

Mena said, "You better hurry up and put a different shirt on. I can see your fresh cuts. Hurry! She's coming."

I quickly pulled off my shirt and put on a longer-sleeved shirt that was in a drawer nearby. Just as I got the shirt over my head, Ms. Mosley burst in and started to yell, but saw that Mena and I were already awake and dressed. She smiled at the sight of us.

She said, "It's good to see that, for once, you beat me to it, Mena. Come on, girls, it's time to get your vitals checked and start the day."

The day started with vitals, then breakfast, and then our Goals Group Therapy session. This was the only time I had to see how many new people had arrived during the previous night. It seemed like new patients were always being admitted to Bent Creek.

On Saturday, Goals Group was with Dr. Pelchat instead of Dr. Finch, and Geoffrey sat in on the group with us as a second mediator. Dr. Pelchat said that this group therapy session was going to be different from our other Goals groups. In this session, we were going to talk about future goals. Goals that we wanted to accomplish when we got out of Bent Creek. He said that they could be long-term or short-term goals. The key was to get us thinking about life after Bent Creek and to help us realize that it would continue on when we were out of here. It scared me to think about going back to work and continuing with my home schooling and then graduating. I knew Mom was going to start talking about me moving out to either go to college or get my own place. She had already hinted at it so many times. But I had other things to think about and try to work out before all of that. I especially had to focus on my treatment. I hoped that Mom would understand that when Dr. Pelchat explained it in our family session.

Tai volunteered to speak first in Goals Group. She stated that her long-term goal was to get along with her step-mother and get to a point where she could really try to respect her as her father's wife.

"Why is that a long-term goal?" Dr. Pelchat asked.

"Have you met my step-mother?" She laughed. "She is not easy to like. But I'm willing to try. It's just going to take some time."

"That is a realistic goal. You really can get along with her if you both put forth some effort. Maybe that is something you will want to bring up in your family session on Monday."

"I will," Tai said. "Dr. Bent and I agreed that it will take us both to agree to get along, and I do want to tell her that I want to try. I mean, I don't have to look at her like a mother. She's not my mother. But she is my father's wife, and I have to respect her as that. As long as she understands and respects that I am my father's child, too."

"Well said," Geoffrey voiced.

"I'll say. Is that really Tai speaking?" Dr. Pelchat commented.

I laughed, along with the people in the room who actually knew Tai. Mena sat back in the chair directly to my left with her arms folded across her chest. She had the "I don't care" look on her tight ponytail-lifted face. The look of intimidation did not stop Dr. Pelchat from telling her to speak up next. He was her doctor, and he was used to her ways.

Mena did not argue or put up a fight. She did take her time answering by making us wait while she yawned and stretched. Then she finally spoke. "I have a long-term goal."

"Please share it with us," Dr. Pelchat encouraged.

She didn't answer until after she had scratched her knee, yawned again, and popped a crick out of her neck. Then she sat back in her seat and proceeded to tell us. "This one long-term goal I have is to own a Triumph Rocket 007."

"What is a Triumph Rocket 007?" Tai asked her.

"It is a motorcycle that has more force than your mouth. It's one of the first motorcycles that will be able to fly. It's going to have transformable wings. But it won't be released for another eleven years. That is why it's a long-term goal."

Dr. Pelchat seemed satisfied with Mena's sharing.

"That's very good," said Dr. Pelchat.

"Yeah," Geoffrey added. "I have to get me one of those. A flying motorcycle? That sounds unreal."

Most of the other people in the room voiced their opinion and agreed with Geoffrey. They started asking Mena more about the motorcycle. She seemed to open up when she talked about things that interested her. She freely answered their questions and, instead of interrupting and telling everyone to quiet down and get back to Goals Group, Dr. Pelchat let them ask more questions. She surprisingly answered them with a smile on her face. I watched Dr. Pelchat. He was leaning back in his chair with his arms folded across his large belly. He was observing Mena intensely. This was definitely going in the chart later.

CHAPTER 50

I liked how laid back Saturdays were in Bent Creek. I spent time in the living room, trying to finish homework that Mom had brought to me from my home schooling. It was hard to concentrate with the pressure of having to see Nick and Alison in a few hours. It was almost three o'clock. I finished the last of my Calculus II homework. It left me with a tormenting headache, just like homework from advanced courses that I'd taken in public school. Mom always pushed me to use my full potential. She said it would be useful later on in my life. She didn't want me to be held back from moving on. Perhaps it was because she felt as if she was being held back. I knew she felt that way after Jack had torn us apart.

It wasn't long after I had finished my homework and closed my textbook that Mr. Anton was standing in front of me. I was still sitting at the table on the main unit. I looked up at him, already knowing what was coming. He was smiling as though he was there to deliver good news. I guessed to some patients it would have been good, but for me it was a reason to be afraid.

"Come with me," he said.

I didn't have time to put my books in the bedroom, so I just took them along with me. We arrived at Dr. Pelchat's office, and Mr. Anton knocked before Dr. Pelchat invited us in. When the door opened, I expected to see Nick, Alison, and Mom, sitting in chairs in front of Dr. Pelchat's desk, and an empty chair there for me, but it was only Dr.

Pelchat behind his desk and one empty chair in front of it for me. I sat down, confused, as Mr. Anton closed the door and left Dr. Pelchat and me alone.

"Where is my mom?" I asked him.

Dr. Pelchat nodded towards the door. "Your family is here. They are waiting in the conference room for us. I wanted to meet with you before we go in."

He didn't have my chart open, though it was in front of him on the desk. I didn't know what to expect from this meeting. I was feeling a little uncomfortable and nervous.

"Don't be nervous," he encouraged. "I think that what you fear is not what you will have to face today. This meeting is not to attack you, but to help you and your family get an understanding of what has been going on with you. There is a reason why you are here, and there is a reason why you did what you did, and we are going to help them understand. Then we are all going to work out what it's going to take on all of our parts not to let it happen again. I think that you are brave, and I think that you are ready. It's going to be all right, Kristen."

I closed my eyes and took a deep breath. Maybe he was right, I thought to myself. Maybe I am a lot braver than I think. I opened my eyes and said, "All right. I'm ready. Let's go."

When I stepped into the conference room with Dr. Pelchat, I didn't have a picture in my mind this time as to how everyone would look or where they would be positioned. I just let Dr. Pelchat open the door, and I followed behind him, trying to feel brave and ready. The first person I saw was Mom. She was sitting in the chair closest to the door at the large, round table. It looked like a room for executive board meetings. Mom smiled sweetly. The way she smiled made me smile. When I stepped forward to approach her, I felt a gentle squeeze around my waist. I looked down and saw skinny arms adorned with gold and silver-toned bracelets dangling around my waist. Alison was hugging me, and her little face was pressed against my back. I sat my books down on the table next to Mom because they had become too heavy in that position. Then I turned around so that Alison and I were facing each other, and I wrapped my arms around her to hug her back.

After a warm hug, I turned to face Nick. Alison wouldn't let me go. She held on to me as I walked over to him. She followed my footsteps with her arms still hanging around my waist. Nick sat on the other side of the table, opposite Mom. His arms hung loosely at his sides. He leaned back in the chair and kept his eyes away from me as if he was purposely avoiding eye contact with me. When I approached him, his eyes shifted in Mom's direction.

I heard mom say, "Alison, come sit next to Mommy."

Alison whined a little, but did as she was told. I kept my eyes on Nick, not caring that Dr. Pelchat was there, observing and probably writing everything down. Nick kept his eyes on Mom. I didn't look her way to see if she was making gestures to him, because I wanted Nick to look up at me, and if he did, I didn't want to miss the opportunity to catch his eyes. I squatted down to his level and put my face near his. He folded his arms across his chest and looked away from me. He was trying very hard to act tough, but I was getting to him. I stayed right beside him and I stared at him. I smelled him, and I looked right through him and saw his anger and his pain. When I got past what I saw and began to feel all of what he was feeling, the tears began to stream down my face. I stood up because I felt my legs grow weary.

Mom called out, "Nicholas!"

"No," I sobbed. "Just let him-"

Nick didn't let me get another word out before he stood up out of the chair and wrapped his arms around my neck. He squeezed me so tightly that I thought I was going to choke. I didn't care. I didn't want him to let go. He was as tall as I was, and yet he was still so young. His hair was longer, tickling my cheeks, and smothering me as he buried his tear-drenched face in my neck. His arms were bulking up because they felt like snakes constricting me. He was growing up, and time was going by.

He squeezed me tighter and said in my ear, "Kristen. I love you. Please don't ever do that again. Please."

"It's okay," I told him through what little breath I had. "Don't cry, Nickyroo. It's going to be okay."

"It's going to be okay." He repeated after me.

"Yes," I assured him.

I gently turned my arms loose of him and, as he felt me pulling away, he did so as well. When we pulled apart for the first time in a long time, our eyes locked. Those large, brown eyes that had haunted me forever stared boldly into mine. They were not pleading and they were not crying. They were strong and supporting. He put his hand on my shoulder and squeezed it hard. At that moment, I felt my heart palpitate from his love. His tears weren't for what had happened to him. They were for me.

"Come on now," Mom said. "Nick, sit down. We have to get started."

Nick and I recovered from our moment and took a chair next to each other. Mom and Alison sat next to each other on the opposite of the round, executive table. I looked over, and Dr. Pelchat was already writing in my chart. I hoped that he was writing something good.

Mom asked him if he was going to get the meeting started.

Dr. Pelchat responded, "It has already started."

Mom didn't say anything back. She stared at me as if I was supposed to say something. I didn't quite know how it worked. It was my first family therapy session. Alison and Nick were staring at me, too. Alison was staring mostly at my arms. I had made sure to wear long sleeves, but I could tell she wanted to get a look to see if I would roll them up.

I looked at Alison and said, "School's starting soon."

Alison squealed, "I get to try out for cheerleading this year."

I tried not to roll my eyes. She reminded me of someone. That was who Alison was. It was better she be like that than like me. As Alison went on about how excited she was to start middle school in a few weeks and how she was looking forward to my birthday, and then hers and Nick's birthday, I started to get back a feeling that I hadn't felt in a long time, a feeling that I had missed. Because I hadn't realized until that moment how much I had truly missed them. I missed my brother, my sister, and even Mom. I found myself laughing and smiling again with my family, and I wasn't afraid to let them see me genuinely happy. I loved them so much.

As the conversation went on about birthdays, and the twins turning twelve and my turning eighteen, it all seemed to be focused on my future and our future as a family. Nick appeared to be fine. It didn't seem like I had caused any traumatic, long-term damage from that terrible night. I had been especially worried about Nick. However, I listened to him talk about middle school, skateboarding, girls, and he responded positively.

I began to understand that Daniel had been right. At the time when he'd told me that saying, *this too shall pass,* I hadn't really grasped those powerful words well enough to take it deep into my heart and make it register in my mind. I'd survived, and so had my family. That terrible time had passed, and here we were, normal again. A month later, and time at Bent Creek had done its job. It seemed as though we were beginning to heal.

PART 3

Eternal Resting Place

By Kristen Elliott

It is believed that when you die

You go to hell.

When in hell

You are made to suffer through your sins

Repeating, systematically.

Hell is a common grave

A place of resting

I will rest

In hell.

It is believed that when you die

you go to hell.

When in hell

You are made to suffer through your sins.

Repetitive

Suffering.

Hell is a common grave

A place of resting.

I will rest.

CHAPTER 51

I didn't want to show any sign of emotion when I returned to the unit. When my family therapy session was over, my group was just getting out of Drug and Alcohol Group Therapy with Dr. Finch and Ms. Mosley. I tried not to let any expression show on my face as everyone scattered and went on to do his or her own thing, as everyone did on Saturdays. I headed straight for the bedroom.

When I was in the room, I fell onto the bed and grabbed Janine's blanket. I curled up with it under my cheek and I tried to take deep breaths and stay calm. The door opened to the bedroom from the hallway and Mena walked in. She started towards her bed, but stopped when she saw me. She smirked.

"How did it go?" she asked.

I lay my head on top of Janine's blanket and shrugged.

"I had my first visit today. Not on Level One anymore," Mena filled me in.

I didn't really feel like talking. It wasn't Mena. I just needed some time to take in everything that had happened during the family therapy session. There was a lot to think about and a lot to accept for my family and me.

During the family session, there had been a lot of apologies. Promises had been made that had to be kept, and there'd been confessions and secrets told that had been kept inside for too long. Tears had been shed and poured out from deep down inside of us until we'd run dry. I was exhausted.

Mena didn't realize this, nor did I dare open my mouth to tell her. She sat down on her bed and faced me.

She said, "My foster mom came to visit. She brought me some clothes. I had asked her to bring me a blanket because it gets too cold in here at night. It is summer time, but it feels like winter in here at night. Of course she didn't bring me one."

Mena continued to talk about her visit with her foster mom. I wasn't really listening to her. I hugged Janine's blanket tighter and thought back to the time after the smiles and laughter had disappeared, when it had been time to talk and be serious.

Dr. Pelchat had begun to talk about the issue of my diagnosis and what it meant. He'd talked about weekly therapy sessions with me, and had suggested that we have an occasional family session. He was particularly interested in Nicholas, and how he was affected by what I had done, because he was the one who'd found me. Nick had a therapist that he saw regularly, up until about a year ago, when his years of intense therapy had been lifted. It wasn't so intense anymore. He didn't have to go once a week anymore. They had reduced it to once a month. Then he was down to just once every three months.

Dr. Pelchat had been pleased to hear that Nick was healing from what Jack had done to him. It was tough. Dr. Pelchat had empathized, to have it happen to him by his own father. Alison had shed a tear or two, but I could tell that she didn't really understand. All she knew was that her brother and big sister had been hurt, and her whole life was affected by it. She'd opened up to Dr. Pelchat by saying that she missed Jack. She hadn't seen him in the years since he'd been put away, and she had hoped that she would get to see him again soon. Mom had stopped her from saying too much with a hard squeeze that I'd noticed, and Dr. Pelchat hadn't. Mom was probably afraid Alison would've said something about Jack's parole hearing. Then we would have gotten into the deeper issue. She wasn't ready for that yet.

Dr. Pelchat had asked Mom if she had any regrets. Mom had said that her regret wasn't marrying Jack, nor was it moving from California, or having the twins or me. She'd said that her regret was not listening to me when I was trying to tell her, and not seeing that it wasn't just Nick who needed help, but that it was all of us, especially me.

"I didn't know that she was in so much pain," Mom had said. "And I didn't know that she was so depressed that she'd want to do something so harmful to herself." Mom had gone on about how much she loved me. She'd said that if I ever felt depressed like that again, she wanted me to go to her. She wanted me to talk to her instead of cutting.

That's when Dr. Pelchat had asked me if that was something that I could do. He'd put me on the spot, wanting me to answer that kind of question right away.

Could I really try to go to Mom to talk to her when I felt depressed? Would she be able to handle it without getting angry with me for being this way?

I'd told Dr. Pelchat that I would try.

Then he'd made me promise. I'd had to look my mother in the eyes and promise her that I would talk to her when I got depressed and if I felt suicidal again. When I'd promised this, I'd wanted to see how she'd react. She'd kept a straight face as she'd nodded and smiled with no tears in her eyes, and millions of them had fallen out of mine.

I'd wanted to believe that I could go to her if I needed to. I'd wanted to talk about Jack and his parole hearing, but there had not been enough time. We didn't get to talk about what had really made me do what I'd done. We hadn't talked about what I'd seen that had drawn me to the pills in the first place.

Dr. Pelchat knew that I was depressed, and so did Mom, Alison, and Nick. I was diagnosed with Borderline Personality Disorder. My treatment and moving forward towards the future was what was supposed to be most important.

Dr. Pelchat had said, "We can't just get everything out and fix it in one session. It's going to take some time, just like it did with Nick."

Dr. Pelchat had asked me a question when we were near the end of the session. Tears had dried up. Smiles had been back on our faces. Alison and Nick had been laughing again, and Mom had looked relieved. She'd seemed relieved to see that I was doing better, and she had probably been even more relieved when Dr. Pelchat had said that our session time was up.

Before we'd gotten up to leave he'd said, "I have just one more question that I want to ask Kristen while all of you are here."

"Yes, Dr. Pelchat?" I had asked.

Dr. Pelchat had asked, "Do you think that you are ready to go home?"

I rolled over and lay on my side on the bed to face away from Mena. I had Janine's blanket wrapped around me, and I pulled my pillow close. With tears dripping from my eyes, I placed my head down on the pillow gently so that my head wouldn't hurt worse than it already did.

Mena heard me crying. She said, "What's wrong?"

I looked up and saw Mr. Sharp. He was sitting on the edge of the night table, next to the lamp, sparkling in the beautiful butterfly wings. My vision blurred because of the tears. I felt almost helpless. I was never going to be better if I couldn't get everything out that was killing me inside. Mr. Sharp stuck out of the butterfly pendant towards me. I didn't want to get it out like that anymore.

"Go away," I told him.

"Fine," Mena said. "It's almost dinnertime." Mena got up off my bed and stormed away, leaving me in the room by myself.

I didn't bother to tell her that I wasn't talking to her. It wouldn't have made sense to her without me having to explain it all. I didn't have the strength.

CHAPTER 52

I didn't go to breakfast on Sunday morning, after the nurse helped me clean up and after my final examination with her. I didn't even bother to say goodbye to Tai or Mena. They were all gone to Group Therapy after breakfast. I stayed behind to pack the last of my belongings into my suitcases. I finished packing and looked around one last time at the room, just to make sure I wasn't forgetting anything. All that was left were the two folded blankets and Dr. Pelchat's book on Borderline Personality Disorder that I had to return to him.

I grabbed Janine's blanket and sat it on top of my suitcase. Then, as I picked up my own blanket, I looked over at Mena's bed. It was neatly made, with the thin, white blanket spread across the top. I remembered my first night in Bent Creek. How cold I was. Then I thought of when I had first met Mena. I didn't think that I could get along with her. She wasn't as mean as I had thought her to be. She was frustrated and depressed, like all of us at Bent Creek. She just showed her depression differently. I was glad that I had met her and had gotten to know her.

When I lay my own blanket out on Mena's bed, I made sure to spread it neatly so that it would cover the thin, white blanket. I folded the corners and tucked the ends so that she would know that I left it for her intentionally. I did not want there to be any mistake.

When I was almost finished, Geoffrey came into the room quietly. He had been so quiet that I didn't realize he was there until he spoke. "Kristen, Dr. Pelchat is ready to see you."

"Okay," I said. I started to grab my bags and Janine's blanket.

"You can leave that there," Geoffrey said. "I will make sure that your ride gets your bags when they arrive. Dr. Pelchat wants to meet with you before you leave. Come with me."

I left my bags and Janine's blanket behind so that Geoffrey could take care of them. Then, I grabbed Dr. Pelchat's book and followed Geoffrey out the door. As we walked, Geoffrey seemed to have something on his mind that he wanted to say, because he kept looking over at me. Before things became awkward, I spoke up.

"I can't believe today is my last day," I told him.

He smiled and sighed heavily. "It's a good thing," he said.

"I think so," I agreed. "Good luck with becoming a doctor."

We stopped in front of Dr. Pelchat's office, and Geoffrey placed a hand on my shoulder. He kept that warm smile on his face and he said, "Thank you, Kristen. Listen, right now it may seem like it's hard to leave Bent Creek, but I know that you will be all right."

"It's not that hard," I told him.

He laughed. "Okay. I know that some people usually have a hard time leaving, but maybe you are different. But, just in case it doesn't hit you until you are out of here, keep in mind that you have made great progress. You've come a long way. I see a real difference in you since the first time I saw you."

His smile and mine were genuine. His words really meant something to me. "Do you really see a difference?" I asked. "I mean a *real* difference?"

"Yes," he assured me. "It is a *real* difference. But there's one thing that hasn't changed, and I don't think you should ever change."

I waited.

"You really are an awesome person. Don't you ever forget it. No matter what you decide to do with yourself after you graduate, know that you are awesome."

I felt a tear shoot out of my eye. Geoffrey blushed when he saw me crying. I wiped my tear away and wanted to hug him badly, but I held myself back. I thanked him as he began to walk away. He waved at me, and I waved back. He strolled down the hall and left me outside of Dr. Pelchat's office, wondering.

When Geoffrey disappeared around the corner of the hall, I turned to face the door. I took a deep breath and entered without knocking. Dr. Pelchat was sitting at his desk with my chart open, writing. He looked up at me as I entered, and a huge, jolly smile appeared on his face. He seemed excited to see me.

"How are you feeling today, Kristen?"

His smile made me smile. I said, "I'm good. How are you?"

He took a deep, happy breath and sighed calmly. With the smile still stuck to his face, he said, "I'm feeling wonderful today. Thanks for asking."

"Me too. Thank you for letting me borrow this," I said as I sat his book on top of his desk. When I sat the book down, a folded sheet of paper slipped out. I snatched the paper from the desk and slipped it into the pocket of my jeans. Dr. Pelchat took his book with gratitude.

"Oh, thanks. You remembered to return it to me. Most of my patients leave with the books I let them borrow. Speaking of leaving, are you ready?"

"I'm all packed."

"I'm sure you are," he laughed.

I had never seen him so ecstatic.

"I do believe that you have outstayed your welcome here at Bent Creek," he laughed on.

I laughed with him. His happiness was contagious. Dr. Pelchat's chubby cheeks turned red as he laughed. It was nice watching him. I began to think about when I had first seen him while Geoffrey and I had been talking at the table. I'd had no idea who this man was. Then, when I had sat in on his group for the first time, he had really come down on me hard about learning about what medications I was taking. I'd thought he was going to be a mean, old man, but I had been wrong. He was a very caring and compassionate doctor. He was the best doctor I had ever had.

Dr. Pelchat stopped laughing and he looked at me. I hadn't realized that I'd rolled up my sleeves. His smile disappeared. "Kristen, what is that?" He pointed to my arms.

I looked down and saw the red wound that was only just beginning to heal. It had a scab, but it was obvious because of the redness. I quickly pulled my sleeves back down on both arms.

"No," Dr. Pelchat said. "Don't do that. Roll them back up."

Sadly, I rolled my sleeves back up to my elbows.

"Hold them out," he said. His stern demeanor was returning to normal. Jolly Dr. Pelchat went back to wherever he'd been hiding.

I held my arms out, revealing my scars, my stitched wrists, and the recent cut that I was trying to hide from him.

"Why, Kristen?"

"I don't know," I said.

"You don't know," he said sternly.

"I mean, I did it because," I forced it out. "I did it because I felt that he was the only one I could run to. But, I know now that I can come to you, and I know that I can talk to Mom. I don't want to run to Mr. Sharp when I feel that I can't deal anymore. I want to be able to talk to Mom, and I want to be able to write out my feelings the way I used to. I don't want to cut anymore. And I don't want to be a loser. I don't! I really don't!"

Dr. Pelchat remained silent. He stared, and it didn't bother me that he was staring at me, because I knew that he was empathizing with me. He wanted to see if I was being sincere. I was sincere, and I meant every word I said when I said it. I wasn't going to stop there.

"You may be wondering who *he* is," I said. "This is probably not a good time to throw all of this on you, because this is my last day in Bent Creek. But I keep this sharp butterfly with me." I reached into the pocket of my jeans and pulled out the pendant. I held it out in my hand so that Dr. Pelchat could see before I returned it to my pocket. His eyes followed in what looked like disbelief.

"That's Mr. Sharp. He lives in everything that is sharp. I call him Mr. Sharp because he's always helped me through this way. He would listen to me, comfort me, and help me breathe when things got too suffocating. It felt like this was the only way. Now I know that it's not. I know that I can do it without him. And I have to live without doing these things. I have to be able to deal without hurting myself. Dr. Cuvo was right. I don't deserve this, and what I did to myself was a terrible thing. When I saw how angry and hurt Nick was, and how much Alison missed me, I knew that what I had done was terrible, and I don't ever want to do it again. I want my little brother and little sister to learn the right thing to do from me, because I'm their big sister and I don't want to fail them. I can't fail, Dr. Pelchat. I can't fail this time."

"You won't fail," he said to me. He was staring into my eyes. His eyes were warm and his words remained sincere. "You won't fail, because everything you just said--I know you mean it."

"You're not mad at me for having this?" I said, gesturing to the pendant in my pocket.

Dr. Pelchat shook his head. "I'm not mad, Kristen."

"And for cutting?"

"No. I am disappointed that this happened, but I'm very proud of you for taking that big step. I know that it took a lot for you to talk about it and to admit you were cutting while you were a patient in here."

"Does that keep me from going on?"

"Not at all. If anything," he said, "It will help you move forward. I don't see any reason why you should stay here any longer as an in-patient, or for you to be sent to long-term. Not everything will be solved in one session. It is going to take time, and you know it. You are ready. You've been through a lot and you've learned a lot. Yes, Kristen, you are ready to go home." Dr. Pelchat stood up from his chair and made his way around the desk towards me. He stuck out his hand for me to shake.

I reached out my hand with every intention of shaking his hand, but something inside of me pulled me forward and my arms wrapped around him. I caught him off guard, because he didn't seem to know how to react. After he realized what was happening, I felt him hesitate, but his arms were eventually wrapped around me, too. He gave me a warm and gentle squeeze, and then he released me.

"Remember," he said, "This is not good bye. I will be seeing you soon."

"You're right," I said. "When?"

"On the sixth," he assured me.

I smiled and shook my head.

"What?" he asked.

"That's my eighteenth birthday."

"Well then, I'll have to see if we can't get you a slice of cake or something," he said.

"Really?"

"Yeah, why not? You'll be the birthday girl."

"That would be cool," I said.

We made our way to the door, and before Dr. Pelchat opened it, he said, "You're now officially discharged."

CHAPTER 53

John's parents, Jonathan Sr. and Mariah, came to Bent Creek to pick me up. Geoffrey carried all of my bags out to their car for me. The only thing that I was allowed to carry was Janine's blanket. Jonathan insisted on helping him, but Geoffrey told him it would be his pleasure to carry my bags. I believe Geoffrey used it as an excuse to see me off. Mariah signed my papers for my release, since she and her husband were considered immediate family.

After Geoffrey was gone and we were in the car, Jonathan turned to me and said, "You all set, kiddo?"

I smiled and nodded at him. Mariah didn't have much to say to me. She looked down at my arms and frowned.

I looked up, still smiling, and I said, "It's now or never."

Mariah didn't seem convinced. I could tell she was uncomfortable because she hardly looked at me, and when she did, her eyes didn't tear away from my arms, even though they were covered by my long sleeves.

When Jonathan began to back out of the parking spot, it hit me. The warm sun that I hadn't felt against my face since summer had begun now beamed through the window, and it warmed me through. I closed my eyes so that I couldn't see Bent Creek grow smaller in the distance. I just wanted to feel the sun and not think about leaving. I was happy to be free of what I'd once considered prison, but it had turned out to be a place of salvation through the kindest peers and the most empathetic and compassionate doctors I had ever met in my life.

My eyes remained closed until I felt it was safe enough to open them again. As I opened my eyes, I remembered the sheet of folded paper that I had found in the book I'd returned to Dr. Pelchat. I reached into my pocket that held it and my butterfly pendant. I pulled out the sheet of paper and unfolded it. When my eyes beheld what was on the paper, the tears that were trying to break free from under my eyelids slid down my cheeks.

The illustration of Daniel's late girlfriend gazed back at me through her dark, pencil-drawn eyes. Daniel's kind words of encouragement from his experiences and growth ran through my mind. It made me sad to realize that my time at Bent Creek was over, and there were great people that I was leaving behind, and ones that were moving on. It was harder than I thought it was going to be to leave.

Going into Bent Creek, I'd had so much doubt. I'd carried in the fears and had walked around with nothing but thoughts of hopelessness. I'd been trapped in my condemnation and restlessness of the past. Those memories had drowned me, suffocated me, and fed my soul to what was trying to destroy me--Borderline Personality Disorder.

It made me feel good to have new memories. I had to think of more things that were positive. Bent Creek had given me much to ponder. I let myself shed a few tears with a smile on my face as I said, "see you later," not "goodbye," to Bent Creek.

Jonathan broke the silence. "Kristen, you must be feeling pretty good right now. Did they help you at all in there?"

"Yes. I do feel like my time was well spent," I answered.

Jonathan seemed as if he was the only one out of the two of them who was listening. I didn't blame Mariah for the way she behaved. She'd never had a child like me to worry about. John was an exceptional person who always made good grades and didn't seem to give them a real reason to worry. Lexus was always beautiful, happy, and her family was wholesome and unbroken. Lexus was the perfect future daughter-in-law for her.

Jonathan tried to lighten the mood in the car as we rode off by turning on the radio. He pulled out a CD and looked in his rear view mirror. I noticed his eyes were on me.

He said, "How about some music, ladies? Let's listen to the tunes of..." He took his eyes off the road for a second to glance down at the CD. A puzzled look came over his face as he read aloud the name of the pop/R&B singer who was most popular for his romantic and catchy love tunes.

I knew immediately to whom that CD belonged.

Mariah laughed. She said, "It's one of the kids' CDs, honey. John and Lexus must have left it in here when they went up to Helen yesterday."

Jonathan glanced at me through the mirror. He quickly looked away.

"Yes, they did take the car yesterday. I remember. Well," he said as he stuck the CD into the player. "If it's what the kids are listening to today, then Kristen will like it. After all, we are happy to have her back with us. Right, dear?"

She nodded her head while looking out of the window.

"Yes, we are," she sighed.

She didn't sound too assuring. I knew that she had always thought that I was a troubled kid. She was right. I didn't blame her for being guarded and unsure about me. I had a lot of mess to clean up, and I had a lot to prove. One of those messes I needed to clean up was with Lexus. There was no doubt in my mind that she had told John, who may have in turn told his parents, about our recent quarrel.

Jonathan said, "I hope you don't mind us coming to pick you up. Your mother didn't get out of work early enough to come get you, but she and the twins should be home by the time we get there."

"It's great," I said. "I'm really happy you came to pick me up. I missed you guys."

Jonathan smiled, and he nudged his wife playfully. She smiled at him. She began to warm up as John Mayer's soulful voice poured out of the surround-sound speakers of their SUV. The acoustics played the sounds of romance. Mariah turned to Jonathan and smiled at him.

She said, "I actually kind of like this song."

Jonathan smiled. He seemed proud of himself. It seemed like he felt he had reached his goal of lightening the mood. His charms definitely worked on his wife. He grabbed her hand and kissed it sweetly as he steered onto the highway. The music was definitely getting to them. I could only imagine what it did for John and Lexus while they were in the romantic and cozy city of Helen, Georgia. I cringed at the terrible and annoying song of romance that blasted from the perfect surround-sound stereo system. I couldn't wait to get home to see my Nick and Alison.

When we arrived, I could hardly wait for the car to stop moving so that I could get out. Mom's car was in the driveway. I knew that everyone was home. I quickly grabbed both of my bags before Jonathan could help me, and I ran towards the front door. I almost dropped everything, being in such a hurry, but I was able to make it. Before I could get my keys out of my bag, the front door flew open.

Two bodies lunged at me with full force. Alison and Nick were both hugging me. I tried my best to hug them back. Jonathan honked the horn at me. Alison and Nick let me go. I turned to the SUV and waved at them. I yelled thank you and goodbye. I started to turn away, but Mariah called out to me. I turned back to them as Alison and Nick grabbed my bags and yelled goodbye to Jonathan. They ran into the house with my bags, calling out for Mom.

Mariah leaned out of the rolled-down window. She yelled, "Tell your mother we'll call her when we get home. We are sorry we can't come in to visit, but we're still planning the engagement party, and we are overdue for the meeting with the party planner. We'll see you soon."

Jonathan added, "It's wonderful to see you home, sweetheart. See you next week!"

When they were gone, I ran into the house. Nick and Alison had left my bags beside the door. I shut the front door and looked into the living room. Alison and Nick were grinning at each other, and then they looked back at me. "What? What's going on?" I said. I knew they were up to something.

Mom came out of the kitchen and into the living room. The sight of her made me feel warm. She was smiling, and I could tell that she was glad to have me home.

Alison turned to Mom and said, "Can we show her now?"

"Yeah! I'm sure Kristen would like to see it," Mom said. "Let's show her."

"Show me what?" I asked.

"Come on!" Alison squealed with happiness.

Alison grabbed my hand and led me downstairs to the basement hallway. Mom and Nick followed with my bags. My bedroom was down there. I could only imagine what she couldn't wait to show me. I opened the door to my bedroom and turned on the light. Nothing in my worst nightmares could have prepared me for what I saw. It wasn't blue, it wasn't orange, and it wasn't even white, like the walls of the hospital. It was pink! My whole room had been painted pink. From the ceiling to the new paint on my old wooden bed frame and dressers. Everything was pink. I held onto Janine's blanket and hugged it, almost scared.

"She likes it!" Alison inaccurately observed.

Nick shook his head when I looked at him. He knew what I was thinking. I looked at Mom, and she was smiling in a way that I wanted to deny.

I made myself walk deeper into that strange room. I looked around. My books were in place. There were new sheets and a new quilt on the bed. My notebooks were as I had left them. Those looked like the only things that were in the right place. Mom turned to Alison and Nick.

She said, "Go upstairs and set the table for dinner. Kristen and I will be up in a minute."

Alison gave me another hug and Nick kissed my cheek. They ran upstairs in a race to try to beat each other to the kitchen. When we were alone, Mom walked over to my dresser. She put her hand on a silver-toned jewelry box. That jewelry box had not been there before I had gone into Bent Creek. It was bejeweled and dazzling to the eye. It looked too elegant to be mine.

"Do you like it?" she asked me.

"Who does that belong to?" I asked.

Mom laughed. "It belongs to you, silly girl."

"Really? But it's so *pretty*."

"That's why she brought it here for you," Mom said.

"Who brought it?"

"Lexus brought it for you when she came over to help us paint your room. Alison picked out the color. I couldn't very well have you come home with your room the way you had it. The walls were covered in black and your sheets were – well, you know. Lexus had the idea to come over and help me get things ready for your return. Since you are better now, we thought you'd start fresh."

I carried my bags over to the closet. I opened the door. I looked up, shocked, when I saw that the shelves and walls were completely empty.

"Where are my ninja swords and the daggers? Where are my knives?"

"Don't you like your jewelry box? Look inside," she said. "You have earrings, necklaces, rings, and other cute stuff. You don't need to collect those knives anymore. Why don't you collect jewelry?"

My head began to ache. "You got rid of them?"

"Don't be angry, Kristen. You'll get them back when I see that you are ready to have them. Now, I don't think it's a good idea for you to have those things in here. Look at this!" She pulled out a gold necklace with a little fairy pendant dangling from the center. The fairy's wings didn't look as sharp as my butterfly pendant. I was sure that was her and Lexus' intentions. Mom came towards me with that necklace. She held it over my head and placed it around my neck. Then she stood in front of me to admire the necklace.

"All right," she assured herself. "I'll let you unpack and get yourself prepared for dinner. Did you thank Jonathan for bringing you home?"

"Of course," I said. I wanted her to leave me alone already.

"Good," she said. "We're going to Lexus and John's engagement party next week." She was smiling her forced and ridiculous smile.

I didn't smile back. I didn't want to be fake anymore. I was too tired, and I was too freaked out by that strange and uncomfortable room. It didn't feel like mine anymore.

As Mom walked out of the room, I began to shut the door. Mom stopped it from closing with her foot. She said, "No. I want this door to stay open from now on."

"I can't shut my bedroom door?"

"No," she said. "I want you to keep it open. Things are going to start changing around here. If I have to make changes in order to keep you from slashing your wrists and being completely depressed, then you are going to work with me and make some changes too."

It started to feel like home again. I knew it wouldn't take too long.

As Mom walked towards the stairwell, I started to close my bedroom door. She turned around and looked at me. I hesitated. She saw me hesitate. She turned away, and as soon as I heard the first stair creak underneath her foot, I slammed shut my bedroom door. I made sure to do it hard and loud enough so that she could hear it. I locked the door and waited. I pressed my ear to the door and, for a second, I heard the stair creak again. I smiled. She was coming back toward the door. But then I heard her storm up the stairs.

I looked around my room. I could smell the nauseating fresh paint. It had Lexus' personality written all over it. I made my way over to the dresser that had no mirror in it. I thought back to the day I'd smashed that stupid mirror with my hands. Mom had never replaced it, convinced I'd only do it again. Maybe I would have destroyed it again if there were a mirror in the frame.

The only thing I saw was that precious jewelry box. The anger inside of me swelled to an unbearable crescendo. Not being able to hold it in any longer, I swiped my hand across the surface the jewelry box sat on. Calmly, I watched it violently crash to the floor. The box disassembled upon landing, and the beautiful jewels that decorated the box smashed and broke apart.

Relief washed over me as the jewelry spilled out of the box. Little pendants and gorgeous crystals and jewels rolled underneath the bed and scattered in other places throughout the room. Pieces of jewels cracked, snapped, popped, and were destroyed. All of the chaos and the new disarrangement defined exactly how I felt inside.

CHAPTER 54

Before going into Bent Creek, I didn't have to worry about Mom being angry with me for keeping my door shut. It was always closed. No one bothered me. I could just sit for hours inside the dark, black walls of my room. Mr. Sharp and I would talk for hours after doing homework, after work, and after Lexus left to go on her dates with John. I closed my door, but I always opened it back up.

It wasn't until the day when I'd found that letter from Jack asking for Mom's forgiveness, that I'd felt I did not ever want to have to open my bedroom door again. Was it hopelessness? Was it fear? Did I fear her forgiving him? Did I think that she really would go to his parole hearing and put Nicholas through that again? Would she really put all of us through that again?

She banged on my door in the morning. The banging was angry and loud. I woke up, startled. Then I realized that this was the moment I had been waiting for since I'd left Bent Creek. The morning of the day that I got my stitches removed.

I could hear Mom yelling from the other side of the door. She couldn't open it. I'd begun locking my bedroom door ever since coming back from Bent Creek.

"Kristen! Kristen! Open this door! Kristen!" She almost sounded panicked.

I opened the door, fully dressed and ready to go. I just looked at the sore expression on her face, almost wanting to laugh.

"Don't you ever -" she caught herself. "Kristen. I thought I told you to keep this door open from now on."

"What do you want me to do, Mom?" I said as I pushed past her. "You want me to get dressed with my bedroom door open from now on?"

She followed me up the stairs. I felt as if she was on my back as she yelled, "Don't start with me this morning! We are not going to be like this. I'm not going to argue with you. You keep the door open, and that's it. You hear me?"

"Fine," I said under my breath.

"I can't understand you. I asked you a question."

"I said that is fine, Mom."

"Good," she accepted. "Come on, let's go. I have to drop Nick and Alison off at the Rec Center before I take you to the doctor." She went to the top of the stairs and headed for their bedrooms. "Nicholas and Alison, let's get going! You're going to be late."

I grabbed my summer jacket off the banister of the stairwell, and as I was slipping it on, I noticed three envelopes on the occasional table that sat by the front door. All three of them had my name on them. I picked them up.

Alison and Nick were coming towards me as Mom yelled for them to go to the car and wait for her. I grabbed the car keys and the three of us went out to the car. When we were in the car, it didn't take long for Nick and Alison to find something silly to argue about. Which of the X-Men was the most powerful?

I blocked them out. I looked down at the envelopes in my hand, and I opened the one that was postmarked the earliest. Two of them were grades from classes I was taking. B- in Calculus I and a B+ in Life Science. I didn't expect to do any better than that in those classes. The last one I opened was dated almost two weeks prior to that day. It was a notice from my school for past due tuition.

There was a late fee plus the tuition that was past due. I hadn't had a paycheck since Mom had come to the hospital with my last one. I remembered that I had endorsed it to her and asked her to mail off what I owed for the month. What had happened?

Mom came out to the car and got in on the driver's side. She looked back at Nick and Alison. Their arguing had somehow turned to them hitting each other. They stopped fighting after Mom yelled for them to stop. She threatened that instead of letting them go to summer camp at the Recreation Center she'd make them stay home and do chores.

I stayed silent as Mom pulled out of the driveway and drove off.

"Kristen," she began, "You hear them back there trying to kill each other. Why didn't you do anything?"

I didn't say anything. I looked down at the notice from my school and held back my temptation to ball it up and throw it at her.

When we were at the doctor's office, I anxiously awaited to be called in. I was eager to see what my arms were going to look like without all of the metalwork and stitching. I was finally inside of the room. The nurse had been kind enough to ask my mother to stay in the waiting room. I didn't want her there while the doctor was removing the stitching because I didn't want her to talk about it or pretend to cry so that she could get sympathy from the doctor.

The little, white room felt crowded with all of the equipment around me. Dr. Mitsen finally came into the room with the nurse, who pushed in a metal cart that held the tools to do the job. I was back in Dr. Mitsen's office because it was time to have the metal-sutured stitches removed. The nurse cleaned the area with Isopropyl, and then the doctor held up the scissors.

"Don't be nervous," Dr. Mitsen said. "You won't feel a thing."

He completely lied to me. I walked out of his office with my arms against my chest. I hadn't had regular, sewn-in stitches. I'd had metal in me that had been supported with the string. The part when he'd cut the string hadn't hurt at all, but removing the metal had hurt, and looking down while he'd done it had made it even worse. I felt like what I imagined a machine transforming into a human would feel like. All of the pain felt so new, and when I looked down at the results, I realized that my wrists looked better with the stitches than without.

"Don't you worry," Dr. Mitsen said. "They will scar over and heal in due time."

I knew he was right, but the way they would scar over would be thick and too obvious. I'll have to wear long sleeves forever, I thought.

After the doctor's appointment, Mom and I were back in the car together. She drove as I sat on the passenger side, trying not to look at her. I wished Alison and Nick were in the car with us. They were having fun at the local recreation center, doing summer camp activities. At least they were enjoying their youth. I was struggling through mine.

Mom sensed something through my silence. I could tell she was frustrated. She could tell there was something bothering me. She started sweet, like she used to do. Then it would turn into her yelling and end with me feeling like a troublesome burden.

"It's really nice to have a day off," she said.

I didn't respond.

"Did you know, while you were in the hospital, I was working almost seventy hours a week? You plan on going back to work soon?"

I nodded.

"When?" she asked.

"I talked to my boss yesterday. She said I can come back to work on Monday," I responded.

"That's nice," Mom said. "At least they don't know why you were in the hospital. She probably would have fired you."

I looked down at my arms. I tried not to let her get to me, but the scars on my arms and wrists only made me feel worse.

"What's wrong with you now?"

"Nothing," I lied.

"Kristen, don't start. Remember, this is how it started last time. We were in the car coming home, and I asked you what was wrong, and you told me that it was nothing. I didn't say anything and I let you get away with it. When we got home, you went down to your room and shut your door. Then the next thing I know, your little brother finds you in your bed with your wrists cut up."

"Thanks for the replay, Mom," I said.

She pulled into our driveway. When she put the car in park, she reached her arm over and slapped me across my face. She slapped me so hard that I thought I saw stars.

I rubbed my cheek, as it stung in pain.

"Don't dare act like you are the only one in pain! Do you know what that did to us, Kristen? Do you even know what *you* did to us?"

"Yes! I know! I'm sorry! Okay? I'm sorry! I know that I did something terrible, Mom. I admit that, and I don't want to do that to you again. I can't take it back, but I was scared."

"Scared of what?" she said with tears in her eyes.

"The letter."

Mom got out of the car as soon as she heard my answer.

I quickly followed behind her.

She opened the front door, and we both entered the house. Mom threw herself down on the couch and I sat down next to her.

"Mom, are you going to the hearing?"

"I don't want to talk about this right now, Kristen."

"When are we going to talk about it? It's getting close. You have to tell me, because I can't sit here and live in this fear that you're going to give in and go and possibly..." my voice trailed off as I could only think of what I was afraid of instead of put them into words.

"What is it?" Mom asked. "You think I'm going to try to help get Jack out of prison? You think I'm so lonely and desperate that I would want that man who hurt my own child to come back into our lives? Is that

415

what you think of me, Kristen?"

"I don't know what to think," I told her.

Mom took a deep breath and wiped the heavy tears that were falling from her eyes. They were real tears this time. I couldn't figure out why she was crying. But she was crying so hard that, each time she wiped tears away, more would fall. Did I hurt her?

I pleaded, "Mom. I'm sorry. I've messed up so much. It's this Borderline Personality Disorder, and it's -"

Mom looked at me with those angry tears. She said, "Don't do that. You've been in that place all this time. And you've had those people to talk to you and counsel you and show you how to deal. But I haven't had that. I haven't had the privilege of having someone to listen to me and take into consideration how I feel about things. I have to take care of your brother and sister. I can't even give any attention to me and *my* needs. Sometimes I feel as if I can't take it anymore. No, it's *most* of the time that I feel this way. So, don't sit there and act like you're the one with all of the problems, Kristen."

"But I do!" I yelled. "I do have problems! Mom! You can't put me on the back burner because I'm almost eighteen! When I turn eighteen, I will still be your child! You can't just expect me to go away and be able to deal with this on my own. I can't. I'm not strong enough to do that. I'm trying to survive, but I can't do it on my own. Don't just ignore it, Mom."

"Shut up!"

"Shut up?"

"Yes, shut up! I can't take this right now. I have to get away from you."

She got up off the couch and headed towards her bedroom. I got up and followed her.

"Shut up," I repeated back to her. "That's all you have *ever* wanted me to do. You wanted me to shut up when Jack was put away and people asked questions. Even when Jack was hurting Nick and I knew and tried to tell you, you told me to shut up."

"Shut up, Kristen," she said.

Tears poured out of her eyes. Her face was red and she pulled at her hair. We were in her bedroom and I stood by the door. There was nowhere else for her to go.

"I swear, Kristen. If you don't get out of my face..."

"You wanted me to shut up because..." I hesitated, but I got out the last words I had said to her that night.

"*You knew, Mom*," I told her. "You knew everything! You wanted me to shut up because you can't admit to yourself that Nick continued to get hurt because you didn't do anything about it. You wanted to live in your perfect, little, naive world. That's why you wanted me to shut up. And now you want me to shut up because you can't take it. You can't take the fact that I could have died last month, and it would have been your fault!"

That was the last straw. Mom gasped. Her eyes grew big in shock. I choked back more words that I could have shot at her, but I kept quiet. She came towards me and grabbed my arm so tight that it felt like I was losing circulation.

"Why don't you just go down to your room and cut your wrists again!" she yelled at me. "If I'm such a terrible mother, why don't you just go do it and make sure you do it right? Or just get out of my house!"

She wasn't crying anymore. Her eyes were red and puffy. She was certainly angry and she was not holding back. She pushed me out of her bedroom with full force. I didn't fight back. I knew what I'd said, and I expected it to make her angry.

"I'm the bad mother because you tried to kill yourself and because of everything that happened years ago. I can't fix it. What's done is done. So, your poor, little, victimized, weak and jaded, teenage self who can't make it on her own will have to settle for a kitchen knife. If you want to kill yourself, you'll have to use that because I sold all of those fancy little knives you wasted your money on. Just do me one favor, Kristen. Don't use my good cleaver knife." She gave me one last push to make sure I was out of her way, and then she thrashed shut her bedroom door.

I went down to my bedroom and I sat on the bed, not sure what to feel. It felt good to get out what I had been holding in all those years, but I had never imagined she would be so angry to the point of actually *telling* me to die. I didn't think she was wrong for feeling the way she did about me, because I was a problem for her, and I had only made things worse. What I'd said to her was true, she knew, and she needed to know that I was aware of it, even if it did kill one of us in the end.

CHAPTER 55

I didn't kill myself by cutting my wrists. In fact, I didn't even call out to Mr. Sharp that night. Mom and I didn't say much to each other over the next few days. I was glad when Monday came around because I was going back to work. Mom was glad too, because she didn't have to work as many hours at her job as she had been working when I had been in Bent Creek.

My boss was glad to have me back at work. I made sure to wear long sleeves. It wasn't too bad, because summer was nearing its end, and the chill of fall was starting to rise into the air. When I entered work, my boss gave me a warm hug. After I settled in, she showed me the new product and had me begin inventory and stocking the shelves with new merchandise. She didn't waste any time on getting me back to laboring.

The morning was slow with customers in the store. There were mostly homemakers coming in, shopping for new clothes and shoes for their children. I was ringing up the last customer in the store for the morning when my stomach growled. It was nearly afternoon, which meant I had a lunch break coming soon.

The customer was leaving the store with her new merchandise and pushing a baby stroller, and as she walked out of the door, I noticed Lexus holding the door open. The woman passed by Lexus and thanked her as she exited the store. I had to blink twice to make sure I was really seeing Lexus. Sure enough, it was Lexus. She was dressed in a blue and white, satin camisole and a pair of low-riding blue jeans. Lexus walked into the store looking beautiful and glowing with happiness. She approached me at the counter with an Abercrombie and Fitch bag in her hand.

She smiled a warm smile and asked me, "Are you hungry?"

I looked over at the clock on the wall, trying not to let her smile get to me. It was too late. I was hungry and I missed her a lot. I felt guilty because I hadn't bothered to call her to tell her that I was home from Bent Creek, even though I knew that she would find out from her parents. And, worst of all, I hadn't bothered to try to reach out to her and apologize for the way I had behaved the last time we had seen each other.

"Give me a minute?" I asked.

"Sure," she said.

Lexus kept that smile on her face that made me feel guilty.

I walked to the back room and opened the door labeled: EMPLOYEES ONLY. Beyond that door was a storage room that connected to the manager's office. There was a cozy couch and a nineteen-inch, flat-screen television. The television sat on top of an orange milk crate near the manager's office.

My boss looked up at me as she lay on the couch. She was watching a talk show on the television.

She said, "What's going on? Did it get busy out there?"

The audience from the daytime talk show cheered as an angry woman pummeled a man on the stage. The studio audience seemed to be extraordinarily excited over this woman's apparent rage from whatever injuries this man had caused her.

I looked away from the television and frowned at my boss.

"No," I told her. "It's time for me to take my lunch break."

"Oh, Kristen," she whined. "Can't you go on your break in fifteen minutes? At least let me watch the rest of this part. I have to see if he fails the lie detector test, and I need to know if he is father of her baby, or if it's his younger brother."

"No," I denied her. "I have to go. I'm starving."

Before she could get out another plea, I went over to the time clock and punched in the time on my card.

"I'm clocked out." I told her, "I'll be back in an hour."

I walked back into the front of the store and my boss dragged herself behind. She had a childish scowl on her face. She couldn't keep me from going to lunch just because she wanted to finish watching some sleazy talk show.

As Lexus and I walked to the food court, she kept looking over at me as if she was waiting for me to say something to her. I knew what she wanted to hear. I just wasn't too sure if it was the right time to say it.

When I didn't say anything, she decided to begin with, "Are we okay, Kristen?"

I nodded. "I think so."

She clasped her hands together with a big smile on her face.

"Good," she said. "There's just so much to tell you."

Of course we were okay again. Lexus didn't hold grudges, and she didn't keep anger built up inside of her. I had always known Lexus to be confident and a sincerely admirable person. Those were just a few of the qualities that I envied about her. She had other friends, too. Friends that were genuinely happy, and they were like her, including John. I was the only negative person in her life whom she considered a best friend. I had always wondered why this girl was my friend, because I was nothing like her.

CHAPTER 56

Lexus and I sat at a small, square table in the food court of the mall. We both decided to settle for sushi from the Japanese restaurant. They were handing out samples of California Rolls and had a special on the Yum Yum rolls. We couldn't resist.

Lexus did most of the talking. I didn't mind, because I didn't want to talk about Bent Creek or anything that was really going on with me. It would have been too much, and it probably would have ruined her good mood. Lexus liked to be happy and she liked to hear good things. I wanted her to be that way. I didn't want to be the cause of distress once again.

Lexus talked about her family and everyone's involvement in her wedding. She insisted on paying for her own wedding dress because she felt bad that her father was paying for everything else, including the engagement party that was coming up.

"It is *my* wedding dress," she said. "I can't believe how much it cost! Can you believe it was almost three thousand dollars?"

I nodded.

"Well," Lexus said with a sigh, "let's not talk about the cost. That doesn't matter. I guess what really matters is that it is finally going to happen."

She was glowing with happiness, and I secretly envied her. I tried to push that unloved feeling away. I wanted to listen to her, and keep the focus and attention on her. This was my best friend. This was Lexus. She deserved to be this happy.

"John proposed to me at a party my parents were having. When he and Dad stepped away to talk, I kind of had a feeling that he was going to ask my Dad if he could propose, but, then again, I had my doubts."

"Why did you doubt?"

"I don't know," she said. "That night was-"

Her voice trailed off as if she had to think about what she was going to say next. I looked at her silently as I waited. She looked away from me and shook her head.

"It's okay," I said, "I know that was the night when I messed up. I know that's why you didn't answer your phone. It was a perfect night, just like you said."

I smiled at her. She had to know that I was not angry at her for being happy.

She wiped a single tear that rolled out the corner of her eye. She sucked back more tears in a deep breath. She cut her eyes back at me for a second, most likely expecting me to be looking sad. When she saw that I was smiling, she looked back at me. She let out a sigh and then began to chuckle.

"Why am I crying?" She continued laughing.

"I don't know." I let out a laugh.

"Kristen," she called out to me. "I am really sorry."

"No," I told her. "You did the right thing. I'm glad you didn't answer your phone that night, because then things would not have gone as they should have for you. Now, everything is as it should be."

Lexus' smile disappeared when I finished speaking. A look came over her. I had never seen the look from her before. It was a look of wonder and amazement. Her eyes narrowed and the color seemed to warm her face. Her cheeks relaxed as her mouth slightly opened. She cocked her head slightly to the left side while staring at me.

"There's something different," Lexus realized aloud.

"What?" The new expression that graced her caught me by surprise.

"I don't know."

As she spoke, her eyes warmed me ever more.

"I'm looking at you," she said, "and I'm listening to you, and you...you're..."

When her voice trailed off again so that she could think about what she wanted to say, I took the opportunity to cut the topic short. I wasn't ready for what Lexus might have said to me. In fact, it scared me to think of what may have been coming next.

She opened her mouth to let out the words that had come to her when I reached across the table and grabbed her left hand. This made her quickly close her mouth.

"Can I see?" I asked her.

"Yes," she said. "It just worked out perfectly. Look at it!"

Lexus stretched out the fingers on her left hand and dazzled her gorgeous, teardrop, white diamond.

I couldn't help but touch it. It was beautiful. I told her that I was very happy for her and that she deserved it more than anyone did.

Lexus smiled and said, "Thank you so much. That means the world to hear you say that."

"I'm sure everyone's told you that," I told her.

"Yes," she said. "But I appreciate it so much more from you."

"Why?"

"Because you're my best friend. And I want you to be one of my bridesmaids."

I unintentionally rolled my eyes.

Lexus caught me.

She explained, "I want to share this happiness with you. You are the reason I know John. We all grew up together. So you, more than any of my other friends, know how special this is. I need you to help me set things up and get ready for my big day. It wouldn't be right without you there beside us."

The sparkle and gleam in her eyes made me say yes.

She reached across the table, and her long arms grabbed me. We both stood up and we hugged each other. I quickly wiped away the painful tear that shot out of my right eye before we pulled away so that she wouldn't see me crying.

As I sat back down in my seat, I felt the metal ball turn in my chest. I ignored it, picked up a Yum Yum sushi roll with my chopsticks, and then ate it.

Lexus was still smiling.

I kept my eyes focused on the food. I knew that if I looked at her she'd see that I wasn't smiling and that rottenness inside of me would somehow seep out and ruin the moment.

"So," she said as she ate a California Roll. "What color should the bridesmaids' dresses be?"

"Oh, I know," I started to answer, but she cut me off.

"Black is not an option," she said.

"Well, I'll have to think about it some more," I told her.

CHAPTER 57

Lexus and John's engagement party was the main event that everyone had been looking forward to. I had to spend most of my check paying off the late tuition from my home schooling program, along with the steep late fee. Mom and I had to split a gift for Lexus and John. The gift didn't turn out to be as elegant as most of the gifts we saw in the piles of gifts from their family and friends who were at the party. We got them a gift card for the store IKEA. At least they would be able to get a few nice things to decorate their new home together.

The event was held at the Marriott Marquis. When I entered the event hall, a man greeted us and took my summer jacket and purse. He asked if we had brought a gift for the soon-to-be newlyweds, and I held up a white envelope that contained the gift card and something witty from Hallmark. The man pointed me in the direction of the gift table that was being guarded by two formally-dressed women. When we approached them, they smiled and greeted us warmly.

"Hi," the one with the biggest smile said. "Do you have a gift for Lexus and John?"

"Yes," I said as I handed over the envelope.

She frowned as she took it from me. "Okay, well," she said. "Enjoy the party. You can go right through those doors there."

She sat the envelope on top of a pile of smaller gift boxes and quickly waved us off to move on to the next pair of guests that were behind Mom, Ally, Nick, and me.

At first, I didn't understand why I had gotten such a snotty response from that woman, but as I passed the next four tables that were covered in oversized and elegantly wrapped and bowed boxes, it all began to sink in. I shook off the minor upset, seeing that it didn't seem to bother Mom or the twins, and we approached the large, dark, double doors to the ballroom. Two professionally-dressed men standing at each side reverently opened the doors. As the men held the doors open for us, we entered the ballroom in complete astonishment.

Lexus' parents had hired a party planner for the engagement party, and it looked like it was money well spent. I immediately noticed the high, hanging chandeliers that rose from the ceiling. Dim, romantic light made the crystals in the chandeliers sparkle like stars in a creamy, vanilla sky. The way the room lit up made everything from the tablecloths to the champagne glasses look like gold. A woman held a wine glass in her hand. When she pressed the glass to her lips and began to drink, it looked like she was drinking pure atomic number 79.

There were tables and bars set up. Servers hurried through the crowds in the most professional attire and manner. They walked from the tables to the kitchen in a maze of party guests. Some of them were going to the bars to collect drinks to take back to tables. They stood tall with their chins and noses up while they were still. When moving, they were swift and traveled with perfect balance in a synchronized rhythm. They didn't seem to spill a drop.

There was a large stage at the front of the hall. Before the stage was a modest-sized dance floor. The crowd of people dancing looked like they were having the time of their lives. The middle-aged and thirty-something-year-old dancers were being serenaded by a jazz band that was conducted by a maestro. The jazz band looked down at the entertained dancers from the large stage as they played instrumental, upbeat music.

What was even more astonishing to me was the effect this formal event seemed to have on the guests. It made everyone in the room look like movie stars, and some looked and even behaved as if they were royalty.

One of those people was Lexus' mother, Clarisse. She was elegantly dressed in a backless, black and white, Christian Dior, silk chiffon gown. She wore heavy jewels around her neck, in her hair, and on her fingers. Jonathan Sr. looked just as nice, dressed in a black tuxedo with a white bow tie and cummerbund. I could only imagine how lovely Lexus and John must have looked.

The two proud parents spotted us entering the ballroom. They had been talking to each other, along with their own spouses. As soon as Mariah saw me, she kissed her husband and walked in the opposite direction. Jonathan and Clarisse were the first people to greet us out of the group of four. As they approached us, Jonathan smiled at me and gave a handsome wink. John definitely got his charm from his father.

"You made it!" Clarisse greeted us.

She and Mom stretched out their arms and gave each other a quick pat on the back without genuinely embracing.

"I'm glad you all could come," Jonathan greeted us.

Mom smiled. She asked, "Where is the newly engaged couple?"

"The kids will make their entrance soon," he answered.

"Look at Miss Alison. You look so cute," Clarisse complimented. She

reached her arms out to Alison, wanting a hug.

Alison sweetly obliged and embraced her.

"Thank you," Alison said. She pulled away and took her place beside Mom again.

"And Nick," Clarisse said to him without reaching out for a hug. "That's a *casual* suit you are wearing."

Nick rolled his eyes at her.

"This is all he can fit into." Mom tried to laugh it off. "He's growing up so fast! I can't get him into anything he owns anymore."

"You should see James. We had to buy him a tuxedo the other day, just for tonight. I'm sure he's going to be growing out of that by next week," Jonathan said. "So I know exactly what you mean."

Mom laughed. I could tell that Mom was feeling embarrassed and self-conscious.

Mom looked relieved as Clarisse took over the conversation. She was probably relieved because Clarisse hadn't commented on what she was wearing. Mom's outfit wasn't completely dressy, but it wasn't casual, either. She wore a solid color, light brown, knee-length, spaghetti strap, v-neck dress with stockings and matching sling-back high heels. Compared to what Clarisse was wearing, I guess it was nothing to brag about.

I was waiting for Clarisse to size me up, but she didn't look at me even once after she saw what I was wearing. Jonathan looked at me with a frown, but quickly caught himself and smiled at me to try to cover up.

"You ladies look lovely tonight," he said to Mom and me.

As Mom talked with Clarisse and Jonathan, and with Alison staying beside Mom, Nick and I slyly sneaked away without excusing ourselves. Nick grabbed my hand and pulled me towards the front of the room. We giggled mischievously, knowing exactly what we were doing.

"Lexus' mom looks hot," Nick said.

"What?" I asked while laughing.

"What? She does!"

"I can't believe you," I said.

We laughed together as we wandered closer to the front.

"Well," he said. "She doesn't look as hot as Lexus, though."

"Where do you see -" I gasped.

Nick pointed towards the stage.

The crowd cheered as the maestro stopped the music to kindly introduce Lexus and John to the stage.

"Everyone say hello to the future bride and groom: Lexus Reed and Jonathan Christian, Jr."

The crowd cheered and applauded in an excited roar as though Lexus and

John were rock stars.

"Let's give these two kids a hand, folks! They are on their way!" he exclaimed gleefully.

Lexus stood on the stage in a colorful and strapless Betsy Johnson floral and tulle dress. John stood beside her in a black tuxedo with a loose bow tie and no cummerbund. His jacket was buttoned and his collar was undone and turned up. His long locks that he'd let grow out over the years handsomely draped his neck. A few strands attractively fell over his cheerful eyes. The breathtaking couple dreamily stared at one another. I believe that they saw no one else but each other at that moment. Their smiles were something to admire enviously and enough to make tears fall out of my eyes.

Nick looked at me as the cheers began to fade and the music started back up.

"Hey, sis. Guess what?"

"What?" I asked while wiping dry my wet eyes.

"She doesn't look hotter than you."

I smiled at him. He was a prince to adore.

"Thank you," I said.

"Come with me," he said as he gently grabbed my hand and began to lead me towards the crowd on the dance floor.

"No, Nick. I am not dancing in these shoes," I told him.

"You wore high heels and that cute, short skirt for a reason. You are going to show them off."

Nick knew me too well. He swung me out on the dance floor. As we moved to the music that had no lyrics, I couldn't help but laugh and let the good time I was having with him take over me. We weren't really into swing music, but that's what was playing, so we made the most of it by doing the best we could, which was our worst. So we made fun of each other and ourselves as we tried to do swing moves that we had seen on television.

"Do this with me," Nick said as he swung his arms wildly at his sides, kicked his feet forward, and back while in place. He did the silly dance with a goofy smile on his face.

I threw my head back and laughed. "There is no way I'm doing that!"

"Get over here," he demanded as he grabbed my hand and swung me into his arms. He and I laughed aloud.

Nick was taller than I was, and he was only eleven years old. He looked like a dashing prince dressed up in a suit with his hair slicked back. We both felt a bit under-dressed compared to the other guests we saw. Nick wore a pair of brown, cotton-blend slacks and a matching jacket. He sported a gold and black striped necktie to compliment. I was wearing a short, black, pleated skirt and a black spaghetti strap top to match. I wore no jewelry except the silver chandelier earrings that I had found under my bed.

When the music stopped, Nick and I held onto each other while laughing hysterically. The people around us probably thought we were drunk from the way we were dancing and making funny faces at each other. It only made us laugh harder.

"I need something to drink," Nick said hoarsely.

"We danced a little too hard out there." I kept laughing.

"Come on! Let's see if we can get a drink without an I.D."

"Nick," I said, as he dragged me along. "Wait." I couldn't stop laughing. "I have to catch my breath."

Nick stopped in his place and put a hand on my shoulder to rest.

"You think they'll give us something to drink?" Nick spoke hoarsely because he was almost out of breath.

"No. I'm not letting you get alcohol. Stay here." I said.

I walked over to the bar and asked for a cup of ginger ale and a cup of cola. The bartender told me he'd be with me in a moment as he placed drinks on top of a waiter's tray. The waiter waited patiently as the bartender tended to him.

I didn't see Mom approach until she began to speak.

"Kristen, where is your jacket? I thought you were going to keep it over your arms."

I rolled my eyes and turned towards her.

"The man took it at the door when we came in."

"You should probably get it back," she said.

"Why?"

"It's not appropriate to have your arms showing like that. It's too much skin."

"So I guess you don't like what Lexus is wearing, then," I sarcastically replied. "She's showing way more skin than me. I think she looks nice."

"You know what this is about. Don't argue with me. Get your jacket back from the doorman and put it on."

"I don't want to," I told her, "I like it like this."

"You are embarrassing *me*," she said.

"I'm sorry I'm not like Lexus, Mom. I'm sorry that I can't be perfect enough for you to show off. I'm sorry that you can't compare yourself to your friends and come out on top. But this is me, Mom." I showed my bare arms to her with my wrists turned up and my scars exposed. "I'm not going to stand here and be uncomfortable and hot in that jacket all night. And if Lexus' mom or any of your friends have anything to say about the scars on my wrists, then you tell them to shut up and go to hell."

Mom bit down on her tongue and angrily stormed away.

The bartender finally came over to me when Mom walked away. "I'm sorry, sweetie," he said with a fake smile that begged for money. "I didn't mean to keep you waiting. What drink would you like me to make for you? Was it ginger ale and a cola?"

"A cup of ginger ale," I said, "and a cup of *rum* and cola!"

"Sure thing," he said with a flirtatious wink.

When he returned with the drinks, he smiled and said, "The bar is paid for, but if you'd like to leave a tip, that's fine." He tapped his fingers on a jar that was sitting on the counter top. The jar had black marker writing on it. It read: PLEASE HELP THE PO'.

I smiled back at the bartender and said, "I'll get back to you on that."

As I walked away, I watched to see if he'd give me a dirty look, but he just kept on smiling. He moved on to the next woman waiting at the bar, who could have been Vanna White's twin sister.

Nick rushed up to me and tried to grab the rum and cola out of my hand.

"No, baby," I told him. "This one is yours." I handed him the ginger ale.

Nick frowned into the cup before he took it and drank it up in only three gulps.

"You were thirsty," I said.

He put his nose close to my cup. He said, "What are you drinking?"

"Just cola," I said. I snatched the cup away from his nose.

"Smells like something else," he said.

"I'm going to the ladies' room."

"Can I come?"

"Shoo! Be gone!" I playfully said as I walked away from him.

Nick laughed. "That's okay. I wanted go look for James."

I didn't look back as he strolled off in the opposite direction, snapping his fingers. Nick was full of life and seemingly high spirited tonight. I turned around when I was sure he wasn't following me, and I saw him running over to James. James was sitting at a table full of young girls. That will keep Nick occupied while I go drink this in secret, I thought to myself.

I laughed as I turned around and continued walking. I wasn't sure where I was going. I found myself outside of the event room. Wandering down the spacious halls of the Marriott Marquis, I was amazed at how tall the walls were. They were distinguished in design and extravagantly lavished in multicultural-looking art. I admired the regal decor from the paintings on the wall to the million-dollar carpeting on the floor. My tour down the hall dead-ended at a large, glass view-port. The glass was so flawless and clear that the door was barely noticeable. I stretched my free hand out and pushed at the door, and it opened gracefully. I stepped out onto the terrace and looked out at the city. The lights on the Marquis twinkled and shined brighter than the stars in the cloudless night sky.

I sipped on the rum and cola slowly. It was mostly rum with what tasted like just a splash of cola. I laughed to myself as I remembered the way Nick and I had been dancing on the dance floor. We must have looked insane compared to the older and more mature people out there.

Then I thought about how gorgeous Lexus looked, and how attractive she and John looked together. Their individual beauty complimented the both of them together as a couple. No one could rightfully say that Lexus was more beautiful than John was or that John was more alluring than Lexus. When everyone looked at them, they saw an enamoring couple.

I smiled at the lights that began to blur. I was getting drunk from the rum. Letting the warmness seep into my chest, I took another sip. I blushed, thinking of John and Lexus finally married. My thoughts were taken over by the alcohol, and I thought about being married to John. Sadness filled my heart, and despair crept into my mind. What if it had been different? What if Jack had been here and hadn't ruined us? Would I be different? Would John have liked me more? Would he have kissed me that day when we'd flown the kite?

The cup only had one gulp left inside. I quickly drank the last of the rum and cola. When I swallowed, the alcohol went down my throat the wrong way, and I started to choke. I coughed to catch my breath. I felt as if I'd never breathe again. It was taking so long to get those tiny trickles out of my throat. Suddenly a hand was rubbing my back gently, and a kind voice was calling out my name.

"Kristen?" The angelic, soft voice of a man called out to me.

I caught my breath at his delicate touch. When I saw his eyes, I almost stopped breathing again. He kept his hand on my back just to make sure I was all right.

"Kristen, are you all right?" John asked. Concern remained in his eyes as I slowly pulled away from him.

"Thanks," I said. "I'm okay now."

"Are you sure?" His wonderful eyes glistened in the twinkling lights.

"Yeah." I turned away from him and looked back out at the sky.

"What are you doing out here? There's a kickass party going on in there."

"I'm just getting some air."

"I see," he said.

He wasn't getting the hint that I didn't want to be around anyone. He moved closer to me and stood right beside me.

Looking up at the sky, he said, "You came out here to drink."

"Don't tell my Mom," I said.

"I won't," he laughed.

"Don't tell Lexus either."

"No worries," he said as he continued to find humor in the situation. He took his eyes off the sky and looked directly at me.

He was making me nervous. Looking at Lexus was wonderful, but when he looked at me, I was sure he wasn't seeing anything special. I put my hand over the right side of my face so that I could cover up and hide from him. Not realizing that I was actually making it worse, I kept my hand up, and he was able to get a good look at the scars on my wrists. When I heard him deeply sigh, I realized I had made a mistake.

He said, "How have you been?"

I nodded.

"What does that mean?" he sincerely asked.

"It means... It means I'm better," I told him. His concern for me made my heart flutter.

It seemed as if he believed me. He let out a sigh of relief before he curled his lips into a satisfied smile.

It was apparent that he was not going to leave me alone, so before he could ask me any more questions, I turned to face him and I said, "So, who are all of those people in there, anyway?"

John laughed. He said, "Honestly, I don't even know half of them. I bet they're all my parents' and Lexus' friends." His smile was terribly adorable.

"Congratulations, John. You and Lexus are going to be great together. I'm really happy for you guys," I said.

John stared into my eyes for a quick moment. In that moment, I felt my knees grow weak. Before I could fall, John grabbed me and embraced me with both of his arms wrapped around me. I hugged him tight. I squeezed him, and I didn't want to let him go.

He slowly started to pull away after that quick embrace that we shared. The moment seemed to go by too fast.

His convincing and handsome smile that I loved so much was present on his face. His enthralling lips curled up perfectly and created a flawless smile that I could never deny.

John said, "Thank you. You know, it really means a lot to hear you say that."

"I'm sure you both have already heard that from everyone here," I said.

"But it means a little more, coming from you, Kristen." He sounded too much like Lexus talking.

I smiled, holding back my tears.

"I have to get back," John said. He looked back inside at the hall. "Have a good night, and remember to take it easy on that stuff." He pointed to my empty cup.

I laughed and said, "I will. You have a great night."

After that, he left me alone, outside on the terrace. I would remember John that way for the rest of my life. He was beautiful, kind, and happy.

That night Lexus insisted that I come to her apartment after the party. She suggested that we have a sleepover, and it would just be the two of us. She said it would be like old times. I said good night to Nick and Alison, and told my mother where I would be. She didn't have too much to say to me, so I left the party with Lexus.

John walked with us out to Lexus' car. I turned away from them as they kissed each other and said good night. My stomach turned at the sounds they were making with their mouths and tongues. Finally, Lexus was able to break free of John's embrace, and we got into the car.

As Lexus pulled out of the parking space, John waved to us and shouted, "I love you," to Lexus. She smiled and drove off. I watched John in the rearview mirror. He grew smaller in the distance until Lexus turned the corner and he was out of sight.

"It wouldn't kill you to smile," Lexus started.

"Yes, it would. It would kill me," I joked.

"Ha, ha, very funny," Lexus said.

CHAPTER 58

Spending the night over at Lexus' house was just like old times. Lexus let me borrow one of her nightgowns, and we both settled down in front of her television once we were out of our formal clothes. We sat on the floor on top of a blanket Lexus had spread out, and we ate frozen yogurt while a late night comedy show played on the television.

"So, was it too much?" Lexus asked.

"I liked your party. It was like a dream," I said.

"That was my mother's idea of what an engagement party is supposed to be like. She wanted something out of a fairy tale. Oh, wait until you see the ideas she gave the planner for my wedding. I think I'm going to feel like Cinderella."

"You're far from being Cinderella," I told her.

"You know what I mean. Not the evil step-mother part. You know, the princess part. When she meets her Prince Charming and everything is *so* enchanting."

"Oh," I said as I scraped up the last of my frozen yogurt out of the bowl.

"You don't think so?"

"Yes, it's great. It's going to be amazing," I humored her.

Lexus laughed. She was truly happy. I listened as Lexus continued to talk about her wedding plans. She went on about herself, John, and their plans for the future. I could only smile to make myself feel happiness to cover up the sadness that seemed to want to weigh heavily in my heart. Some of the things she shared with me were intimate. There were things she said that I didn't really care to know, but I let her go on and tell me because she was on a blissful high. I didn't think it would be fair for me to break her from it.

"I want to tell you something, but it may be TMI," Lexus said with a blush.

"What is it?" I asked.

"I told myself I'd wait until I was married to have sex. I wanted it to be something special for our wedding night. I don't know what happened, Kristen," she said with a smile. "It just felt like the night was too perfect. We did it. But it was only one time. We said that we'd wait until after the wedding to do it again."

I nodded.

"I'm sorry," she said. "You probably don't want to hear all of this."

"It's okay," I told her.

Lexus quieted herself and stared at the television. She laughed at the red-haired man who was cracking jokes on the late night comedy show. He made one last joke and then directed the cameras to his band that played a short intermission to the commercial break.

"That guy is so funny," she said with a laugh.

"Yeah, when I was in the hospital, the only time we got to watch television was during prime time when detective shows and teenage soap operas were on. The TV never stayed on long enough, and we weren't allowed to be up late enough to watch the late night comedy."

"Well," Lexus responded. "You are out of there now. You're home free! And you can watch as much late night TV as you want."

We laughed together. After the laughter, we stared at each other in silence. Looking at Lexus' beautiful face was not a difficult thing to do. It was when I grew self-conscious of what she was seeing when she looked at me, which made it difficult to keep eye contact. I turned my head back to face the television. The commercials were still playing.

Lexus suddenly snapped her fingers, startling me.

"I know it!" she exclaimed when she snapped her fingers.

"Know what?"

"What's different," she said.

"What's different?" I asked.

"Yes," she said. She smiled wide and scooted herself closer to me, forcing me to have to face her now. She was very happy about her sudden epiphany. "You're different." She went on. "You seem happier. I mean, more positive about things. You don't seem so..."

"Negative?" I completed her sentence.

"No. Uh. I mean, yeah. I'm not saying that you were a negative person. You made a change, because now you're just so different, but in a good way."

"I know what you mean. It's okay. Thank you, Lexus," I said.

"You're welcome," she said with a sweet smile.

I hoped that she would leave the subject alone, and not keep going on about it. The comedic late night talk show host saved me. The red-haired, hyperactive, funny man welcomed his next guest to the set. A popular young male actor with a godlike bone structure and suave swagger joined the host on stage. Lexus' attention was now tuned to him.

As she watched television, I watched her. I noticed the sweet beauty mole that rested on her neck, just below her jawline near her left earlobe. I slid closer to her, quietly, not to disturb her. I put my hand on her shoulder and watched her smile. Then, I gently pressed my lips on that mole and kissed it. I held my lips there to make sure she felt my touch.

She didn't flinch or pull away from me.

I pulled myself away. When I looked at her, I was surprised to see that her eyes were closed and she looked peaceful and calm. She was breathing slowly.

As I took in that moment between Lexus and me, things became clear. Lexus really was a good friend. She was there for me as a true friend should be, the best way that she knew how. She did not want to hurt me, or use me to make herself feel good because she was not a bad person. She truly cared about me as her friend.

Lexus and I lived on the same planet, but we were from different worlds. Hers was a world that I did not understand. Lexus' world was full of romance, love, family, John, wedding dresses, and engagement parties. Her story would have been written in an entirely different tone and genre if she had written her story.

My world consisted of trying to heal what had been broken on the inside and outside of me. Even though we came from different worlds and she couldn't fully understand what I was going through, and vice versa, we remained best friends. We loved, supported, and accepted each other.

"Good night, beautiful," I said to her as I pulled a pillow close and then lay down.

I closed my eyes and didn't look back at her again that night. I was sure to pull the blanket over my face so that she couldn't see me crying. I held my breath so that I wouldn't make a sound. I didn't know what she was doing or thinking after that, but I heard a sniffle and a soft sob.

Her warm hand touched my back, and it stayed there for a short forty seconds. She whispered good night just before she removed her hand. The television was turned off. The lamp was turned out. Then I heard her bedroom door shut.

CHAPTER 59

On my birthday, I woke up to Nick, Alison, and Mom singing to me. They serenaded me with the traditional birthday melody, but Nick and Alison topped it off with the best, most annoying soprano notes I had ever heard.

Mom fussed, "It was supposed to be nice. You both killed it."

"She loved it," Nick said as he dashed onto my bed and pulled the covers up from over me.

Alison added as she sat down on the other side of me, "We made it unique. I wanted to hit all of the high notes."

I kissed the both of them on their cheeks. "I did love it," I said.

Mom gave me a blueberry muffin with a lit candle sticking out of it.

"Make a big wish!" Alison said.

I closed my eyes, made a secret wish, and then opened my eyes again. I took a deep breath and was ready to blow, but Nick stopped me.

"Wait," he said. "What did you wish for?"

"I'll never tell," I told him. Then I blew out my candle.

Nick and Alison applauded.

"Okay, kiddies," Mom said. "Go get dressed so that I can drop you off at the Recreation Center."

"Mom!" Alison exclaimed.

"I thought we were going to hang out with Kristen today, since it's her birthday," Nick said.

"Kristen has to see the doctor today," Mom said. "You guys will see her later, after camp."

I couldn't deny the looks on their faces. I told Mom, "I'll pick them up after I see Dr. Pelchat today, if you leave me the car."

"Yeah!" Nick exclaimed.

"Mommy, please," Alison pleaded.

Mom smiled at me. She said, "Okay. That'll be fine. Just be sure you are at the Rec Center by 3:00pm."

Nick and Alison cheered as they ran out of my bedroom and back up the stairs. When Mom was sure that they were in their rooms, she closed my bedroom door. She came over to me.

I sat up in bed, and she sat down next to me. I could tell this was about to be a serious conversation. A sharp pain shot through my chest. I stayed silent, anticipating what was coming.

She reached into her bathrobe pocket and pulled out an envelope. She took a deep breath and carefully said, "This came in the mail for you this morning." She held the envelope out to me.

I took the envelope from her hand. It was addressed to me, and it was from...

"It's from Jack," Mom said.

The metal ball in my chest started to slowly turn, but with the turns came a burning sensation that hurt me more than it had ever hurt before. My heart pounded as if it wanted to escape my chest.

"I don't want this," I said to Mom.

"Open it," she demanded. "At least open it and see what he has to say."

I opened the envelope and pulled out the birthday card that was inside. On the front of the card was an illustration of a brown bear that was dressed up in a business suit and a tie. Beside the bear was a baby brown bear that had a pink bow on top of its head. The baby bear was wearing a pink dress to match the bow. Both of the bears were smiling at each other, and they were inside of a house that I guess they both lived in, since they were supposed to be family. The top of the card read: OH HOW MY BABY GROWS

The card had three inserts inside. The first insert showed the baby brown bear with her papa bear again. This time the baby brown bear looked a little older. The papa bear was tying the baby bear's shoe laces. The second insert showed the papa bear and the baby brown bear. She wasn't a baby anymore. She had grown a little bigger. They both were smiling as she and the papa bear flew a kite together. The final insert showed the papa bear waving goodbye to his grown-up baby brown bear with tears in his eyes. She was leaving the house dressed in a graduation cap and gown.

I didn't want to read the words that were written by Jack at the bottom of the last insert. It was about three paragraphs of his sorry apologies and sad regrets. The damage was already done. I did not intend to forgive him.

I closed the card. As I was putting the card back in the envelope, I noticed something inside. I pulled it out. It was a twenty-dollar bill. Wrapped around the twenty was a thin strip of paper. In Jack's handwriting it said, "I wish I could have sent you more. Happy birthday, sweetheart."

I put the twenty-dollar bill and the card back inside the envelope. Mom watched me. There was more to it, and I knew it. Otherwise, she would have already left me alone. Mom sighed and leaned over towards me. I waited for what was coming.

"Kristen, we got off on the wrong foot when you first came home," she admitted. "We had that argument. You said a lot of things that really made me feel a certain way. And I think we need to talk about this before you go to see Dr. Pelchat."

"Mom," I said, "I'm really sorry."

"No," she stopped me. "Just listen to me. When you said what you said, it really did hurt me. But believe it or not, it did make me think. First off, you should know that you make your own choices. I shouldn't be blamed for your own mistakes. You chose to pick up that knife, and you chose to hurt yourself. You need to take responsibility for that."

"Mom, I do," I said. "I'm sorry for all of that."

"I'm not finished," she said as she put her hand up to stop me from speaking. "I know that you are eighteen now. You are considered a grown-up, but I *do* still consider you my child. When our family broke apart, I know that it was not only hard for Nick, but I know it was hard for you, too. I did push you hard, and that was only because I didn't want you to turn out to be depressed, and I didn't want you to get like this, the way you are now. I thought that I was helping you. I guess all of that pushing turned out to be something else. It turned into a lot of guilt and hardship on you. It was guilt that I had inside of me pushed on to you. It was guilt, which has been there ever since you were born."

I looked at her, afraid of what she might say next.

"You never knew this, but eighteen years ago, when I first found out I was pregnant with you, I almost let your father talk me into having an abortion. It seemed like the only solution at the time to get rid of this problem that we thought we had. We were both young, and we had no idea what was going to happen. But when I got to the clinic, I couldn't do it. Your father didn't want to have a relationship with me anymore, after I told him I had decided to keep you. I felt like I had to really make keeping you worth the sacrifice of losing your father."

I sat silently with my eyes turned away from her.

She continued, "I feel guilty because I feel like I failed you. Ever since you were born, I've felt that I should have waited to have you. I should have waited until I was ready. I was growing up and raising you by myself all at the same time. It was hard on the both of us. When Jack came into my life and showed me what a real family could be like, I thought that I was doing right by you and the twins when I decided to marry him and move here. I wanted to hold onto that and keep that. Even when I saw that what we had was fading, I thought that one day it might change. I wasn't naive. I was just being stupid. And I'm sorry that I failed you as your mother."

I took a deep breath, leaned over, and I hugged her. She hugged me tight.

"I love you, Mom," I told her.

"I love you, Kristen. I'm so sorry, baby," she said as she pulled away.

"I'm sorry too, Mom," I apologized again.

"I forgive you," Mom said as she pulled away.

"Really?"

"Yes. I forgive you for what you did," she said. She gestured to my wrists.

I stayed silent and looked away from her, feeling ashamed.

"And," Mom said. "You should forgive yourself."

I looked at her. Silently I contemplated what I should say in response, but nothing that I could think of seemed right.

"You've said that you're sorry enough for now," she said.

Still speechless, I only nodded.

She noticed that I was dumbfounded and changed the subject, I guess in a way to give me something to think about.

"Are you going to talk to Dr. Pelchat about Jack's parole hearing that's coming up?"

"I don't know," I said. "I don't know what to say."

"Maybe he can help you decide if you should come with us. I've decided that we are going to be there. I'm not going to force you to go if you don't want to. But you need to make a decision soon. I'm going to let you get ready in private. Try not to be too long. Happy birthday, Kristen."

She left me alone in my room with my mind racing. If Mom went to the hearing with Nick and Alison, Jack was going to get out on parole for sure. I could feel it inside of me. It had only been three years, and it was already time for a parole hearing. That disgusting feeling crept back inside of me. Mom wouldn't take him back. She couldn't! Right? She couldn't because she had us: Nick, Alison, and me. Right?

There was no answer from Mr. Sharp. There wasn't anything sharp near me. My butterfly pendant was nowhere to be found, and his voice could not be heard.

This was the birthday I did not think I'd ever live to see.

CHAPTER 60

After I dropped Mom off at work, I drove the twins to the Recreation Center. I got out of the car to open the trunk so that Alison and Nick could get their swimming gear out. Alison grabbed her bag in a hurry. She gave me a warm hug before she ran into the Recreation Center. She had left Nick behind.

Nick didn't seem to want to get out of the car. I got back into the car and sat down beside him in the back seat. He looked sad.

"Nick? What's wrong?" I asked him.

"Nothing," he said.

"You want to just sit here?"

He shook his head.

"Well, come on. Get your stuff out of the trunk, and I'll walk you inside if you want."

"No," he said, "that's okay."

"Well, you have to go, Nick. I have to get to the doctor's office."

"Don't go," he begged me.

"I have to," I told him.

Nick let out a deep sigh. He looked at me with seriously worried eyes.

"What is going on? Is there something that you want to tell me?"

"I have a bad feeling," he finally admitted.

"Why do you have a bad feeling?"

"I don't know. I just do."

"Are you scared?"

He nodded.

I took a guess. "Is it because of Jack's parole hearing? Is it because Mom is making you go?"

He shook his head.

"You're not scared of that?"

He shook his head again.

"Why not?" I asked.

Nick took a deep breath and, looking me straight in the eyes, he said, "I'm not scared because I know that he can't do anything to me anymore. And he'll never, *ever* touch me again."

Nick became my hero at that moment. He replied, sure of himself and brave. He was so much braver than I was, and I believe that he knew that. I didn't know what else to say to him.

"You're so right, Nick," was all I could think to say. "He can't hurt you ever again. How come you're so brave?"

"Because someone listened to me and helped me understand. What happened to me wasn't my fault. Nothing like that could ever be anybody's fault except Jack's."

I wanted to hug him.

He went on, "Did you know that when you save someone's life, it makes you their hero? Did you know that, even if that person is mad at you for saving their life, another person who may have been watching or who may have heard about it could be affected by what you did for that other person, and you could be a hero to them, too?"

I nodded as I tried to take all of that in.

"Yeah, it must be nice to save someone's life," I said.

I had no idea where all of this random rambling of Nick's was coming from. But I figured he just needed someone to listen to him. I wanted to be there for him, even if it was making me late for my appointment with Dr. Pelchat.

He continued, "Kristen, I'm sorry that you hurt a lot."

I looked into his eyes, shocked.

"I'm fine, Nick," I tried to convince him. "What makes you think that I am hurt?"

"I wish that you could be happy," he said. He had ignored my question.

"I *am* happy," I said with a forced smile. "See? I'm really happy. It's my birthday!"

Nick didn't look too convinced.

He said, "No matter what, you have to know that I love you. And now, you have to know why."

"Why, Nick?"

"Because you saved my life."

I held back my tears and took a deep swallow to hold it down.

"I saved your life?"

"Yes," he assured me. "Just like I had saved yours."

"Yes, you did, Nickyroo," I said.

"I don't want you to be mad at me for it, because I'm *not* sorry," he said.

"No, Nick," I said. "I could never be mad at you."

Nick took in a deep breath and let out a heavy sigh, as if he was relieved.

Alison ran back outside of the Rec Center and yelled for Nick.

Nick yelled out the window, "I'm coming!"

"You'd better go," I told him. "You don't want to get in trouble."

We got out of the car and I opened the trunk again. Nick grabbed his bag out of the trunk and started to walk away from me. I slammed the trunk shut. At the sound of the trunk closing, Nick jolted back towards me. Before I could get back inside the car, Nick's arms were already around my neck. He was constricting me again.

"Please be careful!" he cried.

"Nick," I called out to him. "I'll be fine. I am coming to get you and Alison right after my doctor's appointment. Don't worry."

"I'll call Mom if you don't," he threatened as he pulled away.

"That's fair," I said. "I'll see you later."

Nick backed away from me. He walked backwards towards the entrance of the Recreation Center where Alison impatiently waited for him. I got back inside the car. After I closed the door and started up the car, I noticed Nick was still standing by the curb. Alison had left him behind. He looked worried and sad to see me go.

I was happy inside to know that he was free of that painful guilt that Jack had burdened us with. I saw Nick with true bravery written all over his mature and handsome face. Before I drove off, I pulled up beside him and told him that I loved him.

Nick smiled at me lovingly. His large, brown eyes were shining.

He said, "Kristen, you are my hero."

CHAPTER 61

Dr. Pelchat seemed glad to see me. He greeted me with a jolly smile and a gripping handshake. When I was settled into a chair in his office, he began.

"Happy birthday, Kristen. Do you want some cake? I can have Geoffrey bring you a slice from the cafeteria."

I giggled and said, "No, thanks."

"Okay. How are you doing today?" he kindly asked.

"I'm here," I told him.

He responded, "What does that mean? Is that good or bad?"

"I guess a little bit of both. It's good that I'm here."

"Right, but what's bad about it?"

I pulled out the envelope that held the card from Jack, along with the twenty-dollar bill. Dr. Pelchat stayed quiet and waited for me to explain what it was. I took a deep breath, pulled the card out of the envelope, and reached out to give it to him. He took it out of my hand.

"What is this? A birthday card?"

"It's a birthday card from my ex-step-dad," I said.

"What does it say?"

"It doesn't say anything. It's a birthday card."

Dr. Pelchat studied the card. He smiled at the illustrations and laughed a little. He turned the pages of the inserts until he got to the last one. His smile disappeared.

"It does say something. Did you read this?"

"No," I admitted. "I don't want to."

Dr. Pelchat reached out and put the card back in my hand.

"Read it," he said.

"I don't think that I can," I said as I felt the tears trying to form.

"You don't have to," he said. "But I encourage you to."

"Why? What will it accomplish? What's done is done. Right? I can't forgive him. I can't just accept this stupid card like it's going to make up for everything that happened. I can't!"

"Cope," he said.

"What?"

"Cope," he repeated. "What happened can't be changed. But you have to learn to cope. You have to face these things in order to cope. You can't keep doing what your mother has forced you to do all of these years. You can't push it to the back of your mind and hope that it will one day disappear. Pushing it back further until you break will ultimately cause your breakdown and can even cause physical anguish. Let's break you from the pattern you've gotten used to right now! Read it! Face it!"

"You want me to read it now?"

"Yes!" he exclaimed. "There's no better time!"

I opened the card to the last insert. I was taking to heart what Dr. Pelchat had said. I began to read aloud.

"'Dear Kristen,

'I'm sitting here thinking about how much you must have grown. I can't believe that you are already eighteen years old. It seems like time has passed by, and now my baby girl is all grown up. Since you are an adult now, I expect you are going to be in college soon. Kristen, I am very sorry for what I did to our family.'"

Chunks of bile started to rise to my chest. It felt like I was going to throw up right there in Dr. Pelchat's office. Tears welled up in my eyes and already began to fall. I hadn't gotten finished reading, and I felt like I was going to lose what little control I had. I kept on reading even though my body felt like it couldn't take any more.

"'Now you are eighteen, and I have missed the most important events of your life. I wish that I could have been there for your all of your birthdays up until today. I wish that I could have been there to help you buy your first car and to teach you how to drive it. I wish I could have been there for your senior prom. And most importantly, I wish I could have been there for your first kiss. I am sorry that I wasn't there for all of those wonderful events that have come and gone.'"

I wanted to throw the card to the floor and stomp on it until it disappeared. But I held on to the card. There were only a few more sentences to go. I knew that Dr. Pelchat could see that I was upset. It was more than obvious, but he was counting on me to finish reading it.

I closed my eyes and took a deep breath. When I opened my eyes, more teardrops fell from my eyelashes. I continued reading through my cloudy vision.

"'I am truly sorry from the bottom of my heart. I hope to see you at the parole hearing. I want to see my little girl. I love you. Your dad, Jack.'"

I couldn't resist it any longer. I threw the card to the floor and I kicked it. I buried my face in my hands and cried aloud. Dr. Pelchat let me cry and didn't say a word. He handed me a tissue when I finally raised my head. I blew my nose.

Dr. Pelchat said, "It's okay to cry. I know that this is upsetting. It is okay for you to be upset."

"Is it okay to hate him so much?" I asked.

"He did an awful thing to you and your family. It is natural to feel the way that you do," Dr. Pelchat assured me.

I felt that entity creeping around me once again. It scared me.

"I don't want to see him," I told Dr. Pelchat. "I don't want to see him ever again!"

"Then you don't have to. It would be your choice to not go to that hearing."

"Mom is going, and she's making the twins go. What would it look like if I didn't go with them? Mom would be mad."

"Then let her be mad. I feel bad for your brother and sister because they have to do what she tells them to do, but you don't. You're a grown-up and you can make your own decisions."

"Yes, but what if he gets out? It's one thing for them to go the hearing, but what if he actually gets out of there and she wants to take him back? Can she do that?"

"Truthfully, yes. She can take him back."

"What?" I felt myself almost fall out of my chair from the shock.

"Yes, in truth, she can take her ex-husband back, but he would not be able to live with you. He would have to register as a sex offender, and he wouldn't be able to come within a certain amount of yards from your little brother and sister and other kids. But, your mom could see him on her own time."

"What if she wants to marry him again?"

"I don't think that your mother would do that, Kristen." He seemed to be getting a little annoyed. He may not have been getting annoyed at me, but because of the situation. "You have to think rationally. Do you really think that she would do that to all her children?"

"I don't know," I said. I thought about it, and then answered again. "Probably not, but she's going to his hearing." I had to pause to try to breathe. "I have these dreams sometimes, and they feel too real. They are dreams of Mom and Jack being back together, and everyone is happy except me. I'm the only one who is still angry and hurt from what had happened, and everyone else has forgiven him. So I'm pushed out. Then there's the other dream..."

"What's the other dream?"

"I dream about when I caught Jack raping Nicholas. In that dream, I keep trying to kill Jack, but it ends up being too late. He gets away, or something else scary happens. I fail each time, just like I did before."

"How did you fail before?"

"I failed to save Nick. I failed to save us because I knew and I kept letting it happen. The first time I saw him hurting Nick, I just...I just...I ignored it...and I tried to tell myself that it wasn't really what I had seen, that I was just hallucinating or something. Deep down inside, I knew. How could I let that happen, Dr. Pelchat? How could I just..."

The more that I cried, the more wound up I felt. It didn't make me feel any better to cry. I was worse because I didn't even feel like I was crying for Nick. I was still crying for myself.

"I hate that he has this much control over me."

"Control?"

"Yes," I almost yelled at him. "I hate that all of those things he said in that card are still the things I long for. I hurt for him to be here, even though I know that it's too late. I can never have my Daddy back. You'd think I would have gotten over that by now."

"No one expects you to get over it," Dr. Pelchat said. "You have to cope with it, yes, but you do not have to get over it right now. Don't accept what he has done to you and your family, because it was evil. Never accept evil. What you do need to accept is that Jack does not control you. The only one that controls you is you. However, he can influence you. He can influence the way you think, the things you do, how you act. But don't let Jack have this much influence over you.

"Don't let him do it while he's behind bars, and especially when he is out of prison. You have to find that place within yourself that lets you cope with what has happened. That is the only way you are going to be able to control your emotions and your mind in order for you to feel safe. That's the only way you are going to survive."

"I don't know how," I said.

"You will learn when all of this begins to make sense to you. It takes a day at a time. And if you don't feel that you can take a whole day, then give yourself one minute at a time. Keep moving up to five minutes and then ten, an hour, twelve hours, until you've made it a whole day. Then try again tomorrow."

CHAPTER 62

I left his office with those final words playing in my mind. It was hard, trying to survive. I still wanted to know what it meant to survive, and to learn what it would feel like to want to survive. After my individual therapy session with Dr. Pelchat that day, what was left inside of me was a dramatic feeling that I could not yet understand. This feeling haunted me as I made my way to the Recreation Center to pick up Nick and Alison.

The clock was keeping the time, but I was not keeping up with the time. It was ten minutes until three o'clock when I ran out of gas. I was turning onto the ramp that would take me to the Recreation Center. Mom had told me to be sure I was there at 3:00pm to pick them up.

Fortunately, there was a gas station only a few yards away from where the car gave out on me. I turned the engine off and waited a few seconds. I tried to start the car back up, but it wouldn't give in. Mom kept a canister in the trunk in case of an emergency. I would just have to walk to the gas station and leave the car on the side of the road between the ramp and the bridge to the highway that would bring me to Nick and Alison.

I remembered that Mom always kept spare change for gas in her glove compartment, so I reached over and opened it. As soon as it popped open, I reached in and scrambled around for change. The glove compartment was nearly empty except for a box of tissues, a few dimes and nickels, and a large white envelope that had been opened. I did not see any dollar bills, and the dimes and nickels only came up to fifty-five cents. Then I remembered the twenty dollars that Jack had given me. I figured I'd have to use that. I reached into my bag and pulled out the envelope that Jack had sent my birthday card and money in. When I looked at the envelope, I realized that it looked similar to the one that was in the glove compartment.

When I put them side by side, I noticed that the handwriting and return address were the same. The envelope from the glove compartment was addressed to Mom, and there was a letter inside of it. There was a familiar, whispering voice telling me to open it. I listened to him.

The envelope had already been opened and read by Mom. That much I could tell, but I couldn't really bring myself not to snoop so easily. I ignored the sounds of traffic, the passing cars, the thunder, and the rain that began to fall. Fear crept up inside of me as I stared and hesitated. The feeling inside scared me. Everything that Dr. Pelchat had said to me sent mixed emotions through me. If I read it, then I could know for sure what really could happen. I could know what Mom's intentions were for going to the hearing and what Jack's intentions were for wanting her to come.

As I opened the envelope, a large tractor-trailer passed by me to get onto the bridge to the highway. I felt the car shake, but I ignored it while I unfolded the paper.

I began to read:

Dear Love,

I know that I made many mistakes. One mistake was letting my family go. I've hurt all of you in the worst possible way. When I was a child, I would always say that I would never hurt my family the way that my father hurt us, and it turned out that I did exactly what he did to me and Jonathan. What I did was wrong and I admit it. There's nothing I can do to take it back even though I wish I had a time machine to go back and make it right. I can't. But I can make it up to you and eventually make it up to the children.

If you would please come to my parole hearing and bring Nicholas, Alison, and Kristen, then you will see. I won't be able to get close to Nick and Alison yet, but I do want them to see me. I've changed. God had showed me that this is my second chance. This is my chance to make it up to Him and my family. Finding God has really opened my eyes to see the wrong I've done and what I must do to make it right.

If you would give me that chance to make it right then I will. When I get out on parole I would like to see you. But before then I will need you and the kids there at the courthouse supporting me. And when I get out I promise I will support you. It will take a while for me to be able to be around our children again, but God will work all of that out. Please be there. I need all of you. I love you and miss you.

Jack

There was nothing I could do to stop the metal ball from turning in my chest. The ball tore through my lungs and made it hard to breathe again. Tears were falling from my eyes. How dare he? How could he think that he had the right? The audacity! Mom was going to go to his parole hearing, but was she going to be there for him to give him hope? I did not know. What I did know was that I was scared, and I didn't know what I could do to make it not happen. I balled up the letter and threw it to the floor angrily.

The scariest part that remained in my mind was how he really thought that God had given him a second chance. Was God really going to let the Devil back into Heaven so easily? Is that how it worked? You take a life and ruin others, and then say a prayer and you're forgiven? Would Jack be so easily accepted?

If Mom was going to him, then it must have been so...

Coldness seeped inside the cracks of the windows. Rain began to splat heavily on the car. I heard the drops beating down on the rooftop. The air became so frigid that little chill bumps began to form above my elbows. I rubbed my arms to warm them from the cold air on my skin. I rubbed as if I could just wipe it all away. It was no use, because my hands were cold, too. I stuck them in my pockets. When I reached in deep with my right hand, I felt a sharp prick on my finger. I shoved my hand in deeper, and the pain pierced me.

I opened my eyes wider as I let it poke into my finger deeper. I twisted my finger on the sharp, painful object and looked over to the passenger side. That's when I saw him. He was drenched from the rain and shivering uncontrollably. His hair covered his face so that I couldn't see his eyes.

From under his strands of hair, I could see his lips shivering and his teeth chattering. He hugged himself tightly and bunched his knees to his chest.

"I didn't hear you come in," I told Mr. Sharp.

He wouldn't look up at me.

"Are you afraid?" I asked him.

He didn't answer.

I felt the blood drip down my finger. I pulled my hand out of my pocket, and the sharp butterfly fell into the palm of my bloody hand. Mr. Sharp stayed crouched up on the seat. He looked at my hand and his shivering lips would not give me that smile I was waiting for.

"What's wrong? I need you! Help me!"

He bit down on his lip and kept his head low. He wouldn't let me see his eyes.

I pressed the sharp butterfly wing to my hand and twisted the wing into my palm. I screamed in pain as I twisted and made the blood squeeze out.

"You said you'd be there for me! You said you'd help me breathe! I need to breathe! Mr. Sharp! Mr. Sharp, please don't leave me!"

"You have to stop," he whispered hoarsely.

"What?"

"You have to stop," he repeated.

"I can't! I can't breathe. The ball keeps turning, and it's hard for me to breathe."

Mr. Sharp turned away from me and, without opening the door, he stepped outside into the pouring rain. He started walking towards the bridge that led to the highway. I began to open the driver's side door when Mom's cell phone rang. I looked down and saw that Mom was calling from her office. The phone rang continuously. She was calling because it was after 3:00pm, and Nick had promised he would call her if

I wasn't there on time. I looked at the phone, and then out the window that had begun to fog. Mr. Sharp was still on the path to the bridge.

I slammed the door shut when I was out of the car, and I ran as fast as I could in the pouring rain to get to him. When I caught up with him, he was at the top of the bridge, looking down from the overpass.

Mr. Sharp kept his head low as he yelled over the noise of the traffic. "Jack was right!"

"No! He was never right!"

"Yes, he was! You got what you deserved, Kristen, because you failed! He's going to come back and he's going to show you! You'll see! She's going to take him back!"

"She wouldn't do that!"

"Yes, she would, if she knew that it would get rid of you! You are useless! You are ugly! You are a loser!"

"Why?" I screamed out to him.

A car horn honked loud enough to make me jump. I had somehow walked out into traffic. The car swerved and passed me.

"No!" I called out, even more afraid. The metal ball in my chest turned mercilessly. It was getting harder to keep my breath.

Rain poured down on me, and I shivered from the cold. I didn't care about the cars that were honking at me. I didn't care about the sounds of traffic that should have scared me off that bridge. Mr. Sharp was wrong, and he needed to know it.

Mr. Sharp stood near the edge of the wall that bordered the bridge. He leaned over the top of it and looked down. He turned towards me, and this time he lifted his head. His eyes were red and wet with tears and rain. He reached out for me.

"Come with me," he said.

"Where?" I walked towards him, afraid.

"Take my hand," he said.

I approached him. He looked over the wall again, and I looked down, too. We could see cars, trailers, trucks, campers, and other vehicles passing under the bridge down below us on the highway.

The car that had almost hit me had stopped up ahead, and it looked like it was trying to come back. Two more cars stopped and shined their lights on us. Someone was running towards me, but I couldn't hear what that person was yelling.

Mr. Sharp climbed up to the top of the wall. He reached out to me one last time. "Take my hand and take a deep breath," Mr. Sharp calmly said.

I was shaking, cold and afraid, but then he smiled at me. That convincing smile appeared on his scared face. I climbed up and stood next to him on top of the wall. Even though it hurt to breathe, I took one deep breath and I grabbed his hand. The moment when our hands touched, life became surreal. The rain fell at an unrealistically slow pace. The drops were so big and detailed that I could see the exact shape of each one. Mr. Sharp and I were lifted into the air in one high jump. The air beneath me grew steady and my breath became still.

We went up into the air together outside on that bridge, and when we came back down our feet touched the surface of a cold, tile floor. Dry, calm, and warm, we were inside of the old house again. I looked at Mr. Sharp, ready for what was to come this time. He put the knife into the palm of my hand. The tears fell from his vulnerable eyes.

He said, "This is where it ends. You have one last chance not to fail, Kristen. Take it."

I took the knife from him. If I were gone, Jack wouldn't have to come back. He wouldn't come back and hurt them in order to hurt me. It was Jack's entire fault. Jack was the devil, and he had taken my daddy away. He'd taken my family away. I did not want him to come back to hurt any of us. If I went, then he would have to go. I wasn't going to fail this time. I gripped the knife tightly in my hand and turned towards the dark hallway.

Mr. Sharp grabbed my arm before I could walk away from him. He looked me straight in the eyes. In one smooth movement, he leaned in and kissed me gently on my lips. With that virtuous kiss, he whispered without pulling his lips from mine, *I love you.*

I closed my eyes, took his kiss into my heart, and let the painful tears fall out. I had loved Mr. Sharp, too. He knew it.

When I opened my eyes, Mr. Sharp was gone. All that remained with me was the knife in my hand and the door that stood closed in front of me. The sickening sounds of Nick's cries and screams were seeping out from behind the other side of that door. I had had this dream too many times before, since the devil had made it reality. I knew exactly what I had to do.

I opened the door and saw Jack standing in front of Nicholas. Nick lay still on the bed, belly and face down. His eyes were closed, and tears streamed down his face. He was never going to cry again because of this demon, and we were never going to be afraid of it, because I was not going to fail.

As Jack approached me, I raised the knife. Instead of taking it to my own skin, I punctured it deep into Jack's bare chest. No, I did not run this time. I pulled the knife out of the wound. It bled smoke and black tar. As was expected of a demonic creature such as Jack, he cried out in shrieking pain. It was the sound of music to my ears. I could no longer hear Nick crying.

I raised the knife and stabbed him again in his chest once more. The knife came down into where his heart would have been, if he'd had one. This time the tar and smoke swelled up into his eyes, turning them completely black. The smell of soot filled my nostrils. Jack threw his head back, and the sound of his screeching cries was smothered by gurgling. He was trying to breathe.

Hot, lava-like tar burst up into his throat and drained out of his mouth. This was the killer blow. I pulled the knife out and watched Jack fall to the floor. When he hit the floor, his body shriveled up and turned to ashes and smoke. Looking down at that pile of waste made me feel sorrow. It didn't have to be that way, but, yes, it did. I raised the knife once more and then pressed it to my arm. If I could just see Mr. Sharp one more time…

When the blade touched my arm, a scorching sensation went through my skin that made me immediately drop the knife. Scared, I reached for the knife and grabbed it. But before I could try to reach Mr. Sharp again, I began to cough. My chest felt like something hard was ripping away at my lungs. Breathing was harder than ever, because whatever was stuck in my throat would not go down or come up. I coughed uncontrollably and pounded my fists on my chest. I kept on coughing until what was keeping me from breathing finally began to come up. I coughed and coughed until that evil metal ball choked up out of my mouth and landed in the pile of Jack's ashes.

I looked down at the metal ball. The ball was large, round, black, and full of sharp spikes. The ball was gored with pieces of my heart and chunks of blood. It didn't frighten me that it had taken a costly piece of me with it, because I knew that I was still alive, and I knew deep in my soul that it was only for the better that I finally let that part of me go.

I walked over to Nick's bed, but he wasn't there. I hadn't seen him leave the room. The door to his bedroom was open. He must have slipped by me while I was choking up the metal ball from my chest. I went over to the door and looked out. Nick was standing in the hallway with Mom, Alison, Dr. Cuvo, and Dr. Pelchat. They were all smiling and applauding for me. Nick was happier than I had ever seen him, and Mom looked prouder than I would have ever imagined her to be of me.

As they applauded, I could only feel sadness. Shouldn't I have been happy? Shouldn't I have been proud? I saved them. I did not fail this time. I looked down at the tarred knife. Mr. Sharp was really gone. He'd said that I had one last chance not to fail. Then why was I being sucked into darkness? Why was I allowing the door to close on my life?

There was light where they were standing, and there was only darkness where I was standing. I heard Alison's voice calling out to me. I saw Nick waving his hands in the air. Mom screamed my name.

She said, "Open your eyes! Come out of there! Come back to us!"

The door began to close. They stood in the hallway, waving and calling out to me. I wanted to stop the door from closing me in the dark room, but I was almost afraid to step into the light and be with them. What would I do now that I had saved them? Did they really need me? Did they really want me now?

"Please, Kristen," I heard Nick cry out.

His voice sounded so far away as the door begin to shut me in. The door creaked when it was only an inch from the latch. I saw the light on the other side of the door peek in through the crack. Nick cried louder and harder. Mom screamed.

Darkness filled the room and shut me in. The smell of smoke and fire filled the black air, and I grew afraid. A loud noise that sounded like a long beeping siren filled my ears. The piercing sound frightened me even more because I could not see where the sound was coming from in the dark. The siren grew louder, and the smell of the smoke became intense.

With the sound of the siren fading in and out, there was a jolt of electricity that turned the whole room red and then black again. My body was being electrocuted, and with each shock, a red light blinked from above my head. My heart was racing so fast that I could hear it pounding in my brain. My veins felt like they were on fire. The whole scene was frightening.

How do I let go? How do I make this stop? I couldn't figure it out. What I did know was that I wanted out of the darkness. I wanted the electricity, the red blinking lights and beeping sirens, all to stop. I wanted my heart to stop burning rapidly inside of me. It hurt too much.

The room was dark, but I stuck my arms out. I felt the hard, shut door. With all of my might, I pushed my arms forward through the darkness and painful electric shocks. Pushing all of my weight on that door made my skin burn. I continued to push and push until it began to break apart. Cracking and crumbling, that door was breaking down. I did not stop pushing. The hurt in my veins became almost unbearable just before the door finally burst to pieces. When the wood crumbled beneath me, I fell through and hit the floor. The door faded to ashes, and the darkness seemed to wither away. I lay still, and the pain drifted away as I began to open my eyes again. The brightest and most blinding light I had ever seen suddenly filled the room. I could not see clear enough to make out where I was.

The world was completely white.

"She's awake! Mommy! Mommy! Her eyes are open!" I heard Nick's voice so loud and clear.

The sound of his feet pounding on the floor made me cry.

"Her eyes are watering!" Alison said with fear in her voice.

I did not move. I lay still on my back, staring up at the bright lights and white ceiling above me. I couldn't see anyone's face. I could only hear their sweet voices. Nick and Alison's sweet voices made my heart beat steadily again.

Mom was there. I could feel her hands touching my arm and rubbing my hair gently. I heard her crying and sobbing. Real tears seemed like they were actually falling from her eyes. I saw her leaning over me, almost like a shadow. The tears that fell from her eyes landed on my face. It reminded me of the rain.

"Oh, baby," Mom cried from over me. "I'm so sorry. I'm here. It's okay."

"Is she awake?" an unfamiliar voice asked.

Mom looked away from me towards the voice.

"Her eyes are open, and she has tears in her eyes. Does it mean that she's awake? Does she know that we are here?" Mom asked.

Mom was pushed out of the way, and someone else stood above me. It was a woman dressed in a white coat. Her white coat almost blended with the white ceiling above. The bright lights made it hard to make out her face. She shined a circle of light into my eyes from a pen she pulled from her almost invisible coat pocket. It made me blink. She gasped happily.

"Kristen is awake and alert!" The woman exclaimed. "Get Dr. Grayson. Quickly!"

I couldn't hear Nick and Alison anymore, but I heard Mom still crying. I did not know what was going on. All of the excitement from the moment I opened my eyes was exhausting and scary. I closed my eyes and pushed myself away from the white lights and the confusion.

CHAPTER 63

Hospitals have a smell to them. The sickening smell lingers to make you always remember where you are and what you've done. The smell was too familiar. The white, thin blankets were too familiar. I lay in the bed with three of the white blankets spread over me.

That day when I'd followed Mr. Sharp onto the bridge, I knew that we did not intend to ever get off the bridge alive. We'd jumped over the wall to die so that there would not be any time for regret, no way of turning back, and no way for us to be saved.

Or so I'd thought.

After I'd climbed up the wall and had stood next to Mr. Sharp, we had decided we were going to jump. I hadn't looked behind me, and I hadn't looked down. My chest had been tight, but I'd taken the deepest breath I could take and I'd jumped. I'd gone up into the air, but I'd never felt myself go down.

I was told that I had passed out, possibly from fear or shock once I had actually jumped, but, before I could launch myself completely forward, someone had caught me. I never made it to the bottom of the highway where I would have, without a doubt, died. If the 100-foot drop down to the highway below wouldn't have killed me, then I was sure that a passing car or semi would have done the job.

My limp and unconscious body had been pulled back by the person who had been there and quick enough to grab me. When I had been pulled back over, I'd fallen back to the ground and had hit my head on the concrete ground. The person who had saved my life was a man who had been driving the car that had almost hit me. He'd parked his car right there on the bridge, and when he'd seen me climbing up the wall, he'd started running towards me. He had been screaming out to me, but I couldn't understand what he was saying.

As I had been launching myself off the wall with Mr. Sharp, I'd grown light-headed, and then I remembered only seeing black. That's when my savior had gotten a hold of my shirt. He'd told the police that he barely got a hold of an inch of my shirt, just in time. He said that I had been so heavy because I was passed out and unable to move myself or take control of my own weight. He didn't think that he was going to be able to keep me from falling. I was told that he had almost lost his own life trying to save me, because he'd really had to pull to get me to fall back and not make us both go forward and down. He certainly had pulled hard enough, and he'd been able to let me go before we could fall over. That was when I'd fallen backwards and had landed back on the concrete ground of the bridge. I had suffered a serious concussion, but the doctors had said that I was lucky that a concussion was all I had.

I woke up from that concussion a few days later. Mom, Alison, and Nick were there beside me. Mom told me that they would not leave my side until I had woken up. I did not fully regain consciousness for three days after I woke up for the first time. After those three days, I did not have any more blackouts. Coincidentally, the day that I regained full consciousness was the day of Jack's parole hearing. To my surprise, Mom, Alison, and Nick were there at my side. Mom promised me that she was not going anywhere.

She said, "I am right where I am supposed to be."

"What about the parole hearing?" I asked her.

Nick and Alison stood next to Mom, one twin by each of her sides. She squeezed them tightly with one arm each as she smiled down at me. Genuine tears fell from her eyes and, one by one, they made me happy.

"That's not important," she said. "Our family is what is important right now. *You* are important to us."

I knew that this was certainly not a dream. I was wide awake, and what was happening was for real. Everything that Mom was saying was true. Her tears were not fake, and her actions were not of my imagination.

Every tear that was shed between the both of us that day proved that I didn't fail this time. I was given the strength to push myself back into the light. I could not stay in the darkness and let myself rest eternally in hell where I did not belong. That was where Jack belonged, and that was where he was going to stay.

CHAPTER 64

Dr. Pelchat's office was terribly familiar. I sat in the same chair opposite his as he sat behind his big, wooden desk. He had my same familiar chart open with a pen in his left hand. He and I were alone together in that familiar room with the same familiar window that I had a habit of staring out of when I felt too closed in.

"You're a strong girl," Dr. Pelchat said.

His voice crept in and disturbed my silent thoughts.

"I didn't think that you would want to see me this time," I admitted to him.

"Why not?"

"I don't know. I just didn't think so. After all, I did become a statistic."

"No," he corrected. "You would have been one of those statistics if you had actually succeeded in killing yourself."

"You're right."

"Do you remember what happened that day?"

"Yes," I told him. "I let him go. Mr. Sharp is gone."

"How do you feel about that?"

"I'm taking it one minute at a time."

Dr. Pelchat nodded.

"There are times when I wish he would appear again, but I know that he won't. Especially now that you put me back on Risperdol."

"Does that make you upset?"

"No." I shook my head. "I mean, sometimes it does. Sometimes I am very upset because I have to take the medicine, and Mom really pushes me to take it every single day."

"That's good. She is only looking out for you. How are you doing, now that you're at home with your family?"

"I'm doing all right," I told him.

"You will continue to be all right. I've told you this before, and I will say it again. You've come a long way from when I first met you. You've made progress in such a short time. We do have a long way to go, but you are a fighter. We just have to watch out for those moments. Those moments that cause the desperation that you feel when you are about to do something impulsive. As you learned, Borderlines tend to make irrational decisions based off of their intense emotions.

"For instance, when you cut, from the patterns on your arms, I see that you are a fast and compulsive cutter. You slice at yourself in a rage. You make these impulsive, self-abusive decisions. You release your anger all out on yourself at those moments where you feel loss of control and despair. Sometimes the past becomes something you hold on to, and it comes up every time something goes wrong. It doesn't matter if it's something that has nothing to do with your mother or Jack. Somehow, you are able to work it up in your mind that all of these things are coming down on you, and because you don't know how to deal with it, you jump to the most desperate conclusion. The almost fatal conclusion, Kristen, was when you tried to kill yourself. You need to know and understand that when those moments arise, you cannot give into despair. You have to use your coping skills and talk to someone."

"When I'm in that moment," I said, "I feel as if there is nothing in the world that could pull me out. When I did decide to end it all the first time, I thought that the only thing that would give me rest was death! That is how it felt. I wanted to sleep and never have to wake up and feel that way again. When I tried to jump, I needed to get out of the darkness. I was so afraid."

"The darkness was where you felt you had failed. You were afraid of what you thought would happen if your mother had taken Jack back. You see, it did not turn out the way you thought it would. You did not fail because you managed to come out of that darkness. Kristen, you're alive. If you had died that night, you would not be here right now. You wouldn't have had a chance to see that you *are strong enough* to survive. This is your only chance to open your eyes and see the light that you have been searching for. Now that you are aware of what it is - your illness, which is Borderline Personality Disorder - you have to think about what you know and use it for your survival, because this is real. What happened to you and your family was not your fault. Therefore, you shouldn't feel sorry. Stop punishing yourself. Kristen, *this is your life*. It's no more excuses."

I thought back to when Ms. Mosley had told me about the moment when I would truly understand. She knew, just as Dr. Pelchat knew, and they were both right. These weren't just random words from a book or psycho-babble crap that doctors just say to get you in and out of their office. These words were true. There was no way to deny or reject any of it, because there it was, laid out right in front of me, and for the first time I understood.

In realizing this, I felt something change inside of my mind. Something clicked inside. The change that I felt within myself brought on a new feeling, a new way of thinking, and a new understanding. I realized that, this whole time, Dr. Pelchat's words were being used as a potent force. These words were powerful enough to help me out of the darkness, and they began to lead me into a new light. Dr. Pelchat, Ms. Mosley, and even Dr. Cuvo's words all seemed to come together and somehow began to make sense to my mind. It may have been because this was the moment I began to understand that everything that had happened to me and my family in the past was not ever going to disappear, and if I did not want it to destroy me, I had to begin coping and healing so that I could get on with my life. I couldn't use it as an excuse anymore. It was going to be hard, and it was going to take a lot of time, but it had to be done. It had to be done for my family and me. None of these people wanted to hurt me. I didn't want to hurt myself anymore.

This is my life, I thought to myself. Then I realized who I was, and who I was ready to be.

Dr. Pelchat stared at me silently. He was watching me. He was waiting to see if I would respond. Did it bother me that he was staring this time? No.

Without another thought or hesitation, I stared right back at him. I could tell that my direct eye contact with him caught him off guard. He shifted in his seat a little, but he did not take his eyes off of me. In a straightforward and mild manner, I raised my head up higher while keeping focused on Dr. Pelchat's eyes, the way I remembered Dr. Cuvo used to do.

I said to Dr. Pelchat, "I *want* to be a survivor."

EPILOGUE

Her

Her story was one that waited to be told.

In order to tell a story there has to be a story to tell.

There has to be

A beginning,

A middle,

And an end.

For Her,

There was a beginning,

And there is an end.

This is where the story of Her ends,

And my story begins.

ABOUT THE AUTHOR

Felicia Johnson was born in Philadelphia, PA. Felicia is a writer, youth mentor, behavioral health worker, and big sister. She loves ice cream, dancing, and seeing her little sister, Laura, smile. She currently lives in Atlanta, Georgia.

Made in the USA
Charleston, SC
22 November 2016